I0788445

THE KING'S ENEMIES

THE HENCHMEN CHRONICLES

BOOK FIVE

CRAIG HALLORAN

The King's Enemies

The Henchmen Chronicles Book #5

By Craig Halloran

TWO-TEN BOOK PRESS

P.O. Box 4215, Charleston, WV 25312

ISBN eBook: 978-1-946-218-48-3

ISBN Paperback: 978-1-793081-57-5

www.craighalloran.com

Publisher's Note

This book is a work of fiction. Names, characters, places, and incidents either are the product of the author's imagination or are used fictitiously, and any resemblance to actual persons, living or dead, events, or locales is entirely coincidental.

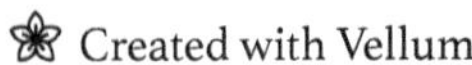 Created with Vellum

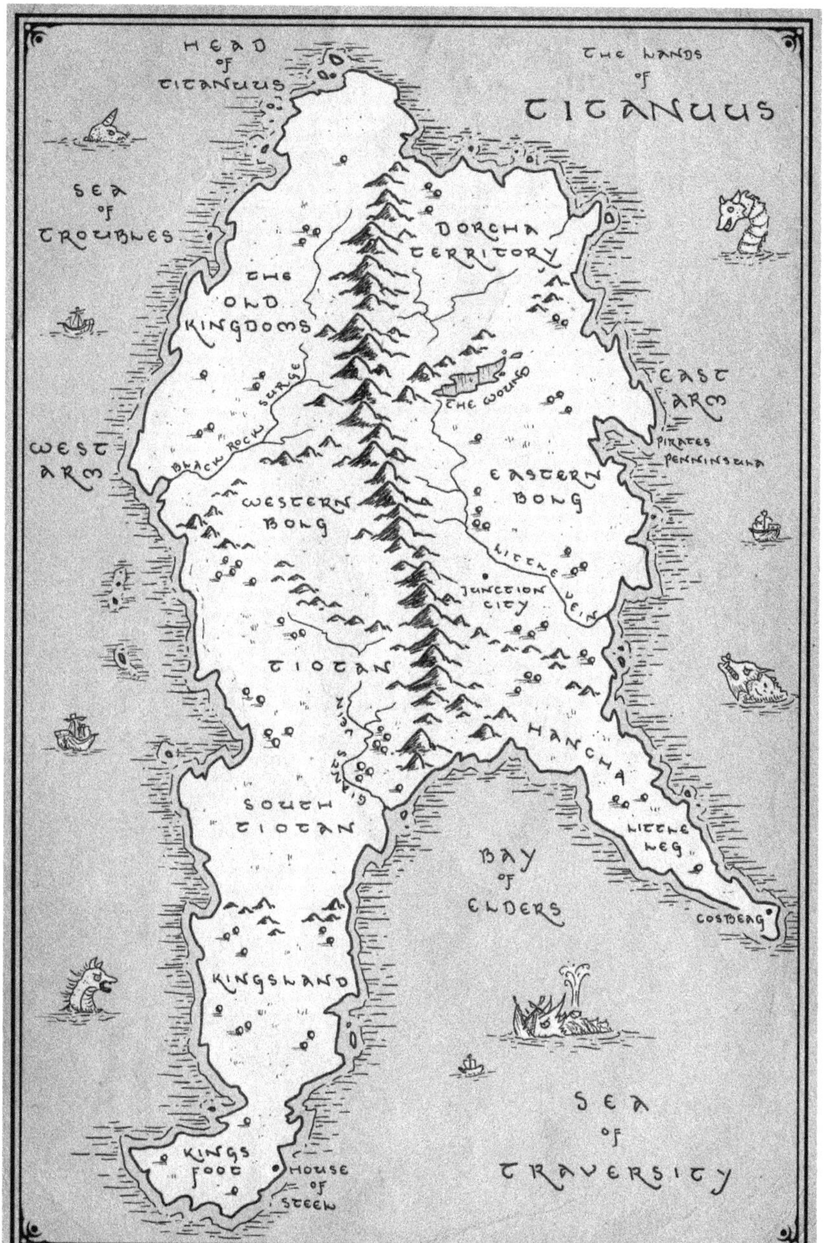

THE LANDS
of
TITANUUS
HEAD
of
TITANUUS
SEA
of
TROUBLES
THE
OLD
KINGDOMS
DORCHA
TERRITORY
SURGE
BLACK ROCK
THE WOUND
EAST
ARM
PIRATES
PENNINSULA
WEST
ARM
WESTERN
BONG
EASTERN
BONG
LITTLE VEIN
JUNCTION
CITY
TIOTAN
VEIN
GIANTS SPINE
HANCHA
LITTLE
LEG
SOUTH
TIOTAN
BAY
of
ELDERS
COSTBERG
KINGSLAND
SEA
of
TRAVERSITY
KINGS
FOOT
HOUSE
OF
STEEN

1

Smoke drifted into Abraham's nostrils. He coughed. Lights burned his eyes. The surrounding room was dark. Dr. Jack Lassiter paced around his table, puffing on a thick cigar. The orderlies, Otis and Haymaker, stood nearby with their stun rods in their big mitts.

Abraham wet his lips and asked, "Don't hospitals have a strict no-smoking policy, you jerk?"

Jack leaned his head back and chuckled, continuing to pace. His eyes were hard as coal, and he spoke with a strong, penetrating voice. "Glad you are back, Abraham." He stopped at the end of the table, where Abraham's toes were covered by a hospital blanket. Jack looked him dead in the eye and scratched the short, curly brown hairs on his head. "I could see it in your face the moment that you woke. Your eyes, they aren't like the other man's. There is a softness to them. The other's are like burning daggers. The jaw isn't as tight either." He huffed out a stream of smoke. "Very telling."

"If only I could applaud your brilliance," Abraham said as he wiggled his fingers. "A true master of psychiatry. I mean, you aren't Freud, Niles, or Frasier Crane, but you have some savvy."

Jack chuckled heavily. He poked a finger at Abraham and said,

"You know, it's good that you have maintained a sense of humor about all of this. It's quite remarkable. The others don't fare so well, making you... unique."

"Momma always told me that I was special." He eyeballed Otis and Haymaker. "And not ugly." Talking smack came easy to him. He used it as a tactic while he tried to gather his senses. The last time he had been back home, Mandi was with him. They were with her cousin, Sidney, and Sidney's mysterious husband, John Smoke. They were in a helicopter when he passed out and wound up back on Titanuus. His nose itched. "Uh, I've got a bad itch that I can't scratch, right on the tip of my nose." He eyed Otis, who was built like a tackling dummy and had a swollen jaw. "How about you help a brother out?"

Otis rapped his stun rod in his hand and said, "I've got a cure for that itch."

Abraham clucked with laughter. He tugged against his bonds as he did so, testing the firm leather straps binding his wrists and ankles. Short of transforming into the Hulk or some other super-strong beast, he wasn't going anywhere. *Where are Mandi, Smoke, and Sid? What the heck happened?* Continuing to delay, he directed his voice toward Otis and said, "You remind me of Luke Cage. Do you know who that is?"

Otis gave him a funny look.

"Mister Jenkins, you can stop with the charades. I already know that your brash attempts at humor are a coping mechanism when you are uncomfortable," Dr. Jack said. He was dressed in camo hunting gear complete with a beige vest, and he had a sidearm on his hip. "I've read your file many times."

Abraham eyed Jack up and down and asked, "So you've been hunting again?" He said this as his thoughts raced back to Titanuus. He'd been with the Henchmen, and they'd just entered the mouth of the Wound. Melris the Elderling was going to lead them into the dark bowels of the chasm to find two more gems of power for the Crown of Stones. "It's been a long time since I've had some venison. I could go for a nice cut of deer steak with a side of scrambled eggs. And some butter biscuits. Like the ones my grandma used to make."

"Otis," Dr. Jack said, "Why don't you come over here and scratch his nose?"

"Oh, it's fine now," Abraham said.

Otis strolled over to the table with a lazy stride. He scratched Abraham's nose and stuck the stun rod in his side. Abraham cried out as his body arched and spasmed on the table.

Otis stuck him again and again, and Abraham's body jumped on the table.

"That's enough," Dr. Jack said.

Otis shocked Abraham again.

"That's enough!" Dr. Jack replied.

With a nod of triumph, Otis pulled his stun rod away and resumed his place by Haymaker with a grin on his face.

Abraham groaned. Painful tingles coursed through his body. The spot where Otis stuck him ached and burned. With sweat beading down his face, he panted and asked, "What's with the *One Flew over the Cuckoo's Nest* treatment? I haven't done anything." He glared at Dr. Jack. "What is your deal?"

Dr. Jack's eyes narrowed. His voice rose. "Haven't done anything? Haven't done anything? You are the one fouling this entire operation up!" He sucked hard on the cigar, making the ashes burn bright red. "I don't know what you are doing in Titanuus, mister, but you need to stop doing it now! Do you understand me?"

Abraham's eyes widened. He'd never seen Dr. Jack lose his cool. The man had become incensed. *The dude is having a meltdown. Good.* "Hey, I didn't ask for this to happen to me. It happened not because of something I did but because of something that you did."

Dr. Jack approached from the right side of the table and said, "You are the only one, the only one, that is giving this operation fits. Why can't you be like the others and butt out?"

"I don't even know what you are talking about?"

"Don't play games with me. You know what you are doing. You are fighting for the king. King Hector." Dr. Jack hit the edge of the table. "You side with him!"

Abraham had no idea what to make of that illuminating statement. His fingers danced at his sides. He looked deep into Dr. Jack's stone-cold eyes, unsure if that was the same person he'd met before or not. For some reason, he was getting a strong vibe that Dr. Jack might have been to Titanuus—either that, or he'd talked to someone that had. Someone like Eugene Drisk. He wouldn't be the only one either.

"If I'm such a problem, why don't you kill me?" He regretted saying it the moment the words came out. The last thing he needed was to suggest his own death.

Dr. Jack blew another blast of smoke in his face and said, "Because, just like you said, you are special."

"But you tried to kill me already."

"Not you. Just the fools that have been helping you."

I've got to find out what happened to Mandi. How did I get captured? What happened to her? "You seem to have a good grasp of what is going on in Titanuus, but what do you want from me?"

"I want to know how you move from body to body. As you've figured out, there are others, otherworlders, like you, that come, but they cannot come and go. Only you." Dr. Jack started to pace around the table again. "Out of all of them, only you have this special talent. We need to harness it. You are the gateway from here to Titanuus." He stopped, turned, and poked Abraham on the head. "Perhaps I can drill it out."

The heat of the cigar burned just over Abraham's eye. His watery eye sent a tear down his cheek. The truth was, he probably could work with Jack Lassiter. It might get him everything he ever wanted. The problem was that he didn't want to. He wouldn't, either. After all, he served the king. *Right is right, and wrong is wrong.* But that didn't mean he couldn't play along. "Look, Dr. Jack, I didn't ask for this, but maybe we can work something out."

Dr. Jack held the cigar over Abraham's eye. "Oh, you want to bargain now. Interesting. The other man inside you, Ruger Slade—he was hard as a stone. He wouldn't mutter a word. Nothing I tried would break him." He pulled the cigar away. "A fascinating case, actually. But he is the bigger problem, it seems. Bigger than you, a washed-up, entitled athlete turned into a worthless trucker."

"Hey, don't knock truckers. They are the lifeblood of this country. Who do you think hauls your twenty-dollar cigars to your humidor and fills your fridge with imported beer?"

Dr. Jack grinned and said, "My wife. And by the way, it's a one-hundred-dollar cigar."

"Good for you." Abraham sighed. "Look, man, I'm tired of all of this. I want to stay home. What do you want to know?"

2

"Good. You are willing to play along," Dr. Jack said with a puff on his cigar. "That might make all of the difference. You see, I'm not a man known for endless patience. I demand results."

"This might go better if I was in a more comfortable position." Abraham flexed his hands. "I'd be lying if I didn't say that I missed your office. Being strapped to a table—well, it's weird. Even talking from behind steel bars would be better. Besides, I have to pee."

"Go ahead. My orderlies will clean you up," Dr. Jack said. "They just love that stuff, dontcha, boys?"

Otis and Haymaker didn't utter a word. They glared at Abraham with their usual dull, heavy stares.

"I think I can hold it a bit longer," he said.

"Tell me, Mr. Jenkins, what happens right before your essence moves from one world to another?" Dr. Jack asked.

He didn't see the harm in answering and said, "Usually, I start to get a headache, you know, like a migraine, right between the eyes. I see those rings too." That was the truth but only part of the truth. The last time it happened, back at the Wound, he hadn't felt anything at all. He was talking with Sticks, and the world became a black swirl.

"A big part of me still has trouble believing that this is real. For all I know, I might be strapped to a table elsewhere, in a coma."

"Does anything trigger these migraines?" Dr. Jack asked.

Abraham managed a shrug and said, "Stress. Normally, I'm in a lot of danger when it happens."

"What sort of danger?"

"You know, the usual fantasy fare. I'm killing monsters with my magic sword, and they are trying to kill me. Just before I arrived here, I finished butchering a ten-foot-tall monster that looked like a man and walked like a dog. They are called Wild Men. The carnage I left would fill this room from one side to the other." He noticed Otis and Haymaker exchange a glance. "It wasn't long after that I fell back here."

"Wild Men, huh? And a magic sword. Interesting. What does this magic sword do? Can you fly with it? Heh heh."

"No. It has strange properties." Abraham figured he might as well lay it on thick while playing a little dumb at the same time. "It's razor sharp, can talk in my head, and sometimes it will shoot a bolt of lightning."

"A sword that shoots fire." Dr. Jack smiled at his orderlies. "Man, this world has it all. Are there flying rugs too?"

"I think you mean carpets, and no, at least, not that I've seen. There are dragons." He swallowed. "Look, my throat is dry, and I'd like a drink, and I'd like to not pee all over myself either. How long have I been laying here? I feel like I haven't gone in days."

"That's about right," Dr. Jack said. "At the moment, you are in a very secure location. No doubt, your friends will try to rescue you. You've picked up some very interesting allies, it seems. It surprised even me."

"Mandi is okay?" he asked sheepishly.

"Since you are attempting to be forthcoming, I'll lend you that branch. Your girlfriend, or whatever she is to you, is on the loose with her peculiar cousin and her husband."

"How'd you get me?"

"Huh, funny that you don't remember." Dr. Jack puffed out a

smoke ring. "You took off in that helicopter you stole. You landed in a field behind a truck stop in the dead of night. Believe it or not, we got kind of lucky. As it turns out, someone called the cops because four strange people walked out of the woods without a car or truck. They ordered a table full of pancakes and milkshakes. Not that that was the oddest thing for a trucker, but the descriptions paid off. We picked up on it right away. The government has eyes and ears everywhere."

Abraham's belly gurgled. "Those pancakes and milkshakes sure sound good about now." He rolled his head toward the orderlies. "Do you think you fellas could whip us something up while we are talking? I like my milkshakes cold and my syrup warm." He turned his attention back to Dr. Jack. "Not a fan of cold syrup. You?"

"I'm an oatmeal-for-breakfast kind of guy." Dr. Jack took another draw on his cigar and said, "It didn't take long for us to close in on you. We managed to be discreet. It seemed that you and your cohorts were planning to roll out with a friendly trucker. It might have worked too if we didn't sniff you out. Lucky for us, Dirty Lyle made that call. No one was going anywhere. We blocked the truck stop and closed in. Colonel Dexter led the charge. He was hungry to get you."

Me or Mandi. "So, did the trucker rally behind us? Did they crash your gates doing ninety-eight? Man, I would have loved to have seen them drop the hammer down."

"Sorry, Rubber Duck, but you gave yourself up."

If Abraham could have sat up straight in an instant, he would have. "Are you serious?" It was a fair question. For all he knew, Dr. Jack was lying to him. It was best to assume that.

Dr. Jack nodded. "In terms for your surrender, we let your cohorts go. But we're keeping an eye on them. You wish you could scratch your head, don't you?"

Abraham nodded. *What in Titanuus's Crotch is Ruger up to?*

3

At first, Abraham wondered if the person hosting his body was Ruger. It might have been another otherworlder from Titanuus. Ruger had been becoming more active, however. Before, Abraham would have lain comatose. Now, Ruger was alive and well. Even Dr. Jack seemed to believe it. He parted his lips to speak, but Dr. Jack spoke first.

"Colonel Dexter agreed to your terms or, rather, Ruger's terms. He came quietly, and when he got here, well, he clammed up." Dr. Jack's jaw tightened, a thin film of sweat building on his brow. "Needless to say, I'm not so happy about that. He agreed to cooperate. He lied."

"It's not as if you are running this secret organization on honesty. And your methods"—he glanced at his bindings—"are far from humane. You've tortured me."

"All for the greater good."

"For some, perhaps, but I seriously doubt for all. Jumping from one world to another—let me tell you, it ain't no picnic. And I don't think you are going to be able to control it."

"We can make anything we imagine happen." Dr. Jack held his pinched fingers about an inch apart. "We are this close. In some areas, we've already succeeded. It's the soul swapping that we haven't mastered. That's what we need you to help us with. We need to learn how to control it."

"Maybe there is an antenna in my brain. Perhaps aliens put it there."

Dr. Jack chuckled. So did his stone-faced goons.

Abraham felt the hair rise on his arms. "Whoa, are you suggesting that aliens are in on this?" His mind started racing. He could hear old man Herb from Woody's Grill joking about the alien sighting in Wytheville, Virginia. Those words came back to haunt him now. He broke out in a cold sweat, and a well of doubt started to swell inside him. *This must be a dream. But it can't be!*

Visions of the zillon dragon riders crossed his mind. He remembered the zillon waitress in Hancha, Anna. She was sweet and pretty in her own unique way. He couldn't help but think that she was a distorted figment of his imagination.

"What's the matter, Abraham? You look pale," Dr. Jack said.

"You realize that this entire ordeal is hard enough to buy into, and now you are tossing in the existence of aliens."

"Is it really so hard to believe now, after all that you have seen? I've heard plenty of wondrous stories about Titanuus, the kind of stories that make my kinky hair straighten and my toes curl. I can't wait to see it. A new frontier ripe for the picking."

"Sure, if you want to take yourself back to the Dark Ages." Abraham played along, wanting to get more answers out of Dr. Jack, who was being very forthcoming. "Listen, there are monsters, literal physical monsters, that aren't going to give their world up without a fight. You can do what you want to do, but you better be careful what you wish for—what you wish for and your associates. It looks like people like you have enough already."

Dr. Jack raised his brow and said, "Well said, from one elite to another. Did you have enough, Abraham, when you bought your father that fancy plane? Or did you want more? A pennant? A World Series championship? A bigger contract perhaps, for Jenkins the Jet?"

"I was grateful for all of it and never wanted for anything more. I just happened to be a great baseball pitcher back then. But one thing

I realized while I was trucking down the road was this: none of those privileges made me happy. The only thing that mattered was what I missed, my family. My world was empty without them."

"Well, not all people feel the same as you. They want their own world to rule. A fresh start. One without all of the red tape." Dr. Jack tapped the ashes off his cigar.

Abraham fought off the urge to roll his eyes. He understood men like Dr. Jack and Eugene Drisk. People like them would become power mad. They thought they knew what was best for everyone else. He'd had teammates, coaches, and owners like that. He'd heard their slants in their boorish meetings. They were the "me" in the "team" that they prattled on about all the time. It was all about their hidden agendas. He said to Otis and Haymaker, "So, what's in it for you guys, a little castle and some pretty wenches? I have a Stronghold. Maybe I'll let you guys see it. You can come over and have a beer."

"I don't drink," Otis said.

"Or blink. Good for you. I'm not so much of a drinker either. I used to have a problem." He lifted his head up. "Jack, I really need some relief and sustenance. I'm cooperating. Do you think you could make that happen? It would go a long way with me."

Dr. Jack rubbed an eyebrow and said, "You think this is a big joke, don't you?" He came closer. "But there is a lot more to this than meets the eye. A whole lot more. You've talked at length with Eugene Drisk, haven't you?"

He nodded.

"We've come a long way since we began what he started. He's just now learned what he helped give birth to." Dr. Jack stoked the fire on the end of his cigar with a few stiff puffs. "We're moving more and more through the working portal that we have. But it can serve a greater purpose. What if I were to tell you that I could send you back in time before you had your plane accident?"

"I'd say those curls in your hair are a little too tight."

Dr. Jack nodded at Otis. "Let our guest in, gentlemen."

The orderlies vanished into the exterior darkness of the room. A heavy door opened and closed, then the heavy footsteps of the bulky orderlies approached. They resumed their spot to the side. No one was with them.

Abraham looked at Dr. Jack, and not having seen anyone, he asked, "Am I missing something?"

"No, not at all." Dr. Jack looked past Abraham.

Abraham twisted his head around and looked upward. His heart jumped in his chest. He was face-to-face with a zillon.

4

TITANUUS

"He's coming to," Sticks said. She held Abraham's head in her lap. She petted the short grizzly beard building up on his face. "A good sign."

The Henchmen stood inside the interior wall surrounding the Wound. A chill, gusty wind came up from the black mouth of the great canyon. Iris and the Red Tunics were mending the wounded with spells and stitches. Dominga and Vern had built a small fire.

Horace took a knee beside Sticks. His beard was caked in both the dried blood of the Wild Men from the Wound and his own. His arms were covered in bloody bandages. He stuffed some tobacco chaw in his mouth and pinched it between his teeth and gum. He sucked his teeth and said, "I hope he's back. I hate it when he goes into the deep sleep. We have a mission."

"Horace!" Iris's voice carried with agitation. "Are you sucking on that chaw again? You know I don't like it. Spit it out."

Horace's bald, bearded, and beefy face soured. "There won't be any time for romance on this mission. I'd appreciate some slack."

"There won't be any romance after, either, if you don't spit that foul foliage out." Iris gave him a demanding glare. "I mean it."

Horace grumbled, took the juicy wad of tobacco out of his mouth, and flung it against the wall. "If it was my dying wish, you wouldn't let me have it either, would you, woman?"

"No, I wouldn't!" Iris said.

Horace sucked his teeth. He winked at Sticks and said, "I always leave a little bit to suck on. She'll never know the better."

Abraham's eyelids snapped open, and he sat straight up. His eyes were alert, like a wary panther's.

"Abraham, take it easy. You'll get a head rush," Sticks warned. The plain-faced woman touched his neck and rubbed it. "You might have a knot on the back of your head from where you fell."

The swordsman quickly stood up, leaving Sticks and Horace gawking at him. The pair exchanged a glance.

"Captain," Horace said, "it's good to see you up and about. Can I get you anything? Food, perhaps. According to Melris, there won't be any food to plunder down there." He cast a look toward the dark belly of the cavern. "Just death, he says."

The rest of the Henchmen were going about their business, tending to the fire and their wounds. Prospero and Apollo were leaning against the wall, eating strips of dried beef. Dominga and Shades joined them.

Sticks took Abraham by the hand. He pulled his strong fingers away. He cast a long glance between her and Horace. A shiver ran down her spine the moment they locked eyes. A fiery intensity grew on Abraham's face. His eyebrows were knitted together, and his shoulders were pulled back. Even though he was looking with his eyes downward, his chin was still up.

She swallowed. "Let me fetch you a skin of water."

Abraham looked as if he hadn't ever seen her before in his life. He reached down and cradled her by the chin with his hand. He lifted her to her feet. His eyes looked over her bandolier of knives. His stare hardened.

The strength of his hand kept Sticks frozen in place. Immediately, she thought of the man that had possessed Ruger Slade before. He was a womanizing maniac who sent his men out like sheep for the slaughter. Her jaws clenched as she battled against the urge to tear her gaze away. This man was not Abraham, but she wasn't sure exactly who it was either.

"Perhaps the two of you need a moment alone," Horace suggested. "I'll have the Red Tunics pitch you a tent and give you some privacy. The heat of battle brings out the lust in all of us in one way or the other."

Slowly, Abraham turned his downward gaze on Horace. In a voice filled with tempered elation, he said, "This flower in my hand I do not know, but I certainly know you!" He released Sticks and caught up Horace in a bear hug. He lifted Horace up off his feet. "Handsome Horace, my, have you grown!"

The moment Horace's toes touched the ground, he took two steps backward. With wide eyes he said, "I haven't been called that in years. Captain?"

Bearclaw, Vern, Apollo, and Prospero approached with cautious looks in their eyes. All the rest of the party stopped what they were doing, including Shades, who slid in behind the four warriors.

The wild raven locks of Bearclaw shook with a nod of his chin. "Do my ears deceive me? Has my old friend returned? Is that you, Ruger?"

"It is," Ruger Slade said as he held his fingers out before him and clutched them open and closed. "For a spell, anyway."

Vern stepped forward and said, "I don't believe it. It's a deception. It has to be."

Sticks watched the men face off with one another. She wasn't sure what to think. She'd never met the real Ruger, but this man certainly wasn't Abraham. It wasn't the demented soul named Eugene either. Her gaze slid over to the baffled Horace. "How can you know that it is him?"

"It's him," Horace said. "I can feel it in my belly. I see it with my very own eyes as well. I would know."

Sticks's heart sank. The thought of Abraham being gone created a cold void inside her. She cared for the man more deeply than she would admit.

Vern swiped his wavy blond locks out of his eyes and said, "Don't get all gooey eyed, Horace. We've been deceived how many times before?" His hand fell on the handle of his sword. "This man might be as possessed as the others." He pulled his longsword. "There's only one swordsman better than me in this group, and that is supposed to be you." He flipped his blade around. "Let's see what you can do, Ruger."

5

Sticks picked up the tattered scabbard containing Black Bane, leaning against the wall. She walked toward Ruger.

"No, no, no, no," Vern objected. "The real Ruger won't need his precious magic sword. Get him another blade. Something on par with mine."

Ruger gave Vern a dangerous look and said, "You're always up for a challenge, aren't you, Verner? It brings me joy to see there is fire in your guts." He eyed Black Bane's scabbard. "Who is the fool that is mishandling my equipment? Never mind." He pulled free a short sword from Sticks's hip. He patted her on the side. "May I borrow this?"

"You're the captain," Sticks said coolly. Ruger's direct mannerisms caught her off guard. He wasn't pushy but polished, direct but polite. He carried a natural charm that was captivating. Her heart sped up. She made an unlikely comment. "Be careful."

Ruger spun the sword by the handle inside the palm of his hand. He flipped the blade side to side and studied its sharp edge. "It's notched. Looks like you've been neglecting to put the stone to it. Has everyone forgotten how to care for their weapons?" He eyed Vern. "Let's hope you haven't forgotten how to fight."

"I don't know where you've been, Captain," Vern said. He got into his sword-fighting stance. "But I've been fighting plenty. What have you been doing with yourself the last few years?"

"A good question. If I could only answer it in its entirety." The company surrounded the combatants. "My, it's good to have hard steel in my hand once again. Come on, Vern. Have a go at it. Make a move."

"Whoever you are, you're going to regret taking a shorter blade. I'll carve you in two." Vern locked his eyes on Ruger, dropped his sword into the ox guard position, and lunged.

Steel rattled against steel as Ruger snaked to the left and batted the longer sword aside with jarring effect.

Vern stumbled sideward, fought for his footing, and faced off again. He licked his puffy lips.

"You dropped your shoulder too soon," Ruger said with a disappointed shake of his head. "Once again, you telegraphed your move. Whoever you have been fighting must not have been very good."

Bearclaw and Horace chuckled.

Vern set his jaw and came at Ruger again. He turned his hips into a powerful swing.

Ruger jumped several feet backward as the edge of Vern's sword tip scraped across the metal covering his chest. "That's the spirit!"

Ruger and Vern exchanged sword-on-sword strikes with blazing fury.

Bang! Clash! Ting! Slice! Whisk! Clang! Clang! Bang!

Vern poured it on.

Ruger parried with grace and power, dropping in tutorial tidbits as he did so. "Your elbows are extended. You flap like a chicken." *Bang!* "I've seen bears with better footwork than you. Are your boots tied together?" *Ching! Slice!* "Oh my, this is worse than I thought. Your skill has deteriorated."

Lathered up in sweat and chest heaving, Vern shouted, "It has not!" He locked both hands on his handle and redoubled his efforts. He unleashed all hell with his steel. He stabbed from the high guard, ox guard, and plow guard. He turned loose a final lethal wrath-guard swing.

Ruger knocked every strike aside in a blink of an eye. Without attacking, he batted aside Vern's snakelike strokes with raw power. Sticks caught her breath. She'd seen Ruger fight before, but it wasn't anything like the display he was putting on now. His form was perfect from head to toe. He was a true sword master.

In a blur of movement and with a flip of the wrist, Ruger knocked the longsword out of Vern's grip and held his short blade on the panting man's throat. "Do you still take me for an imposter?"

Vern's Adam's apple rolled against the edge of the blade. "You are my brother in arms, my captain, Ruger Slade. Of this I have no doubt."

Ruger's eyes narrowed. Tension hung in the air. Every breath was stifled. "You were insubordinate, Vern. You should never question the captain, no matter who is in his skin. I could cut your head off... but I won't. This time." He flipped the short sword back to Sticks. She snatched it out of the air and sheathed it. He grabbed Vern and wrapped him up tight. "'Tis grand to see you, brother!"

"You too!" Vern hugged him back. "You too!"

The often-quiet Prospero threw up a fist stained with Wild Men blood and said, "Slade the Blade returns! The captain of captains is back!"

Ruger embraced all his men with hugs and fierce armlocks. Sticks had never seen a group of men so tight. It was a brotherhood with roots that ran deep.

"I see many new faces, but many are gone as well. Dare I ask?" Ruger said.

"I couldn't keep them all alive without your help," Shades said as he stepped into Ruger's view.

"Ho! If it isn't the Night Possum!" Ruger swallowed Shades up in his long arms and crushed him like a child. "I should have known that you would squirt away from any disaster." He let Shades free of his powerful embrace. He addressed them all. "You'll have to forgive my elation. My rigid demeanor that you're accustomed to escapes me at the moment. I've come from a strange land ruled by greed and despair, polluted by chronic noise that would jangle a troglin's bones... Hello..." His voice trailed off as his eyes landed for the first time on Solomon. "What do we have here?"

Horace put a meaty hand on his shoulder and said, "Captain, there is much to talk about."

"I can see that."

6

By torchlight, the Henchmen ventured on to the narrow ledges and into the icy chill of the Wound. Aided also by a soft glow from Melris's and Iris's hands, the surefooted group navigated deeper into the black terrain.

Ruger led in the front with Horace by his side and Melris a half step behind and between them. Sticks was bringing up the rear, with Solomon and the Red Tunics, Skitts, and Zann. She rubbed her hands together. Frost came from her breath. She brushed against Solomon's furry body and said, "What do you make of our new leader?"

The aged troglin shrugged and said, "I hope Abraham comes back."

Lifting an eyebrow, the normally unflappable Sticks asked, "Why do you say that?"

"I put my trust in Abraham to take me home. I'm not so sure about this man. His purpose might not be the same. To make matters worse, if Abraham does not come back, then that only means that I am stuck here as well." Solomon frowned. "Perhaps it serves me right for getting my hopes up of seeing my home again."

Sticks nodded. She felt for the troglin and could see the lost look in his big brown eyes. "This Ruger is better than the other one. At least we have that. The old guardians have truly embraced him. I don't have much of a problem with it myself, but I miss Abraham."

"Funny, but I still feel compelled to follow this man." Solomon rubbed his chest on the spot where he'd been branded. "It's the magic in the Brand, I guess. I was hoping to talk with him, but Horace wouldn't stop blathering. This Captain Ruger, he really jumped feet first into the king's mission. It was as if he hadn't missed a beat."

Ahead, the group slowed. The shelf that made a path down into the great canyon's interior narrowed to a ledge twenty feet long and just barely big enough for one man. Ruger crossed first with his back against the stone. He tossed a length of rope back to Horace. "Take no chances. One by one. We don't want to risk this shelf cracking.

One by one, the others crossed, holding the rope in hand. Debris on the outer edge broke off and chipped. The small rocks bounced down the rock wall, echoing at first then falling silent.

All the Henchmen moved across the ledge without hardly a one touching the rope. Sticks crossed in a few quick steps. She was followed by the Red Tunics, both of which were carrying heavy packs full of gear. Skitts used the rope, but Zann didn't.

"A bold pair of rabbits, I see," Ruger commented as they crossed. "You should grab the rope. Your packs will leave you off balance, and I don't want to lose any gear."

Skitts locked his hands around the rope. He was facing the wall and sidestepping along the twenty-foot gap. The back of his heels barely hung off the ledge as he moved slowly.

"Will you hurry up?" Zann suggested in his Southern drawl. "Or are you waiting for the ledge to break underneath of you?"

"I'm moving fast enough. You hush," Skitts said with a shaky voice.

"Keep it moving, young fellow. Only a few steps left to go." Ruger slid a look at Sticks. "This place would benefit from one of those elevators from that other world." He extended his arm and grabbed Skitts's pack the moment the Red Tunic came close enough. He assisted him all the way across. "Your heart won't shoot out of your throat so much the next time. You'll get used to it."

"Thank you, Captain," Skitts said as he moved on.

With an impish grin, Zann navigated the foreboding ledge with ease, leaving Solomon and Horace on the other side.

"Go ahead, Horace," Solomon said. "I'll hold the rope."

Horace handed him the rope and started to cross. The portly warrior walked on tiptoe with his free hand grazing the wall of rock. He crossed the gap in seconds.

Solomon tossed the slack in the rope over. He signaled to the others with a casual flip of his hand. "Scoot back. My feet are far too big to walk this dainty ledge."

Ruger coiled the rope over his head and moved back the onlookers bunched up on the ledge. "Let's give him some room. Have at it, troglin."

"Call me Solomon," the old troglin replied. In a single leap, Solomon jumped across the twenty-foot chasm. He landed gingerly on the full ledge. "Easy peasy."

"Well done, Henchman," Ruger remarked. "Though I'm not surprised. I've seen your ilk leap thirty feet like great cats. I was only concerned because you appear old."

"Yeah, well, don't let appearance fool you," Solomon replied with a quick look at Sticks.

"I assure you I don't." Ruger turned.

The shelf that Solomon was standing on broke underneath him. The troglin slipped into the chasm with his claws raking down the chasm wall.

Ruger dove belly first onto the ledge. His strong fingers clutched over the rim. "Horace, anchor my legs—I have him!"

Horace dropped down on his butt and hooked his meaty arms around Ruger's ankles.

Sticks burst into action, grabbing the rope and tossing it over the rim. She flipped the excess rope to the Red Tunics. "Anchor it!"

The Red Tunics fed the rope back to the others. A strong chain of rope and men was set.

"Where is he?" Horace asked.

"I don't know. I thought I had him. It appears I have not," Ruger replied.

Sticks gazed over the ledge. There was no sign of Solomon, only blackness.

7

———

"Is he gone?" Horace said. He took a peek over the ledge as he did so.

"Shhh," Ruger said softly.

Sticks turned an ear. Small chunks of rock were bouncing down the wall. Something scraped against stone. The Henchmen lowered their torches into the black gap.

Suddenly, Solomon appeared, climbing up the wall like a squirrel. A broad grin crossed his face as he shouted, "Waaahooo!" He clucked with thunderous laughter as he climbed up onto the smaller ledge. He fastened himself to the wall with two black fingernails. "Have you forgotten that troglins are the greatest mountaineers in this world? Climbing through this chasm is easy peasy."

"Why don't you climb back down and find the bottom of this abyss?" Horace said as he hauled Ruger back in.

"I'm following orders," Solomon replied.

"As you should," Ruger said as he climbed back to his feet. "Next time, I'll have a better recollection of your skills in mind." He turned and face the group. "Enough gawking. Onward, Henchmen. We have the king's stones to find."

"'Tis a sad day to serve a king that has no stones," Shades remarked.

Many of the Henchmen chuckled.

"Not those stones," Ruger replied as he passed Sticks and shoulder bumped Shades. "Don't quip about the king. It can bring misfortune."

Sticks watched Solomon make his way back to the ledge. He still had a smile on his face. "Did I have you worried?" he asked.

"I never worry," she replied. Her ears perked. "Did you hear that?"

"What?" Solomon said.

She stepped to the ledge and looked downward as a moist sucking sound caught her ear. The fine hairs on the nape of her neck rose. "You didn't see anything down there, did you?"

"It's pitch-black. I can't even see my paw in front of my face." Solomon started forward. "It's probably the blood rushing through your ears."

Sticks gripped her handle of her sheathed sword. "You're probably right. Let's go." She glanced at Solomon just as a moist and fleshy tentacle wrapped around his waist. She pulled her sword and screamed, "Solomon!"

Solomon was ripped from the ledge by the powerful tentacle. The slimy thing had thousands of clutching suckers all over it.

"Gah! Get this thing off of me!" Solomon shouted. He was suspended by the massive tentacle, which plucked him off the wall like a bug. He thrashed against his bonds with his face in horrified agony. "Help! Help!"

Sticks chopped at the octopod tendril but was far from the mark.

The Henchmen, led by Ruger, rushed to their aid.

More tentacles crawled up the ledge and swiped at Sticks's feet. One tentacle had a bulging eye on the end of it. It lunged at Sticks. With a swing of her sword, she cut the eyeball off. She danced between the tentacles, cutting fiercely at everything that moved.

"Gaaah!" Solomon screamed. "Somebody do something!"

"There!" Ruger stabbed his sword downward at a hulking blob

churning up the canyon wall. "Death to the slime dweller, Henchmen!"

Skitts and Zann fired a volley of crossbow bolts into the massive blob. A mouth opened and closed that could swallow a horse whole. The bolts sank into its flesh and disappeared. More tentacles exploded from it and snaked their way up onto the rim.

The Henchmen burst into action.

Horace stabbed his great spear into the tendrils.

Vern and Bearclaw slashed away.

Prospero hurled a burning torch into the monster's mouth.

The monster shrieked as it began to burn from the inside out. Its tentacles clenched and recoiled. The creeping slime began a rapid descent down the wall. It's bulging froglike body glowed with burning fire from within.

"Help me!" Solomon cried out. "Help me!" The troglin was being pulled down into the inky depths. His long, hairy fingers clutched at the air.

Ruger grabbed the rope and hurled it at the troglin, shouting, "Grab hold!"

Solomon grasped the rope with the tips of his fingers then coiled it around his hands.

"Henchmen! Take the rope!" Ruger commanded.

Every able hand in the company grabbed hold of the rope and pulled. Sticks stood behind Ruger, digging her heels into the ledge. Ruger's forearms knotted with muscle. He threw his head back and heaved. Behind her, Horace panted heavily and said, "This thing is heavier than me!"

The creeper wasn't going down without a meal. It pulled against them with unearthly force.

The boots of the Henchmen began to slide across the ledge.

Solomon cried out, "I can't hold much longer. Save yourself!"

"Put your backs into it!" Ruger shouted as he set his feet on the ledge and squatted down. "Death before failure. Hurk!"

Inch by inch, the Henchmen pulled the rope back. Every person holding the line groaned. Sticks's teeth ground, and her jaws clenched. Her back and thighs burned with fire. Out of the corner of her eye, she caught hornets made of rosy-purple fire shooting down into the abyss.

The monster let out a moan that would have turned a softer man's bones to jelly. It pulled down the wall with the strength of an elephant.

The rope burned through Sticks's hand. Horace bumped up against her.

Ruger gave his final order as he teetered over the edge. "No one lets go of this rope but me. That's an order!" He snatched up his sword and dove point first toward the monster.

"Captain, no!" Horace yelled.

Ruger vanished.

The rope juddered on the other side of the ledge. The great weight at the other end broke free a few moments later. The company backpedaled with the sudden change in weight and slammed into the wall. Not one single Henchmen lost grip.

Solomon climbed up over the ledge. His long, hairy arms were shaking like leaves. Sticks and Horace crawled over and hauled him all the way up.

"Thank you," Solomon said with a trembling voice. He looked over into the black expanse. "He dove right in. He dove right into its very jaws." He swallowed. "And like a wind blowing out a flame," he cast a sad look at Sticks, "he was gone."

8

———

Sticks rubbed the raw palms of her hands. Hours had passed since they battled the monster Ruger had called a creeper. Her hands burned like fire. That would pass. The loss of Ruger wouldn't. Nor would the loss of Abraham. If Ruger was dead, she had no chance of ever seeing Abraham again.

"Are you sure you don't want me to have a look at that?" Iris said in her naturally cheery voice. "After all, I've patched up all of the others requiring aid."

"It's only a burn," she said flatly.

The Henchmen had reached what appeared to be the bottom of the canyon. Above was a skylight the size of a fingernail, which showed the night sky. The canyon floor must have been a mile down, perhaps deeper. Sticks wasn't the best judge of such things.

"I'll live."

"Suit yourself. Holler if you need me." Iris moved back toward the rest of the group.

The men were gathered around, grumbling back and forth. Horace's, Bearclaw's, and Vern's heads were down. Vern was cursing. Fingers were being poked at one another. Without the captain, no one was there to control them.

Shades squirted away from the pack and squatted down by Sticks and Solomon. "This is going to be ugly with the captain dead."

"Don't say that," Solomon said. "We don't know that."

"Ruger might have been the greatest sword, but even he can't kill a thousand-foot free fall," Shades said with his usual rugged playfulness. "I imagine that only makes your predicament worse. Sorry, hairy fella."

Solomon shoved Shades onto his backside. "That man saved my life. Show some respect."

Shades climbed back to his feet and said, "You are right. Ruger deserves that. It was good to see him one last time and watch him save our backsides again. Believe me when I say when I grieve, I grieve as much as you."

Sticks sat with her legs crossed and the assault rifle across her lap. Her fingers toyed with the weapon's carrying strap. "I should have shot the thing. Like Abraham taught me. I didn't even think of it."

"Everyone is blaming each other. At least you aren't. I'll let you take full responsibility if you like." Shades grinned. "For a change, no one is blaming me, which is refreshing."

Horace's and Vern's voices started to rise. The loud talking became loud shouting.

"You are not going to lead this expedition. If anyone is going to lead, it is me!" Horace bellowed at Melris. "You are not even a Henchman! We are going to search for the captain!"

"No," Melris replied in his smooth voice that could penetrate a wall. "All of us are under the same order from King Hector. We are to make haste to recover the stones. Ruger Slade would have understood that. The mission comes first. We've been sidetracked once. I cannot allow it to happen again."

Vern jabbed a finger at the Elderling and said, "You listen to me, you little worm, we are in charge, not you!"

With a flick of his finger, Melris hurled Vern off his feet and sent him skidding over the ground. The Henchmen's weapons whisked out of their sheaths. They walled in Melris with shining steel bared.

Horace held his spear tip in Melris's face. "Henchmen don't turn against other Henchmen."

"I'm not a Henchman," Melris replied. His iron rod glowed in his hand. "And you err, Horace. I am in the right. You are in the wrong. The king placed me in charge of the expedition. Captain Slade understood that. Now he is gone, leaving me in charge. Though you can choose a leader among yourselves, you still have to follow me."

Sticks quietly approached the arguing men and said, "He's right, Horace. You know it. We don't have a choice."

"Then you can follow him," Horace said. He yanked his spear away from Melris's face. "I'm going to find the captain. Who is with me?"

Rising back to his feet, Vern said, "I am."

"As am I," agreed Bearclaw.

"We aren't going anywhere without the captain, dead or alive," Cudgel said.

His brother, Tark, nodded.

Apollo and Prospero stood gathered behind Horace. So did Dominga.

"I don't know, Horace," Iris said with her fingers fidgeting by her side. "It's bad luck to split up and even worse to go against the king's orders. "I have to stand by Melris. Methinks any other move will piss the Elders off. We need them."

Horace stuffed his fingers into his pouch and said, "Then I'm chewing my tobacco!"

Shades and Solomon joined Iris behind Melris.

"Well, what in the Crotch are we supposed to do? We just take orders. Who do we take them from now?" Zann asked.

Horace pointed at Skitts and said, "You come with us. Zann, you can go with them." He gave Melris a final hard look. "Henchmen don't abandon Henchmen."

"Henchmen are expendable. That's why they are Henchmen," Melris said. "I'll warn you your chances of survival greatly diminish with your numbers divided. All of you would be wise to follow me. Believe me when I say that I know what I am talking about."

Horace spat on the ground. He eyed Sticks and Iris and said, "I'm disappointed in you." He turned his back and led his group into the darkness of the canyon.

Skitts carried a torch. He gave Sticks and her group one last long look before they disappeared around a bend in the rock and vanished into the darkness.

"I have a bad feeling about this." Zann sucked his teeth. "I'm not used to being separated from my brother. It makes me feel like a dove is flapping inside my chest."

9

Aided by the illumination from Melris's and Iris's hands, the small company moved across the bottom of the Wound's canyon floor. Sticks could make out the rolling dark clouds high above, through a shrinking eye-shaped window. She felt small, tiny, like an ant in a strange but new world that lurked in the ground below. She tucked her hands against her sides and churned on.

Melris was in the front, Iris in the rear. Sticks, Solomon, Dominga, Shades, and Zann walked between them.

"Say, mage," Shades said to Melris. "Do you have a sense of where we are going? All of this place looks the same to me."

"I can feel it," Melris said. "The stones are in this place, deep in the bones of Titanuus."

"What does he mean by that?" Zann said with a frosty breath. "And wouldn't it be wise to make a torch or something? It might keep us a little warmer."

"Strange that it feels so cold down here," Solomon commented. "And where does the wind come from?"

"I don't know," Dominga said as she cozied up to Solomon, grabbed his arm, and draped it over her shoulder. She snuggled into him. "I hope you don't mind, but I hate being cold."

"Not at all," Solomon said.

"I can keep you warmer than him," Shades commented.

"I seriously doubt that," Dominga said.

"Well, I bet I can do a better job than Vern," Shades said.

"We'll never know." Dominga clung to Solomon more tightly, looked up, and gave him a smile.

Solomon smiled back.

Melris cradled his Rod of Devastation in his arms like a man holding a baby. He moved at a brisk pace on ghostly-soft footsteps.

They walked for hours. Sticks's teeth chattered though she tried to control it.

Finally, Melris moved over a rise on the hard rock floor and stopped.

A pale-pink light emanated from a hole in the ground. A slope inside the hole led downward.

Zann stretched his fingers over the twelve-foot-wide gap and said, "It's warm."

"We are going into the bones," Melris said. Without another word, he walked down the slope.

The remainder of the Henchmen stood outside the gap, exchanging glances with one another.

"I don't know about this place," Iris said with her fingers strumming the air. "Something very alive is down there. My very bones tingle."

"I'd rather die warm than be left out in the cold." Sticks hopped into the tunnel.

"Aye, I'm with her," Shade said.

"You don't have to tell me twice," Dominga added.

Solomon and Zann were still standing outside when Sticks looked back over her shoulder. Solomon was shaking his head. Zann was mumbling and nodding.

"Are you coming?" she asked.

"Perhaps we should wait for the others," Solomon said. "Something doesn't smell right."

Sticks sniffed. "I don't smell anything odd."

"Yeah, that's what bothers me," the troglin replied.

"We need to stay together. What's left of us, at least," she said.

"Yup," Zann croaked, "someone needs to protect the rest of them. I guess that's us." He waltzed into the tunnel. "Come on, hairy fella. They need us. And I don't have fur like you. I hate the cold too."

Solomon ventured in, casting his eyes all around. The tunnel was twenty feet high, and the walls were the color of red brick and perforated with holes. He scratched his fingers over the crusty coating of the walls, which were bone white underneath.

"Interesting," he said. "If I were to guess, I'd say that these walls were made of bone."

"Bone?" Zann asked.

Solomon looked at the dried dirt underneath his fingernail then at the strange flooring beneath his feet. The floor was no different from the walls.

"And this is blood or the dried marrow."

That's very observant, Solomon," Melris said. "We are inside the very bones of Titanuus. Feel them." He touched the perforated surface of the wall. "There is still life inside the celestial titan. And where there is life, there is more life."

"Now it's getting creepy," Solomon said.

"Shall we proceed?" Melris turned his back and continued walking down into the tunnel.

The walls were twenty feet high and just as wide. The passage led straight forward.

The small company moved at a brisk pace through the odd corridor. Sticks wondered if what Melris had said was really true about the titans that formed the world. *Are we actually inside the bones of a celestial titan that died eons ago? Is Titanuus still alive?* She rubbed the goose bumps popping up on her arms. *Creepy.* That wasn't something she would have ever dwelled on, but now, the odd circumstances told as stories to excited children before bedtime had become very real. She was on a bigger stage than she had ever been. *I miss Abraham.*

The longer they walked, the more she thought about him. Ruger Slade had come back, but then he died. That meant Abraham was gone, which wasn't something she was prepared to deal with. Her feelings for him ran deep. She didn't want to accept that he was dead. *I hope he still lives on his world.*

Iris drifted back and said to her, "You've got a long face for a girl who shows no expression at all. I figured you'd be feeling better now that we are all nice and toasty." She fanned her glistening face. "Perhaps too toasty."

"I think you know by now that I'm not the chatty type."

"Oh, well, we don't have much else to do, seeing how this walk might go on for days," Iris said.

Plenty of distance remained between everyone. Melris and Shades were in the front, while Dominga, Solomon, and Zann were in the back.

"Come on, have a go at it with me. I know it's your man that's missing."

Without batting an eye, Sticks looked at the pie-faced mystic and said, "I don't want to talk about it."

"Fine, then I'll do the talking. Abraham had you feeling all rosy inside, didn't he? And now, you don't know if you'll ever feel that way again. Well, let me tell you, you probably won't. Those kinds of feelings are fleeting in this world, but consider yourself lucky that you felt them because most don't."

"It won't ever come back," Sticks said.

"I had a fellow once. I felt like I was on a cloud when I was with him. Sometimes, the timing isn't right. Life gets in the way. People move on. It's a very sad thing." Iris offered a warm smile. "I think about him a lot still. I always will."

Sticks nodded. "I only wish I could have said good-bye."

10

———————

BACK HOME

Abraham blinked. The zillon standing beside his table didn't disappear. The alien-like person, unlike in the movies, had a black ponytail hanging from the back of her head. His oval eyes were large and black. A small nub of a nose was set in the middle of his face. She had a mouthful of many straight teeth. The zillon was no different from the ones he'd seen on Titanuus. The only difference was this zillon was here.

"Welcome to Earth," Abraham said.

Dr. Jack Lassiter chuckled. "You're a real funny guy, Abraham. No, this isn't an alien from another world. This is a zillon from Titanuus. Pretty interesting, wouldn't you say?"

In a voice as normal as any human woman, the zillon woman said, "I am Ottum from Hancha. A dragon rider. Do you know the dragon riders?"

Abraham looked the shapely zillon up and down. Ottum was wearing a set of black-and-gray camouflage clothing.

"Yeah. I know 'em. Killed them too. How'd you get here?"

Ottum kneaded her fingertips together and replied, "I came through a portal." Her spacey eyes did not blink. "It was long ago."

Dr. Jack intervened and said, "It's still a mystery how she got here, but we are unlocking more secrets about the portals every day. It's only a matter of time until we have it under complete control."

"Are there more zillons out there?" Abraham asked.

"It's a big world," Dr. Jack said. "We only see what the bigshots want us to see, so it's safe to say that yes, there are plenty of strange beings walking this world."

If Abraham could have sat up, he would have as he thought of Solomon and said, "Like Bigfoot!"

Dr. Jack shrugged. "So, Abraham, what do you think? How would you like to go back and start all over again? With your cooperation, we can make that happen."

"I don't believe that we can travel back through time. That's crazy."

"And you didn't believe that you could travel from one world to another, now did you?" Dr. Jack asked. He eyed the zillon. "But now, you have proof."

A big part of Abraham wanted nothing more than to go back to the time just before the plane crash. If he could do it all over again, he'd never get on that plane. He'd never fly either. He could be with Jenny and Jake again. He would hold them both in his arms and never let go. Life would be perfect. *This is madness. I can't go back in time. Of course, I can't live in two worlds at once either. God help me.*

"You should work with Dr. Jack," Ottum the zillon suggested. "Like you, I too want to return home."

"Well, back in your world, your people are trying to destroy the king of Kingsland. The dragon riders tried to assassinate him with modern weapons." He glared at Dr. Jack. "I bet you knew all about that, didn't you?"

"Come on, Abraham, don't be naive," Dr. Jack said as he puffed out a stream of smoke. "No kingdom lasts forever."

"Except the Kingdom of Heaven."

"Yeah, if you believe that sort of thing. You know your history. Every nation has been conquered at one time or another. Now is our time to be a part of a new world, a world where we can do things right. After all, this world is collapsing. We need a place to escape. There is no telling where this might lead."

"I don't know."

"Think about it," Dr. Jack said. "You saw the movie *Back to the Future*, didn't you? With the DeLorean that went back and forth through time. They set the wrongs right. You can have your life back."

"You make it sound like you have this mastered. If that's the case, why me?"

"I guess it's because you're special. You are the only one that bounces back between both worlds. The others can't do it. They come, they stay, they can't commute. For some reason—I don't know what it is—you can do both. It's causing problems. Work with me, and you can have your life back, and we can get back to our work."

Abraham imagined going back eight years in time. It didn't seem possible. Something inside his gut twisted. His father, Earl, had often said, "Life happens. It's not always good. It's not always bad. But you have to move forward." He wanted more than anything to hold Jenny and Jake one last time. In truth, he hadn't been able to move forward in life without them. He never moved on—at least, not until this maddening twist of fate, where he found himself traveling from one world to another. It had to end. But he had to end it correctly.

"What's on your mind?" Ottum asked. She stroked Abraham's face with a feather-light touch of her long, slender fingers. "Tell me. I want to help you, and you can help me. I understand. You can trust me. I've lost loved ones as well."

"I bet you have."

He tried not to have a grudge against her. Not all zillons were bad —he'd met many. But the zillons had attacked King Hector.

"Listen, I don't think I can handle much more of this," he said. "I'll deal with you, but I want to use the bathroom and have something to eat first."

Dr. Jack gave him a nod and said, "Deal."

11

After Abraham was fed under the watchful eyes of Otis and Haymaker, he was strapped to another gurney and loaded into a green military ambulance and hauled away. Otis and Haymaker sat inside the ambulance cabin with their stun rods in their hands. Neither man took his eyes off him. The ambulance bounced over potholes and swayed on the hard bends in the road.

Abraham had no idea where he was. He opted for small talk. "So, how much does a good orderly make these days? Fifteen, twenty dollars an hour?"

"Shut up," Otis said. He stuck his stun rod on Abraham's nose. "Don't make me shock you."

"I'm not so sure that you want to do that. You might bring Dr. Jekyll out." He eyeballed Otis's swollen cheek. "You have a tough time with him, don't you."

"I'll say," Haymaker said in a cheery country-boy manner. "You tossed us around like bales of hay the last time you switched. But we'll be ready for you next time. We can handle it."

"Yeah, with me strapped up like this, you might." He strained against his cuffs. "Pretty strong, but I think Ruger Slade is stronger. In the other world, I have superpowers. I can snap these bonds like twigs." He shrugged his eyebrows. "Like twigs."

"Yeah, well, if Dr. Jack was smart, he'd let us kill you. You're the source of all the trouble. I don't know why, seeing how you are one man, but they are obsessed with you." Otis sniffed. "They'd be better off without you."

Abraham had no idea why he was more special than the other otherworlders that had soul swapped. He understood that he traveled between both worlds, but why it was him but not the others, he didn't know. *Why me?* For the life of him, he couldn't recall anything special having happened in his life, aside from the plane wreck, when the plane was struck by lightning and he somehow survived.

The ambulance rumbled down the road. It bumped and jostled over rugged terrain. With no windows inside the cabin, Abraham had no idea if it was day or night. Suddenly, the rough road became smooth. The ride went on for a few more minutes, then the ambulance's brakes squealed to a halt.

The double doors on the back of the ambulance popped open. Two soldiers in black-gray camouflage, wearing machine guns strapped over their backs and mesh baseball caps, stepped aside while Otis and Haymaker pushed the gurney out of the back.

The gurney's legs dropped open underneath Abraham. The orderlies pushed him along on the casters. They were inside an old tunnel, the walls made of old cinder blocks. The ceiling was at least twenty feet high. The tunnel was lit by military tree lights. Gas generators made a steady hum. On the walls of the tunnel were more heavy equipment and generators. A Jeep and a Humvee were there. Long black power cords ran along the floor.

"Nice place. Let me guess, Batman lives here," Abraham said.

"No, that's another cave," Dr. Jack said.

Abraham heard the man's voice but didn't see him. He craned his neck around. Aside from Otis and Haymaker, he saw only the two other soldiers. "You aren't really going to keep me strapped to this thing forever, are you? I said I'd help."

"Stand him up," Dr. Jack said.

Otis and Haymaker adjusted the custom-made gurney with a tilt that stood Abraham almost straight up.

He was facing the entrance of the tunnel, where he could see the ambulance, other vehicles, generators, and the other equipment. The bigger, rectangular generators were loud. A fuel tanker truck was pulled into the tunnel as well.

"What is this, one of those underground bunkers like that place in Colorado called NORAD? Or is this NORAD?"

Dr. Jack stepped into view and said, "No, it's not NORAD." He wasn't smoking.

"What's the matter, did you run out of cigars?"

"We don't smoke in this facility." Dr. Jack gave Otis and Haymaker a look and said, "Go ahead, turn him around."

With one arm, Otis spun Abraham around one hundred eighty degrees. Teams of men in white lab coats were strolling through large ground-level computer stations. At least a dozen soldiers were standing guard back against the tunnel's walls. He could make out a few familiar faces. Eugene Drisk, older and frumpy, was talking to Colonel Drew Dexter and Ottum the zillon. Colonel Dexter held an iPad and dotted it with a pen. His moustache twitched when he glanced at Abraham.

Well, if it isn't a couple of my favorite persons. Evil scientist and power-mad military man. "Ah, I see more of my favorite people," Abraham said. "Is this the secret lair of evil geniuses?" He nodded his head. "It's very sinister."

Dr. Jack moved deeper into the tunnel. "You're a funny man."

The orderlies shoved Abraham forward. He noticed some odd lettering on the generators that they passed. In large letters painted white, it read, Drakeland Corp. The letters were configured like a logo, and they ran through a rising sun. *Interesting. This isn't military equipment. It's private industry. I bet Sid and Smoke would want to know about this.*

Dr. Jack shook hands with Colonel Dexter.

Eugene Drisk almost jumped out of his lab coat when he saw Abraham. Shielding himself with his iPad, he said, "That's not...?"

"No, that's not Ruger. It's Abraham. Good ol' washed-up Abraham," Dr. Jack said. "And he wouldn't be here unless he'd agreed to cooperate. He's game for our big plan... Aren't you, Abraham?"

"I just want to get this over with one way or the other," he said.

"Good." Dr. Jack grabbed Ottum's hand in his and said, "Well, what are we waiting for. Let's turn the Time Tunnel on."

12

Eugene Drisk moved over to one of the large computer stations and started punching keys. The five main computer stations were fanned out in front of an intricately crafted metal ring that made a thick hoop inside the tunnel. A new hum carried throughout the tunnel. Small twinkling LEDs in a variety of colors came on inside the loop. Like the stars in the sky, thousands of them appeared.

Abraham saw Haymaker's arm hairs stand on end. His own hairs stood as though they were filled with static electricity. Great power was coursing through the tunnel. The steady hum of the gas-powered generators chugged and suddenly heaved.

Dr. Jack stood with a triumphant smile on his face. "Watch this," he said.

Eugene gave a single finger signal to the other scientists wearing lab coats, standing along the tunnel wall. On both sides, each manned a large electrical switch with a long black handle. At the same time, they pushed the levers upward. The tunnel beyond the hoop filled with light, and the droning hum of lights became louder.

Abraham squinted. He couldn't shield his eyes, but he wanted to.

"It's not on!" Dr. Jack said in a loud voice. The curly hairs on his head were standing taller, as if he'd just walked through a wind tunnel. "It's only warming up!"

The tunnel walls behind the hoop were made up of large tiles of shiny steel. The glimmering tiles stretched back another fifty feet, where a bright ring of yellow light burned at the end.

"Very nice," Abraham said, "but I don't see a passing lane. And shouldn't there be a toll booth? You know, make sure you use one of the EZ Pass services. It makes a trucker's life a lot easier."

"Huh huh," Colonel Trotter laughed. "I might have liked you if you hadn't killed so many of my soldiers."

"What's a trucker supposed to do, let them kill me?" He was referring to the battle near Morgantown, when the choppers came. "It was us or them."

"They wouldn't have fired if you'd given yourself up," Colonel Dexter said. "The rest of it was miscommunication. I wasn't there. With that said, I hope this next trip of yours is a one-way journey. And don't worry about Mandi. I'll take care of her."

"I'm pretty sure you've burned that bridge." Abraham would have knocked the moustache off Colonel Dexter's face if he could have. His heart burned for Mandi. She'd stuck with him through thick and thin, and he hardly knew her. Now, he was thinking about his family, about going back to them, but he didn't believe that was possible. *What about the Henchmen—Sticks, Horace, and my friends? Will I ever see them again?* "So, what's the story, Jack? How does this thing work?"

"I'll let Eugene and his allies handle that. The question is, are you willing to go back and quit this nonsense with the king of Kingsland? You need to tell them to surrender. Tell them that we will give them whatever they want. Just cooperate."

Ottum approached Abraham, put her cool hand on his face, and said, "King Hector is not a good man. He rules with an iron fist. You cannot trust him. The gems in the Crown of Stones were taken from his family for good reason. They are power mad. It runs in his blood. That bloodline must be destroyed."

The inflection in Ottum's voice suggested she believed what she said. Abraham liked the king. He'd been fair. However, the last time he saw him, the king had changed. He had the green and blue Stones of Power, and the air about him had changed. *I hope I haven't been fighting on the wrong side of this the entire time. No, that couldn't be.* He eyed the men surrounding him. *These dudes are a bunch of tools.*

"Abraham, we aren't out to kill King Hector. We aren't out to kill anyone. What we want is the King's Steel. That's how we can keep the portal open." Dr. Jack pointed into the portal. "You notice that some of the plates shine more than the others. That's the King's Steel we've acquired. We need more of it. It keeps the tunnel and the gate intact. There is no metal on Earth like it."

"I don't think I'm going to be able to talk Hector into surrendering. He'll kill me. That would be treason. I'm no good to you dead."

"You're going to have to convince him. But we can help with that." Dr. Jack nodded at Colonel Dexter.

The colonel gave a hand signal to a group of soldiers. In the middle of the tunnel was a set of railroad tracks that led in and out of the tunnel. Behind them, way far in the back, something heavy started to roll over the tracks.

"Otis, do me a favor and turn me around," Abraham said.

"No," Otis answered.

"It's okay—do as he asks," Dr. Jack replied.

"As the gurney turns," Abraham said as he was wheeled around.

A train flatcar rolled down the tracks. It was loaded with a tank, racks of assault rifles, and crates that were marked Ammunition. He paled.

Eugene Drisk snaked his way over to the group and chuckled wickedly. "They've made more progress than I even dreamed of. What I told you back in Pittsburgh was misleading. Progress in this world moves faster each day. It's... uncanny."

Abraham was turned as the flatcar passed by. It stopped right before the mouth of the loop. The army-green tank might as well have been a harbinger of doom. Titanuus was being invaded. They wouldn't be ready for it.

"I know it's only one tank and a few hundred assault rifles," Dr. Jack said. "But it should be more than enough to send a message."

13

"Fire up the Time Tunnel, Colonel Dexter. Let's show Mr. Jenkins what we can do," Dr. Jack said. He looked at Abraham and said, "This part makes me giddy."

Each computer station had several large LCD screens. Most of the images on the screens were of the Time Tunnel shown at various angles. The other screen showed the insides of tunnels from other places. Some of them had traffic passing through them like the Big Walker and East Mountain Tunnel. The other tunnels were abandoned.

"I thought the portals opened at random places and you couldn't control them," Abraham said.

Eugene Drisk overheard him talking to Dr. Jack, walked over, and said, "Your memory serves you well. I can't help but be amazed that this traveling back and forth doesn't jar your memories more."

"Did it jar your memories?"

"No, but I haven't been back and forth so many times as you," Eugene said. He stroked the scraggly whiskers on his chin. "I would think that would make a man crazy. As for the portals, when we turn the tunnel on, sometimes the other portals become active. They are most effective inside tunnels and possibly caves. I believe it has something to do with the contour and the darkness. So far, they are mostly active in the Fort Pitt, Big Walker, and East River Mountain Tunnels, plus some of the smaller railroad tunnels between here and there. That's why we practice this at night, when the roads are not so busy. The portals only open for a few seconds before they close again. We do our best to avoid casualties."

"Is that how I was pulled into all of this? You fired this tunnel up, and I happened to drive through it?"

"It's a theory. But"—Eugene lifted a finger—"we believe these portals have been around a very long time. Anomalies in time and space. We just happened to be the ones that discovered them."

"Good for you," Abraham said.

A black camping trailer over thirty feet long was parked on the left side of the tunnel. A rectangular row of windows ran from one end to the other. Men and women were standing behind the glass, wearing white lab coats.

Abraham tried to dig for every bit of information that he could get. Ruger Slade hadn't surrendered himself for just any reason. He must have wanted to get closer to the operation. Perhaps he had some faith that Abraham would do the right thing too. Abraham knew how clever Ruger could be as well. The sword fighter had an indomitable will, but he was more than that. He was a tactician, which made him dangerous.

"So," he said with a nod of his chin toward the trailer, "who are they? More otherworlders, I bet."

"No, that's the A-Team," Eugene said. "They are the geniuses that kept this project alive when I was gone."

Dr. Jack moved away and started talking to Colonel Dexter.

"Listen, Abraham, I don't know when you are going to speak to King Hector again, but I'll tell you this, it's very unlikely the old man will budge. Kingsland will die with him. As for you, well, you should do what is best for you. Just like I did what is best for me. Believe me, I was trapped inside Ruger Slade for years. It gets old. It can make you crazy, and I tried to make the most of it. The world is inhospitable. But we will make it so much better."

"Wouldn't you rather be here instead of there?"

"These people think that they will make Titanuus a vacation resort for the rich. That's only a ploy for money. There is more at play here, more than what wealth and riches could ever offer. It's a chance at immortality, by moving from one body to another, or rather, controlling time itself."

"We'll see."

"Yes, we will, because you are going to be the first pilot that we send through space and time." Eugene sniffed. "You'll be like the first space pilots that landed on the moon."

"Except many believe that never happened."

"Poppycock. People believe what we tell them."

Red lights mounted on the tunnel's interior walls started to flicker. An annoying buzzer went off.

"It's showtime," Eugene said.

The lab assistants started handing out rubber goggles with dark lenses. Otis jammed a pair over Abraham's eyes and snapped them shut tight.

"Thanks, big fella. Say, are these 3-D?"

"Shut up," Otis replied.

A digital female voice sounded overhead: "Countdown begins mark thirty. Twenty-nine. Twenty-eight."

The gas generators chugged more loudly. Their power cords ran across the ground, along the tracks, and were hooked into two five-foot-high-and-wide metal boxes fixed to the ground in front of the tunnel. Each box had a yellow nuclear-power warning sign. Heavy black power cords, each a foot thick, ran from the nuclear boxes to the Time Tunnel ring. A purple glow emanated from the tops of the boxes.

"Twenty-one. Twenty. Nineteen. Eighteen."

In that instant, Abraham understood what he needed to do. He had to destroy the Time Tunnel on Earth, and the portal gates on the other side of Titanuus had to be sealed as well. Forever. All he could do was hope that the Crown of Stones could do that.

"Twelve. Eleven. Ten. Nine."

The onlookers moved back from the Time Tunnel. They stood behind the computer stations, where Abraham was. Everyone had their goggles on, standing with bated breath.

Abraham's chest tightened. He was about to witness history. He didn't want to see it.

"Five. Four. Three. Two. One."

The LED lights inside the time tunnel switched from multiple colors to a bright purple. The plates inside the tunnel started to glow white hot and spin, slowly at first, then faster and faster.

Cold air blasted out of the tunnel in a hair-stirring *whoosh*.

A bright sun ring formed inside the tunnel. The bristling-cold air started to warm.

An image started to form inside the tunnel. Walls of a cave appeared that had not been there before. Great torches were hanging from the walls. Figures of men and women stood in a background cast in shadows.

Colonel Dexter started barking orders. "Send in the flatcar. Send it now!"

The flatcar loaded with the tank and modern weaponry was pushed into the tunnel.

The people on the other side of the tunnel waved swords in the air and cheered. They were rugged men, barbaric brutes with neck muscles up to their ears. Black tattoos decorated their bodies like snakes.

Abraham's blood chilled. They were Gond. That wasn't all he recognized, either. Standing in the wild crowd was the wraith, Fleece. Right beside him was the horned halfling, Big Apple. Big Apple waved his stubby little fingers. He pointed at the tank and grinned impishly.

The portal closed.

14

"Did you get a look at those guys?" Dr. Jack asked with a shiver of his shoulders. "They were huge. It gave me a chill."

The scientists and soldiers were shaking hands, high fiving, and talking with elation about a job well done.

The light inside the Time Tunnel had cooled. The flatcar was gone. The loud humming in the background went quiet.

Abraham had chill bumps all over. "Do me a favor and take these goggles off, will you?"

Otis complied. With a rough yank, he pulled the goggles from Abraham's face.

"Gee, thanks. So, did you guys see some of your cousins over there? Those Gond are your kind of people."

"Shut up," Otis replied.

"Mr. Drisk," said one of the scientists monitoring the computer station closest to Abraham, "we had activity inside the Fort Pitt Tunnel."

Eugene hurried over to the man. Dr. Jack and Colonel Dexter joined him.

The scientist pointed at one of the overhead monitors. A van decked out in Pittsburgh Steelers logos passed through a bright sun ring that suddenly appeared in the tunnel. The van vanished. A young woman and her small daughter, decked out in Steelers jerseys, sat stranded on the stretch of road. Their eyes were big as saucers. They dashed across the road, away from the fast-moving traffic.

Colonel Dexter got on his phone and said in his deep voice, "We've got two live ones in the Fort Pitt Tunnel. A woman and her girl. Decked out in Steelers gear. Hard to miss. I'll upload more data." He stuffed his phone into his pocket. "Got to go. Let me know if you discover any more of them." He gave Abraham a quick disapproving look and hustled away.

Abraham mulled over his plans for the next hour or so while everyone else scuttled about like a hive of bees, congratulating themselves. He didn't have any doubt that what they did might have been one of the greatest achievements of mankind. *If men like this keep such secrets, then what other secrets do they keep?* "Otis, will you pinch me? I'm having a hard time believing this is real."

"Shut up."

"How about you, Haymaker? You don't look too busy."

"It's real," Haymaker replied. "As real as the hair on my head. I can't wait to get to Titanuus. I'm going to be a baron. Acres of land and many wives."

"You know the women are really hideous over there, don't you?" Abraham said.

Haymaker's bright expression dulled. "What?"

"I mean, if you like the husky, cornfed type, let me say they are aplenty. But don't expect them to have all of their teeth. They don't have toothbrushes, you know. Or running water or television."

Haymaker scratched his head. "I never really thought about that."

"He's pulling your leg," Otis said. "I told you to shut up, Abraham." He waved the stun rod over his face. "You don't want to make me use this."

"I think we both know that *you* are much safer with me than the other guy, aren't you?"

Otis paled. "Shut up."

Dr. Jack and Ottum strolled over. Eugene came with them. "Did you enjoy the show?" Jack said.

Feigning awe, Abraham replied, "So that is what happened to me? I drove through a sun ring, and that's how I became like this. A schizophrenic."

"You aren't a schizophrenic. You are an experiment," Eugene smugly said. "A lab rat."

"A lab rat, huh? I want to be clear about something, and I'm not one to use profane words, but I think all of you are bunch of first-rate arseholes." He eyed Ottum. "Including you."

"*Arseholes*—now that really is a harsh word," Dr. Jack said. "Where'd you come up with that one? Your friends in Titanuus?"

"No, it's from one of my favorite books. It's where guys like you wind up with an axe run through them, but in this case, it will probably be a sword."

"Black Bane," Eugene said.

"Anything can happen."

"What's Black Bane?" Dr. Jack asked.

"It's a sword in Titanuus with magical properties. An artifact of sorts. There is no blade sharper than it in all of the world." A hunger grew in Eugene's eyes. "It cuts bone and flesh like butter. Steel too."

"Hmm... sounds like something I'd like to add to my collection. I don't see why we couldn't acquire it. It's sounds like something that I would love to see." Dr. Jack eyeballed Abraham. "That's another little thing that I'd like to add to the list. Have King Hector stand down, and bring me that sword. Do this, and we can send you back to your wife and kid."

"Not to mention that you'll get back your friend Buddy Parker too. You might even earn a few pennants," Eugene added.

"You know, I've seen you transport people and things from one world to another, but I don't believe that you can send me back in time. Even though I want to."

"Yeah, well, watch this," Eugene said with a cocky smile. "Wheel him over to station one."

Otis pushed Abraham over to the computer station.

Eugene typed on the keyboard, and a new image came up on the overhead screen. It was daytime at an airfield. Jenny and Jake were standing outside Abraham's father's birthday-present plane with smiles on their faces.

Abraham's blood ran cold. The image was clear as a bell, real as could be. "How... how are you doing this?"

Dr. Jack looked right at him and said, "With our imagination combined with magic and technology, anything is possible. All you have to do is believe."

15

braham's heart pounded. Jenny and Jake looked real enough to touch. All he wanted to do was reach out and hug them. Buddy Parker entered the picture on the screen. He hugged Jenny, and she gave Buddy a kiss on the cheek. He picked up a loaf of bread and swung the boy up into the air.

A tear ran down Abraham's cheek. "Stop it. Just stop it."

"What's the matter?" Dr. Jack asked. "Is this a little too close to home?" He nodded at Eugene. "Go ahead. Turn it off."

"If you can travel through time, why don't you just bring them to me?" Abraham said. "That would make it easier for all of us, wouldn't it?"

"We can only work with what we know," Eugene said. "Our Time Tunnel technology allows us to look into the past but not the future. What you just saw is an image created by data we knew of from that very day. Since 2010, modern-day technology has been very accurate. And because you can travel from one world to another without ill effect, we think that you can travel back into time."

Abraham scratched his chin on his chest. He was sweating profusely. Somehow, they were using magic and technology, based on the sound of it, but he didn't know where the magic was coming from.

He didn't have time to get it all sorted out, but at least he was getting closer.

"So, if I am to go back to Titanuus," he said, "you want me to talk King Hector into surrender and bring you the sword, Black Bane. And then you'll send me back in time to my family."

"That's the plan," Dr. Jack said.

He chewed his lips and asked, "How are we supposed to know that I'm keeping my end of the bargain and that you are keeping yours?"

"Oh, well, we'll be sending more weaponry over with very specific instructions. We have plenty of agents that are working with us now in Titanuus. They are doing very well with communicating our agenda. That fella, Big Apple, Edward Gravely... It turns out that he's been a really fine help. We made a deal with him. A pretty incredible story for a man that was once an invalid. Turns out he had great ambition."

"Yes, I've met him. So, there only seems to be one problem left," he said. "I'm still here. I can't really control when I go back. It just happens."

"No, no, I think we've got that one figured out," Dr. Jack said with a wave of his finger. "Just remember—a deal is a deal. And our eyes, even in Titanuus, are everywhere."

"You're talking about the Sect and the Shell, aren't you?"

"Bingo. We made a deal with them some time ago. They all stand to profit every bit as much as us in the bold trek into a new frontier. It's going to be glorious." Dr. Jack pulled a cigar out of his pocket and put it in his mouth. "I can't wait to light up the moment I'm out of here. I'm going to have some bourbon too. Do they have good bourbon in Titanuus?"

"I don't know. I don't drink too much. Not here or there that much. I think you know my history."

"That I do. Try to find out for me on this next go-around."

"Again, I don't think I can click my heels together and go back. But most of the time, there's a headache involved."

Dr. Jack chuckled and said, "Yeah, I know." He nodded at Otis and Haymaker. "Let him have it, boys."

Without a moment's hesitation, the brutish orderlies drove their stun rods into Abraham's ribs with hungry glee all over their faces.

Abraham's toes and fingers curled. He thrashed violently in his bonds and let out an earsplitting scream.

Dr. Jack and Ottum plugged their ears with their fingertips.

Abraham's blood ran hot with lightning like fire. He glared at Dr. Jack's sneering smile. Another moment passed. Fire ran through his heart. His world turned black.

THUMP-THUMP. *Thump-thump. Thump-thump.*

He felt as if someone was driving a nail into his skull. The loud, painful thumping started to slow. Abraham stirred. His burning limbs swam in a warm pile of goo. He fought for his breath. Something squishy suffocated him, covering his mouth and nostrils.

What is this?

Abraham started to swim. He kicked and punched. He spat out something gooey. More rancid goo poured into his mouth.

Nooo!

Something hard was in his grip. His arms and legs were free. He wasn't strapped to a gurney anymore, but he was dying.

Black Bane, help me!

The fiery runes etched in the great longsword glowed. Abraham found himself in something like the body of a jellyfish. He grabbed the pommel of his sword with both hands and started hacking through the blubbery flesh with broad strokes. He carved up the alien body from the inside out. He sliced open a gap and felt fresh air hitting his face.

Freedom, oh sweet freedom!

He shoved his head out of the body. Huge octopod tentacles were all over. He couldn't tell if he was facing up or down. He was attached inside the strange thing.

What is this place? I feel like I am being born again!

Black Bane's light helped, but above and below him was only blackness.

"What kind of monster is this? Did I get eaten?" He squirmed farther from his captor, inching his body out one limb at a time, until he squirted out and fell into the black depths below. "Nooo…!"

16

Abraham hit the ground a split second later.

Thud!

He lay flat on his back, sword in hand, looking upward at a bulging hulk made of tentacles with eyeballs. It reminded him of the monster Elder they'd fought at Crown Island. It was a huge creeper but much smaller. It started rapidly sliding down the rock wall.

"Holy sheetrock!" He scrambled on all fours away from the descending sludge pile.

It hit the ground with a squish.

Abraham gasped. His legs were pinned underneath the bulging hulk. He pushed away from the slimy creature and, with a fierce grunt, finally freed his feet. Panting, he stood up on noodle legs and swayed. He used Black Bane as a crutch.

"Where am I?"

A tentacle with an eyeball coiled around his calf.

"Gah!" He chopped right through the tendril and jogged away. "Blazing saddles! It's still alive!"

With a shiver, Abraham limped farther away from the creeper. In seconds, the monster was gone from sight. He was on a cavern floor. A thousand feet above him was an eye of wide-open sky. *Looks like I'm in the Wound. I wonder what happened to everyone else.* He shivered. "Frosty the Snowman, why's it so cold?"

Step after step, he stumbled over the rises of the black canyon. He didn't hear another soul. The land was cold and barren. Slowly, his natural strength started to return. He moved at an easier gait and tried to remain quiet. He let Ruger's senses do the work.

I can't believe I'm back. Just like that. I wonder how Ruger is doing. He contemplated everything that had gone on in the last several hours. Dr. Jack and Eugene Drisk had revealed a lot. They had a way to get his family back... *Or do they?* He shook his head. *So far on this misbegotten adventure, anything seems possible. I have to end this. It's getting too crazy.*

He wandered—step after step, hour after hour. He had to be able to find the Henchmen. Certainly, they would be near. They had to be.

"Did you say something?"

"Huh," Abraham muttered aloud, noticing that the engravings in the sword's blade brightened when it spoke. "Is that you, Black Bane?"

"I don't think that is my name."

"No, that is the sword's name. You go by another name, but we don't know what that is yet."

"Hmm... did we kill that monster?"

"Yes, I think."

"Interesting. Who are you? You sound different than the other man I was speaking to. Ruger. I like him. You're that other fella. Softer, but serviceable."

"I'm Abraham, and I'm not soft. Are you freely talking with Ruger but not me?"

"We go further back. It's a well-established relationship. But I have some good news."

Abraham held the sword before his eyes, looked at the gently pulsating orange runes, and said, "I can't wait it hear it."

"You sound like someone that doesn't want to know."

"No, I want to know. I'm confused, though. So, you've been talking to Ruger recently?"

"I don't have the same concept of time that you do, but I've spoken with him thoroughly since the last time I talked with you."

"And?"

"I like Ruger Slade. He has the grit of old friends I can't remember, but I can see them like ghosts from the past. He said that I should help you."

"Wow, it sounds like a real game changer," he said sarcastically, recalling that the essence within Black Bane had been extremely unreliable. "So you weren't willing to help me before?"

"I admit, I had my suspicions. Now, if you were an ample woman, there would be no doubt about it. But some strange fellow that holds me by the handle, eh, I'm not warming to that."

"What difference does it make? You can't see."

"Who says I can't see? I can see. I just didn't tell you that I could. But of course I can. I have a strong intuition about things."

Abraham spun the sword in his palm and said, "In that case, can you help me find my friends?"

"Perhaps. Are there any ample women among them?"

Abraham started to say no but switched his thoughts and said, "Of course there are. Some of them are plump, others athletic, but all of them bosomy."

The engravings inside the sword blade flared the bright orange of a fire. *"Tell me more!"*

"Show me the way, and I'll tell you about the triplets."

"Did you say triplets?"

"Yup, and I hope you like piles of silky black hair cascading over heaving mounds of cleavage."

Black Bane moved under its own power, pulling Abraham briskly through the caverns.

"Whoa," Abraham said as he was practically jerked out of his boots. He tugged back on the sword and said, "Slow down. What are you, a dog in heat?"

"No—more like an old dog in heat. Come on, young fellow. We have vixens to fetch. Tell me more."

Restraining himself by giving more modest visual pictures, he accurately described Sophia, Selma, and Bridgett.

"Those are pretty names. I like them all. I can see them in my mind. Black. Red. White. The perfect trio. And you didn't marry any of them?"

"No, I've been married, but now I'm a widower. I had a son too."

"Hmm... I seem to think that I had a son. I'm not sure though. I sense your friends are near. Very near." The sword pulled Abraham at a quick pace then forced him to break into a jog. Finally, it stopped in place. *"Is this them?"*

Abraham moved toward a cluster of standing men. In the dim light given by the blade, he squinted and said, "Horace?"

It was Horace. He was standing like a statue, his body unmoving. He was with Bearclaw, Vern, Prospero, Skitts, Apollo, Tark, and Cudgel. Their limbs were frozen stiff, as if they had been marching in place and suddenly came to a stop. Abraham touched Horace on a cheek. It was frosted with ice and cold.

"No, no, don't be dead. You can't be dead. Not all of you."

17

A braham wiped the ice from Horace's eyes. The big man's eyeball twitched.

"Horace? Horace, are you alive?"

Horace's eye didn't move again.

Abraham placed his hand on the man's chest. He checked Horace's pulse on the wrist. He swore he felt a beat, but it was very slow. "What in the world could have done this?"

"I don't know. Are the women all right?"

"There aren't any women with this group." Abraham walked through the group, inspecting them all. Not a single one of them had a horrified or shocked expression. It was as if they'd been frozen in time. He waved his hand in front of Vern but got no reaction. "Can't you see them? I thought that you could see them."

"I can't see anything. I'm a sword. I don't have eyes."

"You said you could see."

"I can sense things as well as sight. I suppose it's another gift. Hmm."

"Hmm, what?" Abraham tried to take the extinguished torch out of Skitts's hand, but the Red Tunic's fingers were locked around it like a vise. "Do you sense any other people? There should be at least seven more from the group."

"I sense something."

As fate would have it, Skitts was carrying Abraham's backpack. He reached inside the pack and fished out a Zippo lighter. He popped the lid open and flicked the flint wheel. He got small sparks. "Come on." He shook the lighter and flicked it again.

A flame started. He lit the torch, which slowly caught fire. The flame grew, casting soft light over the rigid company.

"That's better. You said you sensed a presence. What sort of presence?"

The engravings in Black Bane cooled.

"Oh great. You're sleeping again just when I need you most. And not like the love song 'I Needed You Most' either. In more of a macho way."

Abraham scanned the area. Nothing was there but pitch-black beyond the torchlight's thirty-foot radius. The chill winds rustled his hair. He moved over to Horace and said, "Hey, big guy, can you hear me?"

"Of course he can... for now."

Abraham spun around, brandishing Black Bane. He peered into the blackness toward the sound of the voice. It was a woman's voice, low, wicked, and gravelly, like an old witch's.

"Show yourself," he demanded.

"What is your name?" the voice in the darkness said. It came from a different location, on the other side of the Henchmen.

He spun around and said, "Show yourself, and I'll tell you."

No reply came. He didn't hear a word.

He envisioned the Frights that he'd first encountered when he came to Titanuus. They were bony pink-eyed women with strands of wiry hair. "Did you do this to my friends, witch?"

"Don't insult me. I am no witch!" The voice darkened. "I am much, much more. What is your name, human?"

"Show yourself, and I will tell you. I think that is fair."

"You invade my territory and now give me orders? You fool of flesh and blood. I will end you..." Her voice was followed by a hiss and a soft rattle. "But I will honor your final request and show my face."

Abraham turned. The woman's voice had moved behind him. Something told him he should run. His knees should have been knocking, but they weren't. Ruger's body held fast. The sword warrior didn't fear anything.

With his heart pounding in his throat, he said, "I'm waiting."

Twenty feet ahead, a light shone on a face in the darkness. It was a woman, fair and beautiful. Her skin appeared radiant and lit up from within. He saw no body, only her beautiful face with haunting good looks.

In a seductive voice, she asked, "Do you like what you see?"

With icy breath and jaw hanging, he said, "Absolutely."

"Good." Her words wrapped around him like a warm blanket. "Now, tell me what your name is."

"Ruger, er... Abraham. Abraham Jenkins."

The face hovered in the darkness, moving gently side to side but coming no closer. "That is a strange name, Abraham Jenkins. But we like it."

"We?"

Another face appeared, just as pretty as the other. Both of them had long, flowing, illuminated white hair that moved as if it was floating in the inky depths of the ocean. "Yes, me and my sister." They spoke as one but changed who was speaking between words and sentences. "Do you find us divine?"

He licked his lips and said, "Certainly. Can I see the rest of you?"

He lowered his guard, and his knees bowed. A cool, fragrant mist drifted through the air and coated his body like dew. His taut muscles started to relax.

"I can't wait to see you."

"Yes, I can't wait for you to see us either. We are called Duplii. We don't receive visitors like you very often." Duplii's heads came closer together. Like Siamese twins, they almost touched cheek to cheek. "Please, relax and let us welcome you to our home."

"That sounds like a good idea," Abraham replied. He'd

completely forgotten about the Henchmen and everything else. He felt as though he was entering a spa of some sort. Swaying a bit, he said, "This is nice, but it's getting chilly. Do you have any blankets?"

"Of course we do." Duplii's exotic faces drifted apart, farther and farther.

Abraham's eyes danced between both of them. The mist coating him started to crystallize on his body. He felt as though he'd fallen into a blanket of snow.

"Are you ready to see us fully?" Duplii said.

"Y-yes," he muttered as a fiery warning started pricking in the dulled recesses of his brain.

Duplii's heads came back together and forward. His heavy eyes widened. Duplii's heads grew bigger the closer they came. They were twice as big as his. He didn't see the sensuous bodies that he expected either. Instead, he saw something else as he watched the heads rise.

"Oh no."

Duplii's heads were attached to the ends of fleshy strands. Those strands were attached to a monstrous hulk that towered twenty feet high. Its jaws were wide open and filled with rows of thousands of sharp teeth. An inky mist came out of its mouth, still covering Abraham like soft rain.

It was the most hideous thing Abraham had ever seen.

"Do you still think we are beautiful?" Duplii said.

"Absolutely not," Abraham muttered as he watched the great mouth full of slavering teeth descend upon him.

18

———

Abraham's grip tightened on his sword, but he could not move. Duplii came closer. Each head was on either side of him. Their icy breath was on his cheeks.

"Relax," Duplii said as one, "this won't hurt a bit, Abraham. Soon, you will be one with us."

Ruger's hot blood started flowing. Abraham couldn't move a muscle. He could barely think. The nagging in the back of his head grew stronger. It had to be Ruger. *I'm trying. I'm trying. I can't think of anything. So tired. So comfortable.* His eyes slid over to the beautiful faces of the alien women. "You're so pretty," he mumbled, "but so mean."

"We are Duplii. Aren't we beautiful?" They kissed his cheeks with soft lips as cold as ice. "You are warm. Warm is delicious."

Abraham fought to keep his mind alert. His eyelids felt heavy as rainclouds. Suddenly, a thought struck him as he stared at the beautiful women.

Black Bane! Wake up! There are two voluptuous women out here! You are missing it!

Black Bane's engravings turned bright fireplace orange.

"Did you say voluptuous?"

With Black Bane's handle hot in his hand, Abraham's sword arm filled with new strength. He lashed out at Duplii's face on the right side of him. He cut the head off, clean through the tendril.

Duplii's monster jaws crashed down.

Abraham dove out of the way.

"No!" Duplii screeched. "You killed my sister! Nooo!"

"Where are these voluptuous women? I don't see any. I only see a monster."

Abraham crawled to his feet and took a swipe at the beast. It didn't have legs like a dragon. It moved on thousands of small black ciliary feet underneath its body. Black Bane took a hunk of flesh out of it. "So you can see! You said you would help me. Help me kill that thing?"

"I want to see the women."

Abraham backpedaled away from the charging monster.

"I swear it! I swear it, you will!"

"All right, you don't have to sound so strained about it. I'm only making a modest request. Let me see what I can do. Give me a moment."

Running backward, he said, "I don't have a moment."

Duplii might have been huge, but the titanic beast moved quickly. "You will die!" the woman's head said as it stretched out toward him. She spat black needles out of her mouth. "Die, Abraham, die!"

A ball of white-hot lightning appeared above them, lighting the canyon floor up for one hundred yards.

Duplii fixed her gorgeous eyes on the ball and asked, "What is that?"

"It ain't a snowball."

The great beast turned from Abraham and looked upward. It roared with its mouth wide open. A freezing mist spewed out.

The bowling-ball-sized globe of energy dropped inside the monster's mouth.

Duplii made a gulping sound and exploded from the inside out with a notable *kah-poom!*

Fleshy guts sprayed all over Abraham. He was covered in gory grit from head to toe.

"Did that work?"

"Like magic."

"Good. I'm going to sleep now. Don't you dare wake me up again without the company of ample women. I swear I won't help you."

Abraham wiped the slimy flesh away from his face and hair and said, "You got it." He flicked the slime onto the ground. "Yuck."

The torch burned in the distance.

He walked toward it. The Henchmen were slowly moving.

He broke into a jog. "Horace!"

The bearish man gave him a dumb look, lifted an eyebrow, and said, "Captain?"

"The one and only. What happened?" he said.

"We were searching for you. That mist fell over us. We didn't even take notice. The next thing I know, we were frozen." Horace rolled his jaw and clenched his fingers. "I see you are back."

"What do you mean?"

Vern walked over, stretching his arms and yawning. He said, "He means you aren't the same captain that we were hoping for. It's a dead giveaway in how you talk."

"Don't start, Vern," Horace warned.

"No, that's all right. So you're telling me that the old Ruger was back in this body?"

Horace nodded.

"You better believe it. He lifted our spirits out of the throes of doom," Vern said.

"We're on the same side, you know." Abraham eyeballed the group. "How is everyone else?"

"Limber again," Bearclaw commented as he swung his axe from side to side. "What happened to us?"

"I'll show you."

He led the way to the fallen hulk called Duplii. The beautiful faces had turned as hard as stone. The body was a ton of mush scattered like mashed potatoes on the cavern floor.

"That's what happened." He noticed everyone seemed downcast. "Look, we're getting closer to getting everything back to normal. I haven't failed you yet. I won't fail you now. Ruger won't either. Now, where are Sticks and the others?"

"We split up hours ago," Horace said.

"Well, wipe those frowns off of your faces, and let's go get them."

19

———

The Henchmen were the best trackers in the land. Picking up the trail of Melris, Solomon, Sticks, and the others didn't take them long. Their prints showed well on the canyon floor. That led them inside the strange wormhole that was filled with natural light and warm and humid instead of cold.

Abraham and Horace led the way, but Cudgel and Tark scouted out front. The flooring inside the strange twenty-foot-high tunnel didn't leave any prints, but it went one way.

"So, what was it like to have the old Ruger back?" Abraham asked.

"No disrespect, Captain. I'd follow you into the Sea of Troubles if need be, but it was a good thing to have him back, even if for only a short time." Horace scratched his eyebrow. "I'm glad he still lives, however that be."

"Yeah, he's living, all right. Listen, there is a lot that we need to talk about, between us and when Ruger comes back." It had become natural to talk about Ruger as if he was a different person who hosted the same body. "And I'm assuming he will. Things are coming to a head. The people in my world are invading Titanuus. We have to stop it." He brought Horace up to speed on everything. Horace wasn't slow by any measure, but he always felt more comfortable telling it to

Sticks. "No matter what happens to me, you have to warn King Hector. The sooner we get back to Kingsland, the better."

"You know I won't let you down. We won't let you down, you or Ruger." Horace grinned. "It's kind of exciting."

"What do you mean?"

"We'd been cast aside so long that we'd become insignificant. Now, well, the fate of the very world might rest on our shoulders. We can take it."

Vern caught up with them and said, "It all sounds like madness to me."

Horace gave Vern a disappointed look and opened his mouth to speak.

"But"—Vern lifted a hand—"I'm in sword deep. Ruger was here. He filled me in. I have a better grasp of the situation. We've got to win this." He put his hand on Abraham's arm and said, "If you ever doubted my sword before, doubt it no more. It's yours. For the king. For the Henchmen."

"You can be my wingman anytime?" Abraham said.

"What does that mean?" Vern said. "I don't have wings."

"It's a thing in my world. I'll explain later."

When they caught up with Cudgel, he was standing at a tunnel intersection that split off in at least twelve different sections. "I have no idea which one they took. There isn't a sign or anything. We always leave a sign. There is not one."

"Where's Tark?" Abraham asked.

"He's running along these ribs, looking for a sign." Cudgel cradled his club in his hands. His eyes scanned the ceiling. "This is a strange place. I don't like it. Watch this." He pressed his hand into the crud caked up on the tunnel wall, leaving an impression. A few seconds later, the impression was gone. "See. You can scrape it with a knife too. I see bone underneath. I think we are inside a living thing."

Tark came hustling back. His smoky eyes were wide, and he was holding a flat knife in his hand. "I found this. It belongs to Sticks. I'm sure of it." He flipped it up and caught it. "You know she never loses a knife."

"Show me," Abraham said.

Tark led them to the fifth tunnel and stepped inside. The tunnels were half as wide as the one they'd been walking in. "It was stuck in the way." He jabbed the knife in. "Like this."

The tunnel gently quavered underneath their feet.

"I hope that's a coincidence." Abraham stuck his sword in the ground, and the tunnel didn't shake. "Good. I'd hate to think I've been eaten again." He looked ahead. "That way."

"Captain, do you want to split up?" Horace suggested.

"No, splitting up the last time is what got us into this mess. You should have stayed with Melris." He eyed the company of men. "We'll talk about that later."

"A punishment is coming, eh?" Horace asked.

"One thing is for sure—no soup for you." He nodded at Tark. "Lead the way."

The farther they traveled, the more the walls dripped with humidity. Sweat dripped from their chins and splashed on the ground. They walked for an hour on a straight path without the slightest bend in the tunnel. They heard no other sounds among their quiet footsteps.

"Captain." Tark had stopped ahead in the tunnel and was holding another small knife in his hand. "Another one."

"At least we are on the right path." Abraham lifted his shoulders. "Keep rolling."

"Sticks doesn't leave her knives unless she's in some kind of trouble," Horace commented. "Methinks that something is wrong—very wrong."

"I know, but how is this any different than any other day. Tark, pick up the pace. The sooner we find the trouble, the sooner we can put an end to it." *I hope.*

The company moved on hour after hour, or so it seemed. Abraham couldn't tell. He had much on his mind during the droning march. He had been asked to betray the king and promised that he could go back to his family. All this madness could come to an end, and he could make that happen.

He looked at his men. Their faces were hard, filled with deep cracks, scars, and lines. Their hands were hard with calluses and as thick as leather. The Henchmen were something, the ultimate teammates. They did what they were told to do without question.

But there was another question. *Are we on the side of right or the side of wrong? After all, what kind of king would brand a man with a hot iron?* The zillon, Ottum, had gotten him thinking. Abraham gave all his men a careful study. Not one of them wouldn't pass for a hardened criminal.

What if—just what if—the king fooled me?

20

———

Tark hurried back to the company, showing a smile of white teeth. "We found something." He cupped his ear. "Can you hear that?"

Abraham bent his ear toward the tunnel ceiling and asked, "Is that water?"

"Yes, there is a large stream that runs in the bowels of the world. But that is not all. You have to see this. Hurry." The warrior took off in long, graceful strides and raced up the tunnel.

"Really, we are running now?" Vern said. "I seriously doubt that the stream is going anywhere."

"A little run never hurt anyone. Henchmen, let's go." Abraham took the lead. He couldn't imagine what could have gotten Tark so excited, but it had his blood pumping too. The journey through the sweltering tunnel had been long enough. The time had come for a change.

Skitts raced up beside him. He sniffed the air. "I can smell them now."

"You can?" Abraham asked.

"I can smell like a bloodhound," Skitts added. "It was hard to smell inside this tunnel. These walls seem to absorb the stenches. It's weird."

"Well, follow your nose," Abraham said. "It always knows 'the flavor of fruit.'"

"What?" Skitts said.

"Nothing. I just had a hankering for a bowl of Froot Loops." He and the Henchmen caught up with Cudgel and Tark.

The black brothers stood on an overlook where the tunnel ended. A steep drop over one hundred feet down led into a forest.

"Whoa," Vern said as he leaned over the ledge. "Are you jesting? There is a giant forest in the middle of the dirt."

For as far as Abraham could see were miles of treetops, shrubs, and other greenery. The cavern went on for miles, possibly leagues. The ceiling of the cavern was speckled with crystalline rocks that glowed like stars. The gargantuan cavern was still dim, but the rocks cast light similar to moonlight. The loud rush of water caught his ears. A smaller river was snaking its way through the underground forest away from them.

"Huh, looks like we are going down. Watch out for dinosaurs and underlings."

The Henchmen climbed down the steep incline with boots slipping and sliding over the wet rocks. Within a few minutes, they made it to the bottom of the forest floor.

A mix of oak and maple, the trees stood thirty to fifty feet high. Many of them had white bark, like dogwood. Their leaves were mostly green, with some maroon and yellow. Small forest critters jumped through the trees' branches. Tiny black birds flew in small flocks from one tree to another.

Abraham squatted beside an orange mushroom as tall as his knee. "That's worth some money." He turned his head and found Tark. Tark and Cudgel were on their hands and knees, running their fingers through the dirt. "Any sign of our friends?"

Tark nodded. "We have prints a blind man could follow." He pointed up the river. "That way."

"What about you, Skittles?" he asked. "Do you smell any trouble?"

"Solomon's scent lingers the strongest. I could find him a mile away. I am smelling plants and the dirt. It's heavy. But I don't smell any other people. I'd have to be in contact with them before I smelled them."

Abraham looked down at the tracks Cudgel had pointed out. "I don't see any other tracks. Just theirs." He looked up and down that path. "Do you?"

"No signs of duress," Tark said. "They move—they move quick."

"What are you thinking, Captain?" Horace asked.

"I'd think there would be trouble down here. It doesn't seem right that we can waltz right down here without any trouble."

Vern cleared his throat and said, "If people live down here, I don't think they'd get many visitors. Who else would come down here if you didn't have to?"

"Good point, but don't take any chances." Abraham drew his sword. "From here on out, we stay close. Let's move."

The deeper the company went, the more Abraham worried about getting out. He'd been spelunking before, when he was younger, and didn't like it. The mere thought of being hundreds of feet below ground and getting trapped left a sinking feeling in his stomach.

Tark and Cudgel led them alongside the stream. The banks were sandy, and the stream appeared shallow. Fish with glowing scales swam quickly underneath the waters. In groups, the fish would follow the company upstream, stop and face them, then move after them.

"Perhaps we should refill our canteens, Captain," Horace suggested. "After that walk in those tunnels, my whistler has become dry as a tomb bone."

The group had walked for hours without taking a drink. Abraham realized he was parched the moment Horace mentioned it. He stepped out to the edge of the water and filled his nostrils with the freshwater air. Then he scooped his hand into the cool waters and sipped. "It's no wonder trees grow down here. Their roots are sucking up this refreshing water." He swallowed some more. "Everyone fill up."

Apollo and Prospero kneeled down and scooped handfuls of water into their mouths. Bearclaw refilled two water skins. Horace and Vern drank straight from the stream.

The fish floated in the stream, facing the men in separate schools.

Abraham eyed them. "Either they don't like us drinking their water, or they are the nosiest fish I ever saw."

"They look delicious to me. Perhaps we need to do some fishing. I wouldn't mind a bite," Skitts said. He rinsed his face off in the surging waters. "I'm hungry."

Horace waded deeper into the waters, eyeing a small school of glowing fish. He held his spear over the waters. "There's nothing like fresh fish meat. These look particularly delicious."

Schools of hundreds of fish surrounded Horace. Abraham's eyes widened as a tingle ran through his bones. "Horace," he muttered.

Horace stabbed into the stream. An unseen force pulled him under.

Abraham shouted, "Horace!"

21

Abraham dove into the spot where Horace had submerged. The fish swarmed him and latched onto his body with sucking mouths. In seconds, he was covered by dozens of them. He fought through the fish, searching for Horace. The fish had latched onto the warrior and dragged him toward a deep cave. Abraham swam after the man.

Horace thrashed underneath the deep waters, jabbing his spear wildly through the murk. He let the spear go and ripped the fish away from his body.

The fish latched onto Abraham's arms and legs guided him deeper into the water's black hole. *Madness! They are pushing me into the cave!*

Horace hit the bottom of the black pit. Bones of men and armor were resting on the stream's deep floor. Bubbles burst out of his mouth. He grabbed a fish and bit its head off.

Abraham reached out and hooked Horace underneath the arms. He tried to swim upward, but the fish forced him down. Bigger fish that did not glow swam out of dark holes. They were bigger than a man's head and had black scales and rings of blue stripes. They had mouths and teeth like piranhas' but were far bigger. He punched one away.

Horace shoved up from the ground. The glowing fish pushed him back down again.

Abraham held his breath, which burned in his chest. Above him, the glowfish formed a blanket in the waters. When he swam up, they pulled him down.

Horace ripped off a piranha that had latched onto his flesh. He choked on water and spasmed.

Warm blood flowed in the inky stream. Horace's eyes rolled into his head.

Abraham's mind screamed, *Nooo!* He locked onto Horace and pushed upward. The fish swam him back down. He was trapped. *This can't be. It can't be!* He gawked at the umbrella ceiling of glowing fish. They'd sealed them inside a watery grave and prepared for the feast.

Skitts burst through the barrier of fish with his arms stretched out. Covered in the glowfish, he plunged deep and grabbed hold of Abraham. Suddenly, like an anchor being pulled out of the waters, he, Horace, and Skitts were being pulled free of the fish trap.

Abraham held onto the beefy Horace for dear life. They burst through the ceiling of scales and were lifted through the waters. Underneath the waters, Bearclaw was latched onto Skitts's ankles, Vern had Bearclaw, and so on. They pulled Abraham and Horace into the shallow waters on the bank. Abraham gasped for air.

The fish jumped up and down in the waters like salmon during the spawning season.

Abraham rolled Horace onto his back. The spearman had turned blue. Abraham started chest compressions. "Don't you die on me, Horace. Don't you die! What kind of man dies at the hands of a little fish?"

"More like a thousand cuts," Vern said. He lifted Horace's limp arm. Jagged bite marks covered Horace's hands. "What did you run into down there, a wolverine?"

"Wolverines don't swim." Abraham kept pumping Horace's chest.

"It was some sort of piranha. I have no idea what you would call them in this world."

"A fish that eats flesh—I've never heard such a thing." Cudgel leaned over Horace. "He is dead, isn't he?"

Horace spat a mouthful of water into Cudgel's face and started coughing.

Cudgel wiped his face and grinned. "I knew that would wake him up. He hates being called dead. Horace is a stubborn man."

Blinking his eyes, Horace said, "Captain, those are some tricky fish. I will kill them all. Where is my spear?"

Tark walked up with Horace's big spear in his hands. "It's all secure." One fish flapped its tail on the end of the spear. "It comes with dinner."

Horace chuckled.

Abraham slapped Horace on the back and helped his friend up to his feet. "I guess those fish were fishing for us."

Blood dripped from his arms into the waters. Minnow-sized fish darted into the shallows and sucked up the blood.

"Let's get moving."

For another hour, they walked in a single column farther away from the stream, where the grass stood ankle high. The trail of Sticks, Melris, and the others was still fresh. It appeared that they hadn't been dumb enough to venture into the waters.

The stream dropped off a cliff, creating a waterfall that crashed down onto rocks another fifty feet below. It formed an underground lake over a mile in diameter. Deer with white skins and black horns drank from the cool waters.

Tark led the climb down the rocks toward the lake.

The deer sprang away.

"I don't understand how life can live without sunlight. How can there be beasts such as this in the belly of Titanuus?" Horace said. "Bats and bugs, maybe, but living creatures?"

Abraham descended to the bottom, keeping his toes away from the lake waters. The rest of the Henchmen climbed down alongside the cascading falls.

Tall reeds and cattails surrounded the lake. The surrounding grasses stood the height of wheat. Abraham could see a new path where the grasses were pushed down.

He caught up to Tark. "Still them, huh?"

"Yes, but this path is well worn. I think it's a path used to fetch water and fish. Look." He pointed at the lake. "There are other footprints, not like deer but a two-toed man."

Abraham took a close look at the impressions in the mud. Each was a large footprint with two big toes and one smaller, like a thumb.

Cudgel put his hand in the print. "I've never seen tracks like this. Whatever it is is very heavy." He eyed more footprints. "They are very heavy, like a bull."

The beating of tom-tom drums carried over the strange valley.

Toom-tah-tah. Toom-tah-tah. Toom-tah-tah. Toom-tah-tah.

Pungent black smoke drifted into Abraham's nose. Somewhere, flesh was burning.

Skitts sniffed and said, "I can't say for sure, but that's either animal or people."

A shrill cry carried over the tall trees.

"That's my brother! That's Zann!

22

Skitts raced down the path toward the wailing sound of pain. The stalking man moved as if his head was on fire. Up one rise he went and down the next.

Abraham and the Henchmen gave chase. If Zann was in trouble, the others would be too. Abraham thought about Sticks. She'd been imprisoned and tortured enough before. He couldn't bear to see it. *Not again!*

The path led them downward to a clearing where several bonfires were spread out over the grounds. Stout men squatted around the flames. They had bald heads, large protruding ears, and big eyes. Their squat heads rested right on the neckless men's shoulders. Barrel-chested and thick thewed, they fanned the flames with big, long, thick fleshy fingers, their thumbs matching their feet.

Other strange men faced a great stone statue standing over forty feet high. Some of the men pounded the drums in a steady beat.

Toom-tah-tah. Toom-tah-tah. Toom-tah-tah. Toom-tah-tah.

The statue appeared to have been cut from limestone, like something one would see in the Aztec pyramids. A large ugly face made the head. One eye burned bright red and the other bright orange inside their sockets. A wheel made up of stone hands slowly spun in the middle of its stone body. Inside those hands were Sticks, Solomon, Iris, Dominga, and Zann. All their arms were pinned to their sides. The pinwheel of arms was slow-roasting them over a huge wooden bonfire.

Zann passed over the flames with his tail end smoking. Sticks was the next in line to pass over the flaming pyre.

"Yaaah!" Skitts screamed with his sword raised over his head.

The Henchmen descended on the corded men like a crashing wave.

Skitts brained the first neckless hulk with his sword.

The neckless brood came to life. They snatched up flaming logs in their great hands and attacked from all directions.

"Tark! Get that wheel stopped!" Abraham ordered. "Henchmen, clear a path! Mow these suckers down!"

He uncorked Black Bane with a lethal swing. The blade sank into the side of one creature's chest. It made the sound of an axe chopping wood. No blood spurted out. An inky smoke oozed out as it clutched at Abraham. He split its face open, and it fell away.

"Keep hacking."

Horace gored a monster on the end of his spear and flung it into the fire.

Vern sliced off their groping hands.

Bearclaw brutalized them with his double-bladed battle-axe. With thunderous overhead chops, he turned the creatures into firewood.

"What in Titanuus's Crotch are these things?" Cudgel cried. He popped a black bully in the head, sending hard chips of its skin flying. Then he stuck his boot in its chest, shoved it away, and hit another. "They are made of rock and wood."

"Slay the granite men!" Horace roared. He rammed his spear through two of the men at once, and smoke bled out of their bodies. He charged into them, pushing them backward one step at a time. With a final heave, he shoved them into a flaming pyre. "Burn the granite men!"

Abraham fought his way toward the wheel over the flames. Tark and Skitts plowed into a knot of the granite men. Their swords rose and fell on the chunky bodies, splintering away the fleshlike bark. The swords chopping into wooden bodies did less damage than the hollow sounds seemed to indicate. The King's Steel started to stick in the odd flesh. The granite men piled onto the Henchmen.

Sticks shouted out from above, "Get this wheel stopped! With every turn, we hold over the flames longer!"

"Henchmen! To the wheel! To the wheel!" Abraham shouted and barreled into the cluster of granite men battling Tark and Skitts. He busted Tark out of the swarm and said, "Stop that thing!"

"Aye, Captain!" Tark squirted out of the pack and began his climb up the statue.

Abraham landed one flashing stroke after another. Skitts slid in behind him. The rest of the Henchmen converged on the wheel. They formed a semicircle in front of the bonfire at the bottom of the wheel.

"How do you turn this thing off?" Skitts shouted to his brother.

"I don't know. Put the bloody fire out!" Zann yelled back.

"With what?" Skitts asked.

"Find a bucket or something!" Zann said.

"Ruger, hurry up!" Solomon said. "Sticks is going to die! She was first on the turn. This next one will be the longest!"

The flames licked upward at Sticks's clothing as she descended closer to the flames, gradually moving down from the five o'clock position to six. Her lips drew back, and she turned her red-hot face but didn't scream.

"Burn my biscuits," Abraham muttered. Only one thing could stop the flames from cooking her alive. "Horace, I'm going in!"

"In where?" Horace replied.

"The woodpile! It's the only way to knock those flames down!" Abraham turned and faced the flames. "Blazing saddles, away I go!" He jumped toward the flames.

Horace caught Abraham by the collar and hauled him back. "No, I'm bigger than you." Like a bull in a china shop, he plowed into the flames. He busted into the piles of wood logs and hot coals and ash.

He made it halfway to the middle when the flames suddenly dropped. Horace stopped as well. The suffocating flames started to consume him.

Abraham shouted, "Death before failure!" and rushed into the inferno.

23

Abraham pushed deep into the searing inferno and plowed into Horace. The white-hot flames scorched the hairs on his body. He thrust forward, shoving Horace toward the other side of the pyre. Suddenly, a great weight plunged into his back.

Over the roaring flames, he could hear men screaming, "Death before failure!"

The Henchmen rammed their bodies through the logs and shoved Abraham and Horace through one side and out the other.

The burning heap collapsed.

Bearclaw and Vern jumped on Horace and patted out the flames.

Abraham coughed as he caught his breath. He smelled like a stick of burning hair. The rest of him seemed okay. He wasn't sure why that was, but he had bigger problems. The granite men continued to swarm on the other side of the flames. They started chucking logs at the Henchmen.

Vern and Bearclaw doused Horace with the water from their skins. The beefy man's beard was smoking, and his forearms were red with blisters.

Sticks dangled from the stone hand that held her fast. Her body hung limp. Sweat dripped from her chin onto the ground. Panting, she locked eyes with Abraham and said, "Thank you."

Apollo, Prospero, and Cudgel kept the hordes at bay. Both Apollo and Prospero battled with a longsword in each hand. They blocked the granite men's flanking advances with the wall of flame between them.

Cudgel defended the other side of the collapsed bonfire. With tremendous overhead swings, he bashed one skull after another.

"Are you going to get up," Vern asked Horace, "or lie there while your chestnuts roast?"

"I can fight!" Horace stood with the help of Bearclaw and Vern. He glanced up. "Hello, everyone. Where is my Iris?"

"I'm here, you big fool! Quit doing stupid things and burning yourself alive," Iris said.

"Why do you say that? I always thought you like your buns toasted," Horace replied.

Tark flagged Abraham down from the stone statue. "I locked the wheel!"

"Find out how to get them out of those stone mitts!" he shouted back.

Skitts had climbed onto the wheel. He hung on the same arm that held his brother Zann. His hands rummaged over the stone hand. "How do you unlock this?"

"You don't unlock it. This thing is real," Zann said. "These fingers move with life of their own."

"Solomon, where is Melris?" Abraham said.

"He left us!" Solomon yelled back. "We haven't seen him since we were captured by those things."

The ground trembled. *Thoooom!*

"What was that?" Abraham asked, peering toward the direction of the sound. Over the flames, he saw a gargantuan granite man walking their way. It stood over thirty feet tall. "Oh, it looks like Daddy is coming home for dinner."

Thoooom! The heavy footsteps came down like thunder. *Thoooom! Thoooom!*

The smaller granite men backed off. They formed a semicircle on the ground, facing the giant granite man, and bowed down. On their hands and knees, they rose up and down and made worshipful moans.

"Look, it's Melris!" Vern said.

Melris was riding on the shoulder of the giant granite man. One hand held on to an ear, and the other hand held his Rod of Devastation.

The giant stopped in front of its group of worshippers and scanned the dead on the ground. In a cavernous voice, he said, "They killed my children! Why did they kill my children?"

From his perch, Melris looked down at Abraham and asked, "Yes, why did you attack Osgard's children? We were in the middle of negotiations."

"Really?" Abraham said. "You were in the middle of negotiations while our people were roasting like marshmallows."

"I was almost finished. Osgard *the Elder* and I struck a deal." Melris gave Abraham a nod that seemed to signify that he really needed to be paying attention to this. "A very favorable deal."

"No deal!" Osgard the Elder said.

"What?" Melris replied. "Osgard, don't let this misunderstanding disrupt our negotiations. The very fate of the world is on the line."

"No one is going to come down here. I don't care. No deal," Osgard said with heavy breath. "You've invaded my home. Slain my children. Now, you must make the sacrifice." He held out two monstrous fingers and thumb. "Crush them, my totem. Crush them all!"

Iris and Zann let out pained cries. Solomon let out a grunt.

Dominga cried out, "This thing is squeezing us to death!"

"Make it stop, Melris! Make it stop now!" Abraham ordered.

"I'm sorry, but it appears that Osgard has made his mind up. There won't be any changing it now until blood is shed," Melris replied. "Osgard, will those people be a suitable sacrifice? Can we have the stones after that?"

"No," Osgard said.

"Sorry," Melris replied.

"You snake!" Iris yelled. "Ugh… my bloody bones are cracking!"

Skitts tried to pry back the fingers locked around his brother. Zann screamed with anguish.

Abraham started to climb up the stone statue. He found a landing and started chopping at the wrist of the hand crushing Sticks. "Hang on! Melris! Do something now, or I swear, I'll cut your head off!"

The purple-clad Melris nodded. "Yes, yes." He stuck his iron rod inside Osgard's head like a Q-tip and said, "Osgard, are you sure that you won't change your mind?"

With his dark eyes intent on the men and women being crushed, the Elder said, "Nooo."

"I see," Melris replied. "You give me no choice." His purple robes billowed out from an unseen wind. His hand and eyes glowed with raspberry fire. A blast of angry flames shot through one side of Osgard's head and out the other.

Osgard's minions cried out. The Elder swayed. His head smoked out of both ears, and his eyes rolled up in his head. He spoke with black smoke pumping like a chimney stack out of his mouth, saying, "Elderling, you will pay for this."

Melris feather walked down the Elder's falling body to the ground.

Osgard fell flat on his back. His minions died at his feet.

24

The Henchmen pried their own kind free from the stone statue's grip. Sticks rubbed her ribs as she was lowered back to the ground. "Abraham?" she asked as he assisted her.

"Yeah, I'm back," he said.

Sticks put her arms around him and gave him a warm hug. "I'm glad. I thought that you might have been gone forever."

"Well, look at you, getting all weepy on me."

"Just because you've rubbed off on me doesn't mean that my heart will break without you." She jabbed him in the ribs. "I'm a survivor. I think you know that."

"Yeah, I love you too."

Solomon dropped his big paws onto Abraham's shoulders and reeled him in for a bear hug. "I thought that was it. I couldn't help but wonder if I was ever going to see a Dairy Queen again. Glad you're back."

"Whew," Abraham said. "Me too, sort of. Man, your fur stinks."

"I got toasted, but my fur is very resistant to fire. Remember the barn?" Solomon said. "Troglins can be cooked, but it ain't easy."

"Yeah, well, I think that goes for all of us." He glanced at Horace.

Even though the big man wasn't in the flames long, he still should have been roasted.

Melris approached with his iron rod cradled in his hand. "You bear the brand. Did you not know that it makes you resistant to fire?"

Sticks lunged at Melris and punched him in the face.

Melris fell flat on his butt. His eyes widened when he found a dagger pressed against his neck.

"I wonder: do you bleed purple, Elderling?" Sticks said.

"There is one way to find out," Melris replied.

"You've got some explaining to do," Abraham said. "You left our men in the lurch."

"No harm had been done until your arrival. Besides, I knew you could handle the fires. I'm really surprised that you didn't know that," Melris added.

"I'd like to find out how fireproof you are," Iris said. The pie-faced mystic kicked Melris in the back. "'Cause those flames sure felt real to me!" She tried to kick him again, but Horace pulled her back.

"We need to secure the stones instead of bickering," Melris said, "The sooner we leave, the more likely we all get out of the Wound alive. You don't think we are going to be able to walk right out of here, do you? Osgard isn't the only Elder in the canyon. There are more."

"Then get your magic wand ready, and be prepared to blow more wax out of their earholes. But I'll tell you this, I've had my fill of Elders for the day. Including Elderlings." Abraham looked at Tark, who was standing on top of the statue. "Get those stones out of the eyeholes and toss them down here."

With a nod, Tark climbed down the giant golem's face and peered inside the eye socket emanating red light. "I don't mean to disregard an order, but is this burning stone safe to touch?"

Melris nodded and told Abraham, "He will be fine. It takes a mystic's touch or royal blood to activate the magic within.

Abraham opened his hands. "Toss it down. According to the purple wizard, you should be just fine. Let's get a look at those Easter eggs."

Tark reached inside the eye socket and pulled out the gem. He held the burning red stone between his thumb and index finger. "This little stone makes a big light." The fire went out. "Or it did make a big light."

Some sort of big bird flew overhead.

Abraham and the others looked up. Something was flying above them. It wasn't alone, either.

"Let's speed it along, Tark," Abraham said.

The other socket that glowed orange cooled. Tark reached inside and grabbed the gem. He held it out for all to see.

"Catch," he said and tossed the stones down.

A black hawk dove from above toward the falling stones.

A crossbow bolt fired. *Clatch-zip.*

The bolt ripped through the big bird's chest. It crashed into the statue just as Abraham caught the stones in midair.

More flapping and fluttering stirred the air above them in the darkness. Echoing squawking began.

"Let's move out, Henchmen," he ordered. "Unless you want to stick around and find out what else wants to eat us."

The Henchmen grabbed their gear, formed two single columns, and followed Tark and Dominga as they always did. With the great birds *ka-caw*ing and squawking and diving at their heads, they ran faster.

Up one rise and down another, they made it to the waterfall and scaled the rocks. Abraham made sure every man made it up. Apollo and Prospero brought up the rear.

The company raced by the stream, covering their heads from the diving hawks. Solomon swatted several of them out of the air. Finally, they made it back into the sweltering tunnels that appeared to be made out of bone. The black hawks did not follow them in, so they slowed to a trot.

A few hours later, they crawled out of the tunnels and back into the icy air of the canyon floor. Melris urged Abraham to stop.

"What?" Abraham asked.

"Now would be a good time to summon your dragon," the Elderling said.

"Why?"

He pointed up at the open sky of the canyon, where daylight showed one thousand feet above. "The Elders will let us pass in the presence of the Elder Spawn. Otherwise, they will try to kill us. For none that enter the Wound have ever lived to escape."

With the chill winds rustling his charred head of hair, Abraham said, "I'm starting to think that your precious Elders aren't gods—they are monsters. Besides, I've already killed one on the way down, some two-headed chick that called herself Duplii."

Melris's eyes grew. "Duplii is dead?"

"Deader than the last guy we killed." He patted his sword on his hip. "You can thank Black Bane for that. He's cooperating now. Oh, that reminds me." He took off his sword belt. "Iris, come here."

Iris hustled over. "Yes."

"I need you to hold my sword," he said to the amply built woman. "Cradle him like a baby."

Iris gave him a funny look and said, "Yes, if you say so."

"Captain," Horace said, "We best hustle out of here while we have light in the sky."

Abraham smiled. "No, we're gonna stroll out of here, 'cause we own this place."

25
____

THE HOUSE OF STEEL

After several long days of travel, the Henchmen arrived back in Kingsland. Abraham and Melris were immediately escorted to the House of Steel by the King's Guardians within an hour of crossing the border.

As usual, they were led through the shining gates of the grand castle that overlooked the Bay of Elders.

The Guardian Commander, Pratt, greeted both of them inside the gate. The oversized man appeared like a giant in his full-plate armor, towering above both men. "You are too unsightly to stand in the presence of the king. Couldn't you have washed up first?"

Abraham looked at his bare arms. The fish bites were scabbed over. Blisters were covered in caked blood and dirt. He eyed Pratt and said, "If you'd like to draw me a bath and bathe me, then have at it."

Pratt snorted. "Come along. Be sure to stay downwind of the king and queen. You reek." He led them up to the large terrace located on the back of the castle, which overlooked the Bay of Elders, the same place where Abraham had first met the king. "Wait here."

"We will, but if you could, will you check with the dry cleaners and see if my tuxedo is ready?"

Pratt sneered at him as he moved up to the upper patio and disappeared through the double door leading inside.

Abraham sat on the edge of the wall overlooking the sea. Hundreds of ships were in the bay, many more than before. He soaked up the sea wind while letting the sun shine on his face. It wasn't home, but being back at King Hector's castle felt good for some reason.

Melris dropped his hood. The ocean winds rustled his fair head of hair. "Four down and only two left to pursue. Impressive."

"Yeah, well, we still have to figure out where the other two are." Abraham fished the stones out of his pocket. The ruby and blazing orange gemstones sparkled in the sunlight. "What sort of special fire do these jewels have? Or do you know?"

"Not all their properties are fully known, but they do reveal themselves to the bearer. They do have names, however. The emerald is the Stone of Truth. The blue sapphire is the Stone of Lightning. The ruby you hold is the Stone of Blood, the orange the Stone of Power. That leaves the yellow amber as the Stone of Piety and the white diamond the Stone of Cleansing. All as one, though, can make chaos or harmony. When the king has them all, he'll be the most powerful person in Titanuus."

"Even greater than the Elders?"

"They aren't persons, but one could make a strong case for that." Melris gazed toward the horizon beyond the sea. "I only hope that King Hector can control this great power. After all, there was a reason why they were split up before."

Abraham thought about the zillon Ottum's warning about King Hector. *I hope I'm not creating another monster.*

Pratt returned, escorting Queen Clarann and Princess Clarice. The women hustled Abraham's way. Queen Clarann looked gorgeous in a short yellow dress the color of sunflowers. Princess Clarice wore the cuirass of a Guardian Maiden. Her long hair was pulled back in a ponytail, and her beautiful eyes were as bright as ever. Both women covered their noses.

"I know—I reek," Abraham said as he dumped the stones back in their pouch. He bowed and moved downwind. "It's wonderful to lay eyes on the both of you again. You both look beautiful."

"Tell me what you fought!" Clarice said as she bounced on her toes. "I want to know everything. I should have been there."

Abraham touched the young woman's chin and said, "I'll tell you everything. Perhaps we can go back to Stronghold. No doubt your fellow Henchmen would love to fill you in."

"You look like a burning behemoth spat you out," Queen Clarann said.

"I feel like it too."

"Are you well? You look grave," the queen said.

"Nothing some soap and suds won't cure." He clasped the queen's hand and gave her a knowing look. "All is well."

The queen lifted her eyebrows.

Prince Lewis and Leodor stepped out onto the patio. King Hector came behind them. The dark-headed prince's black cape rustled in the winds. The wizened Leodor's hands were hidden in the large sleeves of his robes. King Hector stood tall. The bend in his back was gone. Some red had returned to his white beard. He wore a stately suit of black robes trimmed in gold. The Crown of Stones rested tightly on his brow, pinching the skin as if it were grafted to his head.

The king's black garb sent a chill through Abraham.

King Hector threw up an arm and said, "Please, come sit! All of us." He gestured toward a table that held pitchers of wine and glass goblets. Diced fruit, cheeses, and crackers were spread out on platters on the table. "I can't wait to hear about all your adventures in the Wound."

After the queen and princess seated themselves on the right side of the king, Prince Lewis sat on the left. Abraham took a seat at the end of the table, leaving only Melris and Leodor between them.

"Why so far away, Abraham Jenkins?"

"I'm afraid my smell might make you retch."

King Hector let out a hearty laugh. He slapped Lewis on the back and said, "Now, that is a champion if there ever was one." His light tone became more serious. He lifted an eyebrow and shot Abraham a lustful look. "The stones. Do you have them?"

26

―――――

Abraham passed the two stones to Melris, who passed them to Leodor, who gave them to Lewis, who handed them to the king.

King Hector's eyes filled with the color of the sparkling stones. He licked his moustache and removed his crown. Two of the six horns were filled with gems. The blue stone was in the back and the green stone in the front. The king rolled the new stones in his hands, one in each. "I feel the life in them. They are excited. It's as if they are a family being reunited."

"The annals tell of the stones having their own unique essences," Leodor stated. The chinless man continued, "Essences that can be quite persuasive."

Abraham noticed a look of concern growing on Queen Clarann's face. She swallowed, reached down, and held her daughter's hand. Her eyes slid over to Abraham, but she quickly looked away.

King Hector clicked the new stones into the open clawlike prongs in the front of the crown. Left to right, the stones were red, green, and orange, with the blue one in the back. Each precious gem caught the sunlight and twinkled.

"It's magnificent, Father," Lewis said with a nod. "There is nothing that compares to it."

"And to think that it isn't even complete. Imagine how radiant it will be when all of the stones are put back in place," King Hector said. He lifted the crown and placed it back on his head.

A sudden wind whooshed over the terrace. The winds rustled King Hector's beard, enhancing a momentary wild look of power in his eyes.

Abraham shielded his face with his hand until the high wind died down. He grabbed a goblet of wine, filled it up from a carafe, and drank. *I got a bad feeling about this.*

As the windy stirrings at the table settled, King Hector eyeballed Abraham and said, "An excellent idea, my otherworldly friend. A toast! Everyone, grab a goblet. We've much to celebrate." He clenched a fist. "Victory is within *my* grasp!"

"Hear! Hear!" Lewis said.

Leodor echoed the sentiment.

Even Melris took up a goblet and sipped.

Abraham found Melris's actions odd because he'd never seen the Elderling eat anything. He felt eyes on him. Queen Clarann's wary eyes were on him again. He needed to talk to her about Ruger Slade, but for now, that would have to wait.

King Hector guzzled down a goblet and refilled another. "I feel so spry. Like the days of my youth when I hunted the great elk with nothing but a knife and a spear. I yearn to fill my hands with steel again and take it to my enemies." He hefted up the goblet. Red wine sloshed over the rim. "Another toast, to Abraham and Melris. Your aid came in the nick of time."

Neither Lewis nor Leodor spoke this time. Instead, the queen and princess offered their own "Hear! Hear!"

Abraham looked at Lewis and Leodor, the most discontent of all Henchmen. *I see someone still has a bug up their butt.*

"Tell me all that I need to know and more if need be," the king said as he looked between Abraham and Melris.

Melris opened his mouth.

Abraham cut him off. "Your Highness, we cut a bloody path from here to the Wound and back. We journeyed into the belly of the deep. Elders rose up, and now they are dead. All the Henchmen survived. Two stones were recovered. That's the CliffsNotes version. But there are more important matters at hand that need to be attended to."

King Hector nodded. "Yes, of course, we need to find the other stones. Leodor has been neck deep in the libraries, searching for their location. Certainly, it's not a priority."

"No, that's not it." Abraham took a breath. This was the part where he had to decide to tell the truth or not about his being able to go back in time and see his family. All he had to do was convince King Hector to stand down. "It's about the invaders. They are going to come hard and fast. But they have an offer."

King Hector sat up in his chair, put his hands on the table, and leaned over. "I beg your pardon? Have you been consorting with the enemy?"

Lewis jumped up out of his chair, jabbed a finger at Abraham, and said, "I told you that he was a traitor. We should have killed him long ago."

"Melris, do you know anything about this?" the king asked.

"This is news to me," Melris said quietly. "But in Abraham's defense, I do not recall him consorting with any of the king's enemies. Any enemy we crossed, he killed, or we killed, rather."

With a wave of his hand, the king said, "Sit down, Lewis."

Lewis plopped into his chair.

King Hector rolled his hand and said, "Out with it."

"As you know, my essence has been switching between this world and my world on occasion. It is in my world that the enemy created a rift, or dimension door, between my home and yours. They are making great strides controlling a portal or, as they call it, a Time Tunnel. I have seen it with my own eyes, and they are sending powerful artillery the likes that you and your armies have never seen.

"I'm sure you recall the weapon that the zillon dragon riders used to try and assassinate you with. It's called an assault rifle. They shipped hundreds of them, perhaps thousands of them, and are giving them to the Gond and whoever else. There is a weapon called a tank. It's a chariot made out of solid metal and bigger than elephants. It has a nose that fires a missile that would blow a hole clear through any side of this castle. That's just the beginning. There will be more—much, much more. They can't be stopped."

Everyone at the table paled except the king. He rubbed a finger over his chin and said, "We'll see about that."

27

"They want me to make a deal with you," Abraham said.

"A deal?" King Hector huffed a laugh. "Who wants to make a deal?"

"The men on the other side. My world. Dr. Jack Lassiter. Colonel Drew Dexter. Eugene Drisk. He's the man that used to inhabit this body before me. You see, the military in my world created the rift, and now, well, they want to take up full occupancy here."

"Why do they want to come here? Is your world so bad?" Queen Clarann asked.

Abraham scratched the scruff on the side of his jaw and said, "Something like that. My world has a lot of pleasures and conveniences that this world doesn't offer. That's not enough for some. They think they can do better. They want a new frontier to conquer, so to speak."

The king straightened up in his chair and said, "You tell them the next time you see them that this king will never surrender. I say we find this tunnel and we take their world by force." He slammed his fist on the table. "I'll invade them!"

"They don't have the process mastered. They can send weapons and other vehicles over, but they can't send people. It's this essence swap that they need control of." Abraham poked his finger on the table. "There is still time to put a stop to it. We only need to find out where their lair is, and we know that it is in the Spine, but that is all."

"This is outrageous." Lewis gestured toward Abraham. "This fool barters with our enemies, who we haven't even seen, and now he is negotiating on their behalf. He's making up stories, Father."

"No, he's not," the king said. "This otherworlder has done nothing but serve with honor. And he bears the brand. You cannot betray the crown without consequences." He nodded. "There he sits, a true Guardian of Kingsland."

Lewis shook his head.

"I only want what is best for both worlds," Abraham continued. "Even if that means that I don't make it back home. I do think there are more problems than the oncoming invasion that you need to be warned about."

"It gets worse?"

"Apparently, there are more otherworlders like me. They are already working with the people on the other side. Part of that is the Sect. The Underlord, a wraith called Fleece, is controlled by a horned halfling named Big Apple. Big Apple's real name is Edgar, and he's from my world. Somehow, I don't know how, he controls Fleece, who controls the Sect. He also leads the thieves' guild called the Shell. All of those people are under his thumb from here to the Old Kingdom. He has spies everywhere, some from this world and others not. King Hector, you can't trust anyone, except maybe your Henchmen."

Pratt cleared his throat.

King Hector grabbed Clarann by the hand and said, "I can certainly trust my queen."

"That goes without saying," he said though he was thinking about the queen's secret relationship with Ruger Slade and their daughter, Clarice. "You have to be careful who you trust from here on out. Very careful."

"Anything else?" the king said with a bemoaning sigh.

"They want the King's Steel."

King Hector raised an eyebrow and asked, "Why?"

"The metal is precious, unlike any other metal. It contains qualities that they need to manage their Time Tunnel. The more steel they have, the longer they can keep the portal open. It's the key ingredient they are missing." Abraham drank the rest of his wine. "Wherever it is, I'd triple the guard on it."

King's Hector's face sagged. "Oh."

Abraham leaned forward. "Oh, what?"

"Nothing that concerns you." King Hector clenched his fists. "These people in your world—if I find them, I'll put a noose around their necks." He wagged a finger at Abraham and said, "The next time you are in your world, you kill them. That's an order."

"Your Highness, I can't just murder someone in my world. There are laws against that, the same as the laws you have here."

Prince Lewis jumped up. "You will do as the king says! Are you defying his order?"

"No, I mean"—Abraham lifted his hands—"I can't kill in cold blood."

"This isn't cold blood. This is war!" King Hector stood up. "I want the enemy dead!" The gems in his crown burned with new fire. His eyes glazed over. "I will have their heads. And you will bring them to me."

The queen and princess pushed back in their seats.

"Hector, control yourself," Queen Clarann said.

King Hector glared at the queen. "You dare speak to me in that tone? I am the king." He hit the table. "I am the king!"

The table burst into cinders, and a force of energy knocked everyone back in their seats. The queen and the princess lay on the ground, holding onto one another, shaking. Shards of wood were sticking out of their faces.

Abraham rolled over on one side and plucked a splinter from his noggin. Everyone at the table was on the ground with splinters in their faces and specks of blood behind them, except for Melris. The

Elderling sat in his chair, dusting the splinters off his robe and shaking them out of his hair.

King Hector's fierce expression softened the moment he saw Clarann and Clarice lying on the ground bleeding. He dropped to his knees and reached toward the queen. "My love, I'm sorry!"

Queen Clarann slapped the king's outstretched hands away.

28

Abraham returned to Stronghold alone. King Hector and Queen Clarann's spat became an ongoing argument. King Hector had quickly dismissed him, but Melris and the others stayed. As soon as he entered Stronghold's threshold, he greeted all the Henchmen that he saw. The triplets, Sofia, Selma, and Bridgett, gave him welcoming hugs and kisses.

"Master, you stink," said Selma, who wore a short strapless dress. She escorted him downstairs to the dungeon level. "You need washed. Very much."

The dungeon was a basement with stone walls, where one part had hot springs turned into a grotto. Steam made for a warm fog that filled one of the rooms.

The triplets stripped Abraham down. Bridgett, wearing a skimpy white cotton dress, fought to tug his boots off. His bare feet slapped on the wet stone floor. Several large pools of churning water waited for him to enter.

Through the steam, he noticed several figures moving out of the waters. "Horace? Iris?" he said.

"Sorry, Captain, we'll give you some privacy," Horace said.

"No, get back in the tub. Geez, it's not just for me. It's for all of us."

Abraham let the triplets lead him into the waters. He noticed Sticks in one of the other hot springs with Solomon. Shades was in the same one that Abraham got into.

Shades waved a hand and said, "Hello, Captain."

Abraham soaked in the tub. The triplets sat on the edge of the pool and began rubbing him down.

"Uh, that's not really needed, girls. Not that I don't appreciate it, but I really just want to sit here and soak." He nodded at Shades. "That fella there might need a rubdown. The others too."

Shades grinned. "That would be lovely."

"As you wish," Sophia said.

"I'll rub down my own man, thank you," Iris warned.

The triplets split up. Sophia joined Shades, while Bridget and Selma moved in on Sticks and Solomon. Sticks shooed the attractive women away, so they both went to work on Solomon's shoulders.

Abraham lay his head back against the damp towel Selma had laid on the rock ledge. He closed his eyes and breathed deeply. The hot bubbling pool of water was just what his aching body needed. His nostrils flared. The minty steam began to soften his hard muscles. The aches and pains that throbbed all over began to fade away.

This is better. Much better.

Ruger Slade's body was more or less a restless device. The slightest abnormal aberration in the environment would fire up his instincts. He was as alert as a prowling panther, always ready to strike at any moment.

Abraham managed winks of rest. He dozed off while the others talked, but every so often, his nerves would fire, waking him up and putting him on edge. Abraham tried to get the body to let go, to relax. They were safe inside Stronghold.

Relax, Ruger, relax.

Normally, Abraham slept well when he slept, though lightly. Ruger's body could make do on a few hours. Right then, that rest, despite all the creature comforts, wasn't happening. For some reason, Ruger's body wasn't settling down. He cracked an eye open.

Sticks lay with her head back, eyes closed, her creaseless face as expressionless as ever.

Solomon had Bridgett in his lap while Selma sat behind him, rubbing his hairy shoulders. Bridgett's fingers were playing with the troglin's gums and teeth, and Solomon would chuckle.

Horace and Iris sloshed around in their own pool, giggling quietly.

Sophia's legs were draped over Shades's shoulders while she gave him a temple massage. The man looked as if he was in heaven.

The room was filled with happy people, yet Ruger's instincts were still firing. Abraham had been in Ruger's body long enough to know to trust it. *Something's wrong.*

Abraham caught Sticks looking at him. She quickly looked away. He lifted an arm out of the water and waved her over. Quietly, she came. His eyes popped when she came out of the water not wearing a stitch of clothing.

"Why are you looking at me like that?" Sticks asked as she sank back down into the water beside him. She slid a look at the triplets. "Is it because I don't look like them?"

"Uh, no, it's not that. You look great. I guess I was expecting to see you in a bikini."

"A *bikini*?"

"It's something that the women wear when they are in the water back home."

She nodded. "I see. So, you wanted something?"

"I just wanted to see how you were doing."

"I'm fine." She sat so close their thighs were touching. She touched his leg. "You?"

"Feeling better, but it's hard to unwind after a trek like that. We still have a big situation to deal with. The king sent me away, so I don't know where things are going."

Shades jumped into the conversation and said, "So, what did the king say?" He scooted toward Abraham.

All of a sudden, Horace and Iris climbed over from their small pool into Abraham's bigger one. Solomon stretched out from his pool and leaned over its rim, which poured into the bigger pool as well.

"Huh, when King Hector speaks, people listen." Abraham cleared his throat. "I laid it all out for him. I told him about my world and the corporation behind the portals. We gave him the red and orange stones. I think they changed him. Let me ask all of you this: have you ever wondered how you know for certain that you are on the right side of things?"

Horace gave him an appalled look and said, "We always know we are on the right side of things because we serve the king."

"Yes, but there are other kings in Titanuus."

"No, there is only one true king." Horace's brows knitted together. "Captain, I find your words unsettling." He grabbed Iris by the hand. "We have to go."

"Horace, wait," Abraham said. "It's only a hypothetical question."

Horace and Iris vanished into the mist.

Abraham's shoulder sagged. "Crap."

29

"Well, that was really smooth," Solomon said to Abraham. He squinted an eye and said, "A little lower, Selma."

She grimaced as she dug her tiny mitts into the troglin's back.

"Ah, that's the spot," he said. "I swear, for little women, you have magic fingers. Strong fingers, at that."

"The better to please you with," Bridget said.

"Abraham, I understand where you are coming from," Shades said as he squirted water out of his hands. "There are many kings, and every one of them had their own ideas about what is right and what is wrong. I come from Hancha. The rules in that country are oily. I'll say this for King Hector: the people might not like him, but you know where he stands."

"What brought this on, anyway?" Sticks asked.

"Ah, I've been fine with it until my last trip back home. There is a woman there, a zillon named Ottum. She warned me about the king."

Solomon gaped. "A real live zillon? How is that possible? I didn't think that our bodies could travel from one world to another."

"I don't know, and the good thing is that they don't know either. That's a good thing. They plan on moving people back and forth by

369

soul swapping." He sat up and brushed his damp hair away from his face. "Man, the possibilities."

"Was the zillon a prisoner, like you?" Sticks asked.

"No, she was one of them. At least, I think she was."

"If it's any consolation, Abraham, I've never known a man with greater honor than Ruger Slade," Shades said. "If our king did something wrong, he wouldn't stand for it. Believe me, I've seen him do much. With Ruger, the standard is the standard. He is the standard."

"I guess me opening my big mouth did him a lot of injustice."

Sticks hugged his arm. "You have to be you. He has to be him. I know you are a decent man. We all do."

He rubbed the back of his neck and said, "Yeah, I just have a heck of a standard to live up to."

"Horace will stop pouting soon enough. Just remember, a lot of those old soldiers practically worshipped Ruger. That's why they left with him when he fled... even though it wasn't him," Shades said.

Abraham scratched the brand on his chest. The raised crown was thick and tough. He wasn't so sure that King Hector was the bad guy. He'd seemed fair, but power could change people. One thing he was sure about was that Eugene Drisk, Dr. Jack Lassiter, and Colonel Dexter were bad. So was the corporation they worked for.

It's time to suck it up, buttercup, 'cause one way or the other, this thing is coming to the end. Maybe that's why my guts are turning.

"So, what do we do now? Wait?" Solomon asked. "Not that I mind waiting at the moment. I could get used to this."

"I'm sure that we will hear from the king soon enough. We still have two more stones to recover. My guess is that Melris and Leodor are trying to figure out where that is." He rinsed off his face. "Let's enjoy the moment. I'm driving myself crazy thinking about this all of the time."

"It sounds like a fine idea to me," Shades said. "I can let me plums shrivel in this water all day. It would be nice to have some beverages to partake in."

"I'll take care of it." Sophia rubbed Shades's shoulder and took off with her damp pink clothing clinging to the curves of her body. "Any requests?"

"Bring the best that you have," Abraham said. "Heck, we've been successful. Why not celebrate?" He nodded. "And that goes for all of us. Tell Elga and Eileen to bust open the wine cellar. Let's have ourselves a Catalina Wine Mixer!"

THE HENCHMEN BUILT a huge bonfire outside, in front of the Stronghold. The men and women—Henchmen, Red Tunics, and hirelings—were dancing arm in arm and hand in hand.

Skitts and Zann had a talent for playing five-stringed lutes like guitars, and they weren't half bad singers. They sang countrylike tunes about adventures in the fields of farm country.

Solomon carried around a full-sized keg of ale. He poured it straight from the tap into the open jaws of Vern, Bearclaw, and Prospero. Bridgett sat on top of the troglin's monstrous shoulders, tossing her hair from side to side and playing a tambourine.

Abraham strolled the courtyard area, smiling, dancing, and patting his men on the back. He started to drink but thought better of it. If Ruger was the standard, he would be wise to be so as well. Plus, his history with too much drink in the past had proven dangerous, and he had yet to shake a heavy wariness that made him feel that something close was amiss. He made his way over to Horace and Iris, who were standing in front of the new barn they'd recently built. Horace had his arm wrapped around the mystic's waist.

"Iris, do you mind?" Abraham asked.

"Certainly not, Captain. I've been dying to go and dance, but I couldn't get out of this bear's grip." She pranced off with her robes hiked up and joined in a dance with Dominga and two of the triplets, circling and skipping together like children.

He looked at Horace and asked, "Do we have a problem?"

"No," Horace said, his eyes fixed on the cavorting.

Abraham bristled. "No, what?"

Horace growled in his throat and said, "No, Captain."

"Was it hard to say?"

Horace gave a stiff chin nod.

Abraham stood beside Horace and watched the celebration with his arms crossed. Neither man said a word for the longest time.

Finally, Horace broke the silence. "I've heard worse from your lips."

"Pardon?"

"The last one, Eugene. He mouthed off about the king all the time. I wanted to kill him. When you said what you said, it hurt coming from you. How can you believe that King Hector is in the wrong? He is the only king that boldly declares what is right. He doesn't mince words and dance in the middle. Ruger did not either."

"I let that zillon push doubt into my brain."

"What zillon?'

Abraham brought Horace up to speed about the discussion at the Time Tunnel.

"Zillons can't be trusted unless they wear the brand. Did you see a brand?"

"Of course not. She wasn't naked."

Horace harrumphed. "Captain, your actions have shown me your heart. I should know well enough to give your comments a pass." He extended his hand. "Death before failure."

Abraham shook Horace's mighty grip with his own. "Death before failure."

"Abraham!" Tark was standing on top of their war wagon, waving a red handkerchief. He pointed down the dirt road. "Look!"

A white carriage was approaching, escorted by riders, Guardian Maidens.

"More women for the party!" He lifted up a flagon of ale. "Woo-tah-woooo!"

Abraham recognized one of the Guardian Maidens. She was the tall one with raven hair, named Swan. She dismounted and opened the door to the carriage.

Princess Clarice stepped out. She was followed by the queen.

All the Henchmen stopped reveling, bowed their heads, and took a knee.

Abraham's knees locked, and as he saw the distraught face turn toward him, he muttered, "This can't be good."

30

Queen Clarann and Princess Clarice met with Abraham inside the Stronghold, away from the others. They were on the main floor, beside the farm table facing the fireplace.

The queen paced. "Hector is losing himself. Those stones—I fear they make him mad with power."

"Did he hurt you?" he asked.

"No, at least not since he turned the table to splinters." Queen Clarann wrung her hands. "I think that taught him a lesson, for now. Still, he did other things."

"Other things?"

Clarice toyed with her ponytail and said, "He knows."

Abraham's heart skipped. "You mean he knows that you are not his child?"

"Yes, he knows. He used that gem on Mother. Now, he's mad. Very mad. I've never seen him so distraught before. I don't think he likes you anymore."

"Me? I'm not your father. I mean, Ruger is, but not me. I'm innocent."

Clarann's pale-yellow summer dress dragged over the hearth stones and snagged on the corner. She ripped it away, tearing the fabric. "It's that crown. My Hector would understand this, but now, he's hot as fire. He threatened to kill you. Well, Ruger." She sat down on the end of the hearth and clutched her heart. "I'm the one that should swing from a rope, not you."

Clarice clicked her sword in and out of her scabbard. "You should have seen Lewis and Leodor clucking. They think that they are so right and righteous. Lewis moves to turn my father against his queen and me. At least I have the pleasure of knowing that he's not my *real* brother."

"Holy sheetrock, this is bad. So, Hector let you leave?" he asked.

Clarann shrugged. "I don't think he cares what happens to me. Hector has been such a good husband. I know that he only feels betrayed, and it's true. I betrayed him, and I am his queen." She sobbed.

Abraham grabbed a cotton napkin from the table and walked it over to the queen.

She took it and blew her nose. "Thank you, Abraham."

He rubbed her back. "I hate to ask, but do you know what his intentions are? Is he bringing a rope for me?"

"No, when I left, he'd taken up counsel with Lewis, Leodor, and Melris. He is very obsessed with recovering the other two stones. I think he thinks that he can control all of Titanuus with them."

He sat beside her while Clarice pulled her sword and practiced several strokes. "I can kill Lewis now, can't I? I'm going to slice him like an apple."

"You can't attack another Henchman," he reminded her.

Clarice slid her sword into the scabbard and said, "Oh, but I can. My father—er, well... King Hector—removed their brands shortly before we left. Those dogs don't have a leash on them any longer."

Abraham jumped up. "What? He lifted the brand on them and left it on us? But they tried to kill him!"

Clarann grabbed his hand in hers and said, "Hector does not think he has much to worry about. He thinks he's become invincible. I fear that he is blinded by the stones."

Abraham tried to pull free of her grip, but she held him fast and looked into his eyes. "This is not your fault. You are doing the right thing. No one could have foreseen this—not me and not Hector and least of all you. You have been nothing but a good and faithful servant."

Her words didn't make Abraham feel a whole lot better. He had a bigger problem. If Hector was not on his side, then he might not ever get home. He could be trapped in Titanuus forever, with a sea of enemies at his back. He could survive, but he didn't know if he could survive without the protection of the king. He would be on the run all his life.

"No sense in crying over spoiled milk." He found the queen's eyes and said, "There is something I need to tell you. Both of you. I left out this detail before."

"Yes," Clarann said.

Clarice sat down beside him. Both women were joined at his hips.

"It's about Ruger. He and I have been switching places, it seems."

"What do you mean?"

"Did you ever see *Freaky Friday*?"

"Freaky?" the queen asked.

"Friday?" the princess added.

"Bad example." He continued, "In the Wound, my essence went back home to my world. Ruger's essence came back to his body." He pocked his chest. "This body."

Clarann and Clarice threw their arms around him and squeezed him tightly.

31

Abraham woke up the next morning, lying on the farm table. He'd offered his room upstairs to the queen and princess. He sat up, rubbing his stiff back. He smelled bacon and eggs cooking. A few bright coals were still burning in the fireplace.

Prospero was passed out on the right side of the fireplace. His nose twitched. In his sleep, he sniffed. His eyelids started to open. He knocked an empty goblet onto the floor.

Other stirrings started in the room. Vern and Dominga were cuddled up together in the corner. She started to yawn. Cudgel was passed out halfway between the kitchen galley and the farm table.

Elga came out with two canisters with steam coming out the top. The haggard-looking elderly woman stepped on Cudgel as she crossed over to the table and set the pot down. "Fresh coffee, Captain." Turning back, she kicked Cudgel in the gut. "Coffee's on!"

Abraham slid off the table and stretched his arms. He'd talked into the wee hours of the morning with Clarann and Clarice. Clarice was excited to meet her father, once and for all. Abraham felt tired. Once again, his sleep had been restless. He dreamed of being back home, facing danger and an uncertain fate. King Hector entered his dreams. The king was angry, disappointed. He'd sent fiery hounds of hell after Ruger.

Eileen teetered in, stepping on Cudgel as she did so. The rickety-limbed woman set down a tray of earthenware cups. She poured a cup of hot coffee with a steady hand. "This will wake you, sire. As you know, my brew can wake the dead. The meal will be served shortly."

Abraham took the coffee, and the cup warmed his hands. "Thanks." He walked outside.

The morning sun had begun to rise over the lake. The birds sang their morning songs. The Stronghold's estate couldn't have been more perfect. Shades stood by the bonfire, bright eyed and bushy tailed. The guardian maiden, Swan, was with him. The two had hit it off not too long before. The braids in her long black hair were down. She was still hard eyed but, in her own Amazonian way, beautiful too.

"Good morning, Captain!" Shades said brightly.

Abraham approached. He could still feel the warmth from the hot ashes in the fire. "Morning." He took a sip of coffee. "Let me guess. You two have been up all night."

In a mannish voice for a woman, Swan said, "The Guardian Maidens require little sleep if not no sleep at all if the queen demands it."

"Yeah, what a bunch of beautiful bloodguard." He rubbed his face. It started to bother him that he wasn't bright eyed and bushy tailed also. Normally, Ruger's body remained vital as a busy beaver, but he felt drained. *Is it me, or was it Fleece? I just can't get my jump back.*

The rest of the Guardian Maidens were standing on guard in front of Stronghold. Every one of them appeared as formidable as the next, in their bronze breastplates and tight leggings. Each carried a spear, with a rapier hanging on her hip.

"So, how did last night go?" Shades asked with a smile. "Are you and the queen, you know, planning another princess?"

Swan backhanded Shades in the shoulder. "I told you not to mention that. Respect the queen's privacy."

"I already knew. I've always known. Good lord, look at the girl. A blind man can see the resemblance." Shades chuckled. "How the king missed it, I'll never know. Of course, maybe the beard threw him off."

"Yeah, well, the king knows now, and I'm not so sure where we will stand after this." He squatted down, picked up a piece of kindling, and tossed it into the fire. "I think we made our leader mad."

"Which kind of mad?" Shades asked.

"Huh—good question."

Horace and Iris walked out of the barn. Chickens and chicks marched by their feet.

"Well, it looks like someone had a roll in the hay," Shade said. "Lucky you."

Iris smiled as she hugged Horace's side. "It was more than a roll."

Horace slapped her behind. "You can say that again. We're making a family." He sniffed. "And they are hungry!"

"Has anyone seen Solomon?" Abraham asked.

"He was down at the lake last night. We saw him when we took a stroll," Shades said as he grabbed Swan's hand though she jerked it away. "He was with the one in white, and the one in pink, Sophia, I think."

"All right, I'll go find him. The rest of you go and grab some McVittles. I'll be back." He headed toward the large pond. He wasn't halfway there when Solomon appeared on the horizon.

The troglin was walking arm in arm with two of the triplets at his sides. He had a content look on his face. He lifted his arm and waved. "Good morning."

Selma and Bridget gave Solomon a squeeze, smiled at Ruger, and hurried back inside.

"Not as good as yours, apparently," he said.

"Probably not. So, you and the queen didn't...?"

"Lord, no. I'm in enough trouble with the king as it is. Needless to say, that puts our little situation in a bind."

Solomon clawed his fingers through the long hairs under his chin and said, "Yeah, you know, I've been thinking about that."

Some squealing pigs ran by their feet.

"About what?"

"Well, I was thinking, if I go back, I'll be about forty years older, won't I?"

Abraham shrugged.

"That would put me in my seventies, at least, I think. And heck, what sort of shape would my body be in?"

"You're an old troglin now. What's the difference?"

"Troglins live a longer time then men, I think. And I'd be lost, possibly." Solomon shook his head. "Heck, I don't know. Perhaps I enjoyed myself too much last night. This world's kind of funky."

"Yeah, and you be the funky monkey. Look, I don't know what's going to happen, but I do know it's going to happen. I can feel it in my bones. Once we find those other stones, well, either we stay here or go home. And if we stay here, the king might not be so kind to—"

Riders galloping toward the Stronghold appeared, kicking up dust and scattering grazing livestock. They were King's Guardians, riding tall in the saddle, with their full lion-face helmets on. They were led by Prince Lewis.

32

The Guardian Maidens bristled. Their ranks were outnumbered two to one. Swan lifted an arm, and the anxious women stood still.

Prince Lewis dismounted. His black cape stirred in the morning breeze. He had a smug look of satisfaction on his face. Abraham followed him over to the smoldering bonfire.

Prince Lewis held his gloved hands over the coals. "Nothing like a dying fire during the morning chill, eh Abraham?"

"If you say so."

He looked back at the mounted King's Guardians. Pratt had taken his helmet off. The big man no longer wore the badge on his armor that signified him as the Guardian Commander. That badge, birds' claws holding golden maple leaves, was sewn into Lewis's leather armor.

"I see you got a promotion."

"Yes, I have my station back, now that I am no longer tarnished by the brand of the Henchmen."

"Are you going to try to kill your father again?"

"Heavens, no. My father and I have mended our fences. I realized that I have erred in my judgment. But I was youthful and, well, poisoned by the Sect and Raschel." Lewis looked Abraham dead in the eye. "I hate to admit it, but I believe I have your intervention to thank for that."

Abraham's skin crawled as Lewis spoke with a serpent's tongue, with words full of guile. "What brings you here? You aren't going to try and burn it down again, are you?"

"Pfft... of course not. As I've said, I'm a changed man."

The queen and the princess came out of Stronghold's front door. Shock and distrust were on their frowning faces.

"Hello, Clarice," Prince Lewis said to his former sister. He tipped his chin at Clarann. "My queen. Father sends word. He would like you to return to the House of Steel immediately."

Clarann had a blanket drawn over her shoulders and said, "I'll return when I am ready."

Prince Lewis rocked his head from side to side. "That wouldn't be wise. Not that it matters to me. You can live here for all that I care. I've always thought that you were more fit for farming and the outdoor life rather than the majestic setting of a royal courtyard. However, for your own safety and for the sake of the crown, it's best that you come home."

"All of a sudden, my husband cares," the queen said.

"Only the Elders know why, but yes." He reached underneath his cloak and pulled out a white handkerchief. Wildflowers were sewn into the fabric. "He offers this. I imagine it has some sentimental value."

Queen Clarann stepped forward and took the handkerchief. Her eyes watered. She glanced at Abraham then back to Lewis and said, "I made this for him."

"Good. Perhaps you can make him another. You should have plenty of time to practice your embroidery inside the walls of the House of Steel." Lewis smirked. "It's time to return, either of your own free will or by force. Please don't make it by force. My men and I have a long journey ahead. We'd rather not scuffle with your personal guard." He glanced at Swan. "They are vastly outnumbered."

"Did you come here to start a fight," Abraham asked, "or is there another purpose?"

"As a matter of fact, there is." Lewis produced a scroll that had the burgundy wax seal with the king's mark. "I have your orders. And he also told me to give you this." He handed Abraham the Rubik's Cube. It had been solved. "He said that he was disappointed."

Abraham blankly looked at the cube in his hand. It was his son Jake's. His neck tightened. He'd given so little thought to his wife and son. He hadn't even been sleeping with the backpack at his side. An awful feeling sank in: guilt and something else. The thought that King Hector had solved it unveiled a new intelligence.

"Are you going to play with your little puzzle, or are you going to read your orders?" Lewis asked.

Abraham broke open the seal and read the scroll. The written words were as clear as English to him. He read in silence, but his lips moved. He looked up at Lewis and said, "We are going to the Wall? To the border of South Tiotan. To engage the enemy."

Lewis smugly replied, "Yes. After all, you are the most qualified person to carry on the fight. It appears that those iron chariots have appeared outside of our walls. Envoys from South Tiotan's officials, along with the prestigious elite of Hancha, demand our surrender. They are quite emboldened by their new foreign allies. My father wants you to take those iron chariots out or die trying."

Abraham swallowed. His fingertips turned numb. "What about the last stones? We should set out on a mission to retrieve them."

Lewis rubbed his hands together and said, "Viceroy Leodor and Melris are working on that. King Hector has put his trust in them rather than the man that impregnated his wife and deceived him for over a decade."

"But the king gave his word!" Abraham said as his plans crumbled. "We need the stones to control the portal. The king gave his word!"

"I witnessed it, and so did you, Lewis," Clarann stated. "The king would never go back on his word." She snatched the letter out of

Abraham's hand. Her eyes scanned the parchment. "It is his signature."

"Of course it is," Lewis said. "His contract with this man was broken the moment he learned the truth of his bastard daughter. It's nice to be right. It gives me such a warm and fuzzy feeling. And if you read the letter in its entirety, he also mentions that if you travel between this world and the other, tell them he won't surrender. Ever."

33

The Wall stood thirty feet high and ten feet wide. It was constructed of huge blocks of quarry stone. It ran for leagues between the mountains that created a natural barrier between South Tiotan and Kingsland.

There was passage through the Wall, the Shield of Steel. The gate was twenty feet wide and had a grand set of thirty-foot-high solid-steel doors that opened outward and another set of doors that opened inward toward Kingsland. Between both sets was a portcullis made of heavy woven strips of steel.

On the backside of the Wall were tremendous ramps leading to the top of it. Forts that were interlinked on the Wall made up a small city. Thousands of Kingsland's soldiers guarded the wall, from one end to the other. They moved like ants today. Armed with swords, spears, and crossbows, they marched up the ramps to the Wall's battlements and manned the ballistae, small catapults, and vats filled with boiling pitch.

Abraham stood on top of the Wall near the gates with the sun on his face, marveling. He'd never been to the Great Wall of China, but he'd seen plenty of pictures, and the Wall looked very much like it.

He and the Henchmen gazed over the battlements. Lewis and the Guardians were nearby.

The lands of South Tiotan were miles of rich green grasses as far as the eye could see. Now, those fields were littered with enemy camps. Soldiers from Tiotan and South Tiotan were lined up by the thousands out of bowshot distance. South Tiotan's banners, with angled black stripes over a field of yellow, were on one side. Tiotan's flags, with black stripes angled a different way on a field of maroon, were on the other side. Those weren't the only enemy flags posted in the ranks. Flags from Hancha, Dorcha, and East and West Bolg were there. The enemies' numbers had grown to over ten thousand or more.

"The Shield of Steel can never be penetrated," Lewis said proudly. "It is the greatest fortification in the world. The army that stands behind it is invincible. My ancestor built it."

Unlike Ruger, Abraham wasn't a master at military combat strategy, but even he tended to agree with Lewis. Even with all the enemy's armies gathered outside the Wall, outnumbering their troops ten to one, he still felt secure.

"There is a wall just like this in my world. It ran for three thousand miles. It did its job... for a while," Abraham said. He leaned between the battlements and eyeballed the tanks in the field. He counted ten green army tanks. He didn't know one tank from another, but to him, they looked like big ones. "But time and technology caught up. Now, the enemies can fly over it."

Lewis scanned the skies and said, "I don't see any zillon dragon riders. I think we won't have to worry about that." He stroked the furs on the collar of his cape. "Those iron chariots haven't made any noise, and they look quite small from here. What do they do?"

"Blow walls like this to smithereens," Abraham said. He ground his teeth. *If the Drakeland Corporation had sent ten tanks through already, how many more could they send?*

"Well, we can't let that happen, or rather, you can't let that happen." Lewis took off his gloves one finger at a time. "Though, those iron chariots aren't so frightening, like you described. They appear quite minuscule compared to the Wall. Besides, the gate won't fall. The portcullis is made out of the King's Steel. It can handle anything."

"Those iron chariots are called tanks—get it right, *Lewis*." Abraham moved from one battlement to another and looked over the ledge at the Shield of Steel. "That's a lot of steel. Have the tanks fired a shot?"

"A shot of what?" Lewis asked.

He rolled his eyes. "You don't want to know."

Well over a week had passed since he'd departed in essence from back home. He was supposed to negotiate with King Hector and be the back-and-forth between them and the Corporation. But he hadn't gone back and hadn't been able to get word back to them either. That was a problem. If they didn't hear back from him, they would no doubt attack.

A group of riders approached the Shield of Steel on horseback carrying a white banner.

"What's that?" he asked.

"They carry the banner of truce. They want to talk," Lewis said.

"Well, let's see what they have to say," Abraham said.

Passing through smaller doors built into the large gates, Abraham, Lewis, and a host of Guardians rode out to meet the enemy. Abraham's eyes widened when he noticed Lord Hawk among the generals of Tiotan. The savvy-looking leader of the Shell was leaning over his saddle horn with a cocky grin on his face. "I've been waiting for days for you to show your face," Lord Hawk said.

"What's this about?" Lewis asked as he steadied his horse. "Who is this man?"

"This is Lord Hawk, the leader of the Shell. We've crossed paths a few times." Abraham scanned the faces of the generals. "Where's your little friend, Big Apple?"

"One never knows when he might pop up," Lord Hawk said. The rogue with receding blond hair looked between Lewis and Abraham. "I take it you've had time to counsel with King Hector and have disclosed to him our offer?"

Prince Lewis bumped Lord Hawk's horse with his horse. "Listen to me, you thieving rodent. Listen, all of you. Titanuus will freeze over before King Hector surrenders. You best pack up your armies and return home. The Wall will never fall."

Lord Hawk chuckled. "Is that your final answer?"

"What is this, *Who Wants to Be a Millionaire*? Of course it is," Abraham fired back.

"I can speak for myself!" Lewis stated. He glared at Lord Hawk. "This negotiation is over."

Lord Hawk lifted a finger and said, "Before we part, I was ordered to show you an example of what you are up against." He raised a hand high.

The tank closest to the roadway leading to the Shield of Steel churned forward with its metal wheels grinding inside its tracks. It stopped fifty-five yards away from the Wall. The top hatch of the tank opened.

Big Apple popped out. The horned halfling wore a flak vest, smoked a cigar, and flexed his muscular arms. He took the cigar from his mouth and flicked the ashes. He had a grin on his face from ear to ear. He placed some goggles over his eyes and stuck his fingers in his ears.

The hairs on Abraham's neck rose. "Holy sheetrock! Get down!"

The tank fired.

Kaboom!

Every soldier and horse jumped.

A huge chunk of the Wall exploded.

34

Abraham and Lewis retreated back behind the Wall. The prince had paled after that initial cannon shot, and his back quickly straightened. He had given Lord Hawk a hot stare and said with a shaking voice, "We will not surrender! You want a war, then you will have one!"

For the next hour, every ten minutes, all ten of the tanks fired. The missiles blasted in the Wall. Running soldiers stumbled. Cries of alarm went up.

The Henchmen stood on the Wall, watching in awe. The barricade was slowly getting chewed up, one ton of rock at a time. A steady breeze blew stone dust into their eyes. Battlements and the manned ballistae on top were being blown away.

"They are very noisy contraptions," Horace said as he wiped stone dust from his eyes. "How do you kill them?"

"Easy, with an antitank missile," Abraham replied, "but the problem is, we don't have any."

The ten tanks, twenty yards apart, formed a line in front of the Shield of Steel seventy-five yards away. Ballista bolts and arrows shot from Kingsland soldiers bows plinked off the tanks' iron hides.

Prince Lewis's cheeks were flushed red. The white stone dust covered his black cape like falling snow. He pointed a finger in Abraham's face and said, "You will stop those tanks! That is the king's mission!"

"You can't be serious. You can't expect us to ride out there and fight those things. Our weapons are useless against them!" he yelled back.

"I don't care! You are the Henchmen. That is what you do! Now gather your men, and do what you are ordered to do, or I'll hang all of you by the noose!" Prince Lewis signaled to his second in command, Pratt. "Gather the Guardians. We depart to the House of Steel immediately. We must warn the king."

"You mean you aren't going to stick around to watch us die?" Abraham said to Lewis. "Imagine you, tucking tail and running. I'm shocked."

"I don't need to watch. I'll have Pratt stay behind." Lewis nodded at his second in command. "Once they die, you ride."

"And if we don't die," Abraham said, "what does Mr. Pratt do then?"

His words fell on deaf ears as Lewis had already snaked his way down the ramps and was out of sight.

"Wow, he's going to make a fine king someday. Not!"

Pratt and Horace stood side by side, overlooking the battlement together. Both men were shaking their heads.

Pratt turned. "Ruger, or whoever, I've never cared for you much, but I'll tell you this. This is the battle I've been waiting for. Those metal dragons and smoking snouts, hah! Let me ride at them with my own thunder underneath my hips!"

"You are ready to ride with the Henchmen?"

Pratt bent his thick neck back and laughed. "Elders no. Only as a last resort. I'd rather wait and see what becomes of you first. So go on, get at it before this bloody wall falls down."

"It's not going to fall down, at least, not anytime soon," Abraham said.

The Wall was ten feet thick and would hold up against the barrage for days, if not weeks, possibly.

"They are firing every hour. Perhaps they don't have enough missiles in their quivers, and they are hoping to scare us. Let's wait it out a bit and see what happens."

Every hour, the tank guns fired. Every blast chewed up the wall, and the Shield of Steel rattled like a giant saber.

Night fell. The torches of the enemies could be seen for miles.

The tank guns' muzzle fire flashed bright orange and red.

Horace, Sticks, and Solomon stood by Abraham, watching the enemy.

"You know, I protested the Vietnam War," Solomon said. "It seemed like the cool thing to do at the time, and I was trying to impress this girl. I never imagined I'd ever be on the front lines of a real battle. This is crazy. Every time those guns fire, my bones rattle. Never understood how a soldier might feel. I feel bad now."

"Yeah, war is hell," Abraham replied. "My dad told me that more than once. Heck, if I wasn't in Ruger's body, I'd probably be crying like a baby. I really don't have any idea how to stop them."

"You'll think of something," Sticks said.

"What makes you think that?"

"Because you have to."

The tanks were one problem, but Abraham sensed there was another. Something else was eating at him. His enemies were right in front of him, but something was missing. He couldn't put his finger on it. He scratched an eyelid and asked, "Horace, did you see any Gond?"

"No, Captain. The Gond would never fight alongside an organized army. Why?" Horace asked.

Abraham recalled seeing the Gond being armed with machine guns at the Time Tunnel. He'd expected they would appear with the army. *If they aren't here, where are they? Guarding the lair, perhaps?*

Another hour passed.

Ten tanks fired as one, rocking the Wall.

The pit in Abraham's stomach sank even further.

35

The armies behind the tanks would let out a rousing cry every time the tanks fired.

"Those cheers are beginning to annoy me," Horace said.

Dawn broke. Blurry-eyed soldiers of Kingsland patrolled the Wall and kept at their daily preparation duties.

Abraham leaned against the battlement wall with the rest of the Henchmen. They'd been ordered to stop the tanks, but a restless night didn't blossom any new ideas.

Pratt marched up to Abraham, kicked him in the boot, and said, "What are you waiting for?"

"An A-10 tank killer? You haven't seen one flying around here, have you?" he replied.

"Don't jest with me. You need to take action immediately. By sitting here, you accomplish nothing," Pratt said. "The longer you wait, the sooner you will be charged with treason. You are under orders of the king."

"I know that!" Abraham stood up. "And what are you going to do, Pratt? Huh? I'm gone, and all of a sudden, you're going to figure out how to stop ten tanks?"

Pratt blanched.

"I didn't think so," he said.

We have to act, Captain," Horace said while leaning on his spear. "I'll ride out there and stick it with my spear. We can kill them."

Bearclaw came to his feet. "I'm with Horace. We must fight. It's what we do. The longer we wait, the less fortune will favor us."

"I'm not going to stage a charge if we don't have some sort of edge," Abraham said. "We have to be patient."

"The Wall crumbles," Pratt said as he cast his hand outward. "Have you not looked for yourself? Those dragon snouts are chewing holes through the exterior."

"Captain," Shades said. He was sitting between the battlements. "You might want to have a look. The iron chariots' heads are swiveling."

The tanks' turrets started to turn. All the tanks' gun barrels pointed directly at the Shield of Steel.

"Sticks, how long has it been since the tank guns last fired?" he asked.

"It's coming up on that time. Any second now," Sticks said.

All as one, the tank guns blasted out their thunder.

Metal smote metal like a great gong falling to the earth.

BRRRWWWRRROOOONNNGGG!

The Shield of Steel rang like a gargantuan tower bell.

Soldiers fell to their knees, clutching their ears.

Abraham covered his ears with his hands. The ear-shattering sound was deafening.

The tank guns fired again and again.

The armies of Kingsland trembled underneath the blast of that limb-shaking sound.

With his hands pressed tight over his ears, Pratt yelled at Abraham. "You will end this now! Do you hear me? End it now!"

The tank gunfire stopped.

With his ears ringing with a thousand buzzing bells, Abraham leaned over the Wall. The Shield of Steel stood intact. The huge outer doors had huge divots and scorch marks all over, but they remained fully intact.

"That's the King's Steel for you! No power can tear down this wall!" Horace shook his spear in the air. He let out a roar.

Horace's bellowing created a chain reaction and caught on. The King's Army came to life. They belted out wild yells from one end of the Wall to the other. They jabbed their weapons toward the sky.

The tank guns turned. The noses of the barrels started to rise. The tanks fired one right after the other. A steady *ka-poom ka-poom ka-poom ka-poom* followed.

The tanks' missiles ripped through the battlement and tore men from the seats of the giant ballistae.

The King's Army dropped on their bellies, covering their heads and faces.

Pratt stormed down the walk. "Get up! Get up! Grin in the face of death, you hounds!"

The soldiers climbed back again and started shouting back over the Wall.

"That's more like it! The Shield of Steel is invincible!" Pratt yelled.

The tank turrets turned again. The barrels lowered toward the same spot on the Wall, to the left of the gate below where Abraham stood.

Like a woodchuck, Big Apple popped his head out of his tank's hatch. He still had an impish grin on his face.

"Let loose the arrows on that little hedgehog!" Pratt ordered.

The king's archers stretched their bowstrings. Crossbows and ballistae were pointed at the horned halfling.

"Fire!" Pratt shouted.

A volley of arrows and bolts whistled through the sky.

Big Apple waved just before he slammed the tank lid over his head.

Arrows and bolts ricocheted off the tank's metal.

The tank guns came to life and fired.

One missile blast after another blasted away at the outer wall. The tank shells pounded the same spot over and over.

"They're turning the Wall into a tunnel!" Abraham shouted. Ten feet of stone or not, those tanks would be able to drive right through the Wall in less than an hour.

The Wall shook underneath his feet. He watched in horror as bigger sections of the Wall started to crumble.

Pratt grabbed him by the shoulder and said, "Get out there and fight those things, you coward!"

Abraham knocked Pratt's hand aside. "The next time you do that, I'll take your hand from your wrist, and that won't be all." He pushed by the bigger Pratt. "Come on, Henchmen. Our time has come!"

Without a word of complaint or the slightest grumble, the Henchmen, one and all, followed Abraham Jenkins down the ramp to the bottom of the Wall. They stood as one and watched the Wall shake until one missile finally burst through. The barrage didn't stop until the Wall crumbled, leaving a tunnel large enough to drive a tank through.

Abraham pulled his sword. "Death before failure."

36

After the shelling of the Wall stopped and the dust settled, Abraham headed into the tunnel. With Sticks and Horace in tow, he sloshed his way ankle deep through pulverized rubble. Out on the field of battle, five of the ten tanks turned and started rattling their way.

"Does anybody have any big ideas?" he said.

Horace's face was as blank as Sticks's. No one in Titanuus had ever seen a tank before, let alone fought one. Abraham had seen them but never fought one either. However, he had seen movies and read his fair share of *G.I. Combat* and *Sgt. Rock* comic books. Those childhood images sparked some ideas.

"Listen up!" Abraham shouted out of the tunnel. "We are going to let the first tank through. Tark, Cudgel, Prospero, and Apollo, as soon as that tank rolls through, start covering it in pitch. We'll set that thing on fire and smoke the men out."

"What about the others? How are we going to stop them from barreling through?" Horace asked.

Abraham flipped his sword around. "Leave that to me and Black Bane."

The first tank thundered down the road, pointed toward the

tunnel. The other tanks blasted cover fire at the Wall. The tank rolled into the tunnel at twenty miles an hour.

"Now!" Abraham yelled to Tark and Cudgel, who were waiting above.

Tark and Cudgel poured two vats of hot pitch over the Wall and down onto the tank. The hot black goo spattered everywhere. Then Apollo and Prospero hefted bags of pitch and slung them onto the tank.

Small slit doors on the tank opened. The rat-a-tat of machine-gun fire blasted away from within.

Apollo and Prospero dropped to the ground.

Ranks of the king's foot soldiers were mowed down.

The tank gun turned and fired on the largest mass of soldiers gathered near the Wall. A loud booming blast sent men and their dismembered body parts flying.

"Burn that thing! Burn it now!" Horace bellowed.

Shades and Sticks rushed the tank with torches in hand and flung them onto the tank. Flames covered the tank. It rolled on, crushing, shooting, and killing everything in its path.

Gripping his sword in hand, Abraham said out loud, "It's show-time, Black Bane. I need you now."

The second tank entered the tunnel with its tank gun lowered.

"Black Bane?" He shook the sword. "Black Bane! I need lightning! I need it now! Oh man, this is a bad idea. Will you wake up?"

The tank started to pass out of the tunnel.

Abraham pointed the sword at the tank and yelled, "Lightning now!"

There was a momentary pause followed by a calm, *"All right, then."*

A globe of white-hot light dropped out of the sky and plowed into the tank, knocking it back into the tunnel. A jarring explosion knocked Abraham back off his feet. Tendrils of energy created a sparkling net all over the tank. Inside the tank's metal belly were the sounds of men screaming. As the mystic fires died out, the men's dying screams died out as well. The second tank was stuck in the tunnel.

A cry of victory went up from the soldiers on the top of the Wall.

"The tanks retreat!" Cudgel yelled from above. "The tanks retreat!"

The first tank rolled on like a flaming juggernaut. The Henchmen continued to throw on more pitch. The flames and black smoke grew higher. Suddenly, a man popped up out of the tank's turret coughing his lungs out and firing a machine gun.

Skitts and Zann shot the man in the face with their crossbows.

Another enemy soldier squirted out of the tank. The hot flames of pitch seared his hands and face. He dove off the tank. Before he could get up, the king's soldiers cut him down.

The tank rolled on, aimlessly, took a sudden turn back toward the Wall, barreled through a storage building, and crashed to a stop at the Wall.

Abraham breathed a sigh of relief and said, "Thanks, Black Bane."

"You're welcome."

"Now let's go and take those other tanks out."

"I beg your pardon? I'm might be powerful, but I'm not a miracle worker. I can only store up so much energy." Black Bane made a yawning sound. *"I'm spent after that. Good luck with your little skirmish."*

"Wait, how long does it take for you to store up enough energy to do that again?"

"Days. Weeks. It can vary. Say, where is that woman, Iris, that you matched me with earlier? She was some warm and cozy. I'd like to—"

Abraham sheathed the sword and said, "Good night."

He made the climb up the ramps to the top of the Wall. Cudgel was spot on—the tanks were retreating to their initial positions. The king's soldiers cheered in victory.

Pratt spat over the Wall and said, "There are still eight more of them out there. What are you and your magic sword waiting for?"

More ideas started to come to mind. He wasn't sure if they were his or Ruger's. He answered Pratt by saying, "Nighttime."

All day long, the tanks continued their hourly shellacking of the Shield of Steel. For the time being, they backed off from blowing another hole in the Wall. They seemed intent on doing something else. They blasted away at that Shield of Steel's weak spot, the stones around the hinges.

Abraham paced. "Blazing saddles!"

One of the front doors of the Wall stood in place, but it had fallen askew. The tanks continued to hammer away every hour on the hour. The enemy took their time about it. The inevitable began to sink in. The doors would fall, leaving an opening big enough to drive four tanks through. There would be no stopping them.

"So, what's the plan?" Solomon asked. The hippie troglin had a few more creases of worry in his brow. "Why do we wait for the night?"

"Because we have to be sneaky."

"Night is a good time for that. What are you going to do?"

"Something crazy. Did you ever see the movie *Beverly Hills Cop*?"

Solomon gave him a funny look and said, "Another movie reference? Seriously? Well, what's the plan?"

He looked at the tanks and said, "It's banana-in-the-tailpipe time."

37

That night, Abraham asked Sticks, "Are you sure that you want to do this?"

"Of course I do. This is what I like to do," she replied.

"Me too," Shades said. He held a tank shell in his hand. "It's exciting playing with an explosive egg. You must come from a fascinating world."

"You have no idea," Abraham replied. He'd removed several shells from the tanks that had invaded them. The shells looked like giant bullets, more or less. With all the Henchmen gathered around him at ground level, he ran his finger over the tip. "Put them nose first inside the barrel. When they fire the tank guns again, they'll kiss. And then *boom*. No more tank."

"No more tank," Dominga said with a nod. She carefully loaded two tank shells into a leather satchel. "I like it."

Tark loaded two shells into his own satchel. "I like this idea too. I can't wait to see those iron devils go boom."

The Henchmen chuckled.

"We are going to beat those demons, aren't we, Captain?" Horace said.

Yeah, we're going to get them. But we are going to need one heck

369

of a distraction." He addressed Sticks, Shades, Tark, and Dominga. Each of them had two shells. "You listen to me. If they sniff you out, tuck tail and get out of there. We'll find another way. Do you understand?"

The squad of four nodded.

"Come on." Abraham moved toward the tunnel the tanks had created with the Henchmen clustered behind him. The eight tanks remained stationed on the battlefield with their guns still pointed at the Shield of Steel. "Any time now. Iris!"

Iris pushed her way past the others to the front. "Yes."

"Do what you have to do to give them some cover."

"Of course." Iris grabbed Dominga by the hand. "Come with me." She led them to the other side of the tank.

"Horace, bring the horses up. We need to be ready to go," Abraham said. His heart pounded, and he was lathered in sweat. "Man, this is a bad idea."

Solomon wandered into the tunnel and peeked at the sky. "It's a good night for the attempt. Lots of clouds. No moon. Pitch-black. It might work."

"I'm still waiting to hear some better ideas."

"Well, you're asking the wrong person." Solomon patted Abraham on the head. "How's your gut feel?"

"Huh, never better."

The tank guns fired more shells into the Shield of Steel, and the great wall shook. New dust stirred.

Abraham flexed his hands, looked back down the tunnel, and said, "It's showtime."

Horace led two horses to the front. Bearclaw, Vern, Cudgel, Prospero, Apollo, Skitts, and Zann towed their own horses behind them.

Abraham took a horse outside by its leather reins and climbed into the saddle. The horse jumped, stamping its hooves.

"Easy, boy, easy." He led everyone outside.

Iris caught up to Abraham and said, "They are ready."

He looked down over his shoulder. The armor and clothing of

Sticks, Shades, Dominga, and Tark had sprouted tall grasses all over. He moved toward Sticks.

"Don't say it again. We are all in this together," she said.

"I know. Just remember my orders. If they sniff you out, tuck tail and run." He scanned the row of tanks. Seventy-five yards of open field lay in front of them and another hundred yards behind them. The enemy army continued to keep its distance from Kingsland's ranged weapon defenses. "Otherwise, you know what to do." He stretched out his fist.

Sticks bumped his fist with hers. "We got this."

Abraham led the horsemen along the base of the Wall toward the Shield of Steel. Up top, the torches that lit the night had been extinguished, leaving them in the shadows that were black as night. They crossed over from one side of the gate to the other. In the rear, Zann carried a burning torch.

The tanks in the field remained stone-cold quiet. Only the rustle of the tall grasses could be heard.

"Send up the flame." Abraham grabbed the torch tucked into his saddle.

Zann lit Skitts's torch, and Skitts lit Prospero's. From the back to the front, one torch was lit after the other.

Abraham moved forward for all to see. "Follow my lead. All of you remember the chant, don't you?"

The grim-faced men nodded.

"After that, we'll scream our heads off like a wild bunch of Indians. 'Cause if we are going to go out, we are going to go out in style." Abraham used to watch a lot of westerns with his father and grandfather when he was a boy. There would be scenes where the Indians would charge out in a showy fashion, posturing in front of settlers and armies in a show of intimidation. He was fool enough to try the same thing today. "Time to ride out, Henchmen."

They formed a row and meandered on horseback toward the line of tanks with their torches held high in their hands.

Abraham cast a sideways glance. He could barely make out Sticks and the others, forty yards away, low crawling over the grasses.

Ahead, the tank turrets didn't move. The wind whistled over the tanks' gun barrels. He stopped the horse line twenty yards away from the front end of the tanks.

The torch flames flapped in the wind.

Abraham fished a stone out of a saddlebag. He hurled it at the tank where he'd seen Big Apple last. "Listen up, you little billy goat! I'm going to give you to the count of ten to surrender, and if you don't, I'm going to do worse to these tanks than I did to the others. One! Two! Three! Four!"

The turret of the tank in the center turned and pointed its barrel right at Abraham.

38

"Ah, it looks like I have your attention." He moved his horse out of the tank gun's aim. "Listen up, Big Apple. This isn't going to end well for you. I have a secret weapon. A really, really, big one."

"We have a secret weapon?" Horace said as he cast his glance all over. "Where? I don't see it."

"Shhh. I'm bluffing," he said under his breath. "He resumed his count. "Five! Six! Seven! Eight!"

The hatch door of the center tank opened. Big Apple's horned head popped out. He pointed at his ear and said, "I can hear everything that you are saying, you fool. You don't have a secret weapon."

Abraham patted his sword handle. "Of course I do. Would you like to see it?"

"Huh huh. If that were a true threat, you would have used it by now. Besides, you can take out all the tanks that you want, but more will be coming." He pointed his stubby fingers at the Shield of Steel. "And once we have those doors down, we'll have enough steel to keep the Time Tunnel forever. It's over, Abraham Jenkins." He took out a new cigar and lit it with a fancy three-flame butane lighter. He puffed up a hot ring of smoke. "All of this fighting now is nothing more than window dressing."

"Don't get cocky, buckling."

Big Apple blew out a smoke ring and said, "Yeah, whatever. Do you have anything else that you wish to say before I destroy you?"

"Yeah, I do." Abraham tossed his head back, opened up his full voice and shouted. "How many Yankees?"

"Ten thousand!" the Henchmen cheered back.

"How many corn-fed, Southern-bred, never-dead re-e-ebels?" he bellowed at the top of his voice.

"Three!"

"What the hell you gonna do?" he finished.

The Henchmen yelled back with throaty voices, "Charge!"

Abraham kicked his horse into a full gallop, and the Henchmen followed. The group of riders raced around the tanks in a wide circle, waving their torches and screaming wildly.

On the Wall, the Kingsland soldiers gaped and exchanged dumbfounded looks with one another.

Solomon leaned against the Wall with his arms crossed, chuckling.

Abraham chanted loud chants of "Yip! Yip! Yip!"

The Henchmen did the same or worse.

Big Apple followed their every move, turning inside the hatch and glaring.

Abraham knew he looked like a fool. He hammed it up like a bad remake of *The Three Amigos*. He yelled out to his men, "Sew, Henchmen! Sew like the wind! Eee-yah!"

They rode long enough for Sticks and the others to snake through the grass and load the shells into the front of the tank barrels. The daring group finished the job and slunk back off.

If Big Apple caught on to what they were doing, he didn't show it. He continued to laugh and chuckle. He yelled at Abraham as he passed. "Hey, idiot, I've seen *Gunsmoke* before. Are you seriously trying to scare us?"

Abraham gave him a wild-eyed look and squalled, "You may take our gates, but you will never take our *freeedom!*"

Big Apple rolled his eyes. He knocked on the tank and shouted down the hatch, "Ready the machine guns. It's time to waste them." He saluted Abraham, dropped into the tank, and slapped the hatch lid over top of him.

The Henchmen were riding down the grasses, making a clear track in an oval circle. The rat-a-tat of machine guns started from the outmost tanks. Horace, Prospero, and Zann were shot out of their saddles. All three of them tumbled into the grass, and their horses crashed into the ground.

Abraham pulled back the reins of his horse. He charged through the field of machine-gun fire. He grabbed Horace's outstretched hands.

Apollo picked up Prospero, and Skitts snatched up Zann. They thundered back toward the tunnel with a hail of bullets ripping up the ground behind them.

"Yah! Yah!" Abraham galloped his horse into the tunnel.

All the rest of the Henchmen made the Wall's interior safety. The roar of machine-gun fire died down.

"Horace, are you okay?"

"What in Titanuus's Crotch did I get hit with?" The bearded bald man slid off the saddle and back onto the ground. He fell down, holding his thigh. "It burns like fire. Put it out!"

Iris rushed over to her man and said, "Be still, and let me have a look at it."

Horace had a bloody wound showing through his trousers. "What is it? It feels like an entire spear is inside my leg."

"It's a bullet. A big one," Abraham said. "Everyone get out of the tunnel. Treat the wounded." He couldn't see everyone with the tank wedged inside the tunnel. "Sticks!"

"Over here," she called back from the interior side of the Wall. She'd gathered with Shades, Dominga and Tark. "We did as you said. All of the shells were loaded into the noses of the iron beasts."

"It was a good plan," Shades said. He plucked grass out of his clothing. "I don't think that even ol' Ruger could have come up with a better one. But his plans always worked. Let's see if yours does."

A man cried out.

Zann lay on the ground, writhing and spitting blood out of his mouth. The young man's face was ghostly white. His brother fought to hold him still.

"It hurts!" Zann said as he spat more blood. "It bloody hurts!"

"Where?" Skitts asked.

Zann pointed to the side of his red tunic. A bullet had ripped through him from one side to the other. He collapsed on the ground, clutching the wound. "I'm dying, brother. My time has come. I go to kiss the Elders."

"Nooo!" Skitts said. Tears streamed down his face. "Iris, Iris, help him!"

"I'm coming. I'm coming." Iris hustled over with her robes hiked up over her ankles.

Abraham kneeled down beside Zann and grabbed his hand. "Zanex, hang on. Hang on. Don't let that little bullet get the best of you."

Zann stared blankly into the sky. "I can't see nothin'. It's been an honor, Captain. Finish them bastards." He stretched out his bloody fingers and touched Skitts's face. "I'll miss you, brother." He died in his brother's arms.

"Nooo!" Skitts yelled. "Save him, Iris! Nooo!"

39

Abraham stood on top of the Wall with his head down. The Red Tunic Zann was dead.

Zann's brother, Skitts, sobbed behind the battlements. "He shouldn't have gone. He didn't have the King's Armor on. He died because of me. He's just a kid."

"No, he was a man," the iron-jawed Bearclaw said. "A soldier. Soldiers die so others don't have to. He gave his life the same as all of us. There is no shame in it." He cast his dark stare at Skitts. "They are brothers. There is no shame in his weeping. It will pass."

Vern had his boot up on the Wall with his eyes on the tanks. "We should all be dead by now. Every day is a miracle, if you ask me. Sooner or later, the rest of us will have it coming. It used to be that way before you came. You've spoiled us by surviving." He spat over the Wall. "Take heart, and move on."

"I wish it was that easy." If Abraham could've stopped his heart from clenching in his chest, he would have. But he couldn't stop it. He wasn't a general that led thousands of troops into battle to see many if not all slaughtered. Death bugged him. He'd rather no one die at all. He didn't use to be that way either. He was more callous in terms of war, with so many veterans in his family that had done soldiering.

But when Jenny, Jake, and Buddy died, that changed his perspective on life. He realized he cared for people. He cared deeply. Abraham cleared his dry throat.

Vern passed him a skin of water. "Drink the wine, and pray you live to drink again."

"Huh." Abraham drank deeply and wiped his mouth. "You know, back in my world, there were wars where millions of men fought at land and sea. One of the most famous soldiers was a man named General George Patton. My coach used to play his speeches to the troops in the locker room before the games we played." He took another long sip.

Vern and Bearclaw shared a mutual high-eyebrow glance.

"Do you know what he said?" Abraham could feel the eyes of the lingering Henchmen on him. "He said, 'The object of war is not to die for your country but to make the other bastard die for his.'"

Horace was sitting on the back side of the Wall with his leg bandaged. He said, "I like this General Patton. Tell us more."

"Yes," Vern and Bearclaw agreed.

Abraham took another pull from the wineskin and said, "Okay, let me see what I remember." The slightest guilty smile broke out on his face. "My father, Earl, used to quote him all the time too. Hmm... this is kind of therapeutic. Let's see." He started the list.

"May God have mercy upon my enemies, because I won't."

"A good plan violently executed right now is far better than a perfect plan executed next week."

"Wars may be fought with weapons, but they are won by men."

Abraham passed the wine around for the others to share. Skitts tried his wine. Abraham's back straightened, and the strength in his voice slowly returned.

"A pint of sweat saves a gallon of blood."

"Nobody ever defended anything successfully. There is only attack and attack and attack some more."

Pratt was standing away from the company, but he lifted up his voice and said, "Hear! Hear!"

Abraham added a few more.

"Courage is fear holding on a minute longer."

"Americans love to fight. All real Americans love the sting of battle."

"When you put your hand into a bunch of goo that, a moment before, was your best friend's face... you'll know what to do."

Skitts sniffed.

Abraham finished with "It is foolish and wrong to mourn the men who died. Rather, we should thank God that such men lived." He walked over to Skitts and hugged him tightly.

"Hear. Hear," Skitts said as he returned the firm embrace. "Hear. Hear."

"Sorry to spoil the moment." Sticks was sitting between the battlements. "Shouldn't the iron chariots have fired by now? "It's been an hour."

"Has it?" Abraham said. He moved to the spot where Solomon was standing. "I lost track of time. What do you think?"

"Let me check my watch." Solomon looked at his wrist. "Oh, sorry, I left my watch in the Fort Pitt tunnel. Do they still use watches back home?"

"Yeah, sort of."

The tanks hadn't moved, and no one had popped out of the hatches either. The field remained dark and overcast.

"I haven't seen anything budge," Sticks added, her assault rifle laid across her lap. She rolled a bullet between her fingers. "Maybe they ran out of those shells."

"No," Abraham muttered. "Big Apple isn't stupid. Maybe he's on to us." He hated to think that Zann had given his life for nothing. "Let's give them a few minutes. Perhaps we spooked them."

The minutes became an hour.

An hour became two.

The wee hours of the night dragged on.

The morning sunlight peeked over the tall hillsides.

Pratt strode over to Abraham and said, "Your plan bears no fruit. What is the second option?"

"They aren't attacking. That ought to count for something."

Abraham rubbed his temples as a nagging headache was coming on. "Be patient."

"What about your General Patton? He was an attacker. You should attack," the horse-necked guardian said.

"Sure, I'll attack, but only if you are going to let me lead all of your men. How does that sound?"

Pratt rubbed his lantern jaw and said, "No."

"Abraham, the iron chariots move," Sticks said.

The Henchmen leaned over the Wall.

The tank turrets turned away from the Wall. Their rattling treads backed away.

Abraham slammed his fist on the Wall. "Devil's donuts!"

40

"Pratt, turn your archers loose on those tanks!" Abraham ordered.

"I don't take any orders from you. This is my wall and my charge. I won't waste arrows and bolts on an enemy that is retreating." Pratt bumped chests with Abraham. "And if you ever talk to me again, I might toss you over the Wall."

"Really?" In a blur of movement, Abraham grabbed Pratt by the neck and waist of his breastplate and heaved him up over his head. The huge man in full armor must have weighed over four hundred pounds of dead weight. Abraham had forgotten Ruger's great strength. His angry effort surprised even himself. "Is this what you had in mind, Pratt?"

Pratt blanched. He stammered when he spoke. "I don't like heights. Put me down. An assault on me is an assault on the king."

"The king isn't here! It's us against them. Are you going to be an anchor, or are you going to act like a Guardian?" Abraham asked. He shook the man over his head. "The standard is the standard. What is your standard, Pratt?"

The big-eyed Pratt let out an angry grunt. "I'll cooperate, but we will settle this. You and I."

Abraham put him down. "You need to quit acting like Lewis and get off of your high horse. "Now, rally your men. Tell them the enemy is retreating. Unleash havoc on those metal beasts!"

Pratt marched away and flagged down his generals, shouting, "Archers! Archers! The enemy retreats! To arms!"

In a matter of seconds, bows, crossbows, and ballistae fired volley after volley. The missiles sailed up and streaked down, hitting the enemy soldiers' foremost ranks. The ballista bolts landed even deeper, impaling bodies over two hundred yards away.

Kingsland soldiers shouted over the Wall in a clamor of victorious cries. They beat their swords on their shields.

The tanks stopped in their tracks. The tank guns turned, and the green machines advanced back to their original position facing the Shield of Steel.

Abraham pumped a fist at his side. "It's working. It's working."

Kingsland's missile weapons rained down by the hundreds and rattled off the tanks.

"Keep firing! Keep firing!" Abraham said as he moved between the battlements. "That's it, make them mad!"

The eight tank guns took aim at the gate and the archers on the Wall.

Abraham's breath caught in his throat.

Every Henchmen hung over the Wall with eyes as big as mirrors.

"Come on, come on, come on," Abraham muttered.

Big ballista bolts rocketed into the tanks. A few of them stuck in the metal.

The enemy tank guns fired.

Boom-boom! Boom-boom! Boom-boom!

Red-hot flashes exploded from the barrels.

Boom-boom! Boom-boom!

The barrels peeled back like banana peels.

Boom-boom-boom-boom!

The entire field lit up like the Fourth of July. The explosions inside the barrels created a chain reaction. The turrets blasted off the tanks and into the sky. Two tanks flipped over.

Boom-boom-boom-boom-boom-boom!

Strips of metal, barrels, and tank treads flew through the air into hundreds of pieces.

Boom-boom!

The tanks caught fire. Oil and gas burned. Dying men screamed, their charred bodies torn asunder.

An eerie silence fell over the masses on the Wall. Jaws hung open. Once the explosions were over, the King's Army let out a loud chorus of triumphant cheers.

The Henchmen were all smiles. They slapped Abraham on the back.

Abraham couldn't help but grin all over himself. But his eyes were still searching the fiery mess of metal. One tank remained unscathed. It retreated from the rest. It was Big Apple's.

"Will you look at that? The little billy goat is getting away."

Horace limped over to him and said, "I don't suppose they will fall for that one again, will they?"

"Probably not. We got away with one. It will buy us some time."

The rest of the day, the King's Army resumed preparations for the assault. Everyone knew that more trouble would be coming, but for the moment, the invasion of Kingsland had been halted.

South of the Wall, in a meadow where the spring flowers bloomed, the Henchmen had a funeral service for Zann. Skitts dug the grave himself with the shovel Abraham had told him to bring. He offered some comforting words and helped fill the grave.

"He was a good brother in his own way," Skitts said with a long look on his face. "I always figured he could squeeze out of anything. I thought I'd go first, being much slower and all." He wiped his eyes on his sleeve. "I'm going to miss him. I've never lived a day without him."

Abraham swallowed the lump in his throat. He knew exactly how Skitts felt. His bowels twisted into knots. "I know it hurts. I know."

The Henchmen made camp away from the army. They needed rest. They hadn't stopped since having departed for the Wall. Black rings were underneath all their eyes. A campfire burned, and a few of the company set up their tents. Most of them drank and celebrated the same as the soldiers did.

Abraham lay down on his bedroll by the fire, staring up into the sky. His head throbbed. He closed his eyes, but the nagging pain didn't go away.

Sticks took a spot beside him, and so did Solomon. They were both sitting up with their arms wrapped around their knees and the flickering flames shining on their faces.

"Old Blood and Guts," Solomon said.

Abraham shut his eyelids and said, "Yeah, it all came back to me. Like a boomerang. I don't guess a hippie like you was a fan of his."

"Well, I don't know. His brutal philosophy makes more sense to me now than it did back when. Boy, the things you forget about. It gave me a warm and fuzzy feeling, hearing it again." The troglin stretched his long hairy arms to the sky and yawned. "It makes me wonder if I've gone crazy."

"Don't fret it—you have," Abraham said. "Now, get some shut-eye. I figure we'll have another big problem to solve tomorrow."

A galloping horse could be heard thundering up the southern road leading to the Wall.

Abraham rolled over onto his side. A King's Guardian riding a large white horse whipped the beast's flanks. A man was draped over the front of his saddle. That man wore a black cape.

Abraham sat up. "That's Prince Lewis."

41

Prince Lewis sat on top of a barrel inside an infirmary tent. He'd been shot in the leg, shoulder, and side. Lucky for him, the gut shot wasn't critical. He still breathed. He should have been dead.

Iris wound cotton straps around Lewis's muscular frame. "Those things, those bullets, are nasty. They tear holes out of the back end of you." She grimaced. "Never seen the likes."

"Yeah, they tumble," Abraham said. "They are designed that way. Nasty stuff."

"You come from a very vicious place," Lewis said. His face was beaded with sweat. "I feel like my entire backside has been ripped out." He had a bullet in his hand, one that they had removed from the tanks. "How can a little thing do so much damage?"

"It's called gunpowder. At least, that's a more primitive word for it."

The only other persons in the room were Pratt and the Guardian that had carried Prince Lewis back to the Wall. That rider had short brown hair and long sideburns. He was young and unscathed.

Lewis pointed a finger at the young Guardian. "Alshon, I owe you a great debt, dragging me out of the jaws of death."

"What happened, Prince?" Pratt was standing in the corner of the tent with his arms in front of his chest. "You looked like death warmed over when you arrived."

"Well, if that's how death feels, then I don't want to die." Prince Lewis took off his bloody gloves and tossed them away. "We were only a few miles north of the House of Steel's front gate, trotting through the passage between the high hills. Without warning, the bushes erupted with the bright glow of fireflies. The horses jumped and bucked. That maddening popping sound sent the beasts kicking into a frenzy.

"The barbarians charged out of the brush with those weapons firing. I've never seen men so big. They almost make Pratt look normal. Tattoos. Piercings." Lewis grimaced sharply and eyed Iris. "They screamed maddening bloodcurdling chants. One group fired those strange weapons, and the other group came upon us with axes." He dipped his chin and said, "None of us saw it coming.

"Horses went down. Guardians tumbled after them. I had enough wits to tell them to ride for the castle. To stay and fight would have been a slaughter. I spurred my horse in the same direction. One of these bullets, or more, took it down. I went down with it. I came to my feet, sword in hand. I made quick work of two Gonds trying to brain me with axes, but I was cut off from the others.

"I was about to chop off the head one of those long-eared Gond when those nasty metal hornets tore through me." Lewis rolled the bullet through his fingers. "I've felt pain but never pain like that. I thought it was over. That moment was my last duel." He paused and looked at the others in the tent. "I swore off the King's Armor. But I'm swearing it back on again. It's the only thing that saved us from being cut to ribbons. Hmph. Then I was cut off from the others. The barbarians continued to swarm. Somehow, Alshon pulled me out of the flames of Sheol. I don't remember much until we made it back here. It is fortune that we had a horse between us and they didn't."

"How many?" Pratt asked.

"The ones carrying the rifles"—Lewis shrugged—"dozens, at least, but I fear there are many more. I fear the barbarians are invading the House of Steel. We need troops. We need to get back.

Even the Guardians' finest will be outmatched by those…" He clenched a fist. "Weapons!"

"Will the king be able to hold out very long?" Abraham asked.

"The House of Steel has the strongest fortifications in all of the world," Pratt argued. "They can hold out forever."

"Don't be a fool, Pratt," Lewis said. "Where there is one Gond, there are ten more. There might be thousands that we missed. You know that. The castle has two hundred Guardians and fifty Golden Riders. The bulk of our armies are here, at the Wall." He eyeballed Abraham. "Speaking of which, how have you fared against the iron chariots?"

"Nine down, one to go," he said.

Lewis gave Pratt a doubting look. "Is this true?"

Pratt nodded. "I saw it with my own eyes. But the Shield of Steel is severely damaged."

"There will be more tanks," Abraham said. "It's only a matter of time. I won't be able to stop the next round. Do you want me to stay here, or do you want me to go to the House of Steel and help fight?"

"Certainly, you don't think that you and your Henchmen can stop hundreds of Gond?" Lewis asked with a smirk.

"Maybe. Maybe not. But I'm willing to try."

"Try. Ha. It will take more than blind effort," Lewis said.

"Of course." He rubbed his throbbing temples. "But I have an idea."

42

"What do you think?" Abraham asked Solomon.

The troglin was standing beside the tank that had crashed into the Wall a day earlier. Aside from the blackened scorch marks from the pitch, the tank was still in serviceable condition.

"Can we drive it?" Abraham asked.

Solomon held a large tank-operation manual, which looked like a pocket paperback book in his huge hands. He thumbed through the pages and squinted. His long finger ran over the lines. "I don't think it's so complicated. There appears to be a sequence to start the ignition, but the driving will be... kinda easy, I guess." He scratched behind an ear. "Things have really changed since I've been gone. All of the buttons, lights, and gauges are so tiny."

"So, do you think that you can squeeze in there and drive it?"

"Me? I can't jam myself inside there. It's going to have to be you or someone else that we can train." Solomon tucked the book underneath his arm. "If they were able to train those other people, then I don't see why we can't do the same. We might have to do it on the way to the castle, though, seeing how time is pressing."

"Agreed. And it won't be all about the tank either. We have more rifles. That should do us some good."

Sticks and Shades had gathered up four more assault rifles from the soldiers inside the tanks. Canisters of ammunition had been inside the tanks too. They had set up a pile of munitions by the campfire.

Abraham patted the tank's hull. "I find it interesting that these electrical systems operate in this world. My beer truck died moments after I drove through the tunnel. Heck, I can't remember if I even tried to start it again."

"These are diesel-fired engines. No reason it would work an entire electrical system," Solomon said.

"Yeah, that's true. But I doubt the GPS system will work."

"The what?"

"I'll explain later. Come on." He led Solomon back to the Henchmen's camp and stood in front of the fire. "Everyone gather around."

The tight group formed a semicircle around him.

"I want to make sure that we are on the same page. We'll ride with the King's Guardians and soldiers back to the House of Steel. And when I say ride, I mean on horseback and inside the iron chariot. Do I have any volunteers to drive it?"

The Henchmen exchanged many uncertain glances.

Shades and Skitts stepped forward.

"Good," Abraham said.

Four assault rifles were standing up butt down like a teepee, and he picked up one of them out of the pile.

"We are going to be doing some on-the-job training on the trip down south. I want all of you to learn how to shoot these weapons. Four of you will be assigned to take care of these weapons. Now I can pick, or you can volun—"

Dominga jumped forward. "I want one!"

"Me too," Tark said, lifting his hand.

"Anyone else?" Abraham asked.

Vern spat into the fire. "I'll stick with my sword. It's like Ruger taught us—it's the best weapon in the world."

"Aye," Bearclaw agreed. "I'll be having at them with my axe."

"Regardless, every man and woman here is going to learn how to use them."

"Sorry," Solomon said, "but I don't think my finger will fit inside the trigger guard."

Abraham nodded. "We won't get a whole lot of practice in because we need to save ammo, but all of you are plenty apt. You'll figure it out. Once we near Kingsland's border, we'll begin recon. Prince Lewis's troops will stay behind, waiting on our report. As I understand it, the Gond are tribal, so they don't know each other so much outside of the tribe. When we roll in, we are going to look like them."

"Some of us are a little small to be taken for barbarians," Shades said.

"Yeah, well, I think some of us can fit the bill. We're going to slap on black paint and ride to the castle on the tank."

Shades flicked a fly out of the air and said, "The Gond might be as brawny as they are stupid, but they can have a good nose for things. I'd be very wary of that plan. But I'd say that you have a fifty-fifty chance to fool them."

"We are going to get a close look at their forces, get a head count, and report back to Lewis."

"If they have hundreds of those guns," Shades asked, "how do we expect to beat them?"

"We have a tank, guns, and wits, and the King's Steel on our side. We'll figure it out when we get there."

"We can kill them," Horace said. He tapped his spear butt on the ground. "The Henchmen will kill them all."

"Well said." Abraham set down the rifle. "Any questions?" He scanned their hard-eyed faces. "Good. Let's roll out."

To everyone surprise, Solomon, Shades, and Skitts fired up the tank and got it moving. Shades and Skitts could be heard giggling like children inside.

Abraham led the group on the southern road back to the House of Steel. Horace and Sticks resumed their places beside him in the front. All of them rode horses. Dominga and Tark scouted ahead.

They moved day and night, stopping only for a few hours of shut-eye before moving again. With the slow-moving tank, they needed to cover as much ground as possible when they could.

The bridges on the roads wouldn't hold the tank at a few junctions, but the rivers and streams were shallow enough for the tank to plow straight through. Abraham watched the surge of water rising over the tank treads as he waited for it to cross the river.

"It's a mighty beast," Horace said.

"Indeed it is."

They were only one day away from the House of Steel. Abraham shared all his thoughts with his Henchmen and even Prince Lewis too. He wasn't certain, but he got the feeling that Prince Lewis might be coming around. He seemed to show gratitude, and the smart-aleck remarks to Abraham had subsided.

"If I depart, make sure to tell Ruger everything I've told you. Don't leave a single detail out," Abraham said.

"We won't," Sticks said in a voice that seemed more sad than neutral. She seemed to have a hard time looking at Abraham.

"Horace, why don't you fall back a moment," he said.

"Aye, Captain." Horace slowed his horse.

Abraham moved closer to Sticks. Their thighs bumped as they moved forward. "What's on your mind?"

She kept her eyes forward on the green hills in the distance and said, "Nothing."

"I know you well enough by now to know that isn't true. It's Ruger, isn't it? You don't like him?"

"I don't want to talk about it," she said.

"So, something *is* bothering you? Just let it out. We never know when we might get this chance again." He wanted to be fair and address this strange love triangle. He had Mandi back home, whom he felt deeply for. Sticks had more than grown on him, but he'd never seen her laugh. Then there were Queen Clarann and Princess Clarice. The queen was Ruger's lover, and Clarice was his daughter. It all would have made for a great time-travel romance series. But with Sticks, he didn't see any point in putting the matter delicately. "Listen,

Sticks, if I go, I'm really going to miss you. And if I stay, I'd like to stay with you."

"How easy for you to say." She spurred her horse into a trot with her hips bouncing on the saddle.

The haggard-looking Prospero wandered alongside Abraham, smacking his lips and sucking his teeth. With his eyes on Sticks, the man who never said anything said, "I bet that saddle's happy." He led his horse away.

Abraham let out a silly laugh. A bright sun ring with black spots formed in his line of sight. Then he shielded his eyes and fell out of the saddle.

43

BACK HOME

"Wrong! Conan!" said someone with a fierce voice and an Asian accent. "What is best in life?"

"Crush your enemies. See them driven before you and hear the lamentation of the women."

Abraham rubbed his eyes. He was sitting on a sofa facing a large flat-screen TV. The movie *Conan the Barbarian* was playing on the screen. A bowl of popcorn, which was sitting on his lap, fell onto the floor. He was in a strange apartment that looked as if it had been made out of an old gas station. The ceilings were high, and a huge garage door had a phantom-black Dodge Hellcat parked behind it.

"Oh no."

He looked to his left. Smoke was leaning back in a fully extended leather recliner. He wore a black dragon T-shirt, blue jeans, and sunglasses with large lenses. His corded forearms rested on the chair's armrests. He held the remote control in his fingers and was snoring softly.

Abraham twisted his head around to see a kitchenette and full-sized kitchen table. Closed doors led to other rooms. It was nighttime outside. *Where am I? Where's Mandi and Sidney?* He reached down and picked up the bowl. His fingertips were coated with cheese dust. *What have I been doing?*

"You just *Quantum Leaped*, didn't you?" Smoke asked in his mysterious tone.

"Huh?" He blinked his eyes.

Smoke hadn't moved.

"You just said that, didn't you?"

"Yup." Smoke collapsed the recliner and turned the TV volume down. He looked at the TV screen and said, "You have been glued to that movie nonstop since I caught it channel surfing. Well, Ruger has. He is really disappointed in the sword-fighting techniques, but he still likes it. Welcome back, Abraham."

"How did you know it was me?" He set the popcorn bowl on the coffee table, which had a small stack of car magazines on the corner and automatic pistols too.

"I can tell. Your eyes. Mannerisms. You weren't moving as sure of yourself." Smoke swiped his thick black hair out of his eyes and took off his glasses. "So, what's been going on?"

"You tell me. The last time I was here, I was a prisoner." He rubbed his neck. "Now I'm... here? Where exactly?"

"It's my old place outside of DC. We needed a good hiding spot." The tall and rangy man stood up. He eased his way into the kitchenette and grabbed the handle of the refrigerator. "Thirsty?"

"No. How'd I escape?"

"You had some help. When you were in the lair of the Time Tunnel, getting the science-fair show, I was there too, posing as a guard." Smoke cracked open the tab on a can of Coke and took his seat in the recliner. "I was one of the drivers taking you in and out. Once we got back out, I took care of those thug orderlies and brought you here. It's been two weeks since all of that happened." He drank. "It's been busy."

"Busy?" Abraham looked at the TV. "Doing what?"

"Learning." Smoke pushed back into the recliner. "Turns out that your counterpart, Ruger, is a very quick study. Sid and I have been teaching him how to use modern weapons: pistols, assault rifles, M-60 machine guns, LAW rockets."

"LAW rockets?"

"It's a personal favorite of mine. Lots of fun. And seeing how they are sending tanks into Titanuus, I think they would be useful."

"So Ruger can use those things now?"

"Oh yeah." Smoke smiled. "He wanted to know it all. That man wants to war." Smoke crossed his ankles. "We've got to know each other well, and he's told me a lot about Titanuus. I'd like to see it for myself."

"No, you don't. I'm not saying it's a bad place, but I'm not so sure it's a good place. I'll say this: we don't belong there."

"Sid hates it when I talk about it. Keep it between us."

"A man belongs with his family."

"Agreed, but I'd be lying if I didn't fantasize about taking them with me. Dragons and monsters—I've seen my share in this world, but I'd like to take on more of them. Things have been quiet around here lately, until now."

Abraham gave Smoke a perplexed look and asked, "What is it that you do? I thought you were a bounty hunter and Sid was in the FBI."

"I was a Navy SEAL too, but Sid gave up on the FBI not long after we got together. She was my handler."

He cocked an eyebrow and said, "Handler?"

"I was in prison for beating the crap out of a criminal that had a really good attorney and an inside connection with the judge. The FBI was low on manpower for some of their projects, and they didn't want to risk their agents on some of the smaller projects. Sid was assigned to a file called the Black Slate. You know, *X-Files* kind of stuff. I was given a chance to shorten my sentence by helping her." He pointed at the TV. "Man, I love this part."

Abraham gestured with his arms and said, "Well?"

"Oh, yeah, I was pretty cozy, waiting out my term, and I didn't really have any interest in helping the FBI. My past experience with big government entities strongly led me to believe that they all are shady, and I wanted no part of them. You see, I have a knack for sniffing the truth out. But, as fate would have it, the moment I saw Sid, my heart changed. That was a woman that I'd break out of jail for. In this case, I took the free ticket."

"Huh, so did the Black Slate turn out to be anything?" Abraham asked.

"Did it ever. Those things that you don't believe exist in this world... Well, let me tell you, they exist. Heck, some of them might have even come through one of your portals. There were werewolves, giants, harpies, shapeshifters, and clones. It was a deep operation invested in evil. I hate evil."

"You're serious?"

"If you don't believe me, you could ask Sid. She'll tell you. Besides, is my story any more bizarre than yours?"

"I didn't mean any disrespect, but I never would have imagined such things go on in this world." He rubbed his palms on his jeans, which he'd never seen before. He looked at his sweatshirt and read the upside-down lettering, Darkslayer Brew: The Beer for What Ales You. "Where'd you dig this shirt up?"

"Luther Vancross gave it to us."

"You didn't get him involved, did you?"

"Yeah, well, the old man is pretty persistent. He cares. Sounds like a good friend."

"He's not here, is he?"

"No." Smoke finished off his can of Coke, crushed the can, and made a hook shot into the trash can by the kitchen. "I overheard your conversation with Dr. Jack Lassiter."

"Which part?"

"All of it, but the part I was referring to was the part where you could be sent back in time to be with your family."

Abraham leaned back into the sofa and asked, "Yeah, what about it?"

With a fiery intensity lingering in his dark eyes, Smoke said, "Would you do it? Go back?"

Abraham didn't say a word. He'd been so busy fighting to survive that he hadn't had much time to give the matter deep thought. "You know, when I lost everyone, I didn't think I'd ever be able to live without them. I was lost. I'd think of them every day, and the guilt whittled down my soul. My soul was nothing but numb inside." He sighed mournfully. "It took ten years of falling flat on my face before I could lift my head up. I picked up the pieces and started walking again." His eyes started to water, and he dried them on his shirt cuff. "I'd do almost anything to hold them one last time. But I'm not traveling back in time. Even if it's possible. Life moves forward, not backward. Once you start going the wrong way, you die."

Smoke nodded. "I wouldn't do it either. And neither would Ruger, for that matter."

"You talked about this?"

"Yeah, we've gotten to be pretty big buds. I mean, he's a bit rigid, but so was Sid when we met. I've worn him down some. I've got him watching TV, didn't I?"

"The last thing Titanuus needs is more crazy ideas pouring into that world. I fear it's ruined already. I'm not so sure that what we are doing will make a difference."

"Heh heh, it sounds like that portal opened Pandora's Box."

"Based off what I've seen, that world is better off without us, but our invasion is pushing it toward an accelerated ending." He turned his gaze toward Smoke. "We recovered two more gems for King Hector. Now he has four out of the six. But I fear it's making him mad with power."

"How so?"

"He's getting irrational. Oh, and now he knows that Ruger is the father of his daughter, Clarice." He sat right up. "Oh man, I hope Ruger gets the heads-up about that. He's about to be reunited with his family. Well, assuming that they get through the barbarian horde that is raiding the castle." He glanced at the TV. It was showing the scene in the movie where Conan painted himself up in black-and-white war paint. "How do I know that I'm not dreaming?"

"Hey, I saw the Time Tunnel with my own eyes. Trust me when I say it's real. I had my doubts until I saw that thing come on. I saw that horned halfling and those huge tattooed barbarians. Ruger told me about them. The Gond. They all looked real to me. Made my hair stand up on my arms."

"Yeah, I know what you mean. I've got to find a way to shut down those portals."

"We're working on it."

Abraham took a long look around the living room. "Say, where's Mandi and Sid? Nothing happened to them, did it?"

Smoke frowned.

44

Abraham's heart beat behind his ears. "What's wrong? Did something happen to Mandi? Sid?"

"What?" Smoke tore his eyes away from the TV and shook his head. "No. I hate this part when Valeria gets shot. I mean, Thulsa Doom shot her with a snake. Who does that?"

He threw a pillow at Smoke. "I ought to knock you out."

Smoke put the pillow behind his head and said, "I might be big, but I'm not easy to hit. Ruger found that out when he had an episode."

"Episode? What do you mean?"

"Let's just say that I think that this world makes him jumpy sometimes. I slipped behind him, and he, or you, nearly coldcocked me. I have a feeling that, were it his body, he would have got me. He's a warrior, isn't he? What's he look like in Titanuus?"

"Funny that you should ask." Abraham plucked a car magazine from the table, with an old blue four-door Volvo on the cover. He made a funny look and leafed through the pages. "I've only got a good look at myself a few times. Or Ruger. I'm sort of a mix of young Sean Connery and Hugh Jackman on steroids. He's strong. I'm talking animal strong. Moves like the wind and fights like the devil."

"Humph," Smoke said. He stretched his arms out over his head and yawned. "Sounds like me."

Headlights shone through the windows of the remodeled gas station. The crunch of rubber wheels on gravel caught Abraham's ear. The approaching car engine had a throaty rumble to it.

Smoke nodded. "You were asking about the girls. They are here. I can tell by the noise of the engine. It's a SRT8 Jeep Cherokee. It's got a nice groan and rides really smooth on the road. We'll be taking that back." He leaned forward and rested his elbows between his knees with his arms folded. "Say, why don't you play along and have a little fun with them."

"You mean, play Ruger."

Smoke shrugged his eyebrows. "Why not? Mandi's been kinda down, and she'll be thrilled to see you." He turned the volume up on the TV.

The car doors slammed shut.

Abraham leaned back and faced the TV.

"No, you have to sit with your back straight, like Ruger," Smoke said. "I've never seen the man slouch. He's big on posture."

Abraham sat up and put his hands on his knees.

"That's better," Smoke said with a smirk. "And don't say anything. He doesn't talk much. I'll handle it."

The front door opened. It was made of glass with a steel frame. Sid had a brown grocery bag in one hand and a box of Cokes in the other. Bags of cheese popcorn and boxes of Nutty Butty bars were sticking out of the top of the bag. She wore a pink tank top and low-rise jeans that showed off her navel. Her hair was pulled back in a silky black ponytail.

Mandi entered the room and closed the door behind her. She had four large pizza boxes in her hands.

"Hello, lordlings," Sid said in a sarcastic voice. "We have completed your snack run." She dropped the food on the kitchen counter. "How else may we serve you today?"

Abraham watched out the corner of his eye. Turning his head

slightly, he could see the women with their backs to them. Mandi set the pizza boxes on the table. She wore a tight gray top and a pair of low-rise jeans that flowed over her curvy hips and flat belly. Her wavy black hair hung down her back. The intoxicating smell of perfume wafted through the air. As the women turned around, he did also. His body temperature started to rise. *What is with that sexy getup? Where did they go to buy groceries, the Lion's Den?*

"I see he hasn't changed the channel." Mandi walked over, her high heels clicking on the floor. She sat down beside Abraham and glanced between the TV and him. "It's really not that good."

Abraham fought the urge to grab Mandi and kiss her.

Sid walked over and sat down on the right side of the sofa, closer to Smoke. She had a slice of pizza in her hand. "Don't even say, 'Where is mine?' You can get it yourself. It's bad enough we had to run into town to buy your snacks, looking like a pair of hookers." She started unlacing the straps to her high-heeled shoes. "And you thought this idea wouldn't arouse suspicion. Do you know how may catcalls we got?"

"Two," Smoke guessed.

"Huh, I wish it was two. More like twenty," she glanced at the TV. "Geez, Ruger, won't you watch something else? Smoke, show him *The Punisher* or something. *Rambo*, maybe."

"If he wants to watch something else, he'll ask, won't you, Ruger?"

Abraham kept his stare fixed on the TV and nodded.

Mandi took off her high heels and rubbed her ankles. "I wish you loved rubbing feet as much as you like watching *Conan*. Did you ever think we might want to watch something else? I'd like to watch women's Wimbledon."

"I didn't know that you were a tennis player," Smoke said.

"Well, I was—a good one." She shrugged her chest. "A bit too bouncy, but when I played, the stands were full." She leaned back on the sofa's plush arm.

Abraham bent over and lifted her legs up into his lap. Mandi's painted eyes grew as big as saucers. He started rubbing her feet.

Sid gaped.

Smoke grinned.

He winked at Mandi.

She sat up and threw her arms around him and said, "Abraham, it's you? Isn't it?"

45

"It's me," he said with a warm smile.

Mandi dug her fingernails into his back and said, "You sneaky snake! Why didn't you tell me?"

"We wanted to surprise you. Well, Smoke did."

"Of course he did," Sid said. "My man just loves surprises. But they don't always work out." She stood up and said, "I guess it's time to celebrate. I guess I'll serve the pizza."

Smoke slammed the recliner shut, jumped out of the chair, and said, "I'll take care of it. Anything for my queen."

The group dug into the pizza. Smoke and Abraham had their own separate boxes on their laps. The women ate from them.

Mandi held Abraham's hand with one hand and ate with the other. "It's okay," he said, "I'm not going anywhere."

"I want to hold on to you as long as I can. I never know when you're coming back or going again. I just want this to stop." Mandi wiped her free hand on a napkin. "Abraham, tell me you won't leave again."

"I wish I could." He swallowed the last bite of the Hawaiian-style pizza. "Ruger isn't that bad, is he?"

She wiped some pizza sauce off the corner of his mouth. "No, but he's not you. He's more—"

"Intense." Sid patted her flat stomach. "I'm stuffed."

"You only had two pieces," Smoke said.

"Yes, and that's twice as much as I normally eat. The celebration is over. We need to get back at it." Sid moved over to the computer desk in the corner of the room by the TV. She sat down in a black office chair. The screens on the two large monitors came on. "I'll see if Phat Sam and Guppy found anything."

"Who?" Abraham asked.

"Family, co-workers, special people like us." Sid typed on the computer and clicked the mouse. "Uh-huh. That's what we thought."

"What is it?" Smoke asked.

"Guppy confirmed what we believed. Drakeland Corporation is another branch of the old Drake Company. They use the shadow company's name as the Corporation. It's the same old government conspiracies. Powerful men and women hungry for more power. And to think that we thought we got them the last time."

"You've dealt with this before?" Abraham asked.

"People like this, yeah," Smoke said. He slapped two pieces of pizza together and bit into half of it. Speaking with his mouth full, he added, "These evil empires like to team up. More than likely, one of these old corps got wind of the Drake and propped them up. It's old money and old business that we've dealt with—hundreds if not thousands of years old."

"I don't care about the details. I just want to destroy that Time Tunnel and stop all of this from happening." Abraham tossed the pizza box on the table. "I don't have time to sit around and do research either. We know where the tunnel is, and we have to destroy it."

Sid swiveled around in her chair and said, "They know that you'll be coming back. Not to mention that they are already looking all over for you. Trust me when I say we have been putting a plan together, and Ruger has been helping."

Abraham crossed his arms. "Is that so? How? How can he help?"

"Well, for starters, he has a lot of novel ideas on how to kill people." Smoke let out a sinister chuckle. "One at a time, two at a time. Blow them up. Bomb them. Use tanks, swords, and guns. He thought he could do it on his own but wasn't so sure that your body could hold up."

Abraham gave himself a once-over. He'd continued to slim down, but he was a long way from being Ruger. "Hey, he could have done it with me. I used to be a superstar athlete. But if he wasn't going after it head-on, how is he, me, or we going to attack it?" He clutched his head. "Ah, this is maddening!" He kicked the table. "Don't you two play games with me. Spit it out!"

Mandi wrapped his arm up. "Abraham, they are on our side. Believe me, you can trust them, the same as I trust you." She pulled him toward the couch. "You need to hear them out. Be patient. We've covered a lot of ground on this."

He sank into the sofa, pinching his temples with one hand. He broke out in a cold sweat.

"Abraham, you are trembling." Mandi started rubbing his back. "It's okay. It's going to be okay."

"Don't you get it?" he asked in a throaty voice. "It's not okay. It hasn't been okay since my family died. It's not going to be okay either." He flung his hands in the air. "I don't even know if any of this is real. I don't know if you are real." He jabbed his long fingers at Sid and Smoke. "Or if they are real! You aren't the one bouncing back and forth between one reality and another. Are you!"

"Please don't yell," Mandi said in a soothing voice. "I love you. I'm here for you. This might all seem insane, and it does to me, and it scares me, but trust your heart. You know that some crazy stuff is going on. You're in the middle of it for a reason. But you can't do it on your own. Just like your Henchmen help you on the other side, we are here to help you on this side."

"Hear, hear," Smoke said.

Abraham gave the rangy man a hard-eyed look. "What did you say?" he asked with a cracking voice.

Smoke tilted his head to one side and said, "Hear, hear. Why? Is that a secret word or something in the other realm?"

Abraham let out a wild scream and pounced on Smoke.

Abraham landed flat on top of Smoke. The recliner tipped over backward. The men rolled over the floor, over the top of one another.

"Stop it!" Mandi yelled. "Stop it, Abraham!"

Her words did not register with Abraham. All his frustrations had come to the surface. All the doubt and anger swelled up inside and came out. He locked his arms around Smoke's waist and slung the man into the wall.

Smoke rolled up onto his feet and hunkered down with his fingers clutching outward. "Come on, big fella."

"John, don't goad him!" Sid ordered.

Abraham lowered his shoulder and attacked like a charging bull.

Smoke braced himself for impact.

Abraham slammed him into the limestone block wall. A clock hanging on the wall fell to the ground, and its casing cracked. He kept shoving Smoke back into the wall.

Smoke's corded arms flexed. He coiled his arms around Abraham's waist and slung him aside.

Abraham stumbled backward. He lost his footing and crashed into the coffee table. Two of the legs of the table snapped.

Mandi hopped up onto the edge of the sofa. "Stop it, you two idiots! Stop it!"

In a moment, Abraham rolled onto his feet and rushed Smoke again. The fire in his blood was racing. He was mad—mad at everything, mad at the mad, mad world he'd been thrust into. He tipped his shoulder, stopped, and threw a hard punch at Smoke's face.

Smoke blocked the strong punch with his deft hands. The punch still grazed his face.

Abraham started whaling away on Smoke. He brought his hands down like hammers. The hard blows knocked through Smoke's defenses. He connected with chin and nose. He slapped his head into Smoke's mouth.

"Have you gone mad?" Mandi yelled. "Abraham, stop this! Stop this now! Listen to me!"

Her words were drowned out by the tide of anger rushing behind his ears. He kept hitting harder and harder.

Smoke snaked his head away from the heavy punches. He caught Abraham around the waist and held him chest to chest. "Go ahead! Let it out!" Smoke said fiercely in Abraham's ear. "Let it out!"

Abraham beat Smoke's back like a drum. He whaled on the man like a gorilla beating his chest. "I've had enough! I've had enough! How do I know this is real?" He hit again and again. "How do I know that you aren't one of them?" He kept at it. "How do I know? How do I know?"

"You have to have faith," Smoke said. "It's all you got. You're a good man. Don't let the enemy take that from you!"

Abraham's long arms turned to lead. The strength in his limbs failed. His last punches had no weight behind them. He sagged into Smoke's shoulder and sobbed. "I'm sorry." He let out another wet sob.

"Don't be." Smoke led Abraham to the couch and sat him down beside Mandi. He put a strong hand on Abraham's shoulder and said, "You've been at war. It happens to the best of them. Let it out. Have a good cry."

He let out a shuddering breath, straightened his back, and said, "Henchmen don't cry."

Smoke wiped the blood from the corner of his mouth and added, "Maybe not, but they sure can hit." He gave Abraham a firm slap on the back. "How about an ice-cold Coke."

Abraham nodded. He looked between Mandi and Sid and said, "I'm sorry. I bet you think I'm nuts. And why wouldn't you? I think I'm nuts."

Laying a gentle hand on his back, Mandi said, "I always liked the crazy ones."

He choked out a laugh.

Smoke handed him a Coke.

Sid got out of her chair and said, "John, let's give the two of them some privacy. Plus, I need to get out of these clothes." She held up a palm. "Don't say it."

"Say what?" He picked up a pizza and followed her back to their bedroom and closed the door.

Abraham lifted his eyes to Mandi's. "Look at me, sitting here and sobbing like a baby."

"Now isn't the time to doubt yourself. We are getting close to the end. I can feel it. I don't know why, but I do." She reached across Abraham's legs, grabbed the remote, and turned off the TV. "That's better. I think you need some Yacht Rock radio." She dusted the hair out of his eyes. "You need to mellow."

"Huh. Easier said than done. You look great, by the way."

"Thanks." She held his hand. "You sure are full of surprises."

"What do you mean?"

"When you attacked Smoke? I didn't see that coming." She put his head over her chest. "Feel it. My heart's still racing."

He felt the rapid beat of her heart under his fingers. Her perfumed scent wafted under his nose. "I didn't mean to scare you."

"Oh, it didn't scare me. I liked seeing you come alive like that. You gave Smoke a fit. That surprised me. But he handled it well." She kissed his cheek. "It's going to be okay, Abraham. I believe in you. You keep believing in yourself. I know in my heart you are doing the right thing. You should know it too."

"How do I know that my heart is right? Maybe I've been wrong about everything. Like that zillon said."

"You mean the alien woman? Ottum?"

He nodded.

"Yeah, Smoke told us about her. Now, that gave me goose bumps. But let me tell you, Sid and Smoke have let me in on the stuff they've seen. I believe it's real. Stuff like that hides in the dark and wears many disguises." She kissed his hand. "Do you want to know how I know that you are a good guy?"

He shrugged. "I guess."

"You never hit on me, and I get hit on all of the time. That's what got my attention. And you looked like a big ol' teddy bear." She gave him a warm smile. "There was something gentle about you and something broken too. I don't know, but I just knew that you were, well, my kind of guy. My mom, you know, Martha, always told me to find a sweet man. I never listened. My relationships were one drama fest after another."

"And this isn't drama?"

"Well, this is different. You are sweet, Abe, and this is crazy, but I just know that you are a special man. It's not all of this excitement that turns me on like a dreamy-eyed schoolgirl lusting after the latest hottie in *Tiger Beat* magazine. There is something deeper, a spark that I felt. Didn't you feel it too?"

"I suppose, but I'd never admitted it. Because, you know, I felt guilty." He frowned. "I always feel like I let them down."

She wiped her eyes and sniffed. "I'm ashamed to say this, but I did my homework on you. Everything about that accident says that it wasn't your fault. You need to believe it too."

"I try," he said, "but no matter how hard it is, I can't. I think that might be why I like Titanuus. There, I don't have to think about it."

47

"You belong in this world," Mandi said. "You know, I think that maybe that's why you go back and forth. You can't decide between the two. Have you ever thought about that?"

Abraham shrugged. "Maybe. So, what are you saying—that if I concentrate long enough, I can go back to Titanuus?"

"Perhaps. But I don't want you to do that. I want to keep you here as long as I can." She crawled into his lap, straddling him. Cupping his face in her hands, she said, "I want to stare into those soft brown eyes. It's hard seeing you with Ruger in there. His stare is hard as iron —not mean, but penetrating. It freaks me out. Like Martha said, I need a sweet man. A teddy bear. One that I can trust." She started kissing him.

He kissed back. Her soft lips ignited his blood. While he was kissing her, he thought of Sticks. He broke off the kiss.

"Uh..."

Panting with her eyes closed, she said, "What? Don't worry about them. They won't bother us."

"No, it's not that. It's the other women, in Titanuus. I'm close with them."

Mandi slid off his lap. She tied her hair into a ponytail and said,

"Look, let's keep a rule, what happens in Titanuus stays in Titanuus. I don't want to know. Ruger's rambled on a good deal about Queen Clarann. I can't bear to hear any more."

"Well, it's not Clarann. It's—"

She put her hand over his lips and said, "I don't want to know. Believe me, I have a very jealous bone. But we aren't married—or exclusive, exactly. Look, the reason I married Barry was because some other woman made me jealous. I didn't want her to have him. I didn't want her to win. So I took him and regretted it ever since. So for you to do what you need to do, you'll have to decide without my intervention."

"You're a little too cool about that. I mean, it's not like I'm out to fool around. It happens, but it hasn't happened in a while."

Mandi plugged her ears with her fingers. "Nah nah nah. I am not listening. Please quit talking about it. Nah nah nah."

He lifted up his hands in a sign of surrender. "Okay, not a word." He took a long drink of Coke then glanced over his shoulder at the bedroom door. "Do you really think they can help? There is an army out to get us."

"They have a plan. They went over it with Ruger too. He was on board with it."

He tilted his head and asked, "So everyone knows but me?"

"We've been waiting for you to arrive." She bit her bottom lip. "Man, I was hoping to have a little one-on-one time before we got into this. There's another bedroom, you know. The plan would make very good pillow talk."

"I can't believe I'm saying this, but I really need to know what is going on." He ran his stare over her body. "And I think it's best that I don't... you know, until all of this is over."

"Okay, suit yourself." She lifted her arms up, chest out, and stretched. She twisted side to side. "But if you change your mind..."

With a dry throat, he said, "You don't take no for an answer, do you?"

"What do you think?"

"And you said that you didn't want to be a distraction."

"Okay, fine." She eased back into the sofa cushions and curled her legs underneath her body. "I might not be able to explain it as well, but I'll let them explain the details. So if you have questions, they'll have to wait. Got it?"

He nodded. "Okay."

Mandi propped her head on a pillow. "We've been hoping that you would return. At least, that is what we've been waiting for and why we are hiding. Everyone agrees that we need to all meet at the Time Tunnel at the same time."

Abraham lifted a finger.

"No." She pushed the finger down. "Hear me out. From our side, we need to be there when you come from the other side. No, wait— that doesn't sound good." She stroked her ponytail. "When you are in Titanuus, well, you or Ruger, you need to work your way to the place where the tunnel is. Ruger believes the Time Tunnel will have to be destroyed from both sides. Does that make sense?"

"Yeah, it makes sense, but there is one big problem."

"What is that?"

"I still don't know where the Time Tunnel is."

"Yes, you do. You've been there."

"I'm not talking about the one in this world. I'm talking about the location in Titanuus. I don't know where it is.'

"Oh," she said. "Well, that's a problem. We thought you would have known that already."

"Well, I don't." He crushed his Coke can and tossed it toward the waste bin. He missed. "And now, it looks like it's up to Ruger to find out."

48

TITANUUS

"The captain is back! The captain is back!" Horace bellowed. He'd helped Ruger, who had fallen out of his saddle a moment earlier, to his feet.

What now? Sticks thought. She rode back to see what all the commotion was about.

Ruger shook his head, a grim smile forming on his face. He bumped forearms with his original crew, Horace, Vern, Bearclaw, Prospero, and Apollo. Shades sneaked up on Ruger's back, picked him up, and spun him around.

"Ha, I see you are as slippery as ever, Shades," Ruger said.

Sticks managed an uncharacteristic frown. It wasn't that she didn't like the real Ruger, but she missed Abraham. He was gone again. Ruger was different. He walked differently and talked differently. His voice was polished and carried authority. It wasn't that Abraham was bad, but he was a different sort of leader, gutsy and all heart. She didn't know what to make of Ruger yet, but the original Henchmen liked him.

Ruger gazed at the tank rolling up behind the company. He pulled out Black Bane. "The enemy is in our midst!"

"No," Horace said. "We conquered the metal dragon. It rides with us. Skitts, a Red Tunic, is in the belly."

Ruger flipped Black Bane over his hand with a twist of the wrist and stuffed it back in the sheath. "I see. Well done, then."

He eyed Horace and his closest men. They were all painted in white and bare chested. Not a stitch of armor was on them.

"You no longer don the King's Armor? Your appearance is hardly standard or uniform."

Vern stepped forward with a crooked sneer on his face. "Abraham did this. It was his idea to use this disguise to fool the Gond."

"The Gond?"

"The barbarians have laid siege to the House of Steel, Captain," Horace said. "Disguised as them, we hoped to catch them off guard—cut through their forces and attack. We have hornet blasters. Like them."

Ruger glanced at his own painted body. Jagged black striping and white were painted all over. He showed a mouthful of white teeth. "I like it. Now, tell me about the Gond." He slowly spun around with his fists on his hips. "The House of Steel is close, isn't it?"

"Aye," Horace said.

"Abraham came up with a foolish idea to disguise ourselves as Gond, win their favor, and attack," Vern said scornfully.

Ruger stepped over to Vern, looked down at him, and said, "I gather that you take issue with Abraham. Why is that? He is your captain."

Vern swallowed. "No, you are my—"

Ruger swatted Vern across the face with a loud smack. "You follow that captain. Do you understand that?"

Vern shrank underneath Ruger's steely gaze. "Yes, Captain."

"Listen to me, all of you!" Ruger lifted his voice. "There is no time to doubt me or the other. I am the captain. Abraham is the captain! I can see that he has done well to lead you this far. Now, the time has come to finish this quest. Our king, our kingdom, our way of life is in great peril! You cannot doubt. Doubt is death. Do you understand me?"

"Aye, Captain!" the gathering group said.

Ruger marched down the line of men, around the tank, and back to the group. He grabbed Vern by the neck. "I like this plan. The Gond are fierce fighters, but they can be stupid. I would have done something very similar. What would you have done, Vern?"

"I would not have shed my armor. And what happens if they recognize our Brands?" Vern said. "We need a better idea is all."

"So that is it? That is your plan?" Ruger laughed. "Vern, it does not sound like you are a better creator than Abraham. However, I can see immediately where his plan is flawed. The barbarians might be dumb, but it will take more cunning to fool them." He climbed back into the saddle of his horse. "Let us ride while I contemplate. Come, Horace, Bearclaw. Advise me."

Sticks fell to the back of the company with Solomon, out of earshot of Ruger.

With his long, hairy arms swinging by his sides, Solomon said, "A tight-knit group. It looks like you're now on the outside, looking in."

"We're probably better off," she said dryly.

"I think you should insert yourself. Ruger needs to understand your value." The crease between his eyes crinkled. "I would."

"Maybe you should insert yourself."

"No, that's not my style. I'm more of a follower than a leader."

The tank rolled up beside them. Smiling, Shades ran up to the slow-moving tank and climbed on. He saluted Sticks and Solomon and dropped back inside the hatch with Skitts.

"Ruger really does lift them up and out of their boots," Solomon said. "I like him. He's different, very military, but I can respect that. I think he's a man of his word."

"Yeah," she mumbled.

"You are a hard one to figure out, do you know that?" Solomon said. "I've known a lot of women, but you don't wear your heart on your sleeve, do you?"

Sticks gave him a look and said, "Life is what it is. I learned long ago that there isn't much I can do to change it. I do prefer to stay with one personality over another. Is it so bad that I'd like to have continuity?"

"In this crazy world? Huh, I don't think it is possible. Of course, my world was crazy too." He reached over and patted her on the back. "I think you need to assert yourself. Horace will back your play."

Sticks tugged the reins, turning the horse's head aside. Without a word, she drifted farther back from the group, unable to shake the gnawing inside her stomach. She wiped the corner of her eye and looked up into the heavens. *Come back, Abraham. I miss you.*

49

"Good evening," Ruger said to Sticks.

She was sitting alone, away from the camp the Henchmen had set up. She was sharpening a dagger on a stone. The day had been long as they pushed over the rolling hills of Kingsland, trying to gain as much ground as they could. She nodded at him.

"May I sit?"

She shrugged.

Ruger planted himself beside her and leaned back on his hands and looked into the sky. "It's a beautiful thing, seeing my stars again. In the other world, they are very different." He cleared his throat. "Horace tells me that you have been second in command of the Henchmen, alongside him." He raised an eyebrow at her. "Yet you avoid your station."

"It seemed to me that moment changed when you arrived. You and the other men are better acquainted."

"True, and I'm happy to see them. But I need to get to know the rest of you as well. I imagine it has been very odd dealing with the same man who has shared many different personalities."

She switched one dagger out for another from her bandolier. She ran the blade's edge across the stone. "It is what it is. I do as I'm told."

He nodded. "The other one, the one before Abraham, his real name was Eugene. You spent most all of your time with him, eh?"

"Intimately and unfortunately."

"I am aware of his exploitation of the Henchmen. He dishonored this body, my body, and used the Henchmen like fish bait." He balled up his fists, and his knuckles cracked. "I will kill that man."

"Isn't he in the other world?"

"Yes, but I'll be going back. I don't know when, but like the sands of an hourglass, the time for this is running out."

She scraped her knife over the stone while stiffening at the same time. Ruger was right. He could sense it. She could sense it. Their mission was coming to an end.

Ruger unslung a backpack from his shoulder. It was Abraham's. He unzipped the backpack and pulled an item out. It was a small card with a picture on it. It was a decent-looking man, clean shaven, cheeky, wearing a strange cap with a bill. He held a smooth club over his shoulder. "That's Abraham. Had you seen that before?"

She slid her knife into her leather bandolier, set down the stone, and took the card. She squinted. "He looks a lot different."

"Oh, that was a long time ago. He looks much worse now. Bearded and shaggy, and in very poor condition. It's been very challenging to overcome the disadvantages of that body." He dusted the hair from his eyes. "A broken body of a broken man." He lifted a finger. "But he has heart."

She flipped the card around and asked, "Why are you showing me this?"

"I thought you would want a good look at the man that you are in love with."

"I'm not in love." She flicked the card at Ruger. "Not with him, anyway."

"No, but you are in love with the him in me. It's a twisted scenario. I know something about that. I'm in love with the bride of my king." He leaned his head down and sighed. "The only thing harder than war is love. War I understand, but love I don't."

"I guess Horace filled you in. I think the king is pretty mad at you." She looked him in the eye. "He's probably going to kill you."

Ruger chuckled. "Yes, and yet I ride to save him." He rubbed shoulders with Sticks. "I saw her first, you know. He snatched her away from me, though I do not blame him. I cannot wait for the moment when I cast my gaze upon my own daughter. All of these years, and I never knew."

She drew her knees up to her chest and said, "I wouldn't have told you either."

"Yes, I don't blame Clarann. Though I would have liked to have had a hand in raising my daughter. I hear that she is a fine sword."

"Feisty like a raccoon too."

He tossed his head back and laughed. "That she gets from her mother. Anyhow, Sticks..." He picked up the card and put in inside the backpack. "Why don't you hold on to this for Abraham." He stood up. "And don't be a stranger. I need your counsel the same as before. Rest well."

She watched Ruger amble back toward the main camp's fire. She cradled Abraham's backpack to her chest. Ruger seemed to be everything the others thought him to be, an honest knight and compassionate leader. No wonder his men followed him with such fierce loyalty.

Sticks unzipped the backpack and fished out the card again. She took a long and hard look at the image. She traced the face with her finger. *Who are you?*

The image of the man wasn't anything like the man she'd become accustomed to. She wondered what it would be like in Abraham's world. *Would I be out of place? I can't make something like that work. Why would I want to? What's wrong with me?* She tucked the card into one of her pockets. *I need to forget about this. I need to let go.* She rubbed the brand on her chest. *Once this is over, if I live, I no longer want to be a Henchmen. I want to be my own.*

Sticks lay down on her bedroll and closed her eyes. She fell fast asleep. She'd never dreamed before, but she did that night. She saw Abraham fighting Ruger, each with a sword in hand. They were the same but different. Steel flashed. Thunder rolled. Ruger's sword pierced Abraham's heart in two.

"Wake up! Wake, Sticks! Wake!"

She sat straight up, gasping for breath.

Shades was in her face. The new dawn had come. "Time to move." He helped her to her feet and swatted her behind. "Game on, girlie. Game on."

Sticks rolled up her bedroll, fingers trembling. She couldn't shake away the image of Abraham dying.

50

A smoking ball of flame sailed out of a small catapult and over the perimeter wall of the House of Steel. The Gond barbarians let out a chorus of wild cheers. Not one of the bare-chested painted warriors stood under six feet in height. Dozens of them towered over seven feet tall. Their bodies were packed with hard muscle. They carried crude weapons, swords, battle axes, and machine guns. They loaded another decapitated head into another catapult. They lit the skull on fire and let it fly.

"How many do you count?" Tark asked. The athletic black warrior was lying flat in tall grasses. His smoky eyes moved over the sea of savage men dancing and screaming outside the castle.

Dominga was hunkered down on one knee with a spyglass over one eye. "It would help if they didn't move all the time. But I'm counting over five hundred. You?"

"About the same," Tark said, his head slowly turning from side to side. "I don't like Ruger's plan. I don't like it at all. Those men are bloodthirsty. So many of them, too."

"They aren't men." Sticks low crawled over to Dominga and took the spyglass to view the camp below.

Many bonfires were spread out along the castle walls, burning thirty feet away. They'd been made from wood and the flesh of men. A Gond warrior dragged a dead man by his head of hair and tossed him on one huge fire. The road leading up to the castle had been dressed on both sides with severed heads spiked on poles.

She swallowed. "They are Gond."

Dusk was nearing. The shining sun was setting behind them, which made for perfect cover from anyone looking their way.

The trio watched the Gond fire the assault rifles at the castle guards that popped up on the high wall. A guard fell over the twenty-five-foot-high wall, clutching his neck. Two Gond rushed the wall and dragged the kicking man away. One held the soldier down while the other Gond cut his head off and held it high for all to see.

The House of Steel wasn't without its defenses. Crossbows were fired out of arrow slits, but the ballista towers were no longer manned. They'd all been shot to pieces.

The distinct popping of weapon fire came and went in spurts. The moment a castle soldier showed his face, a burst of gunfire followed.

Dominga rubbed her arms. "Those brutes are giving me chill bumps. They are heartless." She looked at her assault rifle and ran her fingers over the stock. She forced a smile. "But I like the idea of being able to kill them from one hundred yards away. It doesn't seem possible." She stared down the gun barrel's sight and closed and eye. She made a gunfire sound and said, "At least they are big targets."

"I know," Sticks said. She held out her rifle. "Do you both remember how to reload and fire this thing? I can show you again."

"No. We got it." Tark bumped forearms with Dominga. Sweat glistened on his forehead. "Personally, I can't wait to shoot one of those Gond. Look at them. They kill without discrimination. They are evil beasts."

"Just wait for the signal," she said.

"What is the signal?" Dominga asked.

"You'll know it when you see it." Sticks crawled down the bank.

They were positioned just over one hundred yards away from the castle. The surrounding plains were grassy, with a few small trees scattered about. The castle sat on the highest point of the gentle slope that led to the steep sea cliffs behind it. The castle's towers had a perfect view of anyone that approached its walls. When the Henchmen came, with a tank in tow, the Gond and the castle would know it.

Sticks crawled over the next rise, and with the sun in her eyes, she ran low to where the grasslands dipped and the castle fell out of sight. She jogged over a mile and didn't stop until she caught back up with the Henchmen, who were waiting by the tank. She reported to Ruger.

"What did you find?" he asked sternly.

"Roughly five hundred Gond lay siege to the castle and many citizens. Half of them are armed with rifles. They mass near the front gates, mocking the king by catapulting burning heads of the dead over the Wall."

Ruger stroked his chin. "I see. And Tark and Dominga are in a secure position?"

"They are planted right where you said."

He nodded. "Henchmen, gather."

The company quickly formed a semicircle around Ruger, who stood with his back to the treads of the tank. "The Gond are waiting on this hunk of metal." He slapped his hand on the tank. "They wait for the tank to come and blast the House of Steel's gates to a thousand pieces, but we'll have a surprise for them... won't we?"

"Aye!" Horace stated.

Solomon and Sticks exchanged a quick look.

The plan had changed. Not all the Henchmen were disguised as Gond. The war paint had been washed off. Ruger wore his breastplate. Vern, Cudgel, Apollo, and Prospero wore their tunics over chainmail. They looked like soldiers, nothing less and nothing more. Horace, Bearclaw, and Cudgel remained painted up and barechested. All of them were big men. Bearclaw was the most Gond looking of them all.

Skitts and Iris were inside the tank.

Shades roped up Ruger, Vern, Apollo, and Prospero. He tied knots around their wrists and put ropes around their necks. None of the men appeared to be armed. Shades tugged on the rope. "One jerk here, and they'll pull free. "Elder's Fortune to you, Captain." He climbed up into the tank and vanished inside the hatch.

Ruger waved Sticks and Solomon over. "I want you to get word to Prince Lewis. Let him know my plan. If we engage, I expect his full support. I hope he brought some."

"I'd rather stay close," Sticks said.

He put his hand on her shoulder and said, "Ride now, and I hope that it isn't over before you return." He looked at Solomon. "There is a large black case on the back of the tank. I need you to look into that."

Solomon gave him a curious look, shrugged, and said, "Okay."

With a frown, Sticks rode away.

51

Sticks caught up with Prince Lewis over a league away. Lewis and Pratt were marching a force just over two hundred men over the grasslands. They were all knights in full suits of armor, riding on horseback. The banners of the House of Steel flapped in the wind.

"Five hundred Gond, you say?" Prince Lewis said. His face was ashen and his shoulders slumping. He held one hand over his side and the other on the reins of his horse. A stiff breeze rustled his hair. "And Ruger rides into the jaws of death. So like him." He glanced at his second in command. "What do you think, Pratt? Do you care to taste the sting of the lead hornets?"

"Those cowardly barbarians fear a straight-up fight." Pratt shook his head. "If it is true what you say, that one man can kill many from a great distance, then I say we need a fuller army."

Lewis scratched an eyelid and said, "True." He eyeballed the rifle slung over Sticks's shoulder. "Why, she could take you out, Pratt, at close range."

Pratt blanched.

"I'd never assault the crown," Sticks said as she continued to ride alongside the prince. She didn't know what else to say. She'd already given the prince all the information she had at her disposal. She'd

369

shared Ruger's plan too, which was, for lack of a better word, insane. "Prince Lewis, might I ask what you are thinking? I should return quickly."

Prince Lewis leaned his head her way and said, "It's a big decision. And I'd be lying if I didn't admit that I didn't want to face those rifles again." He tapped his chest. Underneath his cape, he wore a full breastplate made from the King's Steel. A helmet of the King's Guardians hung from the saddle. "The things I have to do to become king."

They kept riding, eyes ahead, without saying a word.

Pratt finally broke the silence and said, "I like this part of the country. I prefer the seaside for retirement, but I must admit, after this trek, the fields of wildflowers are growing on me."

"Is that all you think about? Retirement?"

"I'll be old someday," Pratt replied. "My bones groan. My father told me when your joints start feeling as stiff as wood, the old time is coming."

"You aren't going to have an old time. You'll be the Guardian Commander, protecting me and my family. Assuming I get the chance to have one." Lewis waved his hand at a pair of men riding not far behind him. "Derek. Gravely. Come."

Two rugged men rode up into the group. They were Guardians in full armor. Derek had a full smile on his face. Gravely was stone-faced and ashen.

"My finest scouts," Lewis said to Sticks. "They will ride with you and report back to me."

Derek gave Sticks a flirty nod. Gravely didn't even look her direction.

Prince Lewis sucked his teeth. "If you chance upon Ruger, tell him that we'll get there when we get there. Oh, and one more thing. Don't get ambushed."

"Thanks for the advice." Sticks whipped the reins of her horse and galloped off with Derek and Gravely right on her tail. She didn't know what to make of Lewis's response. He didn't seem eager at all to engage in full battle with the Gond. She didn't blame him either. The Henchmen were in way over their heads.

What in the Elders is Ruger going to do? If the Gond sniff us out, they'll slaughter them.

She spurred her horse onward, faster and faster. They rode nonstop before slowing to a trot.

"Why did we slow down?" Gravely asked in a dry voice.

Sticks felt spiders crawling up her back. The prairie breeze died down. Ahead were long fields of tall grasses. She'd ridden through it once already, but something seemed different. She slowed her horse to a walk.

Derek exchanged a look with Gravely. "Say, pretty, what's got you all twitchy? Didn't you just pass through here?"

"Yeah." She unshouldered the rifle and flipped the safety mechanism from Safe to Fire. "That doesn't mean something might not have crawled in there since I passed. I have a feeling. Keep your eyes open."

She led the trio into the high grass. The stretch of field was hundreds of yards long. She followed the flattened path in the waist-high grasses she'd plowed through over an hour earlier.

A spotted deer burst out of the grass.

Sticks and the men jumped in their saddles.

Derek chuckled. "Now my heart is moved by the sight of a comely woman. Heh heh heh. If there is something in this grass that's not a bug or varmint, I think we'd be better suited to speed along."

Sticks led her horse in a zigzag pattern, keeping the rifle barrel pointed ahead and downward. She noticed small trees sticking up only a few feet out of the high grass. She didn't remember seeing them before. She pointed her weapon at the trees.

Derek and Gravely acknowledged her signal. They pulled their swords free, split away from each other, and moved toward the little trees. Both men stopped short of the trees. Leaning over their saddle horns, they looked at the trees and shrugged.

Sticks took a close look at a tree sticking up out of the grasses. She could have sworn it had just been planted there, but nothing about it was remarkable.

"Perhaps you overlooked them when you rode straight through," Derek said. "Who's going to notice a little tree?" He glanced about. "I see many."

Gravely led his horse forward.

Sticks did the same, but she could have sworn the trees hadn't been there before.

They cleared the high grasses, and the tightness in her chest eased. She put the rifle on Safe and slung it over her shoulder. The terrain was clear ahead. She walked her horse forward and lifted the reins to snap them, then her instincts caught fire. She twisted her head around.

Gond sprinted out of the edge of the grasses and launched javelins into the trio's horses.

Sticks flew out of the bucking horse's saddle and landed hard on her back.

52

With the wind knocked out of her, Sticks pulled a dagger free of her bandolier the moment a Gond leapt on top of her. She punched a hole in the painted man's belly and ripped him open. Warm blood ran over his fingers. The barbarian whaled on her with mighty fists in his death throes. She twisted the blade inside the man.

The Gond died on top of her.

Sucking for breath, Sticks pushed out from underneath the heavy warrior.

Another Gond rushed her from the thickets. He carried a crude war axe cocked over his shoulder and came on with a fierce swing.

Sticks leapt to one side, ducking underneath the swing. She poked a hole behind the Gond's ribs.

The savage warrior whirled around and let out a bloodcurdling cry. The wild-eyed warrior closed in with an over-headed chop.

Sticks sprang away. Striking like a snake, she slashed him across the wrist.

The Gond let out a throaty chuckle and clamped his big fingers around her neck. He lifted her off the ground and shook her like a rag.

She pulled another dagger free and stabbed the wild man in the throat.

His knees buckled, and he released her. She stumbled away and fell flat on the ground. He bled out in the field.

Coughing and clutching her throat, Sticks spun around to the clamor of battle. Derek was fighting sword against axe with a Gond. The barbarian stood a half a foot taller than Derek and swung his battle axe with might. A powerful blow smote Derek full in the chest and sent the Guardian scout spinning to the ground.

Sticks pulled the rifle to her shoulder and aimed at the Gond. She pulled the trigger. The weapon didn't fire. "Titanuus's Crotch." She flipped the safety to Fire.

The Gond's axe came down. Blood spurted up.

She fired.

The bullet blew out one side of the Gond's head. The axe fell free of his fingers. He fell over dead.

Sticks rushed over to Derek. His smiling face had been split open by the axe. She ground her teeth and shook her head. She put the rifle on her shoulder and searched the fields.

Gravely lay on the ground, twitching.

A Gond wandered the field with a sword jutting from his side. He turned his heavy gaze on Sticks. He pulled the sword free of his wound in a blood-dripping grip and charged.

Sticks blasted a hole in his heart.

The last Gond fell.

She kept her aim on the tall grasses and walked toward Gravely. She counted eight dead Gond on the ground. Derek and Gravely had chopped up two apiece but couldn't overcome the third. She knelt by Gravely. He spat up blood. A deep cut had opened his neck. His eyes fluttered. His cold gaze froze on the clouds above.

Sticks cursed. Two of the horses lay dead on the ground. Her horse had galloped away. She would have to complete the journey on foot. She shouldered her weapon and ran east toward the House of Steel.

She moved at a brisk jog, stopping to rest only a few times. She reloaded her magazine clips along the way and kept her rifle ready. The Gond had set up two ambushes that she knew of. She'd just survived one of them. For all she knew, the Gond were privy to Ruger's plan.

Maybe they don't know. Those barbarians might not have joined the rest. Either way...

An hour into the run, her legs were aching, and her lungs burned. She wasn't used to carrying much of a load, but the rifle tightened the muscles through her shoulder blades. She moved on at three-quarters speed, making her stride as long as she could.

Night had fallen. The thick clouds made the sky pitch-black.

Finally, Sticks caught up to a muddy spot in the back roads where the tank and the Henchmen had passed. She gathered her wind and raced to the spot where she'd left Dominga and Tark. The pair lay deep in the grasses and pointed their weapons at her. Panting, she lifted a hand and said in a low voice. "It's me."

"Well, *Me*, the next time you sneak up on our backside, you might want to signal sooner," Tark said. "I about took your head off with this rifle."

Sticks lay down in the grass between the pair. She sucked for breath. "Oh, I think if you shot me, I'd feel a lot better. I don't think I've ever run that far before."

"What happened to your horse?" Dominga asked. From the prone position, she eyed the activity at the castle with a spyglass.

Sticks briefly shared the story of the battle.

"There are more Gond behind us?" Tark said.

"I didn't come across any more. It might have been a patrol, or they were on their way to join the rest. I don't know," Sticks said. She took the spyglass from Dominga. She could see the tank sitting fifty yards away from the castle's main gate. "It's quiet down there. What is happening?"

"They rolled up with the tank a few hours ago," Tark said with an impatient sigh. "Ruger and the others have been lying on their bellies ever since. Do you see them?"

Sticks saw a row of men lying in front of the tank. It was Ruger,

Vern, Apollo, and Prospero. All of them lay with their faces down in the dirt. She scanned the area and found Bearclaw and Horace talking with a huge barbarian that appeared to be the leader. He towered a full head taller than Bearclaw, who was taller than Horace. The barbarian had a mighty frame covered in tattoos and piercings. They appeared to be arguing. "That is a big man."

Tark nodded. "You can say that again. And I don't think it's going well either. They've been arguing back and forth the entire time. The Gond keeps pointing at the tank and motioning at our men that are kissing dirt."

"What do you think he wants?" she asked.

Speaking innocently, Dominga said, "I think he wants that iron chariot to run over them."

53

Ruger Slade lay in the dirt with his belly on the ground. The Gond would spit on him and his men when they walked by. Regardless, he kept his head down, his eyes and ears open. He was glad to be back on Titanuus. *But for how long?* He moved his head slowly to one side and faced Vern. No barbarians were within earshot.

He said, "Glad to see things haven't changed."

"Yeah." Vern twisted his thick lips into a smile. "Just like back in the day. Glad it's you. So are we going to lie here all night?"

"Patience."

So far, Bearclaw and Horace had managed to fool the Gond leader. The wild warriors were craftier than they were smart. Ruger could hear bits and pieces of the conversation carrying under the clamor of the siege going on at the Wall. Bearclaw was making a case that more armies and tanks were coming and that the Gond needed to wait. The Gond leader, a grizzly of a man named Glaag, had taken command of the tribes. He was calling the shots. The other leaders that had opposed him were dead. That was the story Ruger had caught.

Glaag led Bearclaw and Horace over to the tank. The roaring

369

bonfires cast dark shadows on all their faces. The barbarian rapped his knuckles on the metal and pointed at the machine and at the Henchmen lying on the ground. "Iron chariot run them over." He spoke in a bearish voice. "I want to see their heads pop from their shoulders. I want their bodies to squish. I want King Hector to hear the bones in their bodies pop."

"I want my tribe to see it too!" Bearclaw argued. "They be here at the dawn. More armies come with the Shield of Steel down. I say that we should wait."

Glaag thumped his muscular tattooed chest with his fist. "Don't try me. I am in command. Roll the iron chariot now!" He had an assault rifle slung over his shoulder and carried a single-bladed war axe in one hand. He put the flat of his big blade in front of Bearclaw's face. "Do you want to challenge me?"

Bearclaw lifted his eyes to meet Glaag's iron gaze with his own. "Yes."

Horace pulled Bearclaw away by the collar. "We are here to conquer the House of Steel, not one another! You can play your games later!"

The wild-eyed Glaag thrust his axe into the air. "The challenge has been made! I accept!" He pointed his axe at Bearclaw. "Do you change your mind and cower?"

Bearclaw brought his twin-bladed battle axe around to his front, slapped his chest, and said, "No!"

"What is Bearclaw doing?" Vern said under his breath.

"Buying time. You aren't in a rush to get trampled by that tank, are you?"

"No," Vern replied.

Ruger twisted his head around for a better look at Glaag. He and Bearclaw squared off in front of the tank. The Gond gathered in a huge circle, yelling and chortling at a fever pitch. They'd forgotten about their prisoners for the moment and chanted for their leader.

"Glaag! Glaag! Glaag! Glaag! Glaag!"

Horace dared a look at Ruger. Ruger pointed his lips at him, telling him to wait for his signal. Horace nodded subtly. The plan was still on. How he was going to execute the plan was another thing. He had to wait for the moment and hope it came.

"Be ready," he whispered to his men.

Glaag waved a big arm over to one of his men. "Bring the shields."

A Gond with a long braided ponytail handed a small round shield to Glaag. Glaag beat his axe against the shield's steel. He tossed it to Bearclaw. Brimming with confidence, Glaag said, "To make the match last longer." He took the other shield offered to him, tossed his head back and yelled, "Haaa-hoooom!"

Bearclaw's eyes narrowed. He lowered his gaze to the top rim of the shield and spun his war axe by the handle.

Glaag charged. He brought down his battle axe on Bearclaw's shield with bone-jarring impact.

Bearclaw's knees buckled underneath him. He shuffled backward and struck out with his axe. The blade's edge clipped Glaag's shield.

The Gond leader moved smoothly and easily for such a large man. He fended off Bearclaw's attacks with well-timed ease.

To the hungry howling of the tribes, the titanic, wild-haired, tattooed warriors danced back and forth. They exchanged a flurry of axe blows to the shields with quick and resounding effects.

Ruger tensed. Glaag's powerful and precise strokes beat on Bearclaw like a hammer. The metal and the wood on Bearclaw's shield started to chip away. His friend groaned underneath the barbarian's superior strength and weight.

"By the Elders, that is a barbarian of barbarians," Vern said with a gasp.

A Gond guard rushed over to Vern and kicked him in the ribs.

Vern let out a groan.

Bearclaw snaked in a few strikes at Glaag's belly. The barbarian backpedaled and knocked the jabs away.

Glaag let out a wild, howling scream and yelled, "I will drink your blood, brother!" He unleashed a windmill chop that blasted through Bearclaw's shield.

Bearclaw dropped to a knee.

The clustering Gond horde let out earsplitting screams.

The well-knit Bearclaw, large in stature for a normal man, could not match Glaag's greater length and superior strength.

The weight of Glaag's axe, powered by muscle as hard as iron, bore down on Bearclaw's shield.

Bearclaw lifted his shield.

Glaag knocked it down. He twisted the direction of his axe. With a hard swipe, Bearclaw's shield was ripped out of his grip.

Bearclaw chopped at Glaag's knees.

The barbarian knocked Bearclaw's axe aside with his shield. He tossed his shield away and spun his axe in the air. "Come! Die!" he said with throaty words.

Gasping for breath, Bearclaw came to his feet. Sweat dripped from his hair into his eyes. His broad shoulders sagged. He gripped his war axe with two hands and rushed Glaag.

Axe heads met and locked with a sharp *clank* of steel.

They wrestled back and forth chest to chest, with the bigger man leaning on the other.

In one fierce motion, blades locked together, Glaag ripped Bearclaw's axe out of his grip. The barbarian flattened Bearclaw with a hard boot to his chest.

Standing right in front of the tank, Bearclaw fell on his backside. He clutched his chest. His head hung down.

To the shrill howling of the blood-hungry throng, Glaag lifted his mighty axe high in the air with both hands and let out a triumphant bellow.

54

The moment had come.

Glaag stood in front of the tank, preparing to deliver the death blow to a broken Bearclaw.

Ruger sat straight up and, over the clamor of the crowd, shouted, "Shades, fire now!"

The tank gun squared up right behind Glaag's broad back erupted with a deafening *kaboom!*

Glaag's body sailed head over heels past a ducking Bearclaw and slammed into the barbarian crowd.

The silenced barbarians had hunkered down. Their eyes were big, and fingers plugged their ears.

Inside the tank, behind the gun slits, the Henchmen opened fire with their machine guns. Bullets ripped into the shell-shocked Gond. Tattooed and painted bodies were ripped to pieces.

Ruger was on the move. He, Vern, Apollo, and Prospero had slipped out of their knots. They hustled straight to cover behind the tank.

There, Horace waited. Their weapons were strapped up in burlap bags on the tank's sides, and he fished their swords out for them. "It's fighting time."

Ruger ripped Black Bane out of the scabbard, not stopping to chat. He sought out the closest barbarian and attacked. He tore the first Gond attacker's head from his shoulders then disemboweled two more. Black Bane became a living weapon in his hands. He split skulls to the chin and severed limbs with single strikes.

The tank started to move slowly. Inside the metal cabin, Skitts and Iris were firing the machine guns, mowing down the barbarians. It kept the savage men's fever-pitched advances at bay. The strategy wrought confusion.

Ruger, Vern, and Horace defended from the front of the tank.

Apollo and Prospero fought at the rear of the tank with swords in each hand.

Horace punched his spear into one bare-chested attacker after another.

Vern gutted the exposed abdomens of his opponents.

Ruger hacked off more limbs.

Without Glaag to lead them, the Gond were in complete confusion, but hundreds of them stood against only a few Henchmen.

Shades shouted from inside the tank. "Fire in the hole!"

Ruger, Vern, and Horace split away from the tank gun.

The long gun barrel exploded.

Many of the Gond dove to the ground. Others died in pieces.

"Keep that fire coming!" Ruger lunged and stabbed his sword through a Gond's chest. He yanked it out and poked through another man. "Get away from the gate!"

"What?" Shades yelled from inside.

"Away from the gate! Away from the gate!" Ruger shouted back.

The tank stopped and started rolling the opposite direction, westward. The big gun fired again. The blast blew away a host of Gond.

The barbarians fought on with swords and axes. They rushed the Henchmen in a disorganized throng, fearless of the skilled carnage the Henchmen wrought on their bodies.

Three Gond charged Ruger at once. He parried a sword and caught the axe hand of another, while the third painted reaver tried to split him in half with an axe as he cocked back to swing. A war axe brained Ruger's free attacker.

It was Bearclaw. The bearish man was back on his feet and smiling.

Ruger ended the men he was engaged with in a single stroke. "Outstanding execution, brother!"

"Did you ever doubt me?" Bearclaw replied as he brained one more Gond.

"Of course not, I knew that you could take him." Ruger sliced an attacker's sword arm off. "You wield the best axe in Titanuus!"

"Perhaps. That Gond was good. I've never seen such a large man move so well!" Bearclaw chopped a man down by the legs. "I'd rather have had a fair crack at him."

"Methinks you were losing!" Vern cut a barbarian in the neck and stabbed a hole with a dagger in another. "That big fella bowed you over like a spoon."

Bearclaw let out a fierce harrumph and killed another man.

The tank gun fired again.

The Gond that weren't blown to bits scattered. A loud howling like a whistle started, and the Gond broke away from the tank.

"What's happening?" Vern asked as he slung blood from his sword.

"They are regrouping." Ruger could see the Gond grabbing their assault rifles. Someone had finally taken charge. "And rearming themselves. Stay close to the tank." He banged his sword on the side. "Shades, stop." He pointed at the ground. "Everyone grab a dead body and get under the tank."

55

Through the spyglass, Sticks watched Bearclaw and the Gond leader battle. Beside her, Tark and Dominga were squinting, each having taken a knee.

"What's happening?" Dominga asked over and again.

Sticks gave a dry description of the events as they unfolded.

Tark's head slid side to side on his shoulders. "I don't like this plan. I don't understand it. Wait for a signal? What signal?"

The tank rocked backward on its treads. The Gond leader disappeared from the scene. A loud *boooom* carried across the field.

"That's the signal." Sticks dropped the spyglass and shouldered her weapon. She flipped off the safety and started firing into the cluster of shocked savages gathering themselves one hundred yards away.

Inside the tank's slits, muzzle fire flashed. The barbarians were being ripped to pieces and dropped like flies. Ruger, Horace, and Vern fought the hordes at the front, and Vern and Apollo fought at the back. Sticks fired into the men attacking the front.

"Fire at the ones in the back of the tank!" she ordered.

Tark and Dominga supplied deadly cover fire on the tank's backside. The Gond dropped in threes and fours.

"Am I killing them?" Dominga said with growing elation. "This is so easy. They fall like raindrops!"

Tark had a big grin on his face and said, "Now this is a crossbow!" He fired bullet after bullet until the clip emptied. He loaded another and charged the rifle's chamber.

"Don't talk. Keep your breath. Make every bullet count," Sticks demanded. She squeezed off round after round until her weapon emptied. She reloaded another magazine, took aim, and fired.

Bullets whizzed overhead. Bright muzzle flashes erupted, pointed in the trio's direction.

"Looks like we are going to have some visitors."

A large group of Gond barbarians broke away from the main army and ran toward them. The element of surprise was gone. Sticks started firing at the score of men running at them. The long-limbed raiders were closing the one-hundred-plus-yard gap quickly.

She whacked Dominga on the shoulder, pointed, and said, "Aim for them! Aim for them!"

"What about Ruger?" Dominga said.

"We can't help them if we are dead." Sticks picked off one Gond after the other. Some of the Gond took a knee and fired their guns. Others charged on, full speed, with edged weapons bared and mouths wide open, screaming as if their heads were on fire.

Many of the big men fell to the firepower. Some of them got up again and kept running. None of them turned back.

Sticks shot at one black silhouette after another. A bullet whizzed by her head, causing a sudden stir of her hair. "Aim at the men with weapons in hand. I'll take on the ones with rifles!" She aimed at the muzzle flashes. In the darkness, the attackers that fired dropped.

"Sticks, I think I have a problem!" Tark said. "This is my last magazine." He kept firing. A steady *pop-pop-pop* sounded out over the plains. "What do we do?"

She emptied her clip. The magazine pouch on her gun belt was empty. They'd taken down at least a score of the berserk warriors. Another score were coming. She pulled her short swords free, and all she could think to say was, "Fight."

56

Underneath the tank, dead bodies were being turned into piles of goo. Ruger, Vern, Bearclaw, Apollo, and Prospero had crammed themselves underneath the tank the best they could. Bullets ripped into the dead Gond, which were stacked up like bags of sand.

Ruger returned fire with a rifle Shades had given him through the escape hatch on the tank's underside.

Bullets blasted from the machine guns inside the tank.

The Gond fired back at the tank from all directions. Bullets clattered off the steel bulk, followed by the sound of bullets that ricocheted in the air.

Shades shouted down through the escape hatch and said, "Captain, we have room for more inside. Climb up!"

Horace lay flat on his back and peered at the portal. "If you want the hole plugged, then I'll say that's what I'm good for. One of the slighter men can go."

"Get in there, Vern!" Ruger ordered. "And pass another rifle down!"

Shades dropped a rifle into the hole.

Ruger passed the rifle to Apollo. "Start shooting."

Bearclaw let out a pained grunt. A bullet hit him in the shoulder.

Prospero belted out a howl right after him.

Ruger laid down a line of suppressing fire. His last jaunt with Smoke and Sid had served him well. They'd taught him a lot about modern weapons, which gave him an edge over the raving Gond attacking him.

"We are going to get ripped to pieces lying down here like pigs stuck in a mudhole," Horace said. "If it's no different to you, Captain, I'd rather die on my feet."

"No one goes anywhere until I say so," Ruger said. He cracked off round after round. Barbarians fell on their faces with gaping holes in their backs. "We'll hold out as long as we can." He pounded the ceiling above him. "Shades, use that cannon!"

The tank gun fired.

Something nearby exploded.

Body parts fell down like rain.

Again the tank gun fired.

The loud *boom* sent the tank rocking back.

Ruger could sense the barbarians gathering their forces. They were putting a plan together. Some Gond fired weapons. Others streaked over the grounds and jumped up onto the tank. A full-fledged wild-man assault had begun. That wasn't all. They started lobbing burning logs and bodies at both ends of the tank. Their efforts were covering the ground with smoke.

The men underneath the tank started to cough.

Ruger's eyes watered.

They were being smoked out.

57

Sticks, Tark, and Dominga crouched down in the grasses. They were only seconds away from locking into mortal combat with men over twice the size of the women. The Gond even made the strapping Tark appear smallish in build.

"Go for the guts," Sticks said.

She could take care of herself in a fight, but hand-to-hand combat wasn't her strength. She would have to fight smart, but the barbarians would overwhelm her in only a short matter of time—seconds, possibly.

A presence fell over her shoulder. Someone with a deep but friendly voice said, "Stay down."

Dominga looked over her shoulder and gasped then dropped onto her belly.

A distinct *whirring* sound started up. The superfast *rat-a-tat* of a machine gun followed. Suddenly, the charging Gond started dropping like flies. Their bodies were chewed up and ripped in half.

Sticks dared a look over her shoulder.

Solomon stood tall, taller than ever before. He carried a huge machine gun in his mighty paws and wore a red bandana around his head. The round gun barrel spun like a pinwheel and glowed like fire. The troglin had a long bandolier of ammo strapped over one shoulder. A fierce grin was on his face.

"How's this for some hippie power! Come get some!"

"Sweet Elders!" Tark said with an elated and horrified look. "What is that thing?"

Solomon kept firing. "It's called a Vulcan." He led the march toward the castle. Everything Gond that moved toward him died.

Sticks had never seen the likes of it before. Men were torn to pieces. Their bodies were shredded like wheat.

She pointed at the tank, which was surrounded by smoke and fire. "We have to free them! They are trapped in there!"

"I'm going! I'm going!" Solomon said. The Vulcan machine gun took out the Gond in twos and threes. Their bodies started to pile up by the dozens. "So this is war. I think I like it!"

The barrels of the Vulcan machine gun stopped spinning.

The large trigger housing started to click.

"Uh-oh," Solomon said.

"Uh-oh, what?" Sticks replied.

"No more bullets," he said

"No more bullets?" she asked.

Over a hundred Gond lay dead on the battlefield thanks to the power of the Vulcan machine gun. The problem was that there were still hundreds left. The scattered horde began to cluster again. They pointed down the gentle slope at the Henchmen below the rise. They raised their weapons and rifles and charged.

"Do the Henchmen ever retreat?" Solomon said.

"Death before failure," Dominga quietly said.

"I was afraid that you were going to say that." Solomon picked the Vulcan back up. "I guess I can use it as a club. Just remember, I'm not a man of violence—not at close quarters, anyway."

Sticks swallowed the lump in her throat. She'd been through her share of bloody skirmishes, but not many without Ruger by her side. They were going to lose, just as they did with Eugene Drisk, who'd inhabited Ruger before. This time, they were going to lose big.

She spun her swords and said, "I just want everyone to know that it's been fun."

"You can say that again," Tark said. "I just hope that they leave enough of us to be buried."

Bullets started whizzing by their bodies.

Solomon flinched as he took a bullet in a shoulder. With a snarl, he said, "I'm not standing around for this. Charge!"

Before he took a step, loud war horns from inside the House of Steel blasted. The great brass horns made a *poom-pooow*.

The front gate of the House of Steel quickly rose. Guardians on white horses rode out by the dozen. They wore full suits of armor plated in gold. White manes of hair flapped like banners behind their lion-faced helmets. They lowered lances and spears and thundered into the swarming barbarian hordes.

"The Golden Riders!" Tark exclaimed.

The Gond charging Sticks set their eyes on her group and kept coming.

Another series of loud horns carried over from the west. Suddenly, the sound of more galloping horses caught their ears.

Sticks turned around. Prince Lewis and Pratt were leading the King's Guardians and dozens of other riders right at them. Armored in full plate, they rode with their swords raised. In a heartbeat, Sticks wondered what side Prince Lewis was on when he looked upon her with narrowed eyes. She set her feet.

The regiment of Guardians rode right past the group and galloped roughshod over the barbarians.

Solomon let out a sigh of relief as he watched the last of the riders pass by. He stretched out his arms and said, "Thank you, Lord Almighty!"

Tark lifted his sword high and said, "Ha ha! Let's go!" He and Dominga ran stride for stride toward the heated battle.

Solomon tilted his head down toward her and asked, "Are you going?"

"It's not really my style." She rested her short swords on her shoulders. "We'll make sure that no one slips through."

"I like the way you think." He patted her head with a big paw.

Together they watched the carnage unfold.

The Gond became an unglued, undisciplined mass of disorganized bodies. They fought like wild demons and jerked the knights out of their saddles. They ripped helmets off and pounded them into submission.

"I used to abhor violence. I'm kind of used to it now. I guess the overt exposure has desensitized me to such things," he said.

Two Golden Riders gored a Gond with lances as they charged from different directions.

The barbarians countered the ground pounding they took by firing their assault rifles. Bullets bounced away from the armor made from the King's Steel. Other men died beneath the hail of gunfire.

Tight groups of horse riders trampled the enemy.

Not one Gond fled from the field of slaughter. They died on their feet, bloody from head to toe and swinging. An hour later, every last Gond was severely wounded or dead. Their bodies littered the blood-stained battlefield. The wounded were finally slain.

"Show's over." Solomon walked toward the castle.

"No, I get the feeling the show has only just begun."

58

BACK HOME

S *till here. Still here.*

    Abraham rode in the back seat of Sid's Jeep Grand Cherokee, staring out a window. Mandi sat in the back seat with him, leaning her head against her window with her eyes closed. Sid drove. Smoke was in the passenger seat, humming to a soft-rock song playing on the radio.

He counted the mile markers and watched the hills and leafless trees pass by. Only the pine trees scattered through the woodland showed any green at all. He knew these roads. He knew them well. They were on the hilly climbs and twisting interstate curves of the West Virginia Turnpike.

The car slowed. They were in a car line backing up at the tolls.

Smoke leaned forward in his seat, lifted his sunglasses, and stared hard at the toll signs. "Four dollars. The toll is four dollars."

"Yeah, and we have three more to go unless you want to take the back roads," Abraham suggested as he tapped his knuckle on the glass. "But that will take twice as long."

"No thanks," Smoke said. "I heard that Hank Williams died on those roads."

"Are you saying that you don't trust my driving?" Sid asked.

"No, I'm saying the road might be in poor condition." Smoke dropped his glasses back down and pushed back into his seat. "You might hit a lethal pothole or something."

"You got that right," Abraham mumbled. "It's bad enough that they have trouble taking care of this toll road."

Smoke started to sing out loud the lyrics to the song "Into the Night."

Abraham continued, "You know, there is only so much yacht rock a man can take. I mean, it's nice and soothing for a while, but every couple of hours, you're either getting slammed by Barry Manilow or Benny Mardones again."

Smoke chuckled.

"I wouldn't mind some country," Mandi said, her eyes still closed. "As long as we are in West 'by God' Virginia, I think some mountain music would be fitting."

"No," Sid said flatly.

"She's not a country music fan even though she does look like a giant Shania Twain," Smoke said.

Sid punched him in the leg. "I do not, and I told you to stop saying that."

"I'm sorry. You're right," Smoke replied coolly. "You are much prettier than she is."

"*And* I'm not a giant either."

"Well..." Smoke muttered.

Sid punched him again. "Don't push it, buddy."

"You know that I'm just teasing."

"Oh, I know, but that doesn't mean that I like it."

Abraham's deep thoughts drowned out Smoke and Sid's playful banter. He had more important matters on his mind. He'd just had a mental breakdown a couple of days before. Now, he was getting into the middle of God knew what. He couldn't stop thinking about his friends in Titanuus either.

I was riding on a horse, and boom, here I am. The question is, where are they now? Is Ruger taking care of the Henchmen? Do they even need me?

He didn't have any doubt in his mind that Ruger was better

equipped to handle these high-risk and dangerous situations. But Abraham hadn't done half bad on his own.

If I only had his body in this world, I'd be better off. The kind of stuff Ruger is made of is incredible. But I used to be a top athlete. I could run and hit with the best long before I mastered pitching.

Abraham glanced at Mandi. Curled up in the seat, she snored softly. He couldn't let her get hurt. She'd somehow gotten dragged into this, which was the last thing he wanted. Every time he left and came back, she was deeper into the adventure. He couldn't let that happen again, but she clung to him.

What she sees in me, I'll never know.

He dug his fingers into his palm. He couldn't know when he might switch back over to Titanuus. When he'd left, they were heading back to the House of Steel, under siege by the Gond. He only hoped Ruger was back in his body to help them. His own plan had been pretty thin.

I wish I knew what was going on. I wish I knew for certain that I wasn't crazy.

He scratched the scruff on his neck and yawned and closed his eyes. Part of him wanted to stay home. Part of him wanted to go back to Titanuus.

Perhaps all I need to do is make a choice. Home or Titanuus?

Abraham rested. He didn't sleep, and he only opened his eyes when they slowed to pay at the toll booths.

Sid didn't stop the black SUV otherwise. The ride was smooth, the cabin quiet. It seemed as though everyone had a lot on their minds.

Finally, the Jeep dropped off the exit ramp near Bluefield, West Virginia. The blacktop on the main highway was bumpy, but the Jeep absorbed the bumps well. They followed the old highway a few more miles and turned right at an old brown sign that read Country Roads Microbrewery.

They pulled into the gravel parking lot of the small beer distributor that Abraham worked for. The time was after seven in the evening. Several beer trucks were parked on the lot. Otherwise, the place was abandoned, save for one man that came out of the main two-story building. It was Luther Vancross. He wore a vest over a flannel shirt and a pair of jeans. He was at least seventy years old and mostly bald, with a neatly trimmed goatee.

Abraham got out of the car. He and Luther shook hands.

"It's good to see you again." Luther looked him up and down. "You look well. Better."

Abraham shrugged his eyebrows. "I don't know about that. So, are you really wanting to do this?"

Luther smiled. "I'm old. Why not?"

59

TITANUUS

"Make sure that they are all dead," Horace said. He jabbed his spear into the heart of a Gond whose leg was cut off and who had a few bullets in him.

The Gond were the heartiest of fighters. They might be mortally wounded or crippled, but they would still try to kill. One of the king's soldiers had found that out the hard way when a barbarian shoved a hidden knife in his back.

Horace walked over to a huge barbarian that lay twitching on the ground. "Ho ho ho, look at this one. Isn't he the Gond leader?"

Bearclaw and Vern walked over to the spot where the man lay on the ground in spasms.

Bearclaw grunted. "That's him. I should know. I fought him."

The Gond leader, Glaag, clutched his big bloody hands open and closed like clamps. His remaining eye bulged inside its socket. His chest was caved in, and ribs were sticking out of the wound.

Vern made a sour face and said, "Ew. How is the man still living?"

"He's a Gond. They don't know when dying is good for them." Horace stuck the tip of his spear in Glaag's face.

Glaag knocked the spear aside with a shaking hand. His body shook like a leaf. He breathed bubbles of snot out of his nose.

Iris scurried over to the Gond. Her eyes were as big as saucers. "How can this be? Wasn't this barbarian shot with that cannon thing? The fact that he breathes defies reason. I'm the one that pulled the trigger."

"A shame. He'd have made a fine Henchmen," Horace said.

"Agreed. He could swing an axe like no man I've ever seen." Bearclaw looked at Horace. "Should I do the deed?"

"You fought him. If you want to show mercy, show mercy. If you want to let him live—and suffer—so be it." Horace spat. "This Gond deserves no better."

Bearclaw rubbed his chin. "I can't help but be curious. Iris, is there any chance that he'll survive?"

She looked at Bearclaw as though he was crazy and said, "Elders no. He'll be dead by the dawn. His innards are scattered all over. I'm still scratching my head as to why he's not in pieces. It's as if the shell bounced off of him or he bounced off of it."

Bearclaw took a knee in front of the Gond. He stared into the man's bulging eye. "Do you want mercy, Gond? Eh? Blink twice if you do."

Glaag stared right back at Bearclaw with a defiant and unblinking eye.

Bearclaw nodded. "So be it. You can die on your own then." He stood up and shrugged. "What now?"

Horace looked at the House of Steel. Ruger, Prince Lewis, and a host of Guardians and Golden Riders had returned behind the closed gate. He clenched his jaws and said, "I suppose that we wait."

60

Inside the House of Steel, Ruger stood on the king's terrace. His gaze hung on the shining waters of the Bay of Elders. Warships patrolled the choppy waters over a mile away from land. The boats, docks, and beaches were a hive of activity. Supplies were loaded onto ships by men and women that appeared as tiny as ants.

Ruger breathed the salty air in deep. It smelled like home. He could taste it though he knew it was temporary.

Prince Lewis and Pratt were the only other men on the terrace. They were both sitting at the table on the raised patio by the doors leading back inside the castle. They were drinking wine and eating from plates of food that had been brought forth.

With a leg of turkey in one hand, Lewis walked over to Ruger and offered it to him. "You must be hungry. That was an impressive feat you pulled off against the Gond. Care to share your strategy?"

"Simple. Cut off the head of the snake, and the body goes crazy." Ruger wasn't hungry, but he took the turkey leg anyway, not wanting to insult the prince. "Thank you." He picked off a hunk of meat with his blood-stained hands and ate. "It's good."

"You always did have a knack for getting things done quickly. Cut off the head of the snake. Hmm. I like it." Lewis drank from his goblet and set the cup down on the terrace wall. Looking down at the boats below, he said, "I hate sailing. I'd rather do anything else." His handsome face soured. "It leaves me queasy. And my footing is uncertain. Is that how you feel, Ruger? Or is it Abraham?"

"No, it's Ruger, and I'm not sure that I understand the question."

Lewis tilted his head from side to side and said, "Moving from one body to another. Never knowing what world you are going to wake up in. Isn't that like loose sand underneath your feet?"

"I suppose it is." He took a big bite of turkey leg and chewed.

Lewis leaned against the wall, rubbed his eyes, and yawned. "Riding all night isn't as easy as it used to be. Especially when bullets ripped your backside out." He fixed his stare on Ruger. "Tell me, isn't what you are going through... maddening? Frankly, I think I would go mad."

Ruger lifted his shoulders. He wasn't sure what Lewis was angling at, but he answered honestly. "I focused on one thing."

"And what's that? Wait, don't answer." Lewis snapped his fingers and pointed at Ruger. "Getting home."

"That's part of it. But I always focus on what I have always focused on. Serving the king."

Lewis raised an eyebrow. "How can you serve a king when you exist on another world?"

"By doing whatever I can to get back."

Lewis quickly shook his head and said, "I envy you, Ruger. Perhaps I always have. I'm the king's own flesh and blood, but you've been a better son to him than me. But my perspective has changed."

"How so?" Ruger asked.

"When I discovered that you had a flaw, I delighted in it. Now that the king knows that you are the father of Clarice and that Clarann is your mistress, I don't feel as... hmm, how shall I put this?" The prince grinned. "*Unfavored* anymore."

"I didn't know," Ruger said. "I never did."

"True." Lewis took up his goblet and drank. "But we both know that won't matter to my father. Will it? And speaking of change, well, the king has changed too. I'd be worried about that." He threw the goblet over the wall. "Very worried."

Ruger picked more meat off the bone and flicked it to the sea birds hovering nearby on the wind. The ones that missed the meal dove after it. He picked the bone clean and flicked it over the wall.

Lewis and Pratt remained seated at the table, talking quietly from time to time. At least two hours had passed with no sign of the king.

That gave Ruger time to think. He needed to figure out the next step. First off, he needed to locate the lair of the Time Tunnel on Titanuus. He knew it was in the Spine, but the Spine was very dark and unexplored territory. His best chance would be to track the enemy's armies back to the location. He couldn't do that if he was in Titanuus. He had no idea what King Hector would task him to do either. The king might kill him.

Ruger wiped the grease off his fingers on his blood-soaked leggings.

This is no way to stand in the presence of the king.

The curtains parted behind the patio table. A beautiful woman stepped through, dressed in the armor of the Guardian Maidens. Prince Lewis and Pratt stood.

"Leah!" Lewis said with a broad white smile on his face. "Forgive me for not wrapping you up in my arms, love, but as you can see"—he fanned out his battle-marred cape—"I'm all bloody."

"It suits you well, Prince." Leah gave Lewis a peck on the cheek. She shifted her attention to Pratt. "Good to see that you are alive and breathing."

"Another day. Another battle to come," Pratt replied grimly.

Leah's golden-brown braid hung down her back. She was as fit as she was pretty. She turned her attention toward Ruger and said to Lewis in a quieter voice, "The king comes."

Lewis opened his hands and said, "That's what I've been waiting for." He patted her on the lower back. "But not as much as you, of course."

"Of course," she said. "Is that... him?"

"Yes," Lewis replied. "Ruger in the flesh. For now, anyway. There is no telling when the next possession might take over."

Leah marched toward Ruger and stopped right in front of him. "It's been a long time. We haven't spoken since before your fall from grace. Do you remember me?"

"Of course. I remember everyone that I trained," Ruger replied. He noticed the lioness insignia on the strap of her breastplate. "You've come a very long way. The commander of the Guardian Maidens. Perhaps I did something right."

"Don't be modest, Ruger," Lewis said with his thumbs hitched in his belt. "You trained all of us, and look, we are still alive."

Leah patted Ruger on a shoulder and said, "I just wanted to say that it's good to see you again. I hope to fight by your side one day."

"I wouldn't hope too much. It might happen sooner than you think."

"Well, that is what you trained us for."

Lewis cleared his throat. "Ahem."

Leodor and Melris walked out onto the patio. The older and wizened-looking Leodor wore the customary robes of the viceroy. He maintained the same froward, tired-eyed, and chinless expression.

Melris the Elderling wore the same purple robes and carried the cast-iron Rod of Devastation cradled in his arms. His hood was down, and he maintained his short tawny hair and youthful face. The irises of his eyes were light purple.

The newcomers made a beeline for Ruger.

Leah stepped away.

"Who is with us today?" Leodor asked brightly.

"Ruger," he replied.

Leodor tilted his head side to side and gave him further study. His eyes landed on the hilt of Ruger's sword. "I need to retain your weapons. All of them."

Ruger unbuckled his sword and dagger belt. He tried to hand them to Leodor.

"Elders, no. I'm not touching those things." Leodor lifted a fragile hand and snapped his fingers with a loud pop. "Pratt. Make yourself useful."

Pratt hustled over, his armor jangling. He took the sword belt from Ruger and moved away.

"That's better," Leodor said as he hid his hand back inside his sleeves. "I'm going to need you to cross your hands behind your back."

Ruger gave Leodor a doubting look but complied. He caught a hint of surprise on Lewis's and Leah's faces.

"Please understand that King Hector can't take any chances these days," Leodor continued. "As you have seen, there are many persons of interest trying to kill him."

Unable to contain the edge in his voice, Ruger replied, "I wear the King's Brand, for Elder's sake. I'd never lift my hand against the king."

"Times change. And we can't take any chances that you aren't you." Leodor nodded at Melris. "Secure him."

Melris's hands glowed like purple sunshine. A coil of ropelike energy bands formed inside the palm of one hand. He stepped behind Ruger and bound his hands.

The mystic coils constricted and burned hot without searing the flesh.

"Do not strain against your bindings," Melris said softly. "The more you struggle, the more they will hurt." He moved back beside Leodor.

Leodor nodded at Ruger and said, "Now, get on your knees and bow for the coming king."

<h1 style="text-align:center">61</h1>

R uger took a knee and bowed his head. He heard the rustling of armor and clothing as the others on the terrace also took a knee. The hairs on his forearms stood on end. He wanted to look up but dared not. The sound of soft footsteps approached, and the hem of robes dusted over the terrace's tiles. Two polished boots made from black leather appeared underneath Ruger's nose.

The king's robes were black and trimmed in gold.

In a voice with the strength of a lion behind it, King Hector said, "Rise, my subjects, including you, Ruger."

Ruger slowly rose. His gaze ran over the black sword belt tightly wrapped around King Hector's waist. It held no sword, only a dagger in a sheath with tiny gems encrusted in the hilt. It was the Dagger of Death, the only weapon Ruger had ever seen King Hector carry, and that was rare.

He met eyes with the king for the first time in a long time. King Hector's eyes were as hard and bright as diamonds. The bow in his back had straightened, and he stood almost as tall as Ruger. The graying hair had been filled with brown, and his once-sagging angular jawline had hardened. On the king's head was the Crown of

Stones. Four stones—red, orange, green, and blue—twinkled in the dawn's early light.

Ruger nodded and said softly, "Your Majesty."

King Hector crossed his arms but cupped his elbows in his hands. He looked Ruger up and down. "You always were a glutton for punishment, Ruger. Look at you, bathed in blood and still standing strong as a mighty oak. Normally, this would be the part where I would say that it is good to see you. I would celebrate our victory over the barbarian horde. But greater evil is afoot. For there is no wound so deep as when one friend betrays another."

Ruger had no doubt what the king was talking about—Ruger and Clarann's affair and their daughter, Clarice. For over fifteen years, the king had been fooled. When he found out, it must have been humiliating.

Ruger avoided the king's heated stare. Something disturbing lurked in the king's eyes. It made Ruger's spine tingle. This was the king, but it wasn't the king he knew. He couldn't help but feel that it was someone else. "I never knew."

"I wish that I could take your word for it." King Hector spoke into Ruger's ear. "But you know me. Ignorance is not an excuse." He stepped back. "If I would have killed you months ago, this never would have been an issue. Yet I found it so strange the Clarann desperately came to your aid. It all makes sense now."

King Hector's hand fell to his dagger. He slid the blade quietly out of the sheath. He touched Ruger on the cheek with the flat of the blade. "One prick from the tooth of this dagger will kill any living thing instantly. Instantly! I've used it before to end my troubles. Given the circumstances, I foresee myself using it again."

"You are the king. Do as you will."

King Hector spun the blade in front of Ruger's eyes and said, "I won't waste it on you, Ruger. That would be too simple. It's crude by my standards. Now, I have much more sophisticated weapons at my disposal." He sheathed the blade.

Ruger looked the king in the eyes. The irises in the king's eyes shifted from brown to an emerald green. He had the appearance of a man possessed, a man consumed by unfathomable magic. Ruger's jaw tightened. He tried to look away but could not.

"Now, you will sample my power. Now, you will share the truth," King Hector said.

By an unseen force that was not his own, Ruger's body rose up on tiptoe. His back suddenly arched, and his body became rigid. Slowly, in midair, he began to spin. He spun around once and stopped again in front of King Hector. Their eyes locked. The intensity in the king's emerald eyes bore straight into Ruger's soul. Ruger let out an agonizing scream.

King Hector probed Ruger's thoughts. He rummaged through the warrior's memories. He saw everything he wanted to see about Ruger and the queen and more. He saw torture, blood, war, monsters, and devastation, but most importantly of all, he saw full glimpses of the other world.

Ruger fell from the air and landed hard on his knees. He trembled like a leaf and broke out in a cold sweat. His strength was drained. He fell over and slumped against a wall. His entire life had been exposed.

The emerald gleam in the king's irises faded. His broad shoulders slumped, and he staggered back a step.

Leodor and Melris, who were standing behind the king, grabbed hold of his elbows and steadied him.

King Hector jerked away from both of them. "Unhand me!" He looked at Ruger and pointed a finger at his chest. "You spoke truly that you did not have knowledge of my daughter. And I must say I am disappointed. Your guilt would have made this easy. I could have turned you to dust. Instead!" He retracted his finger. "I see all you have done. So much you have suffered. All for the sake of the Crown. Where most men break, you never gave in. Your service is without question. Yet I stand here, still wounded." King Hector let out a heavy sigh. "Ruger, you will live. In what capacity, I do not know."

Ruger caught his breath. He forced himself back to his knees. He felt as if his soul had been ripped out and stuffed back inside of him again. *Is this what Clarann went through? Where is she?* He wanted to ask but dared not.

The king turned his back to Ruger and addressed the others. "I have seen this other world. I find it fascinating." His fingertips sparkled with mystic power, which flared up. "These invaders attempt to conquer us. Perhaps it is we that should conquer them!"

62

King Hector addressed his constituents with grand ideas of new world conquest. Prince Lewis, Pratt, and Leah hung on every word. Leodor and Melris stood by the king, quietly nodding in agreement.

He's going mad, Ruger thought. *It must be from the stones. This is not the King Hector that I know.* He remained in place, kneeling quietly, not wanting to draw any attention to himself. He needed a greater understanding of what Hector had in mind. He needed to find a way to talk the king out of his quest—either that or knock the Crown of Stones off his head.

As King Hector rambled on about the visions he'd seen in Ruger's mind of a new world, Leodor interrupted when the lathered-up king caught his breath. "Your Majesty, are we abandoning the quest for the other two stones?"

King Hector turned on Leodor, his eyes filled with anger. He glanced at Ruger and calmed. "I have more than enough power with four stones. Besides, I thought that you and Melris agreed further pursuit of the stones is futile."

"It is only futile because I do not sense the presence of the other stones. It is possible that they are lost or destroyed. Their where-abouts are unknown," the soft-spoken Melris said.

Ruger could no longer maintain his silence. "How are you going to close the portal, then?"

King Hector glared at him and said, "Haven't you been listening? I am not going to close the portal. I am going to use it to invade the other world."

"Your Majesty, please listen. I have been there. That world is vastly bigger than this one. Ten times, a hundred times, perhaps a thousand times. You don't want to try this," Ruger pleaded.

"It only takes one man to change the world," King Hector retorted. "Perhaps this world needs a more suitable ruler." He adjusted his crown. "One filled with wisdom and omnipotent power."

"We don't know that our powers work in that world the same as ours. There is no evidence of it," Ruger said. "My king, you must trust in what I say."

"Despite your brave deeds, Ruger, I no longer trust you. You or Clarann. Perhaps in the other world, I will find a more suitable queen."

Ruger's chin dipped to his chest. *He's gone mad. This I am certain.*

"Your Majesty," Leodor said, "perhaps the time has come for you to meet with the Elders. As Melris suggested."

King Hector's fingers needled his palms. "Ah yes, the Elders. I think that it is high time that I meet with my equals." He looked at Melris. "Can you arrange this?"

"Certainly," Melris said. "After all, it was the Elders that sent me to aid you. It will take some time, but if I depart immediately, I can arrange a rendezvous in the next few mornings."

"Take your leave, then," the king said.

Melris bowed, walked over to the wall, and jumped off the ledge.

Leah gasped as the Elderling fell out of sight.

Melris rose up from behind the wall and sailed away to the north, over the handle of the sword of the House of Steel, and vanished behind the blankets of clouds.

"Whoa," Leah said with her mouth hanging open.

King Hector put an arm around her waist and said, "Oh, that is nothing. Wait until you see what I can do. Son," he said to Prince Lewis, "get yourself cleaned up. I want to meet with the leaders in the War Room."

Prince Lewis nodded. "And what about Ruger? What do we do with him?"

King Hector gave Ruger a long, unforgiving look and said, "Take him to the dungeon. I'll deal with him later."

Lewis looked at Pratt and said, "You heard the king. Take him to the dungeon and lock him up in a cold, damp, and smelly cell with the rats, where he belongs."

"My pleasure," Pratt said. In a few big strides, he crossed the patio and yanked Ruger to his feet. He shoved him ahead, using the outside exit of the patio.

Ruger caught a slight smile of victory in Lewis's face. Leodor stared at Ruger with a darker intent. Something was truly off with him.

Black Bane remained propped up against the wall.

Pratt added two more guards and took Ruger to the bottom of the castle. He locked him inside a cell in the very back.

"Listen to me, Pratt. You know that the king is not right. What he is planning is madness. He will get everyone in all of Titanuus killed." Ruger pressed his face to the bars. "You saw those tanks. Those weapons. They will have thousands of them. We have to find a way to close the portal. It's the only way!"

Pratt looked down at him and said, "Though I might agree, that does not change the fact that I serve the king. Where he says march, I march. What happened to you, Ruger, you who never questioned the king, the one who held the standard and the one that never failed? You have become a disgrace. I think the king should put a noose around your neck and hang you for all to see." He chuckled. "But I have a warm feeling that the king's thoughts are headed in that direction." He started to walk away, turned his head over his shoulder, and added, "Enjoy your stay."

Ruger backed up against the wall, sat down on a bed of rotting hay, put his head between his legs, and sighed.

63

BACK HOME

"You know, if I switch with Ruger when all of this goes down, we might have an issue," Abraham said.

Smoke had stitched a small tracking device—like a tiny fuse—underneath the skin of his forearm. "At least we can keep track of you this way. You and Ruger, that is." He bit off the string. "Perfect. They'll never suspect a thing."

Abraham was inside Luther's office. It was the same place where he'd interviewed not so long before for a job as a trucker. Luther was looking out his window at the truck lot, his hands behind his back.

"Luther, I really hate to see you getting involved in this," Abraham said. "There might be another way."

"Don't think anything about it. I'm only making a phone call," Luther said in a reassuring voice. "How dangerous can that be? Besides, it's been a long time since I've done anything meaningful. I want to help."

"To a lot of people, making beer is pretty meaningful," Abraham said while he rubbed his stitched-up forearm.

"True, but you know that's not the kind of meaningful that I mean. Anybody can tap a keg and serve beer." Luther turned around and sat behind his desk. Abraham and Smoke sat in the chairs across from him. "Should I make the call now?" Luther smiled nervously. "I have to admit my fingers are itching like the first time I unhooked a bra."

"Just hold on," Abraham said.

"You know, I knew this was big trouble when those three men showed up," Luther said as he leaned back in his leather office chair. "Colonel Drew Dexter, Eugene Drisk, and Dr. Jack Lassiter. I won't forget them. They were the pushy kind. I never like a pushy kind, unless you're selling me something. I can respect that. But they were threatening me without saying it."

"A pretty good sign that they are the bad guys." Smoke grabbed a can of Coke off the corner of Luther's desk and drank.

Luther made a sour face and said, "I'm surprised that a fit fella like yourself drinks that. That crap will kill you."

"Every man has his poison," Smoke said.

Mandi and Sid entered the office and closed the door behind them. Like Smoke, they were wearing bulletproof sweetheart suits that looked like skintight scuba suits. The two women were drinking bottles of original green Gatorade.

"We are all packed," Sid said.

Abraham gave Mandi a sheepish look. She sat down on the arm of his chair and rubbed his back. "You really need to get that worried look off of your face. We are all going to be fine."

"Somehow, I get the feeling that is the suit talking," he said. "Mandi, you can't be a part of this. It's too dangerous." He glanced at the others. "None of you need to do this. Ruger and I will have to figure it out on our own."

"There won't be any turning back now," Smoke said as he grabbed Sid's hand. "That's not our style. Besides, I really want a peek at Titanuus."

Sid tugged the back of Smoke's hair. "You need to avoid any more thoughts of your crazy vacation ideas. As for Mandi, don't worry about her. She's going to be in a very safe place."

"I'd feel better if she wasn't wearing the suit and was on a plane to Texas," Abraham said.

"Sorry, honey, but I don't do long-distance relationships." Mandi took a long drink. "Man, this stuff really makes a difference."

"We added some more electrolytes to the formula." Sid looked at the phone. "I guess it's time to make the call."

An awkward moment of silence passed.

Luther jumped in his seat and leaned forward. "Oh, I guess that's my cue." He picked up Drew Dexter's business card and dialed. He cupped his hand over the phone receiver. "No one picked up. I'm getting a recorded message."

"So leave him one, short and sweet," Sid said calmly.

Luther's forehead beaded with sweat. "Uh, hello, this is Luther Vancross. You stopped by my place a few days ago. Um, I have some information. He's here. Acting kinda crazy. Oops, got to go." He hung up quickly and smiled. "How'd I do?"

"Fabulous." Smoke stood up. "Now, that's our cue to go."

Abraham shook hands with Smoke and Sid. "Good luck."

The husband-and-wife team nodded, shook hands with Luther, and left.

"Uh, Luther, can Mandi and I have a moment?"

"Sure, sure." Luther hustled from behind his desk and out the office door.

Abraham sat down and pulled Mandi into his lap. He touched foreheads with her. "I really wish I understood why you were doing this for me. But I guess I'll never understand." He looked into her eyes. "I'm honored, Mandi. I don't know how I can—"

Mandi put two fingers on his lips and said, "Don't think so much, just do."

He kissed her fingers, moved them aside, and kissed her fully on the lips. He reeled her body in closer as her fingers grabbed a handful of his hair. Her heart beat against his. Their lips locked in a more passionate kiss.

Someone knocked on the office door's frame. "What is this, a Big Red commercial? I've been standing out here ten minutes already."

They broke off the kiss.

Outside, someone was honking a car horn.

Mandi crawled out of his lap with her chest heaving. "Boy, this suit really does something for the libido. No wonder Sid has such a happy marriage." She caressed his face and kissed his cheek. "It's going to work out. Have faith. Believe in yourself. I do." Mandi gave Luther a hug and left.

From the office window, Abraham and Luther together watched the black Jeep Cherokee drive away.

"Now what?" Luther said.

"We wait."

"Hmm... How about some coffee?"

64

Luther sat in his chair, leaning back and staring out the window. He sipped his coffee. "You know, I was working on moving into a new line of business. I was going to make coffee—something super dark that would keep you up all night."

"Don't they have enough coffees in the world to choose from?"

Abraham was looking at Luther's desktop computer. They had the security cameras on. It was Sunday morning, and the office was closed.

"Eh." Luther shrugged. "It's all about the branding. You know, I should be in church right now. They're going to miss me. I'll tell you, miss one Sunday, and they are all over you the next like a pack of wolves with dentures. I like that. Don't really have anything else. It's good to know someone cares."

"Yeah, I suppose it is." Abraham toggled from one camera view to another. Three hours had passed since Luther made the call, and they weren't very far away from Facility 117. "For so long, I figured everyone in the world hated me."

"Our nation has become an incubator for hair-trigger emotions. Is it like that on Titanuus?"

"No, and it won't be if we can prevent it. Huh."

Luther leaned forward in his chair and turned toward the monitor. He put his glasses on.

Abraham pointed at the screen. "You have a black SUV pulling up to the entrance gate. Another one behind it." Soldiers with machine guns spilled out of the vehicles and dashed into the woods. "They're here."

Luther shivered. "I hated the *Poltergeist* movie. My late wife took me to see it. I never liked scary."

"That wasn't a very scary movie."

"Says you!"

Outside, the distinct sound of a helicopter could be heard above: *wuppa-wuppa-wuppa-wuppa-wuppa-wuppa...*

"I'm starting to think that letting myself get captured wasn't such a good idea." He glanced out of the window. The chopper was landing on the distillery's grounds. "I need to make a run for it."

A man was sitting in the back of the helicopter, pointing a grenade launcher at the window. It was Colonel Drew Dexter—there was no mistaking the moustache. Drew saw Abraham standing in the window and fired.

"Get down, Luther!" Abraham yelled. He dove over the desk and knocked Luther to the ground.

The glass window shattered. The grenade round exploded with white gas.

"Smoke grenade," Abraham said.

Luther broke out in a fit of coughing. "Go!" he spat. "Go!" He coughed more. "Oh my, this is awful. Worse than I remember."

Abraham couldn't see a thing. He fumbled his way through the office doorway and headed down the stairs. He coughed and hacked. His lungs burned like fire, and tears streamed down his face. He couldn't avoid the smoke.

More grenades rocketed into the lower floors of the building and exploded. More white smoke flared up, but it was worse.

Tear gas!

Abraham's eyes watered up. His breathing choked. Holding his breath, he stumbled blindly through the mist, knocking over whatever he bumped into. Unable to see a thing, he swam through the smoke. A man popped up in front of his eyes. He grabbed the man by the mask and ripped it off.

The soldier sucked in a painful breath of air and clutched at Abraham's clothing.

Abraham shoved the man aside. He barreled straight forward and smacked into a wall. His fingers felt along the edges. All he wanted to do was escape.

A pair of men came out of nowhere and tackled him. He wrestled over the floor with one of them. The second soldier cracked him in the skull with the butt of his weapon. Abraham saw stars and collapsed. The soldiers in gas masks hooked him underneath the arms and dragged him out of the building.

Abraham couldn't have been happier. He coughed and hacked while sucking in the fresh morning air. Tears streamed down his face as he spat the foul-tasting mist out of his mouth. Someone cuffed his legs together. His hands were locked behind his back and strapped.

"That was easy," Colonel Drew Dexter said.

Abraham was stood up face-to-face with Drew. He got a good look through his watery eyes.

Colonel Dexter tilted his head to one side and said, "Who are we dealing with today? Hmm?"

A soldier brought Luther out of the building in a fireman's carry. He set the old man on the ground while he hacked his lungs out.

"Make sure the building is clear. There might be three more persons of interest," Colonel Dexter said. "Go! Go!"

Abraham didn't say a word. He wanted Drew to think he was Ruger. He set his watery eyes on Luther. He felt sorry for the old man writhing on the ground and coughing his guts out, but he glared at the old man anyway.

"Not speaking, huh?" Colonel Dexter asked with a twitch of his moustache. "Don't worry, we'll find a way to make you talk. The same as we always do."

Abraham glared at Colonel Dexter. He fought against the men

that held him and snorted. One of the soldiers cracked him in the back of the knee with the butt of his rifle.

"Easy—no need to bust him up too bad. We need him." Colonel Dexter pulled out his phone and made a call. "It's me, Jack. We have them. What do you want me to do with the old man, Luther?" He looked down at Luther. "Uh-huh. Uh-huh. You're the boss." He put away his phone and pulled out his pistol.

Abraham tensed.

65

"Only a coward would kill a defenseless old man. Do you kill women and children too?" Abraham asked in as stern a voice as he could muster.

Colonel Dexter spun the automatic pistol on his finger and studied Abraham's face. "The way I see it, this is war, and war has casualties." He gave Abraham a harder look. "I didn't have any plans to kill him. I was more curious to see how you would react to it. Seems like the two of you are friendly. Makes me think that it might be you in there, Abraham, and not Ruger." He stuffed his weapon back in his holster.

Abraham—still pretending to be Ruger—said, "I'm not that soft-bellied goat. But I live with honor. I don't slaughter the weak for sport. It disgusts me. Take these shackles off, and I'll be more than happy to show you which man I am. I challenge you Gin-gin!"

"What is Gin-gin?"

"A duel. Have you ever fought with a blade, or do you always cower behind your tiny crossbows?"

Colonel Dexter chuckled. "All right, load this head case onto the chopper. Gin-gin. Huh." He pointed at Luther, who was still gagging and spitting. "Take the old man too. Dr. Drisk wants him."

Handling Abraham and Luther roughly, the soldiers secured them in the seats of the large chopper.

Colonel Dexter loaded in and shut the door.

The chopper lifted off, and into the sky they went.

Four seats were in the back of the chopper. Abraham was in the backseat with Colonel Dexter seated beside him. His growing disdain for the man was as bad as the foul taste of tear gas in his mouth. He spat on the floor.

"Don't do that," the colonel said.

Abraham spat again.

Colonel Dexter didn't say another word for the rest of the trip.

Abraham stared out the window. Just over an hour into the trip, he noticed streaks of purplish lightning coursing through the sky. A tempest was forming over the mountains. The hairs on the nape of his neck stood on end.

What in the world?

It was the same sort of lightning he had seen the moment before his plane was struck by it and he crashed.

"What the hell are they doing?" Colonel Dexter asked as he peered through Abraham's window. "Those idiots shouldn't be tinkering with the tunnel when they know we are airborne. Get this chopper lower. Get it on the ground ASAP! Somebody's going to get an ass chewing!"

Abraham kept his eyes fixed on the flashing sky. He wanted to ask Colonel Dexter how long this had been going on, but in his heart, he knew the answer. His blood started to rise as everything came together. The plane crash hadn't been his fault. Men like Eugene Drisk, Jack Lassiter, and Drew Dexter caused it with their experiments. They were the ones that killed Jenny, Jake, and his best friend, Buddy Parker. And all this time, he'd blamed himself. With his temperature rising, he clenched a fist and looked Colonel Dexter dead in the eye.

Colonel Dexter shrank under his gaze, said, "What?" and looked away.

They landed in the parking lot of Facility 117.

Abraham and Luther were hurried into the building. They were separated at the elevators. Otis and Haymaker appeared, hard scowls on their faces. They took Abraham to a padded cell, put him in a full-body straitjacket, and lay him on a rolling table. He wriggled against their efforts, just for show.

Otis grabbed Abraham's face in his big black hand and squeezed it. "Welcome back, Looney Tunes." He nodded at Haymaker.

Haymaker held a stun rod and smacked it into his hand. He had a twisted smile on his face.

"Dr. Jack has special orders for you. Very special," Otis continued. He removed Abraham's boots and socks. He eyeballed Otis. "Hit him."

Haymaker jabbed the stun rod against the bottom of Abraham's foot.

Abraham arched his back inside his bonds. He convulsed on the table and let out a loud scream. Every nerve inside his body caught fire. He shivered head to toe.

"Look at that. Shaking like a leaf. You aren't so tough, are you, Ruger?" Otis asked. He glanced up in the corner of the cell where a security camera hung. He grinned. "Or is it Abraham? So tell us— what are the king's plans?"

Abraham clammed up. He needed to play it tough like Ruger.

Haymaker hit him with the stun rod again.

He jumped on the table. He started to see bright spots and stars. *No! Don't go back, Abraham. Don't go back. Hang in there. We are getting close. Play along.*

Haymaker hit him with the stun rod time and again.

Otis peppered him with heated questions.

"What is your name?"

"Tell us the king's plans!"

"Do you want to see your family again?"

"Where is the sword?"

Abraham kept his mouth shut. It was what he thought Ruger would do if they tried to break him. He had to sell it. Maybe he would have broken before, but not now. The tide had turned inside him. His lingering doubt had been crushed. He focused on the purple storm in the sky, and the lust for vengeance fueled his body.

They killed my family. Now it's payback time.

The torment went on for over an hour. Abraham hung tough. His sweat-drenched hair dripped onto the table.

Otis and Haymaker dabbed their shiny foreheads with cloths. Haymaker was about to hit him with the stun rod again when the padded cell door opened.

Dr. Jack Lassiter and the zillon woman, Ottum, entered. Dr. Jack nodded at the orderlies and said, "I'll take it from here, gentlemen."

The brutish orderlies departed, and the door closed behind them.

"You are tough," Dr. Jack said as he leaned over Abraham's face. "But no one beats the needle."

Ottum stuck Abraham in the neck with a needle longer than his finger and depressed the plunger.

Nooo!

66

TITANUUS

C hains rattled and scraped over the ground. The air smelled damp and musty. The floor was cold. Something nibbled on his fingers.

Abraham woke up. He knocked a large rat away from his fingers. The creature skipped over the floor and scurried away. He sat up and wiped sticky straw away from his face. His head was splitting. He rubbed his temples. From the hallway flickered a dim source of light that he could see through the steel bars.

He crawled to the bars and peered outside. He was in a dungeon, as medieval as it could get. The floors were coated in a film of slime and mold. The place smelled like mold. Water ran down the limestone walls. He touched the breastplate armor on his chest.

"Great, it looks like I'm back in Titanuus."

A chill went through him as he rubbed his head. He had a sinking feeling that Dr. Jack Lassiter had figured out how to send him back and forth. Perhaps the zillon, Ottum, had helped him.

Where am I?

The last time he'd been in Titanuus, he was preparing the Henchmen to fight the Gond at the House of Steel. Perhaps they had lost and he was a Gond prisoner. He had no way of knowing where he was without seeing someone. He called out loudly. "Hello!"

His voice cracked. He thirsted, and his throat was as dry as a bone. He searched the dungeon cell. A wooden bucket was tilted over, and he saw no sign of water or food.

How long have I been in here?

"Hello!" He grabbed the bucket and banged it against the cell bars. "Hello! Hello! Hello! Somebody, please!"

His words echoed hollowly down the hallway. No response came his way. The dungeons were deadly quiet, abandoned to the lingering gloom and stench of death.

Abraham rifled through his recent memories. He'd gained more knowledge since his last trip back home. The lightning that had struck his plane was man-made. The time had come to forgive himself. The time had come to make the monsters that had done that pay.

How many other innocent deaths have the monsters of the Corporation caused?

He shook his head.

I'm getting closer, but I need to get out of here.

He jerked on the bars. He kicked them.

Ruger's body was strong, unnaturally so. He grabbed the inch-thick corroding steel bars in two hands and pulled. The metal peeled back a fraction of an inch. He put more muscle into it. His back muscles knotted up. He let out a loud groan.

Somewhere in the dungeon, a door squeaked on the hinges.

Heavy footsteps came Abraham's way. He let go of the bars, sucking for breath. His belly growled, and he felt weak. His knees buckled underneath him, and he slid down the bars.

"Are you making racket again?" someone with a gruff voice asked. The heavy-set man behind the voice appeared down the hall. He waddled more than he walked and carried a short sword on his belt. "Still trying to bend those bars, eh? Goodness sake, no man can bend them. Those are the King's Steel. You of all people should know that, Ruger."

Abraham studied the pudgy man's face. He was built like Horace but fatter. His forearms were chubby, cheeks flabby, and chins saggy.

He narrowed his eyes on the man and asked, "Do we know each other?"

"Boy, you really are daffy, aren't you, Ruger? Of course. I rode with you over a decade ago. We talked about this, remember? A myrmidon cut the back of my knees out. Haven't been very able ever since. No spring in me boots. Can't climb that saddle either." The jailer made a chipper face. "But I'm here and thankful. Make the most of the worst circumstances, like you always said." He searched Abraham's face. "You really don't remember, do you?"

"Uh, what is your name again?"

"Carlton. Boy, you really have taken too many lumps on the noggin. I never thought I'd see the day when you'd deteriorate. But it happens to the best of us. Look at me. Fat as a cow, and I don't even drink. Well, not at work. Usually."

"What about the standard, Carlton?"

"Ain't no standards down here. None. Just me and the rats. The king tends to kill more that cross him than let them live. Now, you keep it quiet. I'm trying to sleep."

"Carlton, what about the Gond?"

"What Gond? The ones you slaughtered on the other side of the Wall? Why, they are all dead. Fertilizer, as I understand it." Carlton swiped his hand over his greasy black combover. "I miss all of the action. I only hear what I hear if they tell me." He leaned his shoulder on a bar and looked away from Abraham. "They treat me like I never wore that armor before, but I tell them I did. The laugh because I can't fit in it."

"How long's it been since we fought off the Gond?"

Carlton turned his head and said, "By the Elders, being incarcerated really takes a toll, doesn't it? That was three days ago." He counted on his fingers. "Three days since you've been here. You've mostly been quiet. Model prisoner." A distant look came over him. "Sometimes I feel like a prisoner."

Abraham got the sinking feeling that Carlton might be crazy, but he didn't notice a key ring on the man's belt either. He carried only a short sword, and his hand stayed on the pommel.

Carlton moved away from the cell bars. He eyed Abraham suspiciously. "I know what you are thinking. You want to escape. Well, that's impossible. You have to get by me, and ten more Guardians are waiting on guard if you get by me. Plus, you can't get out of the cell without the key because I don't keep the key on me." He tapped his finger to his head. "You see, I am smart. Very smart."

"Carlton, what about King Hector? Where is he? I need to speak to him."

"No, I won't tell you that either because I don't know, and I wouldn't if I did. It's just like you said—ignorance is bliss. Well, I'm chock-full of ignorant."

67

Inside the Stronghold on the first floor, Solomon watched Horace pace around the farm table. He'd kept to himself, listening to what the others had to say while worrying about Abraham.

It's not the same without him, Solomon thought.

Horace punched a hand into his meaty fist, saying, "Need to know! 'Need to know,' the Prince of Cowards says! We have a right to know where Ruger is!"

"Don't let your mind bubble." Iris was sitting on one of the benches at the farm table, knitting a blanket with needles. The rest of the Henchmen were present except for Shades and Sticks. "You know that Ruger, or Abraham, whichever, for I can't keep up, can take care of himself."

Horace pointed at the wall behind the fireplace and said, "An army marches to the Spine, and we are not with it. That is preposterous! Ruger should be leading it. The world ends. All we do is sit here and watch."

"We need to break Abraham out of the House of Steel," Tark suggested. He was sitting at the table, beside Cudgel, sawing up his food with a knife.

"No, that's just what they want," Vern said after he finished a sip

369

of wine. "That's why the prince provokes us. He wants to hang all of us. He always did."

"So, what do we do?" Cudgel asked, wide eyed. "We can't continue to sit here."

Solomon sat in the corner of the room nearest the grand fireplace. He'd been listening to the bickering for days, but he didn't have any answers either. He was as lost as the rest of the Henchmen. "We need to wait for Shades and Sticks."

"What if they are dead?" Vern asked.

"Don't say that," Dominga fired back, nudging him with an elbow.

"Why?" Vern shrugged. "For all we know, Ruger is dead too. I hope not, but why wouldn't they kill him? Especially if the king has gone crazy."

"He's not dead," Horace growled. "Shame on you for saying so."

"I'm being realistic," Vern said.

Prospero, who was digging a spoon into a bowl of stew, let out a loud belch.

"I share his sentiments," Cudgel said. "Vern, your outlook is deplorable."

"Deplorable, huh? Well, nothing wrong with being deplorable if I'm still living and breathing. We have to face the facts: the world is changing, and none of you even know what side we are on."

"We side with the king!" Horace grabbed a log and flung it into the fireplace. "We cannot doubt it, or we are lost!"

RASCHEL

"I hate this place," Prince Lewis said.

He, Leodor, and Leah were in the crypts underneath the largest of the Sects cathedrals in the city of Burgess. It was the same crypt where Leodor had arranged a meeting with Arcayis the Underlord before. He swiped his hand through a cobweb. "Please get on with it quick. I prefer the company of the living and not the dead."

Leah moseyed through the temple's underbelly with a seductive gait. She bent over and lifted a very tall candlestand. "I like gruesome places. I walk by a sarcophagus and wonder how a person died. After all, death is my business."

Lewis opened his arms to the woman, who crossed the room and filled his arms with her body. He kissed her deeply. "It's so very comforting to have you by my side again, Raschel. It was a shame to put an end to Leah. I was very fond of her. But I'm much fonder of the crown."

Giggling delightedly, Raschel opened her hand and showed off the ring on her finger. "Yes, the Ring of Tarsus makes my evil deeds so much easier to execute. Literally. You should have seen your former love when I drained the life from her bones and took it for my own. Talk about gruesome."

"If the two of you are quite finished bragging about your exploits, I could use your hands over here," Leodor said. The older mystic tugged on a great cloth hanging over a very tall mirror. "It's snagged."

Lewis and Raschel yanked the cloth away and dropped it on the backside of the huge mirror. Lewis snarled at the twisted figures wrought in iron around the rim. "I hate this twisted thing too."

"I don't know," Raschel said as she tapped her fingernails on her chin. "I think it would look very nice in my new chambers inside the castle."

"Yes, when you are queen, you should need a mirror that will match your ego." Lewis put his arm around her waist, lowered his hand to her rear, and said, "And when will I get to see my ravishing Raschel again? This body is fine, but yours is much more... sensual."

"When it is all over... and that should be soon."

Leodor finished setting up all the candlestands. Each one had a small skull on its top. He said a mystic word, and a green flame came to life in the shape of a tiny burning imp that danced. It jumped from candle to candle until all the stands were aflame.

"Everyone stay within the triangle," Leodor said.

Lewis and Raschel stepped inside the frame.

Leodor drew invisible symbols in the air and chanted at a feverish pace.

The trio's reflection in the dark mirror warped and twisted. The dull colors swirled like a vortex and slowed, then a new image formed and became clear. Standing inside a cavern was a very tall hooded wraith in dark ghostly robes. A man with receding blond hair, maroon shirt, and black vest stood with a pistol on his hip. They were accompanied by a bare-chested horned halfling who bulged with muscle and smoked a cigar.

Leodor cleared his throat and made quick introductions. "I am Viceroy Leodor, once banished, now reinstated mystic of the Sect. This is Prince Lewis of Kingsland and our colleague, Raschel, from the Brotherhood of Ravens." He bowed. "We are humbly at your service. Especially you, Great Fleece, Master of Shadows and the Sect."

"Let's not forget who the true master is here," the halfling said as he ran a finger inside his collar. He huffed out a smoke ring. "I'm Big Apple, and this is Lord Hawk, leader of the Shell." He hopped up onto a wooden crate. "Tell me all that is happening. I don't need any more slipups like the last time."

"Us being branded was an unforeseen circumstance, but now that King Hector has liberated us from the Brand, well"—Leodor shrugged his scrawny shoulders—"we are back in business. The moment this happened, we did not hesitate to contact you either."

"And you were wise to do so," Big Apple said. "So, where is King Hector now?"

Leodor chuckled. "He and Melris the Elderling are seeking counsel with the Elders. At the same time, King Hector rallies his armies. He plans to march on the Spine to roust you out once he learns of your location."

Big Apple and Lord Hawk chuckled and grinned at one another. "Feel free to let them know exactly where we are. At the tip-top peaks at the bottom of the Spine. Let him try to march an army all of the way through South Tiotan, where we are strongest."

"He'll send ships," Prince Lewis stated.

"Let him. We'll be ready and waiting for him," Big Apple huffed out rings of smoke. "And how is King Hector these days?"

"Everything is going according to plan. The crown's stones are too powerful for him to manage. They are making him mad with power. The Crown of Stones's gems are only meant for individual use or to function as a whole. Otherwise, they create a great deal of imbalance to the wielder's mind. That is why King Hector removed the Brand from us. He was overconfident in his power. Unknowingly, he exposed himself. Still, there is the matter of the other stones. I would not be surprised if he doesn't petition the Elders to help seek them out."

"Oh, don't worry about that. The king can search all that he wants, but he will never find them." Big Apple grinned impishly. "The white diamond and yellow fire gems do exist, but they are not in this world. They are secure in the other world, called Earth, and he will never find them. Heh heh heh."

Leodor gave an approving nod. "It's no wonder that we have not been able to locate them."

"No, we have been working on this conquest a long time. I've thought of everything," Big Apple said. "I can't believe that King Hector is so delusional that he wants to invade my home. This couldn't have worked out more perfectly. The old fool rushes to his death. But feel free to kill him at your earliest opportunity." He looked at the assassin, Raschel. "I'm sure you'll have a dozen opportunities between now and then."

"Dozens, actually," she said. "I'm only waiting on the perfect moment to strike."

Prince Lewis pushed forward. "And the Crown of Stones—what is to become of it?"

"That is not something that you need to concern yourself with," Lord Hawk said. He had his thumbs hitched in his gun belt. "We'll take care of the crown. After all, there will be a new king ruling all of Titanuus."

Prince Lewis puffed up and said, "But I get Kingsland and the House of Steel. That is the arrangement, correct?"

"You will have your little castle and the southern tip of the lands," Big Apple said. "Things will happen so fast it will hardly matter. A new era comes to Titanuus. It will be amazing."

"And what about these otherworlders that are invading? What are their plans?"

Big Apple shrugged. "We'll guide them as we please. The important matter is securing the functionality of the Time Tunnel and the other portals."

"I thought the King's Steel that I sent you was more than enough to get it working," Prince Lewis said.

"Oh, it's an ample supply, but the more we have, the longer we can keep the tunnel open, the more we can make. The process is almost perfected," Big Apple said.

"Almost?" Prince Lewis stated. "I'd assume it was finished."

"The tunnel is, but there is still one part that the men of my world have not mastered. But I think they have almost figured it out. That's why we still need Abraham Jenkins and Ruger Slade alive. They hold the key," Big Apple said. The image in the mirror warped. He glared up at Fleece. "Can't you keep it open longer?"

The towering figure clad in dark wavy robes slowly shook his head.

"This will be the last time we have to speak," Big Apple said. "Let us lure King Hector into a false sense of security. Lead him right to us in the peaks. We'll leave a trail to our location. Once you make it to the lair, we will see you there. Oh, and bring the sword too. Our new alliance would like a trophy."

"What about the Elders?" Leodor asked. "Is it not possible that they will help?"

"Those monsters? I hardly think so. They are very selfish, but one never knows. If they get involved, we will be ready," Big Apple said.

"And Ruger Slade? What do we do with him?"

"After we kill the king, we'll deal with him later. Let him rot in his cell for now."

"And the Henchmen?" Prince Lewis asked.

"Pfft," Big Apple laughed. "They are useless without their leader."

The images in the mirror faded.

The bright candles went out.

As the trio of villains covered the mirror, Prince Lewis smirked and said, "I just can't wait to be king."

69

Sticks remained huddled against a corner wall inside the crypt. She watched Lewis, Leodor, and Leah depart. She'd seen and heard the entire conversation. After the group was several minutes gone, she slid from her hiding spot into the darkness of the crypt, which was also used for storage.

"That was an earful, wasn't it?" someone else said out in the darkness.

Sticks made out the faint outline of Shades. He'd hidden himself on the other side of the chambers. The two of them had been keeping tabs on Lewis and Leodor since they'd left the castle.

"It answers a lot of questions, doesn't it?" she said.

"The sad thing is that I thought Prince Lewis might have turned a corner. I guess once a bad seed, always a bad seed." Shades bumped into Sticks on his way out.

"Watch your hands," she said.

"Pardon me. It is dark, you know."

"And I know you know your way around the dark better than anybody but me," she said.

"True." He made his way toward the stairs. "At least we know that

369

Ruger is alive and in the castle. That's good to know even though it will be near impossible to get him out of there."

They walked up the crypt stairs shoulder to shoulder. "I don't think a mad king will heed our warnings either," she said. "Talk about a rock and a hard spot. No one is going to believe us."

A heavy stone door sealed the entrance to the crypt. Shades put his shoulder into it and started to push it open. "Cripes, this thing is heavy. I could use some assistance."

Sticks leaned on the door. "We can get Abraham out of the House of Steel, can't we?"

"I think it would be far easier to reach out to the king."

"But he won't listen. He doesn't trust Abraham or the Henchmen anymore," she said as she shoved the door.

"True, but if we can get that crown off of his head, he might begin to see clearer."

"I thought the king was a good man. Now, he's ruined."

"He's probably still a good man. The power is corrupting him. It happens to everyone these days." Shades grunted as he pushed the door open. "Except for humble men like me." With the door wide open, he stepped aside. "After you."

They were in the back end of the great temple, in the rooms behind the altars.

Sticks moved out of the crypt stairwell. "Back to the Stronghold?"

Shades started to push the door shut. "Oh, crap on this door. Let someone else shut it." He turned, and suddenly his eyes widened.

Sticks pulled a dagger free and spun around. Raschel ran a knife deep into her gut. Sticks sliced the woman across the cheek, but her strength quickly fled her.

Shades pulled out a short sword just in time to have his sword hand cut off by Prince Lewis, who was lurking behind the curtains. Shades gaped as his missing hand and sword dropped to the floor. Blood spurted from the wound. Prince Lewis sank his sword deep in the man's chest.

Sticks sagged to her knees, clutching her belly. Her jaw hung open. She looked up at the woman in Leah's body.

Raschel smirked as she wiped the blood on her blade on the shoulder of Sticks's cloak. "The wound is fatal. You'll be dead in a few minutes. Any last words that you would like to share? I like to keep a record. It provides for excellent reading with a bottle of wine."

Sticks didn't respond. She tried to stand but could not. With tremendous effort, she knee walked over to Shades. His eyes were wide, and his hands clutched the wound in his chest. He spat blood out of his mouth.

Leodor stepped out from behind the curtain. "Did you really think that interlopers like you could sneak into a house of the Sect and not be noticed? Tsk tsk. Our eyes are everywhere. Even the likes of you could not avoid them."

"And to think you were once one of us," Sticks struggled to say. "You'll get yours."

"I like that quote," Raschel added. "I might even write it down in your own blood."

"Leodor, what are we doing? Watching them bleed to death?" Lewis asked. He wiped his sword blade off on one of the curtains. "We have more pressing matters to attend to."

"Of course. Put them in the crypt. It's a fit place for them to die. The servants of the Sect can dispose of the bodies later, after the rats have nibbled down to the bones. They are excellent when it comes to cleaning up."

Lewis sheathed his sword, grabbed Shades by the collar, dragged him to the top of the stairs, and rolled him down the steps. "A very light little fellow. He must have bones like a bird."

Sticks tried to pull a knife out of her bandolier with her numb fingers. The burning fire in her gut kept her doubled over. The strength in her limbs failed completely. Helpless, she let Prince Lewis grab her by the braids and haul her to the top of the steps.

"Hmph, I think you are heavier than Shades was." Lewis gave her a quaint smile. "It was a pleasure working with you for a time. I'll always cherish the memories."

Sticks offered the prince one last burning look and said, "We saved you."

"And I'll always be grateful. 'Tis a shame that I won't be doing the same for you." With a shove of his boot, he rolled Sticks down the steps, where she landed right on top of Shades's body. Prince Lewis waved his gloved fingers. "Ta ta."

Sticks watched in burning misery. The wicked trio stood at the top of the stairs, gloating. With a shove that made closing the stone door look easy, Lewis sealed them inside the crypt to die in darkness and their own blood.

70

Water dripped from the dungeon's cell beams onto the stone floor. Abraham sat with his head sunk between his legs, listening to the steady, maddening drip of water splashing on the floor. He didn't know which was worse, being locked up in the cell or wrapped up like a pig in a blanket in a padded room.

Switch. Switch. Switch.

A big part of him wanted to go back home the longer he sat in the murk. His trips to Titanuus had at one time been very appealing, but now, its treachery had gotten old. The time for normalcy had come.

Maybe Ruger can put an end to all of this.

He let out a wet cough. Typically, when he was in Ruger's body, he felt a wellspring of endless vitality. Now, he felt drained. He'd never been the same since the wraith—the Underlord, Fleece—drained him. Perhaps all the back and forth between bodies had worn him down. Maybe Ruger's body had begun to take on Abraham's body from back home.

He leaned his head back and bumped it against the slime-slick wall.

Ah man, this isn't good.

369

A rat crawled into his cell. Its long whiskers twitched as it stared at Abraham with beady red eyes.

"Don't even think about it. I'm not dead yet." He flicked his fingers at the rat, but it remained frozen in its spot. "Getting bolder, eh? Maybe you can see that I'm dead already." He sniffed. "Maybe I am and I don't know it. This better be real."

If he'd had some idea of what was going on, it wouldn't have been so bad. He'd left his friends at home in the lurch. Luther was in danger, and thanks to Abraham, he'd been dragged into everything. Mandi, Sid, Smoke—all of them had endangered themselves too. And there were the Henchmen.

What in Titanuus had happened to them? What if King Hector had disbanded them? He wouldn't have killed them, would he?

The large rat with little white feet scuttled out of the cell and vanished in the hallway.

The grinding of rusting door hinges echoed through the dungeon.

Abraham heard Carlton's heavy footsteps. The former Guardian-turned-jailer rambled on like a deranged man during his visits. He remained steadfast about his duties, as he was still sharp enough to not reveal anything to Abraham. Whenever he pressed for information, Carlton would button his lip and storm away.

"Are you thirsty, Ruger? Hmm," the hefty Carlton said as he appeared in front of the cell. "Fresh water from the king's own spring." He rattled a wooden ladle inside the bucket, sloshing the water out as he did so. "You can have water but no food. Those are my orders. Do you want a drink, my old friend?"

"Of course I do. I'm dying of thirst, and I'd be grateful."

"Hum-hee! You would do the same for me—I know that. I'm not here to make you suffer. No, no. I only make sure that you don't escape. Now, you stay back. Any sudden moves, and I'll spill it." Carlton stuck a key in the keyhole and stared at Ruger with a bulging eye. "No no no!" He yanked the key out. "I see what you are thinking. You will try to overpower me and escape. I won't have that!"

"I'm not moving," Abraham said calmly.

He had no idea how Carlton had been assigned as his jailer. The man appeared inept. But he didn't come across as someone worthy of living in the House of Steel. Perhaps Ruger had arranged it long before. "I am very thirsty. I swear on my honor that I won't move."

"Ha! Henchmen have no honor! You said so long ago to me." Carlton slammed the bucket down on the ground. Precious water splashed up over the rim. "You can drink through the bars. Good day, Ruger! I'll be back tomorrow." He waddled away, and somewhere far down the hall, the door slammed shut.

Eyeing the bucket, Abraham crawled across the cell.

Probably sewer water.

He stretched his fingers through the bars far enough and squeezed his thick forearm muscles through. With two fingers, he grabbed the bucket and pulled it over to the bars. To his surprise, the water inside the wooden pail was clear as rain. Parched, he grabbed the ladle and drank. He licked his cracked, dry lips.

"Ah..."

Through the bars, he sucked in ladleful after ladleful until he couldn't scrape any more out of the bucket. He picked up the bucket, tilted it up, and drained the last swallow.

He let out a throaty "Ah!"

He'd never enjoyed water so much before. Something about it was exquisite. The throbbing in his body eased. Hot blood raced through his system. He eyed the inside of the upside-down bucket. Only a drop came out. The bucket was drained.

Abraham clutched his fingers in and out. A spring of hot energy coursed through his limbs.

Blazing saddles! What is going on? I feel like I could run through a wall!

Something was afoot. Someone somewhere was helping him. Perhaps Iris had spiked the water with her magic. He couldn't think of anything else at the time.

He grabbed hold of the bars and heaved against them. The muscles popped in his mighty forearms. Blue veins rose like corded snakes. He put his feet against the wall of steel bars and pulled hard against it. The corroded metal started to bend.

King's Steel, my big ol' butt!

He tossed his head back and threw his back into it. "Hurk!"

The entire wall of bars ripped out of its frame and fell on top of him with a loud *bang*. For a long moment, he was trapped underneath the wall. He fought the urge to giggle. He'd meant to bend the metal, not rip the entire wall down. He crawled out from underneath the bars and said, "Conan, eat your heart out."

He didn't make it two steps down the hall before crossing a woman wearing a dark-red cloak barring his path. She brandished a razor-sharp sword.

71

The woman cloaked in red dropped her hood. It was Princess Clarice.

"What are you doing here?" Abraham asked.

"Rescuing you, uh..."

"Abraham," he said.

She stepped around him and looked at the fallen wall of steel bars. Bewildered, she asked, "What did you do that for?"

"To get out."

She picked up the bucket and turned it upside down. A key was attached to a claylike material on the bottom of it. "Easy peasy?"

"Ah. I thought the water—"

The jailer's dungeon door opened.

"Let's go!" Clarice whispered. She grabbed his hand and led him to another dungeon passage. At the end of the passage, a stone wall was partially split open.

Abraham pulled free of her grip. "You go. I'll catch up. I have to deal with him."

"But..."

He took off back to his cell. He stepped inside, lifted the wall of bars up, and fit them back into the frame. Metal scraped loudly against the stone fitting.

"Har! What is that racket?" Carlton jogged on heavy feet to Abraham's cell. By the time he made it to the cell, he was lathered in sweat and puffing for breath. With his hands on his knees, he eyeballed Abraham. "What did you do?"

"Me?" Abraham asked innocently as he leaned into the dungeon bars, holding them nonchalantly in place. "Sorry, I dropped the bucket. It made such a clatter. Did you hear that?"

"The deaf in Burgess could have heard it." Carlton eyed his surroundings. "What are you doing? You have a sneaky look about you." He eyed the bars and the lock. Rubbing his flabby chin, he said, "Something stinks down here."

"It's been a time since I last bathed," he said even though Carlton smelled so bad it could knock over someone with unprepared nostrils. "Sorry."

Carlton pulled his short sword. "Step back."

"Why?"

"Do it!"

Slowly, Abraham stepped two steps back, thinking he could have handled the situation better. But he needed to fool Carlton. Otherwise, the guard wouldn't hesitate to alert the soldiers of his escape. He didn't want to kill the man either. *Why didn't I just knock him out?*

"Step back further, to the back wall!" Carlton said. The moment Abraham moved back, Carlton grabbed the bars with one hand and tugged on them.

The bars teetered.

"Huh?" Carlton said.

The cell's bars tipped all the way over and crashed down on Carlton, pinning him underneath.

Carlton let out a loud scream.

Abraham jumped over the fallen cell bars and said, "Sorry, Carlton, but I have to go! But try to keep it down, will you?"

"I'll get you! Guards! Guards!"

Abraham didn't wait around to see if the guards showed up. He dashed down the dungeon hall and into the secret passage.

Clarice met him on the other side of the wall. She closed the passage door and dropped a locking bar behind it. "Well, that was a stupid idea," she said. "Come on."

Moving quickly, he followed her through the darkness with her hand fitted in his. The narrow passage wound through the castle's interior in an endless maze.

"Where are we going?" he asked.

"Shhh, the walls can be thin in spots." Clarice hustled onward. "We've known about these networks since we were children. I think most have forgotten about them. We go outside. Horses wait for our escape. There is a ship ready at the port."

He pulled her to a stop and said, "No. We go to the Stronghold. That is the first place they will look. We have to warn the Henchmen."

"But it will be certain death," she said.

"That's why they have to know. Besides, we are Henchmen. We take care of our own."

They made it outside into the pouring rain and stood underneath the northernmost wall of the castle by the sea cliff. It was night, and the waves crashed hard against the rocky shores below.

"Where are the horses?" he said.

"I'll show you," she replied.

Loud brass horns and moaning whistles erupted from inside the castle walls. The clamor of soldiers running along the castle walls began to grow.

Abraham could hear the grinding of the front gate opening. Horses and riders by the score rode out of the castle with hooves sounding like thunder.

"Blazing saddles! They are heading to the Stronghold. I know it." He let out a regretful sigh. "We'll never beat them there. God help them. God help me."

"Abraham, we must go. There is not anything we can do for them now," Clarice said as she dragged him through the darkness. "They are Henchmen. They can handle themselves. Maybe they won't be there. They are savvy, are they not?"

"Yes, but I won't abandon them," he said as he ran over the rain-slick grasses. "I'll help fight."

"But you don't have Black Bane." Clarann stopped running as soon as the castle was out of sight. She caught her breath. "The horses are ahead." She pointed. "See?"

Four horses were there. Two of them had riders. One of the riders was the amazon of a woman, Swan. He could only guess that the other was Queen Clarann. They all met up.

"Ruger?" Clarice asked.

"No." He climbed into the saddle. "Listen, ladies, it would be best if you went back. They are looking for me, not you."

"Where you sail, we sail," Clarann said.

"Sorry, dear, but we aren't sailing. I'm thankful, but I am going to the Stronghold. I have to beat the king's Riders there."

"You won't beat the Golden Riders," Swan said. "They have the fastest horses in the kingdom. They ride like the wind."

With the rain in his face he said, "Then I guess I will have to do the same thing." He felt like a new man and looked at Clarice and said, "What was in the bucket of water?"

"The Guardian Maidens aren't without their own mystical resources. That was ahber root. It restores vitality. Feeling yourself?"

"Sort of." He nodded at the women and tipped his head. "Ladies, I have to go. You need to lie low until it's o—"

"Golden Riders!" Swan said. "We've been spotted."

A half score of the men in full suits of golden armor rode like bats from hell through the rain. They were less than one hundred yards away and closing fast.

"It looks like we are all going the same way now." Clarann snapped her reins. "Eeyah!" Her horse bolted away.

The small group rode like thunder.

Abraham looked over his shoulder. The Golden Riders would ride them down in minutes. He dug his heels into his horse. "Yah! Yah!"

The foursome rode into the brush where a large tree had fallen. Clarann's horse leapt it first, landed hard on the other side, and tossed her from the saddle.

Thunder popped with a loud boom. Lightning streaked across the sky.

Clarann's horse kept running.

Abraham, Clarice, and Swan gathered around the queen. Clarann was holding her ankle. A hard grimace was on her face.

He jumped off his horse and said, "Tell me it's not broken."

Clarann frowned as she nodded and said, "Ride! Ride on!"

"It's too late now." Standing behind the fallen tree, he faced the oncoming riders. He stretched out his hand. "Swan, tell me you brought an extra sword."

"No," Swan replied, "because I only need one." She lifted her sword high, and her horse reared up with a lightning bolt streaking the sky behind her. "Yah!" Her horse jumped the log, and she thundered toward the Golden Riders.

"She's crazy!" Clarice pulled out her rapier and got a wild-eyed look. "I'm crazy too."

"Clarice, don't you dare! Abraham, stop her!" the queen said.

He took a swipe at the reins of Clarice's horse and narrowly missed.

Over the log went the queen's daughter.

The Golden Riders lowered their lances.

Empty-handed, Abraham watched in horror. *They are gonna die!*

A giant black shadow passed over him and the queen.

Gazing up with eyes bigger than saucers, Clarann said, "What in Titanuus's Crotch is that?"

Abraham pumped his fist and said, "Holy sheetrock! It's Simon the Fenix!"

The Fenix dropped in front of the Golden Riders, wings spread wide like a black cloud of death. The fearless knights thundering out of the House of Steel didn't slow their charge. With lances lowered, they spurred their mighty beasts onward at breathtaking speed.

Simon—the Elder Spawn—opened his great mouth. With his eight large eyes narrowing on the charge, he unleashed a stream of misty breath. The white cloud of geyserlike mist covered the charging knights from head to toe.

One of the Golden Riders evaded the stream. His lance busted off of Simon's shoulder with a loud snap.

The horses snorted and bucked as they slowed their pace. They wriggled their mighty necks as if shaking away a swarm of stinging insects. Covered in the milky grime sprayed by Simon, the horses' efforts slowed. The knights climbed out of their saddles at an agonizing pace. Many of them fell from their horses and no longer moved.

Abraham picked up Queen Clarann, climbed over the log, and moved to a spot where he could get a better view.

The horses that didn't fall lay in the grass, frozen stiff. The same could be said for the Golden Riders. Many were stuck in their saddles as if frozen in time. Others were on the ground, snoring loudly and asleep.

He caught up with Clarice and Swan. Both women walked through the field of sleeping men and beasts. Their jaws were hanging open.

"Should I kill them?" Swan asked. Her nostrils were flared, and her chest heaved behind her breastplate. "I wanted to kill something."

"Count your blessings, and let them be. They aren't our enemy." Abraham looked at the queen. "I need to set you down."

Clarann nodded and gave him a quick kiss on the cheek. "I'll be fine."

Clarice steadied her mother.

Abraham approached the great beast, which had nestled on the ground. "My, you just keep on growing like a weed, don't you?"

Simon snorted. He was an ugly creature that looked more like a gargantuan hammerhead bat than anything else—an eight-eyed bat, that is. He was covered in brown fur that appeared coarse.

Abraham touched the Elder Spawn. The thick coat of fur was soft. He petted Simon's flat head, which was almost as big as an entire horse. "Your timing couldn't have been better." He looked at the Golden Riders, not one of which moved a muscle. "Thanks for not killing them. Let's see how this shakes out because you might have to snack on them later." He climbed onto Simon's back.

"Wait! What are you doing?" Clarann asked.

"I'm going to the Stronghold to warn the Henchmen. With Simon, I can easily beat the king's forces there."

With Clarice holding her side, Clarann hobbled over. "We have nowhere to go. We are coming too."

"I'm not getting on that thing," Swan said with a disgusted face. "I'll keep an eye on the Golden Riders. You can all go."

"Are you sure?" Clarice asked her friend.

With a raised eyebrow pointed at Simon, Swan said, "Oh, I'm sure —unless you're going to order me to do so."

"No, I wouldn't do that." Clarice hugged Swan and moved over to the Elder Spawn's monstrous side. "There should be a saddle and stirrup."

"Sorry, ladies," Abraham said as he reached over Simon's side. "Grab some fur."

Abraham, Clarann, and Clarice positioned themselves uncomfortably behind Simon's head. Clarann wrapped her arms around Abraham, and Clarice wrapped her arms around her mother.

Taking in the bizarre situation, Abraham said, "This is crazy. This is crazy!"

"What's crazy?" Clarann asked.

"Nothing. Just hang on. The Stronghold is over a league away. Let's just hope we can beat them there." He firmly patted Simon on the back of the head. "Simon, we're ready for liftoff!"

Simon's monstrous bat wings spread out. He leapt into the sky, let out a ferocious screech, and bolted toward the Stronghold.

73

Simon landed in the Stronghold's muddy courtyard in a matter of minutes. Sopping wet from head to toe, Abraham, Clarann, and Clarice barreled through the front door, taking everyone by surprise.

Clarann and Clarice sat by the fireplace, underneath wool blankets, shivering like leaves. The flight on Simon's back had proven to be a gut-wrenching journey as they flew high and fast through the icy sheets of rain.

Abraham embraced his men with forearm bumps and the women with wet hugs. Everyone in the household was gathered, including the triplets and the servant hags, Elga and Eileen. He stood at the head of the farm table with a foot propped up on his chair. "We have to get out of here, all of us. King Hector's soldiers are looking for me, and they'll be here within the hour."

"Where are we going to go, Captain?" Horace asked. "There is no place in Kingsland for a Henchman to hide. If we flee now, we can never come back."

"We only need to lie low for now." He lifted his voice and scanned every face in the room. "Listen, all of you. Everyone must go. They'll stop at nothing to find me. They'll torture you to find out. I'd think most of you would be thrown back into Baracha." He wiped his face on a towel that Dominga handed him. "There is no choice but to split up and run."

Vern slammed his fist on the table. "We are Henchmen! Sworn to serve the king. We can't go against him whether he is a mad king or not. Perhaps we should turn you in. That would be best for all of us."

"I'm going to break your neck!" Horace said as he stormed around the table toward Vern.

It took Bearclaw and Cudgel to bar his path.

"Easy!" Bearclaw warned. "We aren't against each other."

Abraham had already explained his meeting with the king. He cast a hard look at Vern, who was still seated, and said, "Is that what you want? Is that what most of you want? If it is, I can turn myself in."

No one said a word.

Vern broke the silence. "It's always going to be your word against the king's. Siding with you is a threat to my longevity. If you were Ruger, well"—he shrank in his chain-mail armor—"I'd be more apt to believe you."

"I believe you, Abraham," Cudgel said loudly. "You've never led us wrong. Ever."

"Maybe it would be best if you got on your ugly dragon and flew out of here." Vern got up. "I'm not going to stand around here and wait to fight soldiers from my kingdom either."

"I'm going to kill him!" Horace blurted out.

Bearclaw pushed Horace back and said, "He speaks from the heart. There is nothing wrong with him having doubt. But we all need to remember that this is still the body of Ruger Slade. And if he were here, I think he'd say the same thing."

"The only truth that I can give you is my word," Abraham said. His backpack was on the table, and he hung it over his shoulder. "Perhaps it might be best if I did go. We can meet somewhere else." He scanned the table and found Sticks's seat empty. He'd been so busy that he hadn't even noticed. "Where's Sticks? Where's Shades?"

"They were following Prince Lewis, but they haven't come back," Iris said. "It's been days, and no sign of either of them."

The muscles between Abraham's shoulder blades tightened.

Outside, a horse let out a shrieking whinny.

"They can't be here already!" Abraham jumped onto the table and ran for the door. Solomon beat him to the door and rushed outside right before him.

Simon had a horse frozen in its hooves. One rider leaned over the body of another that was slumped over the saddle.

Even through the heavy rain, Abraham could see they were smaller people and not heavily armed knights. He immediately recognized the shape of one figure and called out, "Sticks!"

She fell out of the saddle and into the mud.

Abraham raced to pick Sticks up. She was pale as a ghost, with clammy skin. She clutched at her bleeding gut. He scooped her up and rushed her inside and set her on the table. "Iris! Iris! Do something!"

Solomon walked inside and set Shades down on the table, head to head with Sticks. "His hand's missing," the troglin said. "He's not breathing."

Shades had a crude bandage wrapped around his bloody stump. He was out cold. Sticks, on the other hand, was barely breathing, and her eyes fluttered open and closed.

Holding Sticks's hand, Abraham said, "Talk to me. Talk to me, Sticks! Who did this to you? Prince Lewis?"

Sticks managed to say a soft "Yes."

Iris leaned right over Sticks and asked, "Did you use the salve I gave you?"

With a nod, Sticks said, "On Shades. He was worse than me. Did I save him?"

"Doesn't look like it," Vern said.

Everyone glared at Vern.

"What? Look at him. Death happens. We're all lucky we made it this far."

Iris tore Sticks's shirt open. "Oh my, that's bad. Why didn't you use the salve on yourself? Don't answer." She held her middle and index finger together. They glowed with a red-hot rosy fire. "This might hurt a bit. Hold her still, fellas." She plunged her fingers inside Sticks's wound.

Sticks's back arched like a bridge, and her wide eyes bulged, but she did not scream.

74

With a groan, Sticks sat up with Ruger and Iris's help. A cold sweat ran down from her forehead to her cheeks. She panted and said, "Thanks."

"Don't do anything crazy," Iris warned. "I sealed your guts with magic fire. It will hold, but it's gonna hurt like the Brand for a while."

Sticks leaned over and touched Shades. "Is he... dead?"

"I'm afraid so," Iris said as she laid her head on the small man's chest. "Not even a beat."

"I tried," Sticks said with a straight face.

Abraham could still see the agony lurking behind her eyes. "What happened?"

Sticks swallowed as everyone gathered around the table, from the stunning Clarann to the scraggly Eileen. "We followed Prince Lewis, Leodor, and Leah to Burgess. They went back to the Cathedral of Elders. Down in the crypt. They uncovered the mirror and lit the candlestands."

Abraham's skin crawled. He remembered the last time he'd been down in the crypt.

Sticks went on. "Images of Big Apple, Fleece, and Lord Hawk appeared. They spoke and talked about their plans."

"You heard all of it," he said.

She nodded. "Lewis and Leodor have already turned on the king. As soon as King Hector removed the Brand, they went back to their old ways."

Clarice spoke up and said, "Leah is with them. I can't believe that. She'd never betray the crown. Never."

"Leah is dead," Sticks said quietly. "The Leah you see is not the one that you know. Raschel the assassin used the Ring of Tarsus to take her form."

Clarice let out a gasp, and her eyes watered as her mother put a comforting arm around her shoulder. "I'll kill Lewis. I swear it!" she said through gritted teeth.

"What else?" Abraham asked.

Sticks cleared her throat.

"Get her a drink," Horace ordered.

"Big Apple is waiting for the king. He wants to trap him in the Spine. Their lair is located at the bottom of the Spine, west of Titanus's Crotch." Sticks grabbed Abraham by the forearm. "Leodor has greatly deceived King Hector. He says that the stones are only meant to be used individually or as a whole. The king is going mad with power, and he will eventually destroy himself if the Sect doesn't first."

"We need the other stones," Abraham said.

She shook her head. "You will never find the stones. Big Apple took them out of this world. I believe he hid them in your world."

"He wouldn't be hiding them if they didn't matter." Abraham stroked his chin. "I need to get back home and find them." He put his thoughts aside. "What happened to Leodor, Lewis, and Raschel?"

"After they thought they'd killed us, they sealed us in the crypt, leaving us for dead. I had enough of Iris's salve to keep us alive and escape."

"So, they think that you are dead, and they don't know that we know this," he said.

"I don't see how. They won't have contact again with Big Apple either until they make it to the lair."

"You know this for certain?"

"Big Apple said so."

Abraham moved from the table and paced around it. "Finally, we have an advantage that they don't have. We have to find the king and warn him."

"He marches to the Spine. No doubt that Prince Lewis will lead him to that trap," Horace offered. "Will the king take your word over his own son's?"

Abraham glanced at Clarann. "Probably not. Does Prince Lewis still have Black Bane?"

"He does," Sticks said. "Big Apple says the other side wants it as a trophy."

"Yeah, that's the same thing they told me."

"You'd think they'd want the crown as a trophy," Shades said.

Everyone looked at the dead man on the table. Shades's eyes were still closed.

"What's everyone looking at?" he said.

The Henchmen exchanged shocked, bewildered looks.

Iris put her ear on his chest. "His pumper beats again."

"Of course it does," Shades said. "I managed to slow my heart rate down so that I wouldn't die. I've just been resting." He kissed Iris on the top of her head and sat up. He held his stump before his eyes. "This is a wee bit of a problem, though."

Sticks embraced Shades and said, "I never thought I'd say this, but thank the Elders you're alive."

Shades stroked her hair. "I'm the one that owes you." He swung his legs over the table and kicked Vern in the nuggets.

Vern doubled over. "I guess I had that coming."

"Captain, what about the Golden Riders? They'll be here soon. It's time we departed and met at the Rendezvous."

"The Rendezvous?" Abraham had never heard of the place before, but a part of him thought it sounded familiar.

"Aye, our hiding spot. It wouldn't be the first time we've been in poor light with the king and many others," Horace said.

The sound of horses galloping through the rain caught everyone's attention. All of them turned toward the door.

"Looks like our time is up," Solomon said.

"No, I have a better idea." He approached the door and smiled. "Simon can keep them at bay. For a long time."

He flung the door open, expecting the see Simon the Fenix guarding the courtyard. The rain came down in heavy drops. Simon the Fenix was gone. Only two score riders remained.

He closed the door, put his back to it, and said, "Henchmen, we have a problem."

75

Vern stared out one of the portal windows and said, "I'm not fighting them again, only to be hunted down and get my neck stretched later." He eyeballed Abraham. "No offense. I believe the story, but will they? I doubt it."

Abraham quickly got over the shock of Simon being gone, realizing he shouldn't have been surprised, for the Fenix came and went as it pleased. He said to Horace, "I need a banner of negotiation."

"Aye." Horace hustled away.

"They'll kill you if you go out there," Vern said. "The Golden Riders are a death squad. They don't accept surrender."

"Maybe they'll accept some reason." Abraham looked out the portals. The Golden Riders' steel armor was trimmed in gold. They wore great helmets fashioned like the heads of lions. The rider in the very front was very big. "Is that Pratt?"

"It's got to be. There's no bigger man in the Guardians than him," Vern replied. "What are you going to do, go out there and shake his hand? He'll kill you." Vern took off his sword belt. He handed it to Abraham. "Take this. You'll need it."

Abraham put a hand out and said, "No, I'm fine."

Horace returned to the room, holding a small flag. It had a thin orange stripe in the middle of a white field. "I'll go with you."

Sticks hustled over to Abraham. She was bent over slightly. "Me too."

Together, the three of them strode out into the rain.

Abraham stopped twenty yards from the row of knights. Holding the banner, he said, "Wait here." He moved ten yards closer to Pratt and lifted the banner high. "I want to talk."

Pratt removed his helmet and handed it to the rider on his left. Glowering at Abraham, he said in a rugged voice, "Golden Riders don't negotiate with traitors, escapees, or anyone else, for that matter."

"You might not like me or Ruger Slade, but when have you known either one of us to lead you wrong?" Abraham lowered the flag. "Can you say the same about Lewis and Leodor, two men that you know tried to kill the king? King Hector took the Brand from them. They are up to their same old tricks."

"I don't care," Pratt said.

"You always were looking for a fight, Pratt," Horace said.

"No, I'm looking forward to retirement." Pratt eyeballed the Stronghold. "This might make a suitable place."

"You can have it," Abraham said, "if you hear me out. And if you value your men, as I do mine, we can part ways without any blood on our hands. Listen, and if you don't agree, I'll come in peace. All of us will."

"Let me guess, if I don't, you'll fight all of us to the death." Pratt chuckled lowly and rubbed his lantern jaw. "Hmm... I can respect that. Spit it out."

Sticks rattled off everything she'd told the Henchmen minutes before. She didn't miss a single detail but added a few.

Tall in the saddle, Pratt sat in silence.

"Come on," Abraham said. "You saw those tanks. The machine guns. That's going to take over Titanuus if we don't stop it. We are the only hope King Hector has."

Pratt flexed the metal gauntlets covering his hands. He scoffed. "I hate to miss out on an opportunity to fight, but the woman's words ring with truth. Bloody blades!" He shook his head. "What are you going to do?"

"I have to try to warn King Hector."

"Ha, you won't get within a mile of him," Pratt said.

Abraham eyed the knights, grinned, and said, "Yeah, but I have an idea."

76

"May fortune favor the foolish," Abraham said.

He wore a suit of Golden Knight armor. So did the rest of the Henchmen as they rode north toward the Spine.

"Who said that, someone in your world?" Sticks asked. She rode to the right of Abraham, while Horace and Pratt were on the left.

"Captain James Tiberius Kirk," Abraham said. "*Star Trek IV, the Voyage Home*. He quoted another person. I think it was Latin, but I don't know who said it originally." Oddly enough, he found his situation similar to the *Star Trek* movie, where the whittled-down crew of the *USS Enterprise* had to time travel with two whales to save the world. "It wasn't the most popular movie in the series, but I liked it."

"Humph," Sticks said quickly.

The Henchmen, along with a handful of Golden Riders, hadn't stopped moving since Pratt agreed, surprisingly, to the idea. The big, gruff man had a better head on his shoulders than it appeared. The next tricky part was getting close enough to King Hector while hoping the king hadn't completely lost his mind to the power of the Crown of Stones.

"There isn't any hiding where they are going," Horace said.

Tark and Dominga were still riding far out in the front on scout duty.

"They march thousands of soldiers. They even took more from the Wall."

The moment when the Henchmen rode through the Shield of Steel was bleak. The great doors were gone. The enemy had taken them. The forces of Southern Tiotan, however, were nowhere in sight. The King's Army scouts stated that they'd moved back north, toward the sea. They left the path to the Spine wide open. As far as Abraham was concerned, King Hector was being led into a trap.

Making it to Giant's Vein River took over three days of hard riding. The company crossed the river and moved toward the Spine. Late on the third night, they made camp.

Sitting by the campfire, Horace said, "The King's Army moves slow compared to us. We will catch them late in the day tomorrow. But I'd say that they will be in the bottom of the Spine by them. I wouldn't want to navigate those mountains with any army. The terrain is too dangerous."

"The king thinks he is invincible," Abraham said. He chewed on a piece of dried meat and drank from his water skin. "No doubt Lewis and Leodor have caught up with him. I am sure that he has the king's pride puffed up."

"What sort of son could betray such a father?" Pratt said. He was lurking nearby, sharpening his sword with a stone. "King Hector is a good man. It is something I never understood about Lewis. He was treated well."

"Perhaps too well," Clarice said as she and her mother joined Abraham by the fire and sat down. "Lewis has always been an entitled brat. May the Elders help Kingsland if he ever gains the crown."

"And I thought he might have turned the corner the last time we saved him," Abraham said. "Listen to me everyone. If Ruger comes back, you know the drill."

"We'll fill his ears with your plans," Horace said. "We understand now."

"I need to go back. I need to tell them what is going on," he said. "If I could only control it."

"Isn't that the problem? Isn't that what the Sect wants to do?" Clarann asked.

"Yeah. Be careful what you wish for."

He warmed his hands at the fire. The rain had stopped a day before, but he was still damp all over. The armor, though light, was heavier than what he was used to as well. Even the queen and princess had armor on as well. It wasn't a good fit but was good enough to fool someone from a distance. Not all the Golden Riders were tall, only most of them.

"Everyone get some rest," Abraham said. "The crack of dawn will be here before you know it."

The present company moved away. Some of them lay on their bedrolls and others underneath a blanket. Clarann and Clarice were both yawning when they left. Pratt had set up a tent for them to sleep in.

Only Sticks and Horace remained with Abraham. "I said 'everyone.'"

"We aren't everyone," Sticks said.

"Look, I'm going to get some shut-eye too." He scooted back to a spot where his feet were several feet from the flames. He lay his head back on his bedroll and looked up into the odd pattern of stars. "Do you have names for the stars in the sky?"

With a heavy upward stare, Horace said, "They are named after the Elders." He pointed at the sky. "That's the Elder of Turtles. That's the Elder of Flowers. That's the Elder of—"

"I get it." Abraham closed his eyes. "It's not very different from back home. Our stars are named after legends and heroes from an age long ago. Geez, I can't believe I'm talking about this. Those aren't my stars, but they should be, and if they are not, then I must be at least a galaxy away from home." He sighed. "This can't be real."

Solomon plopped down beside Abraham. "Now isn't the time to start doubting. Not when we are so close to the end. It's real. You have to believe it's real. I have to believe it's real."

Abraham clicked his steel-shod boots together, yawned, and said, "There's no place like home."

"If only it was that easy," Solomon said. "But I don't think those ruby slippers would ever fit on my feet." He lifted a hairy two-foot-long foot. "That would be expensive."

"I bet. Try and get some sleep." He settled in for the night.

The campfire's embers crackled. The soft rustling of the company settling down surrounded him. The fire's warmth ran from his head to his toes. With a soft breeze passing through the night, he drifted off into a heavy slumber.

He woke from his sleep, sitting up and gasping for air. The stars in the sky were long gone. So were the Henchmen.

77

BACK HOME

Dr. Jack Lassiter slapped Abraham rapidly on the cheek. He snapped his fingers in front of his face. "Who do we have with us today?" He made a throaty laugh. "It's very hard to tell who I am dealing with when I inject you."

Abraham's veins were burning like fire, but they started to cool to an icy feeling. His eyes shifted side to side. He could see Dr. Jack and the zillon woman, Ottum. They were riding in the back of an ambulance on a bumpy road. He was strapped in to the gurney.

Don't say a word. Figure out your circumstances first.

Dr. Jack kept his finger in Abraham's face and said, "Watch my finger."

Abraham glared at him.

"Hmm... look at those brooding eyes. I think this is Ruger. What do you think, Ottum?"

The zillon woman leaned over Abraham. Her voluminous, pitch-black, probing eyes searched his. "I think it's Abraham."

"Really, why so?"

"I see softness, perhaps panic."

Dr. Jack shook his head. "I saw more softness that last time we shot him. Of course, we can't say for sure if this experiment is working at all." He pinched Abraham's cheek. "Of course, you aren't going to tell us, are you? You're being stubborn, aren't you?"

Looks like me and Ruger are on the same page. They don't know who is who. That's a good thing.

The bumpy ride jostled the cabin.

Dr. Jack slipped into his seat. "Heh heh heh." He grabbed a black strap that hung from the ceiling. "It's like riding in the back of a deuce."

"What is a deuce?" Ottum asked.

"A big military transport truck. I used to be a soldier. Spent time in the jungles in Vietnam. God, I'm old."

Abraham kept his heated stare on the man. He didn't hate many people, but he hated Dr. Jack.

A soldier, huh? Maybe he'll pick up a sword so I can kill him. One slice, and off with your big ol' tater head.

The truck's brakes squealed, and it came to a stop.

Abraham's gurney bumped to the front of the cabin.

Seconds later, the back doors were opened by Otis and Haymaker. They hauled Abraham, gurney and all, out of the ambulance with their long, powerful arms.

He didn't look at either one of them. His eyes slid from side to side. He was inside the abandoned train tunnel where the Time Tunnel had been set up.

I wonder where Luther is.

A few seconds later, he got his answer. Luther was strapped in a gurney just like his. Both of them had been placed behind the five computer stations standing in front of the Time Tunnel. Luther was hooked to an IV with orange fluid. Propped up at a forty-five-degree angle, the old man was twitching his fingers underneath his wrist restraints. Abraham wanted to scream. *What have you done to him?*

The Time Tunnel was in full operation. The lights in the main center ring glowed like blue star fire. Inside the ring was the tunnel made up with the metal plates of King's Steel. More plates were there this time. The patches in the tunnel had been filled in. It ran deeper into the mountainside. A row of train cars loaded with tanks and racks of assault weapons was being pushed into the tunnel, where citizens of Titanuus waited.

Dr. Jack stood beside Abraham, watching the railcars crossing from one world to another. "Amazing progress, isn't it?" He pointed at the stacks of goldlike bars that looked like the King's Steel. "And that's what made it all happen, thanks to Prince Lewis winning back favor with King Hector. He shipped it out immediately. Now, here we are. The Time Tunnel is complete, and only one thing is missing."

Abraham kept his lips sealed as he searched the area. He saw Colonel Drew Dexter and Eugene Drisk milling about with the other scientists. They were checking computer screens and giving orders. Dozens of armed guards were there too. The tunnel was a hive of activity. He didn't see any other familiar faces—no sign of Smoke, Sid, or Mandi, which gave him some relief.

"Come on, Abraham, talk to me. I know it's you," Dr. Jack said. "I've had plenty of patients with schizophrenia. Enough to know the difference between you and Ruger." He put a cigar in his mouth. "Man, I wish they'd let me smoke in here."

Seeing Luther spasm, Abraham's heart softened, and he broke down and asked, "What are you doing with Luther? He's no part of this. Let him go."

"The moment he got involved, he became a part of all of this." Dr. Jack looked at him with his dark beady eyes. "There is no way out now. Besides, being older, he's a prime candidate to start a new life on Titanuus."

"What do you mean?"

Dr. Jack pointed at the Time Tunnel. A smaller tunnel had been built to the left of it, standing about seven feet high. It was pitch-black inside, but the small outer lights of the metal ring glowed orange. "That's a portal, one of the random ones that pops up randomly in the tunnels. We caught it, so to speak, thanks to our friend on the other side, Fleece. You see, he has mastered combining the magic of his world with the technology of our world. Heh heh heh." He rolled the cigar from one side of his mouth to the other. "That's the test gate."

Abraham flexed against his bonds. "Then test it on me!"

"No, we want to see how this goes first. And we are using your friend to let you know that we mean business." Dr. Jack flagged down Colonel Dexter. "Are we ready?"

Dressed in a black suit of camouflage clothing, Colonel Dexter said, "Absolutely."

Dr. Jack looked at Luther and said, "Then take him away."

Luther cast a nervous look in Abraham's direction and said, "I'll be all right." Otis and Haymaker unhooked the IV and pushed him toward the tunnel.

The black image inside the smaller Time Tunnel twisted with vibrant colors. An image formed, showing Fleece standing on the other side. His hands glowed with white fire inside the sleeves of his robes.

Standing behind the computer station closest to the small tunnel, Eugene Drisk pounded away at the computer keys. "The moving portal is intact. Now is the time to cross. Go now!"

Otis shoved the horrified Luther into the doorway.

Fleece grabbed the gurney on the other side and ripped him through. The image on the other side of the tunnel went black.

Eugene feverishly tapped the keys. "Where did he go?"

Abraham craned his neck. He could see Eugene's monitor clearly from his position. The screens were all black.

"We put a tracking fluid in him. It's supposed to send us his vitals from one side to the other. In theory, that is. We only have the inanimate mastered. Not the living."

"Couldn't you have tested on a rat?" Abraham yelled.

"We aren't in business with rats. We are in business with people. People with a lot of money, something the animal *and* plant kingdom can't offer."

"I don't have any vitals. I don't have anything," Eugene said. "It's as if he disappeared completely."

"No, wait." Colonel Dexter pointed at the larger tunnel.

Fleece stepped into view from the other side. He dragged the gurney behind him. Luther lay on the bed with his head rolled to the side and eyes closed. He didn't move a muscle.

Colonel Dexter walked right up to the Time Tunnel and stood across from Fleece. He looked toward Luther and asked, "Is he dead?"

The shadowy hood of Fleece nodded.

"I'm going to kill you, Jack," Abraham said. His jaws clenched, and his fists were balled up. He'd never ever had any urge to kill a man in cold blood until he met Jack.

"Don't be so dramatic. Luther was old. Chances are that he had a heart attack." Dr. Jack pulled Abraham over to Eugene's computer station. "What happened?"

"We are checking the readout." Eugene glanced at Abraham. "A shame about your friend. He could have been a true pioneer. Like us." He rubbed an eye. "It's possible that he might still be alive. He could have soul swapped, but we'll never know." He punched the keyboard. "Bloody systems should have worked."

"Why don't you go through it? You've been through before," Abraham suggested.

"That's what we brought you for, you blundering fool," Eugene said.

"You know, you're going to die. Ruger is coming for you."

Eugene paled. "Shut up!"

"It's only a matter of time."

"The only reason that you or he is still alive is because you are the only one coming back and forth through the soul swap. But once we are able to keep the tunnel open for the living, that won't matter anymore. You'll be dust in the wind once this is over."

"Quit bickering and get this thing working," Dr. Jack said. "Otis, get Mr. Jenkins out of the gurney. He can walk, but keep him bound up and all eyes on him." He kicked the gurney's wheels. "I'm tired of rolling this thing around."

Abraham was moved upright. The orderlies left a straitjacket on him and kept their stun rods ready in hand. Abraham could run, but he had nowhere else to go. He had to see things through.

Colonel Dexter flagged Jack and Eugene over. Drew stood in front of the Time Tunnel, eyeing Fleece. Big Apple and Lord Hawk had joined the wraith.

"What is it?" Dr. Jack asked Big Apple.

The horned halfling huffed on a cigar and said, "We believe it is going to take more magic to keep the portal open and be able to get it to work as you wish."

"How do you know this?"

"Fleece is the most adept user of magic in all of Titanuus. He can sense what the issue is. He knew the moment that this man died." Big Apple pointed at Luther. "You need power on our end that is more permanent. You'll need to harness the Crown of Stones's power."

"The king's crown, you say?" Dr. Jack said. "I thought that wasn't a factor."

"So long as it is incomplete, then no man can wield it, but"—Big Apple glanced up—"if you use it to power this ring, it will strengthen the tunnel. Bring me the two that you have in your possession. Perhaps that will be enough to give it a try."

"What about King Hector?" Dr. Jack asked.

"He's marching on the lair, but he is being taken care of. I wouldn't be surprised if he was dead already. But we'll know soon enough. I have scouts in the sky." Big Apple eyed Ottum. "Zillon dragon riders will be reporting soon. And we should have your trophy, the sword Black Bane as well. Perhaps you can kill Abraham with it. Ruger too."

"We'll shoot Ruger before he makes it within one hundred yards of me," Eugene said. He eyed Dr. Jack. "This plan is worth a try. The addition of magic might be just what we need. I can rig something up for Fleece."

"Do it," Dr. Jack said. "Big Apple, keep me updated on the king's location. I don't want any surprises."

"What do you want us to do with him?" Big Apple asked of Luther.

Dr. Jack replied coolly, "I don't know—feed him to a dragon."

Even though Abraham couldn't see Fleece's face, he could see his diamond-hard eyes boring into him like a drill. A moment passed as their eyes locked. Fleece broke off the stare and looked down at Big Apple. His shiny eyes fixed on the collar. Then he dragged Luther's gurney behind himself as they moved away.

What was that? With a strange shiver up his spine, he pushed by the orderlies as he moved after Dr. Jack. "You know, you are really sick. Aren't you sworn to help people?"

"If you are talking about the Hippocratic Oath, well, yeah, you'd be right. But that was written centuries ago, you know, before universal health care." Dr. Jack grabbed a chair outside one of the trailers and sat down. He propped his feet up on the table. "Sit down, Abraham. Relax. Who knows? Maybe when all of this is over, we'll find you a cozy place to live in one of Titanuus's prisons."

Abraham sat down in a folding chair. "I didn't ask for this. Luther didn't ask for this either. This all happened because of what you did."

"There are always incidental consequences on the journey to universal greatness. Don't you realize what we have done? You, of all people, should understand. We've created a gateway to another world." Dr. Jack dabbed his forehead with a handkerchief. "You could have had it better than anybody if you only cooperated. You could have been an ambassador to both worlds."

"Just so you know, I gave King Hector your offer. So I kept my end of the bargain. You can't blame him for wanting to fight it out. That's what any one of us would do."

Jack wagged his fingers. "No, no, no, read your history. Most kings compromise."

"Oh yeah, that's right. I forgot those scenes in *Braveheart*. Thanks for reminding me, Longshanks."If he wasn't in a straight-jacked he would've wagged his finger at Jack. "And how did that end?"

"Robert the Bruce took England out," Otis said.

Jack glared at Otis and said, "Will you shut up?"

"Sorry, Dr. Jack." Otis stepped away.

"Listen to me, Abraham, this fight is over. There isn't stopping progress like this. We've either opened a gateway to another dimension or created a bridge across the universe."

"Or all of this is a part of my imagination. I'm hoping for the latter, considering my fate is sealed." He crinkled his nose. "Say, Otis, could you scratch my nose? I've got a bad itch."

"How about I break it? It won't itch after that," the orderly said.

"You really have a poor bedside manner."

Jack pulled a small case out of his pocket and opened it. It contained another syringe. "You know I can send you to Titanuus whenever I want and bring you back the same. It's only a matter of time before I master it. All I know is that the lightning strike made you special. It changed your DNA." He eyed the needle. "But I think that DNA can be replicated if all else fails with the portals. Once we control them, I think I'll be able to code the body that someone jumps into."

"Aren't you full of clever ideas, playing God and all?"

"We are talking about immortality. What is more godlike than that?"

"No one lives forever in Titanuus either, moron. In case you hadn't noticed, they have dragons over there!"

"Otis. Haymaker. Secure him." Dr. Jack plunged the needle into Abraham's neck. "Next time you see a dragon, give him a kiss for me."

79

TITANUUS

Abraham woke with his face in the dirt. Someone was shaking him.

"Captain! Captain!" Horace said, rolling Abraham over onto his side. "Are you well? You appeared to faint."

"Yeah, I probably did. It's me, Abraham."

The sun was shining overhead.

"Oh." Horace lay on his belly.

They were on a bluff, looking down upon a valley below the base of the bottom of the Spine. The King's Army had gathered down there, numbering in the thousands. They were making a steady march toward the winding hills of the Spine. Foot soldiers led the way, followed by heavy cavalry and support troops.

"So we caught up with them?" Abraham asked. "Have we made contact with the king?"

"No, this just happened. You, or Ruger, hadn't made up your mind on how to approach it." Horace took a knee and stood up with a grunt. "What do you think?"

"I think we'd better act quick." He eyed the sky. "Keep a lookout for zillon dragon riders. I know they are out there. The other side told me." He put a hand on Horace's shoulder. "And keep an eye on me too. They have me jumping back and forth like a frog on a lily pad. It's getting old." He made his way down the hill where he met up with the others.

Pratt stepped forward and asked, "What is the plan, Ruger?"

"It's Abraham—ah, heck, never mind. Does it even matter at this point? Man, I feel like the Tin Man in his suit of armor." He pinched the bridge of his nose. "Anyway, we won't stand here, watching from a distance. The King's Army will see us if they haven't already and get suspicious. The sooner we meet with him, the better."

"What are you going to do? March up to the king and tell him that his son the prince betrayed him again?" Pratt said.

"I wanted you to do that?"

"Prince Lewis will skin me alive," the Guardian said.

"We all need to get as close as we can. It's the only way to keep King Hector from getting slaughtered." He glanced at the distant hills. "The Sect will be waiting with an army of guns and big tanks. We have to stop the king. Now, they want the crown to keep the tunnel open. We can't let them have it."

"Why don't we destroy it?" Horace said.

"If there is no other way. This is the only way. It's going to have to be done one way or the other. Who's with me?"

"Death before failure," Horace said.

All the Henchmen nodded. Even Pratt.

Solomon brought Abraham's horse over. "This is big, isn't it?"

"Why do you say that?"

"I can feel the hair standing up on my neck. I've been lost here for decades, and I've never felt a feeling like this. If it happens, it happens." He offered his huge hand to Abraham. "I just want to say thanks for trying."

Abraham shook his hand and said, "Do you still want to go home?"

"I'm not sure. You?"

"Honestly, I think I'm ready to go back now that I know my past wasn't my fault. It was theirs. There's no telling how many lives they ruined. I just know that I have to stop it."

"I support you." Solomon looked at all the people dressed in the full armor of the Golden Riders. "Man, I wish I could have fit into a suit of that cool armor."

"Well, stay out of sight."

"Don't worry about me. Once we hit the Spine, they'll never find me. Besides, I have an idea."

Abraham raised a brow. "You do? What is it?"

"I'll surprise you."

Led by Pratt and Abraham, the Henchmen, with full helmets on, rode onward and joined up with the King's Army. The soldiers they passed saluted the Golden Riders as they trotted their horses by them. Many of the king's men let out encouraging cheers as they headed deeper into the front ranks.

Pratt cleared his throat and said to Abraham, "I'm not the sort of man that is good with crafty words. Never in my life would I wish to accuse the king's son of treason. I cannot lie either. What should I say?"

"Tell him that you have a message about Ruger, just for him."

"I'll never get by Prince Lewis if he is there. He'll demand to hear the words himself, and he is my commander." Pratt shifted in his saddle. "I'd rather fight a dozen Gond than do this."

"Tell them the truth. Tell them that Ruger escaped the prison and that you felt he should hear it directly from you. That's not a lie, now is it?"

"Well... no, I suppose." Pratt turned his head aside and pointed. "Ah, there is the king's banner." Pratt kept looking around as though he was nervous. He continued to shift in his saddle.

"Play it cool, Pratt. You have to do this for king and country."

"What does *play it cool* mean?"

"Being more like Shades."

"Ah, I think I can understand."

Abraham caught the first glimpse of King Hector. Surrounded by a host of the King's Guardians, he wore a black suit of armor trimmed in gold plate, with a white fur cloak over his shoulders. The Crown of Stones shined dully in the sunlight. Melris, Prince

Lewis, Leodor, and Leah were all riding close to his side. His heart jumped.

Prince Lewis was the first to turn around at the sound of the Henchmen's approach. He wore his black cape and had Black Bane strapped between his shoulders. He cut through the Guardians with Leah in tow. "Pratt, what are you doing here?"

With his helmet still on, Pratt bowed and said, "I bear a message."

"Take your helmet off, fool! I can't understand a word you are saying."

Pratt removed his helmet, hooked it underneath his arm, and said, "I wanted you to know that Ruger Slade has escaped from the House of Steel. Our forces are searching for him now."

"Did you search for him at the Stronghold?" Lewis said with growing irritation in his voice. His gloves tightened on his reins. "Well?"

"Er... uh," Pratt blanched. "It was the first place we looked, to no avail." He scratched his thick sideburns. "They were gone. Er... escaped and hiding."

Abraham watched as new sweat trickled down the side of Pratt's cheek. *He's cracking like an egg. Too late to abort now.*

Lewis scanned the ranks of the Henchmen disguised as Golden Riders. His stare moved from one person to another. With a froward expression, he said, "Take off your helmets. All of you." He slid his sword from his sheath, but Black Bane remained fastened to his back. "Now!"

80

Slowly, Abraham took his helmet off as the other Henchmen followed suit. With a smile, he said to the shock-faced Lewis, "Surprise." He flung his helmet at Lewis and shouted, "King Hector! You are in danger!"

Lewis knocked the helmet aside with his hand. "I am no such thing!"

King Hector stopped his forces and turned around.

Pratt called out in a booming voice, "It is true, Your Majesty! Your son betrays you!"

"Traitor!" Lewis stabbed the unsuspecting Pratt through the heart with his sword. "Die, you lying dog, die!"

Pratt fell out of the saddle with his eyes frozen wide open. He hit the ground with a loud thud.

"Kill the traitors! Kill the traitors!" Lewis screamed.

"Henchmen! Protect the king!" Abraham spurred his horse forward. He rammed Raschel and knocked her from the saddle. He galloped by the Guardians that were still drawing their weapons and headed toward the wide-eyed king. "King Hector, you must listen! You are in danger!"

The ground exploded underneath Abraham's horse's feet, courtesy of a purple bolt of power hurled by Melris.

Abraham flew out of his saddle and hit the ground like a bag of bricks. He popped up to one knee and found himself surrounded by a ring of spears pointed right at him. The King's Guardians had him dead to rights. He lifted his hands over his head. "King Hector, you must listen! Lewis and Leodor betray you again. I have proof!"

"You have nothing!" Lewis said with rage. "Guardians, kill him!"

"Hold!" King Hector said in a voice that froze everyone in their tracks. His eyes burned with inner fire. The stones in his crown twinkled with mystical life. He moved his horse closer to Abraham and glowered down on him. "This time, you try to assassinate me. How deep will your betrayal go?"

"You must believe me, King Hector. I have been on your side always. You march into a trap. The Sect is waiting."

"Don't listen to him, Father! He is an otherworlder, like them, a possessed man that has only brought you trouble." Lewis slid out of his saddle with his sword in hand. "Let me kill this dog myself."

"I'll handle it this time," the king said. He opened his hand and slowly closed his fingers in a crushing manner.

Abraham choked. His full suit of armor constricted as the king's distant fingers crushed him like a can. His face reddened, and his eyes bulged in their sockets.

"Hector! Stop this madness!" Queen Clarann cried out.

The fiery stare in King's Hector's eyes cooled.

Abraham fell to the ground, gasping. His armor's breastplate had a deep bend in the middle.

All the Henchmen were disarmed, dismounted, and brought to their knees. They were set down in a row beside Abraham, including the queen, who kneeled in front of Hector.

"My king, you must listen to them. They do not lie," she said.

"Of course they lie," Leodor said quickly. "All of them are otherworlders that serve the Sect. We have proven this. The only solace you will find is in their execution. It is the only way to defeat the enemy."

With Clarice by her side, Clarann said, "Search your heart, Hector. I know that you are far too wise to fall for the poison that spills from Leodor's lips. Trust me once more!"

King Hector flicked a hand. The subtle motion flattened the mother and daughter on the ground. "I've heard enough talk from you. Bind them all up. Hands behind their backs. Guardians, ready your swords. I'll end these interruptions once and for all."

"You heard your king. Bind them up," Lewis said with a victorious smirk.

The Henchmen's hands were bound behind their backs, and they were set on their knees, including Clarann and Clarice.

The King's Guardians stood behind them with their swords ready to strike.

King Hector stood on the ground, with Melris, Lewis, Leodor, and Raschel disguised as Leah by his side. They talked quietly among themselves.

A few Henchmen down, Vern leaned forward and said, "Great plan, Abraham."

The Guardian behind him cracked him in the back of the head with his pommel and said, "Silence."

Farther down the row, Tark said, "It's been an honor to serve with you, Abraham. All of you!" A Guardian blindsided him with a mailed fist.

The king turned and faced the Henchmen with a glowering stare ripe with madness. "You are interlopers, invaders, traitors, other-worlders, and betrayers." He glanced at Queen Clarann. "As the king, I am the judge, and I am the jury. The sentence for your actions is death. In my mercy, I will allow one of you to speak a final plea for all. Make it short."

Abraham exchanged a look with Clarann, whose lip was split and shoulders slumped. "Maybe you should."

"No," she said softly. "I can feel his anger. He won't listen to me. My words will only wound him. It must be you. Speak as Abraham."

Down the row to his right, he noticed Sticks leaning forward and staring at him. Her face was expressionless as ever. She winked at him and gave a stiff nod as if to say goodbye. He nodded back to her, to Horace, to all of them. "God help us." He lifted his eyes to the king. "May I stand?"

With his nose in the air, King Hector flipped up his fingers.

Abraham cleared his throat. "I am not Ruger Slade, I am Abraham Jenkins, from another world. Since I have been put into your service, I have faithfully served your will. First, I ask for mercy for my friends. They will fight for Kingsland always. Second," he looked at Lewis and Leodor, "I beg that if you will not believe my words, then use the emerald of truth to test my accusations that Lewis, Leodor, and Leah are all traitors that once again serve the Sect. It happened right after you took the Brand from them."

Lewis stepped forward, gestured at Abraham, and said, "Father, this is preposterous. We've been through all of this. He is a snake, a liar, a curse from another world. I move that you let me strike his head from his shoulders immediately!"

"Have my actions ever shown me to be untrue?" Abraham pleaded.

King Hector lifted his hand. "Silence. You have had your say. My mind remains unchanged. Execute them."

81

braham's heart thumped inside his chest. If ever there was a time to jump back home, that time had come. The king was going to execute him, and the queen couldn't bail him out this time either. She was going to be executed too.

He glared at the smug expressions on Lewis and Leodor. "Boy, the seed of evil must run deep in you."

"That will be enough out of you," King Hector said as he lifted his arm in the air. "Guardians, lift your swords and prepare to strike."

Clarann's shoulders trembled beside his.

"I'm sorry," he whispered to her.

"It's not your fault," she said. "It's mine. I should have always been truthful."

The King's Guardians' swords scraped out of their scabbards. The blades caught the sunlight as they were lifted over the Henchmen's heads.

Abraham swallowed. He hadn't even gotten a chance to explain all that the king was facing. He hadn't warned him about the stones, and he'd never see Mandi again either. He kept his head up.

"It's over," Lewis scoffed.

Abraham started to say, "It ain't over until it's over," but he knew it was. The king had him dead to rights.

An earsplitting shriek that shook bones sounded off in the sky above.

Everyone's heads turned upward.

Simon the Fenix made a slow spiral in the air a couple of hundred feet above.

"It's a sign from the Elders," Melris the Elderling said to the king. "Remember what they said: 'The Spawn of the Elders will heed the call of the one that saves the land.'"

King Hector blinked as though a part of him that had long been dormant had awakened. His arm slowly dropped, and he said, "Guardians, sheathe your weapons."

"Father, what are you doing?" Lewis demanded.

The king's eyes burned like green wildfires, and he said, "I will have the truth!" He spread his fingers out.

Lewis and Leodor were lifted a foot off the ground as their bodies arched backward.

"Who do you serve?"

"Father, nooo!" Lewis cried out. He shook and convulsed as if his soul was being wrenched from his body.

"Your wicked heart is exposed!" King Hector said. "I have seen the truth! The truth has set me—"

Raschel sneaked up behind the king, snatched the Dagger of Death from his scabbard, and stabbed him in the belly.

King Hector threw his arms wide, staggered, and fell down.

"Nooo!" the queen and princess screamed. They ran to the king's aid. Melris knelt beside them.

Prince Lewis landed on his feet and quickly regained his composure. Seeing his dead father on the ground, he climbed onto his horse and said, "I am the king now! Follow my orders! Kill the Henchmen!" He pointed at Raschel. "Bring me that assassin! But kill the Henchmen!"

Loud explosions echoed through the valley, coming from the mountains in the Spine: *Boooom! Booooom! Booooom!*

Groups of the king's soldiers were blasted off their feet.

The tank gunfire kept coming. The deadly shells came down.

Prince Lewis's face drew up with shock. A split second later, he was ripped from the saddle by a tank shell.

"The king is down!" the Guardian behind Abraham cried out. "The prince is down as well!"

"Who is in charge now?" asked the Guardian behind Horace amidst the explosions.

"I am," Leodor called out. "As the king's viceroy—"

"The queen is in charge now!" Horace belted out. "Every Guardian should know that!"

"No, I am!" Leodor said.

Princess Clarice stood up and kicked him in the gut. "Shut up, you old fool!"

Out of the corner of his eye, Abraham caught Raschel sneaking up behind Queen Clarann, her dagger poised to strike. He came to his feet and dashed toward the assassin. "Move! Clarann, move!"

Clarann turned just in time to see the assassin's dagger coming down.

Sticks dove into Raschel and grabbed her wrist in both hands. The pair wrestled over the ground.

Abraham tried to free his hands. He twisted his strong hands free from the knots.

Raschel flipped on top of Sticks and punched the dagger down.

Abraham caught the woman's quick hands just in time to save Sticks from being gored. He wrenched the dagger free.

Sticks took the Dagger of Death out of his hands and jabbed it into Raschel's chest. "Remember me!"

Raschel let out an abrupt croak. Her body spasmed. Her face turned from that of Leah to the face of the dusky beauty Raschel, and she died.

"Thanks," Sticks said as she tucked the dagger into her belt. "Time to get out of this armor." She started stripping it off.

The tank fire continued to erupt all around them.

"Captain, what do we do? We need a leader, or we are doomed." Horace said.

Queen Clarann clung to King Hector. She rocked him in her arms with tears streaming down her face. "He was a sweet man. Honest. This foul crown corrupted him."

"Your Highness, you must make a decision," Abraham said. "Your soldiers are being slaughtered."

"Certainly." With plenty of witnesses among the Guardians and the Henchmen, Queen Clarann said, "I declare Ruger Slade is the full-fledged Guardian Commander." She eyed him. "End this madness. Save Titanuus."

He nodded at her, turned his back, and said to the Guardians, "Cut the Henchmen loose. Get on your horses." He slapped his hand on Horace's back. "Get them organized. We have to get away from those tanks."

From the high peaks of the Spine's jagged hills, a small wave of ten zillon dragon riders flew over the army. They soared over one hundred feet in the air and dropped small objects from their saddles.

"What are they doing?" Sticks asked.

The objects plummeted to the ground and exploded among the troops.

"Holy sheetrock! They're dropping hand grenades!" Abraham said. "Crap, I need to get up there. He waved his hands, searching for Simon, but he saw no sign of the Fenix. He caught the dragon riders' eyes and stopped waving. "Oops, that was a bad idea. Incoming! Incoming!" He dove to the ground and covered his head.

Boom! Boom! Boom! Boom!

The ground exploded. Bodies went flying. Soldiers started dying. Abandoned horses bolted.

The King's Army was being bombarded.

82

Abraham climbed to his feet and saw Tark and Cudgel waving him over. He ran to them. They were huddled over what was left of Prince Lewis. His body was missing between his head and legs, a sad demise for Prince Lewis. The master swordsman had shown promise, but his heart deceived him.

Tark picked up the battered scabbard of Black Bane. The sword and casing were still intact. "You'll need this, Captain."

Abraham buckled on the sword belt. "Thanks." He checked the skies and saw no sign of the Fenix, but the dragon riders were turning for another pass. "Listen to Horace and get his army out of the tank guns' range. Get the archers shooting at those dragons." He hurried back to the queen.

Queen Clarann wiped the tears from her face. "I can't help but think it is all my fault. He didn't deserve this."

"No, he didn't. He was firm, but he was fair. I'd do anything to bring him back if I could." He glanced at Melris. "Can't you do something?"

"I've done all I can to preserve his body from decay. There is little more that I can do. The dagger's tooth is fatal." Melris surveyed the scrambling army. More tanks and troops were advancing from the

Spine. "It seems the Sect had no plans to work with the likes of Lewis and Leodor very long. They come for the Crown of Stones now."

The crown was still grafted to King Hector's head.

"Well, make sure that they don't get it. You are on our side, aren't you?" he asked Melris.

"Yes, I was sent to aid the king—or the queen—by the Elders."

"Don't they want to play a part in all of this? It's their world being invaded, you know. They could lend a hand."

"They did lend a hand: me," Melris replied. "The Elders spoke with King Hector and decided to not get directly involved. That would only bring war between the Elders. They would rather see how matters unfold."

"So much for tradition." Abraham didn't know what else to do. He put his fingers inside his mouth and whistled. "Come on, Simon!" Another bombardment of grenades exploded all around. "I need you! Those fish-eyed fiends are going to blow this army to pieces."

A dark blot with wings appeared in the sky. It was Simon. He dove to the ground and landed, startling the King's Army.

"It's about time." Abraham hustled over to the huge Fenix, which was the size of at least three zillon dragons. He grabbed a handful of hair and climbed up. He sat in an odd nook in the Fenix's back that was perfect for his legs. He spoke down into Simon's earhole. "See those tiny dragons? Go get 'em!"

With the pounding beating of his wings, Simon launched himself into the air. Abraham watched the field of battle dwindle away below him. A bright twinkle beside the queen caught his eye. His heart skipped. A portal opened between Clarann, Clarice and Melris. Fleece stepped halfway out of the portal, snatched the king's body in his long ghostly arms, and pulled him into the portal. The portal closed. The king was gone, leaving Melris with his jaw hanging.

The queen and princess screamed.

Abraham cried out in disbelief, "Bloody biscuits!"

83

With an aching heart, Abraham took to the sky on Simon's back. He watched the King's Army retreat from the tank's heavy fire. Soon they would be out of range, but the new army of the Sect was still coming. More tanks and foot soldiers of Tiotan and Gond were marching out from the Spine. With the heavy modern weaponry on the ground and in the air, the king dead, and the crown in the enemy's possession, there would be no stopping the enemy. He had to act quickly.

Below, the queen and princess walked with the retreating army, arm in arm, with their heads hung low.

He turned Simon toward the wave of dragon riders bombarding the army. "Simon, get after them. Let's put those lizards to sleep! Permanently!"

Simon bent in the sky, and his bat wings pounded the air. He made a beeline for the flying pack and closed in from behind.

With the wind tearing through his hair, Abraham pulled his sword free of his scabbard. "Black Bane, can you hear me?"

"Of course I can hear you. I am not deaf. Old, possibly. I'm not really sure. How can I help you?"

"I have about ten dragon riders that I could use some help taking out," he said.

"Hmm... that's a lot. Don't you have any other options?"

"Well, I have a Fenix," he said with irritation growing in his voice. He shook the sword. "We are closing in. Do something!"

The zillon dragon riders looked back over their shoulders. Their alien faces filled with shock. They narrowed their eyes and barked orders to one another, and the flock split up.

"Crap!" Abraham said.

Simon snaked through the air after one of the dragons, sticking to its tail end like glue, and quickly caught up.

The zillon on the dragon's back twisted around and threw a hand grenade at Abraham.

Simon bent away from the grenade, opened his jaws, and bit down on the back end of the dragon, taking its tail and legs clean off. The zillon and dragon fell from the sky and blew up when they hit the ground below.

"One down. Only..." Abraham searched the skies, "nine to go."

Three dragon riders dropped in behind him. Each of them was carrying an assault rifle and fired.

Simon barrel rolled through the sky.

Abraham hung on for dear life with his fingers clutching the Fenix's pelt. He twisted his head over his shoulders. The dragon riders raced after the Fenix. Bullets blasted from their barrels.

He had an idea. "Get lower, Simon! Get lower!"

The Fenix dropped and turned back toward the King's Army.

Abraham flew them right over the ranks of hundreds of archers below.

The archers let loose a volley of hundreds of arrows. The feathered shafts ripped through dragons' wings and bodies and impaled the zillon riders. All but one of them plunged to a violent crash on the ground. The king's foot soldiers slaughtered them.

Abraham led the chase after the last two dragon riders. The riders turned in their saddles and fired at him. "Black Bane, now would be a really good time for you to lend a hand!"

"If only I did have a hand. Now, that would be useful. How about this?"

A ball of blue light dropped out of the sky. It crackled with energy like lightning. Keeping pace between the two dragon riders, its sparkling tendrils lashed out. The strands of energy tore through the zillons and dragons. They shook, smoked, and started to burn, their wings and limbs on fire. They dropped out of their saddles and crashed to the hard ground below.

"Yes! Good job, Black Bane!"

"Certainly. Is there anything else?"

The ball of blue energy flew alongside them. Abraham noticed the tanks on the ground still firing and said, "Can you take those tanks out?"

"What's a tank?"

Five tanks were below that Abraham could see. "Those metal chariots on the ground!"

"Oh."

The ball of energy careened downward and smacked right into a tank. It exploded with a loud *boom*. The energy ball disappeared.

"Did I kill it?"

"Yes! But there are more of them."

"I'll see what I can do. After my nap."

"What?" Abraham shook his sword. "Wait. We are in the middle of a war!"

The presence inside Black Bane checked out.

He tugged on Simon's fur and said, "I guess we need to do this on our own. Simon, let's take those tanks out."

Simon landed by the nearest tank, which was nestled at the bottom hills of the Spine. Huge by comparison, the Fenix bit down on the barrel, bent the metal like a spoon, and ripped the gun turret clean off the tank.

The eyes of the three men inside the tank were big as saucers. They climbed out and attacked with short swords in hand.

Abraham hewed them down with three quick thrusts of Black Bane. He searched the area for the other tanks, looked at the monstrous Fenix, and said, "Let's finish them!"

Simon the Fenix took off on his own. He jumped on the top of one tank; sank his clawed feet into the metal; beat his wings, lifting it off the ground; flew toward another tank; and flung the one tank into the others.

The tanks bashed together, turned side over side, and rolled down from their perches in the hills.

Three tanks were down, with two more to go. Abraham raced across the base of the hills, where a tank gun turned toward Simon's backside.

He shouted out a warning: "Look out!"

The tank fired, and the shell hit Simon square in the middle of his back. His wings spread out and quavered. He fell flat on his ugly face and spasmed.

"Nooo!" Abraham raised his sword high. He closed the gap between himself and the tank. With a mighty swing, he chopped clear through the tank barrel, which dropped to the ground.

A soldier popped up from the top hatch of the tank, firing an assault rifle.

Abraham dove underneath the tank and crawled to the other side. He sneaked up on the man, who was craning his neck side to side. The soldier turned Abraham's direction too late. He split open the soldier's skull, grabbed his rifle, and fired into the hole. The tank gunner died.

Simon climbed back to his feet and shook his neck like a wet dog. All eight of his eyes narrowed on the last tank. The tank gun fired at him, and the shell exploded on his chest. He stumbled backward, let out an angry, earsplitting shriek, and stormed the tank. Glowering at the vehicle, Simon expanded his chest. A blast of red-hot fire erupted out of his mouth and curled the metal barrel of the tank gun.

Abraham pumped his sword in the air. "Now that's a Fenix!"

A shadow passed over head.

He glanced up and saw another dragon rider in the sky. This time, a zillon wasn't in the saddle—it was the burly horned halfling, Big Apple. The pair of adversaries locked eyes.

Big Apple grinned devilishly and tossed two hand grenades down at Abraham.

Abraham dove for cover toward the rocks. The world exploded around him.

84

A rustle of armor caught Abraham's ear. His head pounded, and his body ached. He felt as though he had tiny burns all over. He opened his eyelids. The pie-faced Iris had a pair a tweezers. She was picking shards of rock and metal out of his leg.

"Well, look who decided to join us," the mystic said happily. "Glad to see that you had a good nap."

Abraham touched the bandage on his hand. The sky was dark and filled with stars.

"How long have I been out?"

"Only since this afternoon," she said.

He didn't know whether to be surprised or relieved that he was still in Titanuus. Normally in such tragic events, he was boosted from one world to the other. They were in a typical camp, with fires burning nearby, soldiers and Henchmen huddled in groups everywhere.

He noticed Solomon sitting beside him. "How's it going?"

Solomon flipped his big paw at him and said, "Better now that you have awakened, I think. When I plucked you out of a pile of rocks, I thought you were a goner. The King's Armor saved you. I wish I had a suit that could fit me." He shrugged. "Sort of."

Sticks huddled nearby, rocking on her toes. Shades and Horace were with her, sharing a log for a seat.

"So, what is going on?"

"Bad news, Captain." Horace scratched his meaty neck with a finger. "Armies from Tiotan have us boxed in from the south. They outnumber us too. The only way out one way or the other is to fight."

"What about the lair in the Spine?" he asked.

"I can navigate those hills better than any," Solomon said. "I took Dominga and Cudgel with me. We found the lair. It's a huge cave entrance, forty feet high at least and half as wide. A wide channel like a highway leads straight to it. It's guarded by tanks on the road, Gond and soldiers positioned down the length of the road. It's the only way in or out." He shook his head. "It looks impossible to march an army through there. Plus, more tanks and weapons are coming out."

"Yeah well, the Henchmen never needed an army before, did they?" he said.

The group nodded.

He rubbed his face. Dr. Jack, Eugene Drisk, Colonel Dexter, and Big Apple had everything they wanted. The only hope Abraham had was that their theory for completing the Time Tunnel wouldn't work. If that was the case, he'd be stranded. He winced as Iris pulled a strip of shrapnel out of the meat of his calf. *I don't suppose it matters what world I live in. Evil is evil. I have to stop it in one world or the other.*

"I'm ready," Sticks said. Her gaze landed on his. "Just say the word. It all has to end sometime."

"Well, that's the last of the shrapnel," Iris said as she began stitching up his leg. "I'll put some salve on it, and you should be good to go kill something."

"Great. I can't wait." He craned his neck. "So, is the Fenix gone?"

"Yup," Solomon said.

"What about my sword?" He felt the scabbard underneath his hand. "Oh, there it is. This ought to do it. A magic sword, the King's Steel, the deadliest fighters in the world... Who can stop us?"

A military helicopter flew overhead.

Wuppa-wuppa-wuppa-wuppa-wuppa!

"No, no, no, no!"

The Henchmen and armies stared up into the sky.

"What sort of dragon is that?" Horace said.

Abraham forced himself to his feet. He kept it simple. "It's called a chopper."

Solomon stood behind Abraham's shoulders and said, "This is bad. Really bad. Isn't it?"

"It's certainly not better." He buckled on his sword. "Henchmen, gather around."

The Henchmen formed a circle around him, including Clarann and Clarice. The hard-eyed group hadn't softened a bit since he'd first met them. They looked as invincible as ever in their armor.

"This is it. Last call. The final hour. A do-or-die mission. I don't care if any of you back out. You can even though I know you won't." He pointed toward the Spine. "The end is near, and it's in there. We're going to find it!"

"Hear! Hear!" Horace said.

"We are going to beat it!" He slung his son's backpack over his shoulder.

More Henchmen joined in. "Hear! Hear!"

"Because the King's Army has never been defeated, and it won't be defeated today!"

The Henchmen let out battle-hungry grunts.

He lifted his sword high. Everyone joined him, pointing their weapons high into the sky. United, Abraham and the Henchmen shouted, "Death before failure!"

85

Solomon led the trek into the jagged hills of the Spine. The Henchmen, including Clarann and Melris, moved through the night like a snake slithering up a rut. All of them were in full armor but no helmets as they made the rugged climb.

Down on the battlefield, the King's Army attacked at first light. Led by the King's Guardians, under the queen's orders, the soldiers stormed the channel leading into the Spine. They had no choice but to engage as the chopper flying overhead, with dragon riders in tow, whittled away at the army with machine-gun fire and bombardments of grenades.

Abraham could hear the explosions and clamor of battle as the brave soldiers marched forward to their doom. They would be slaughtered if some sort of help didn't arrive soon. He searched the skies. *Simon, where are you?*

He tried summoning the Fenix with whistles and calls but to no avail. Possibly the Elder Spawn had moved on. Still, he kept trying by concentrating. He didn't want to make more noise after they crossed a gap and started down the other side of the mountain. The journey took hours, and the longer it took, the more soldiers died.

Solomon flagged him down.

He slipped up to the front ranks, where he met with Tark and Dominga. She carried a spyglass and handed it to Abraham. They were on a ledge that overlooked a chasm five hundred feet down. The channel deep in the middle made for a perfect roadway.

He put the spyglass to his eye. "Blazing saddles."

The channel road dead-ended at the entrance to the tunnel leading inside the lair. Tanks were positioned down the road thirty feet apart as far as he could see. Gond savages and Tiotan soldiers in suits of chain-mail armor were positioned along the road and hidden in the rocky shelving above them. Hundreds were there in all, but thousands would be needed to penetrate their strategic positioning.

"It doesn't look good, does it?" Solomon said.

"We can kill them," Horace said.

"If we can sneak in behind them, we can fight our way in. That's the only way I can think of," Abraham said. He turned his ear toward the sky. "Everyone get down."

The Henchmen pressed against the rocks as the chopper flew overhead. It hovered for a long time then moved back down over the channel.

"Do you think they saw us?" Clarann asked.

"Doesn't seem like it. Listen up, everyone. We need to make our way closer. Follow me."

Abraham led the way down the slippery slope. The company wouldn't be entirely defenseless. In addition to their weapons, they'd managed to pack away some grenades and assault rifles from the fallen dragon riders. The company made it within two hundred feet of the tunnel entrance.

The morning mist and shadowed canyon shielded them from the sun. Now, they were within earshot.

"Horace, get a message down to Melris and Iris," he said.

The Elderling and the mystic were at the far end of the company.

"Tell them we are going to need some cover."

"What sort of cover, Captain?" Horace asked.

"Fog. Smoke. They should know—something subtle."

A minute later, fog spilled over the rocky ledges where the

Henchmen waited. It came from Iris's and Melris's fingers. It wasn't enough to fill the huge chasm, but it would do for better cover.

Abraham nodded his head at Sticks, Shades, Dominga, and Tark, who weren't wearing the heavy armor. "Lead the way, but if it gets too hot down there, fall back behind us."

"Aye," Tark said.

"You're the boss, Captain," Shades added.

Silently, the group crept down the mountainside.

The chopper came flying up the channel with six dragon riders in tow. They made a beeline on Abraham's position. The fog created by the mystics was blown out of the channel. The chopper hovered right in front of the Henchmen. The alerted Gond and soldiers popped up from their hiding spots and climbed the mountain by the score, with blood in their eyes.

"Everyone get down!" Abraham ordered.

The chopper's machine guns opened fire.

86

With chunks of rock being busted up all around him, Abraham shouted, "Good lord, where is my Fenix when I need him?"

Overhead, dragon riders dropped bombardments of grenades. The Henchmen scrambled over the rocks. Bullets ricocheted off metal armor. Men cried out and cursed.

On his elbows, Abraham crawled behind the lip of the rocky ledges and hunkered down in a crack. The chopper hovered only fifty feet away from them. Its machine-gun bullets pounded the mountainside.

"Take cover! Take cover!" he shouted.

Dust and debris blossomed all over. The more the bullets and grenades chewed up the rocks, the more smoke arose.

Having had little wartime experience, he finally remembered that the Henchmen had their own guns and shouted, "Return fire! Return fire!"

Nearby, the sound of machine guns rattled away. A zillon rider fell from his dragon and fell to a jagged death below.

Melris moved out to the end of the ledge with his purple robes billowing in the wind. He held out the Rod of Devastation. A bolt of scintillating purple energy blasted from the top of the rod and tore into the chopper's body. The chopper veered hard left and spun in circles before crashing and exploding below.

The Henchmen let out a triumphant chorus of cheers.

A grenade fell from the sky landed and beside Melris. The explosion blew his legs out from underneath his robes. He lay dashed against the rocks and bleeding.

"Melris!" Iris called out and rushed to his aid.

Horace walled off the mystic and the Elderling. He screamed at the dragon riders in the sky. "Fight like men, you cowards!"

With the chopper out of the way, Abraham moved out of his cover and scanned the surrounding scene. The armies in the trenches moved like a swarm of ants. Hundreds of enemy soldiers were in the rocks, climbing quickly up the steep banks. They fired their assault rifles and howled for blood.

Tark and Skitts lay on the ledge, firing downward at the swarming foot troops.

The tank guns turned and pointed toward the Henchmen.

"Devil's donuts! We're going to get blown to bits! Everybody move! Everybody move!" Abraham led them away from the gunfire.

"Come on, Iris!" Horace said. "There is nothing you can do for Melris now. Let the Elders take care of him."

Above, the dragon riders made another pass. They closed in quickly with grenades poised to drop from their bony white hands.

Like a black bolt of lightning shot from the sky, Simon the Fenix slammed into the dragon riders. His great jaws clamped down on zillon and dragon. The other dragon riders veered away and scattered.

Down below, Sticks, Tark, and Dominga shot three more dragon riders out of the air. Simon chased away the others.

A tank gun fired. The rocks two dozen feet behind Abraham's head exploded. Rocks started to slide down the mountain.

"Keep moving! Keep moving!" Abraham yelled.

"I'm tired of running. I want to start fighting!" Horace said.

With a glance at the barbarians and soldiers scrabbling up the slopes, Abraham said, "You'll get your chance."

They were outnumbered at least thirty to one, which didn't include the tanks and the other scores of soldiers guarding the tunnel entrance that had yet to move. A bullet whizzed by his face and ricocheted off the rocks behind him.

"Keep moving!" he shouted. "They can't keep shooting at us once we are engaged."

The Gond raced up to the higher ledges in a flanking move. They moved like squirrels over the rocks and positioned themselves in the rocks above the Henchmen, rapidly sealing them in, shutting off their escape from all directions. The Henchmen were trapped.

"Well isn't this a dung heap of fun!" Abraham led them to a small plateau on the mountainside that gave them a good view of the activity below and above.

Sticks, Shades, Tark, and Dominga scrambled up to the spot. They had nowhere else to go. They shot at the enemies aboveground and below. The savages and soldiers fell, only to have three more overtake their positions for each one fallen.

Abraham gripped Black Bane in hand and said, "Well, Horace, you wanted a fight. Now, you're going to get it."

Horace spat juice on the ground and said, "We can kill them."

Simon soared overhead in a black streak. A dragon and rider were crushed in his mouth. Behind him, two more choppers gave chase with machine guns firing.

"Devil's donuts! They have more of those things!" Abraham's heart sank as he watched Simon's tail end take a barrage of bullets.

The Fenix tucked his tail and curled away before disappearing over the ridges. He'd hoped the Elder Spawn would have taken out the tanks and ground troops.

"Run, Simon, run," he muttered.

Bearclaw spun his double-bladed axe. Eyeing the enemy, he said, "It will be a great fight."

Prospero and Apollo drew their pairs of swords.

Vern filled his hands with sword and dagger.

Cudgel readied his two-handed mace.

The advancing enemy stopped. The gunfire ceased. A silence fell over the chasm.

Abraham scanned the faces of their enemies. High and low, the soldiers had halted, poised to attack. He sought out why and quickly discovered the reason. Two of the tanks on the road below had their tank guns pointed right at them. His jaw dropped. The tank guns fired.

The shells rocketed into the small cliff beneath the Henchmen. The shelf gave way as the company was tossed from their feet and dropped into the rocky carnage below.

87

Abraham gasped for air. His wide eyes beheld the Time Tunnel. Otis and Haymaker were on either side of him. He'd been strapped to the gurney again. Ottum stood beside him with a needle in her hand.

She tossed the needle into a waste bin. "How do you feel?" she asked.

"Like punching you in the face." He was upright and positioned behind the five computer stands. Dr. Jack, Eugene Drisk, and Colonel Dexter stood behind the center station with triumphant smiles on their faces. "And them."

"This isn't something that you need get upset about. It is a glorious day. The tunnel is working, and I can go back home."

"What do you mean, it's working?"

"See for yourself." She turned him away from the computer and directly toward the Time Tunnel.

He could see Big Apple, Fleece, and Lord Hawk talking amongst themselves on the other side. Lord Hawk pointed at the fiery gemstones from the Crown of Stones mounted in the ring. They were placed in order at the one, three, five, seven, nine, and eleven o'clock positions. A chronic hum came from the Time Tunnel, almost as loud as the diesel generators.

"It works?"

"No one has passed through it yet, but in theory, according to your experts, yes," she said. She petted his face. "It's a shame that you picked the wrong side to be on. But don't feel bad. Ruger did too."

Dr. Jack and Colonel Dexter broke out in laughter. Eugene Drisk had a gleeful look on his face.

Jack turned and looked at Abraham. "Bring him over. He needs to see this."

The orderlies wheeled him over to the central computer station.

"This is Abraham, isn't it?" Jack asked.

Brushing Abraham's hair out of his eyes, Ottum said, "Yes, it's him."

"Yeah, it's me, jerk. I'm surprised you didn't know that."

"I've been busy." Jack pointed at the screens. "Look at what we have here." He chuckled.

The images were moving on the screens. The images showed aerial views of the canyon leading up to the tunnel on some screens, while Abraham could see soldiers standing on the rocky ledges on the other monitors. They were the same ones attacking the Henchmen. The second screen showed what appeared to be a chopper chasing after the Fenix. Ripped-off flesh and blood dripped from Simon's body. The third screen showed a dusty scene of the Henchmen, including Ruger Slade, half buried in rubble. Abraham's stomach turned into knots.

"Those are drones," Jack said. "I don't know why we didn't think of it earlier."

"I thought of it," the older Eugene Drisk said. He pushed his glasses up the bridge of his nose. "I thought of everything. And thanks to the retrieval of the Crown of Stones, not only will we be able to move back and forth in our own bodies, but we can use the smaller door to soul swap as well. Two men enter at the same time and swap. Just as easy as *Freaky Friday*."

"Why would you want to do that?" Abraham asked with an incredulous look.

Eugene tossed his head back. "Ha! You of all people should know why after being in Ruger Slade's body. Oh, how I can't wait to take it back." He studied the monitor. "I hope the last round of fire didn't damage him too bad."

Jack flipped his hands out and said, "There you have it. A new world awaits. And we have it all under control."

"We who?"

Jack pointed at Big Apple's trio. "The Sect, the Shell, the Corporation, or Drakeland. Does it really matter at this point? We won. We are the conquerors of a bold new world."

Abraham laughed. "Be careful what you wish for. Titanuus is full of surprises."

"I think we've seen them all," Jack said.

"So what do you need me for?"

"Funny you should ask. Quite possibly, we don't, but you make for an excellent test subject," Jack said. "You know, with your special connection to Ruger. After all, you are the one that led us to all of this. If it wasn't for you, we never would have realized the potential to swap our essence from one body to the other." He looked at Colonel Dexter. "We need to fetch Ruger. Bring him here."

"My pleasure," the deep-voiced Colonel Dexter said. He gave Abraham a cocky look. "It's going to be fun catching up with Mandi."

"Look at this!" Eugene pointed at the screen. Simon huddled in the rocks with his wings shielding his back. The chopper's gunfire was tearing him to pieces. "And to think that flying rodent had me worried. It looks like their doom is sealed." He motioned toward the Time Tunnel. "Come on, everything is in order. Titanuus awaits."

With nothing but the Time Tunnel ring between them, the two groups on either side faced off. Ottum stepped forward and stood right beside the tracks leading inside. "I would like to go first." She lifted her narrow shoulders. "I really don't have anything to lose."

"Be my guest," Dr. Jack said.

"Red rover, red rover, let the zillon babe come on over," Big Apple said as he blew a smoke ring from his side to the other side. "He clapped his stubby hands. "Come on, now."

Ottum hopped from one side to the other. She swooned, started to fall, bounced up, and showed a big smile.

Jack clapped his hands. "Hot dog! We've got it mastered."

Abraham dipped his chin to his chest. *This can't be happening. What happened to Smoke and Sid? Are they captured? Somebody has to stop these madmen! I have to do something!* Behind Fleece, Luther and King Hector were lying on separate gurneys. The crown looked as though it had been ripped off King Hector's head. A sick feeling formed in the pit of Abraham's stomach. *Somebody needs to pay for this!*

"Dr. Jack!" a scientist said from behind the central computer station. She pointed at the monitors. "You should come and see this."

A wellspring of hope built up inside Abraham as Jack hustled over to the station.

Jack's eyebrows lifted. He put a cigar in his mouth and lit it. "Well, will you look at that? It appears Ruger Slade has surrendered."

88

What?

Abraham couldn't believe his ears. Ruger wouldn't ever surrender. Nor would the Henchmen.

This can't be right.

"Come and take a look, Abraham," Jack said.

Otis and Haymaker wheeled him over to the station. Sure enough, the dust had settled, and Ruger had his hands and weapons raised over his head. Soldiers were climbing up the rocky trails with swords in hand to greet them.

Jack slapped him on the shoulder. "Tough loss. My gain." He lifted his voice. "Say, Eugene, looks like your new body is coming. He surrendered."

Eugene had stepped to the other side of the Time Tunnel's frame. The smile on his face vanished. He hurried back to the other side. "It's a trap. Ruger Slade never surrenders." He studied the screens and grunted in his throat. "He still holds the sword! Take it from him!"

As soon as the nearest soldier stepped into striking range, Ruger's blade flashed and took the man's head from his shoulders.

Eugene pounded the keyboard. "I told you! I told you!"

"Relax," Colonel Dexter said. "They can't take out five hundred soldiers with assault rifles, and don't forget about the tanks." He fixed his eyes on the monitors. "They don't stand a chan—" He stiffened. "What the hell are those things?"

Abraham watched as the ridges in the Spine's canyon erupted with new life. Terramen, the race of men that looked and walked like snapping turtles, sprouted up all over. Their shells were naturally camouflaged with rock and brush. Their stout arms and legs were thick with scales. Their jaws snapped off hands at the wrists and feet at the ankles. With powerful claws, they tore through chain mail, skin, and chest bone.

"What are those things?" Jack demanded.

Abraham shrugged. "Ninja turtles?"

In a moment, the script of the battlefield flipped. The cameras in the sky caught it all.

Barath, the twelve-foot-tall leader of the terramen, stood down on the road and turned over tanks like they were boxes.

Eugene jabbed his fingers into the screen. "What is that thing? Kill it, Drew! Kill it!"

"Let me get my choppers on it," Colonel Dexter said. He touched his earpiece. "Eagle One! Eagle Two! Is that giant bat dead?" He nodded. "I need you to break away. We have a, uh, well, the thing looks like Bowser. Fly down there and turn it into turtle soup!"

Big Apple crept over to the bunch, jumped on an office chair, and asked, "What seems to be the problem, gentlemen?"

Dr. Jack gave Big Apple a surprised look and said, "It seems we overlooked something. Do you know how to stop those... turtles?"

"Kill them," Big Apple responded.

"That's what I'd do," Lord Hawk added.

The group broke out into a heated argument.

On the screen, the runes in Black Bane's blade glowed red hot. Ruger Slade chopped through soldiers and Gond like a hot knife through butter. Abraham never imagined a sword blade could move so fast. Each stroke took life and limb, heads from shoulders. The Henchmen were rolling. Abraham grinned. *Come on, guys! Come on!*

"Look at this massacre! The Henchmen are going to be here in minutes!" Eugene yelled. "Send more reinforcements! Send more now!"

Colonel Dexter threw up his arms and stormed toward the Time Tunnel. He pointed to the armed guards in the gray tunnel. "Go! Go! Go! Don't let anything or anyone make it into the tunnel!"

The soldiers ran into the tunnel and joined the ranks of the Tiotan army at the end of the funnel.

Abraham caught a glimpse of Fleece hovering between Luther's and King Hector's gurneys.

The Underlord had his bony fingers stretched over both of their faces. He held their faces a moment and pulled his fingers away. He stood tall, tattered ghostly robes drifting around his body. His diamond-hard eyes locked on Abraham then slid toward Big Apple, and he ran his finger across his neck.

Huh?

Big Apple yelled at Colonel Dexter. "How hard is it to kill a man with a bullet? Just shoot him!"

Colonel Dexter poked Big Apple in the chest. "Listen to me, you little billy goat! You don't talk to me like that. I'll stuff you in a suitcase and ship you out of here!"

Big Apple rammed his horns into Colonel Dexter's groin, doubling the man over. "Watch your tongue, fool! In this body, I can tear any man up!"

"We don't have time for this! We have to stop Ruger and stop him now!" Eugene flagged down Ottum. "Put another shot in Abraham's neck! He's not the kind of killer that Ruger is!"

Ottum ran over to the gurney. Otis handed her a shot. She stuck the needle in Abraham's neck and depressed the plunger.

Abraham's head snapped back. His blood churned. Star streaks raced through his eyes. He stood in the heat of battle. Black Bane crashed against another blade. The smelting fires in the sword's engravings cooled. His legs wobbled beneath him. *Crap! I need time to adjust!* His body didn't respond to his thoughts. He and Ruger weren't one.

A Gond jumped from a ledge above him and planted himself on Abraham's back. They tumbled down the hill, rolling without stopping until they hit bottom.

He cracked his head on a rock. Blood ran into his eyes. Black Bane slipped from his fingers. The bearded, burly, wild-eyed Gond grabbed a handful of his hair and punched him in the head over and over.

RUGER FOUND his essence transported back into Abraham's body. His nostrils flared the moment he saw Eugene Drisk.

Eugene, Jack, and Lord Hawk let out a chorus of cheers. They threw up their hands and slapped them together.

"Perfect! Perfect! Ruger is done for!" Eugene shouted.

"You're going to die, Drisk," Ruger stated.

Eugene's and Jack's heads snapped around. Big Apple and Lord Hawk faced Ruger.

"Well, look who's back—Ruger Slade," Eugene said in a gloating manner. "Guess what, Ruger, now that I have you trapped in Abraham's body, I have no need for you anymore. I want the body on the other side." He looked Abraham's figure up and down. "Not this trash heap. So I can kill you and swap with your body next."

"You always were a coward," he said.

"Like any of that matters now. I'm going to be filthy rich for all eternity." Eugene typed on the keyboard as he watched the screen. "Look at that. Look at that. The choppers are taking it to the giant turtle man. I like it! The game is almost over. Someone kill him, will ya? I don't want to ever sense his presence again."

Lord Hawk pulled his revolver. He spun the gun around on his finger. "I'll do it." He pointed at Ruger's head and cocked back the hammer. "Sweet dreams."

"Don't shoot him here. I don't want blood all over my equipment. Stop being such a savage," Eugene quipped. "Take him over to the wall and blast his brains out."

A blaring alarm sounded. Flashing red emergency lights lit up the tunnel.

"What is going on?" Jack said.

"I don't know!" Eugene hammered at the keyboard and shouted at the female scientist beside him, "Fix it!"

She gave him a blank stare.

He shoved her out of the chair. "What idiot set the alarm off, huh?" He pecked away at a few keys. The alarms and red light went off. "When I find out who did that, I'm going to kill them! This was intentional. It was a hack!"

Someone let out a *woo-hoo* whistle. Everyone turned toward the source.

Smoke stepped out from behind a railcar. He held a pistol in one hand and small box in the other. "Listen up, everyone. In my hand is a detonator. And while you slappy happy bunch of idiots have been high-fiving each other, me and my partner, well, my wife, have been planting remote bombs all around.

Eugene's, Drew's, and Jack's wary eyes searched all over.

Smoke pointed his gun at the orderlies. "Listen up, big fellas. Let my friend loose before I put a hole in you."

Otis retuned Smoke's stare with a glower of his own.

Smoke shot the man in the shoulder. "Don't make me ask again."

The orderlies started to free Ruger from his restraints.

"No, no, no, no, don't you dare let him loose!" Eugene pleaded. "Lord Hawk, kill him! Kill him now!"

Lord Hawk smiled at Smoke. He still had the cocked gun pointed right at Ruger's head. Smoke had his weapon pointed at Otis.

"No one is that quick," Hawk said. "But you are welcome to try."

Smoke winked.

Blam!

Everyone jumped as Lord Hawk fell to the ground with a bullet in his head.

Smoke hadn't moved.

Sidney stepped out of the shadows with vapors coming out of her gun barrel. She put her gun on Haymaker's neck. "Finish untying my friend."

Haymaker undid the straps holding Ruger in place.

Ruger jumped away from the gurney and hit Eugene in the face so hard that his neck snapped backward and he hit the desk. The old man was out cold.

"All right, all right, let's all talk here," Jack said as he wiggled his fingers in the air. "What do you want, huh? Just take it. There is too much here to give up."

Colonel Dexter eyeballed the area and said, "There's no bomb in here. I don't see one."

"Oh yes, there is." Smoke held up his phone. "They are hidden."

"He's bluffing," Colonel Dexter said. "He wouldn't kill himself anyway. Or his deceptively pretty lady."

Soldiers were racing back from the front end of the Time Tunnel. They took a knee and aimed their guns at Smoke and Sid.

"John," Sid said. "Show them!"

Smoke pressed a button on his phone. Computer station one, farthest left of the tunnel, exploded. "I have a lot more where that came from. Care to try me?"

"I do," Big Apple grinned. "Fleece!"

Smoke, Sid, and Ruger were yanked up off their feet. They sailed a foot above ground and were violently slammed together. Their weapons were ripped from their fingers by an unseen force. Limbs tangled, they stuck together like glue.

Puffing on his cigar, Big Apple strode over to them, blew smoke in their faces, and said, "Nice try, fools!"

A SPEAR BURST through the chest of the Gond attacking Abraham. Horace flung the savage warrior aside.

"The fighting isn't over yet, Captain!" Horace punched his spear through two Tiotan soldiers at once and ripped the shaft free. "Grab some steel, and dance like you taught me!"

Abraham rolled to his side and plucked Black Bane from the ground. The handle ignited in his hand. With energy surging through him, he pounced back to his feet. "Abraham's back. It's time to attack!" He set his burning gaze on the tunnel down below. He'd had enough of the enemy. It was time to end them all. "It's time to burn some couches. Let's gooo!"

The Henchmen stormed down the mountain, creating a river of blood on their way down.

The bare-chested Gond were split open like ripe melons by the heavily armed fighters swinging steel with lethal precision.

Vern sliced open a Gond belly clean through the spine.

Bearclaw chopped skulls into bloody bits and pieces.

Cudgel busted a man's knees and cracked his face open.

Apollo and Prospero whittled down the enemy with ease.

Nothing could stop the seasoned fighters cloaked in the King's Steel.

Solomon hurled a Gond head over heels. He beat his chest and yelled, "Hairy hippie power!"

Two helicopters dropped down into the channel. One of them started spitting out bullets at the terramen leader, Barath. With bullets ricocheting off his face, Barath picked up a dead Gond and threw it at the chopper. The body flipped over in the air and fell short of the chopper by one hundred feet. The bullets began to chew Barath up. He tucked his body into his shell.

The second chopper aimed its guns at the Henchmen. The machine guns tore through Gond, terramen, and Tiotan soldiers, making a pathway to them. Apollo and Prospero were caught in the fire. Bullets ripped into their bodies and knocked them down.

"Take cover! Take cover!" Abraham shouted, moving in front of Sticks as she fired her rifle at the chopper. "Get down! You don't have any armor on!"

"No," she said, pulling the trigger over and over.

Chopper bullets spat their way up the road, making a beeline for Abraham. Like a statue, he stood in front of Sticks, facing the heavy fire. "Fine. Keep shooting then. Lord protect us!"

Warriors locked in battle fell before his eyes. Calls of the dying went out.

Simon the Fenix streaked across the sky and slammed into the nearest choppers. The chopper's blades broke off against his hide. The chopper spiraled to the ground and crashed into a ball of flame.

Abraham let out a shout. "That's what I call an entrance!"

The second chopper rose out of the channel and fired bullets into Simon.

Shredded wings beating fiercely, Simon curled away from the stream of bullets and rammed the chopper in the side headfirst. The chopper was knocked out of the sky and hit the mountainside in a fiery boom.

The gore-coated Henchmen let out a new elated battle cry: "Death and devastation!"

The great Fenix worked his way down the channel. A geyser of flame blasted from his mouth into the tanks and sea of bodies below. The road began to burn as far as the eye could see. He left nothing but charred bodies, roasting metal, black smoke, and flames in his wake.

The Gond scrambled back into the hills with the terramen giving chase. The soldiers of Tiotan scattered as the King's Army made its way up the channel.

Abraham couldn't believe his eyes. The enemies fled like water being shed from a dog. They'd won.

He grabbed Sticks by the arm and aimed her toward the tunnel. "Let's go."

A small force of soldiers guarded the entrance. Standing behind shields, they fired assault rifles.

The terramen gathered into a stampeding cluster. Barath was back on his feet and led the charge. The fierce terramen fighters hit the enemy soldiers like a wrecking ball hitting a wall.

Abraham swung Black Bane into the swarming enemy with wroth force. Sword blades shattered against his might. Bullets ricocheted from his spinning steel. The sword's engraving burned like hot coals. He waded deeper into the tunnel, leaving a path of the dead behind him. He didn't fight like Abraham Jenkins any longer. He fought like a man possessed. He fought like Ruger Slade.

"Death before failure!" Horace bellowed out. He gored a man and slung him aside. "I told you we could kill them!"

With blood in their eyes and with wild howling, the Henchmen stormed the Time Tunnel.

One hundred feet away, at the front end of the Time Tunnel, the Underlord Fleece stood waiting.

<hr>

MANDI SAT inside the cabin of the ambulance parked near the front end of the tunnel. She'd watched everything that happened up to the point when Abraham's, Smoke's, and Sid's bodies were ripped from the ground and slammed together.

"Oh boy," she said as she nibbled on the tips of her nails. That was something that she never did. Now, she sat in the stuffy ambulance cabin, sweating like a whore in church. "Oh boy."

Smoke and Sid had ordered her to stay in the ambulance. She was supposed to have it ready when the time came to run. Slipping inside had been tough, but all of them were disguised as soldiers, wearing blue-and-black camo with black ball caps.

She took a sip of Gatorade and decided to drain the entire sixty-four-ounce jug. With her heart pounding in her chest, she got out of the ambulance. Pistol in hand, she said to herself, "Here goes nothing."

Inside the Time Tunnel, she saw the ghostly, tattered robes of the wraith whipping about his body. Her skin crawled. Spiders made of ice scurried down her spine.

"I hate ghosts. I hate ghost stories." She swallowed an emerald-green supervitamin. A moment later, her blood ignited. Her slumped shoulders pulled back, and her eyes narrowed. She looked at her gun. "I can do this. I can do anything."

Mandi snaked down the tunnel wall, using the cover of shadows and railcars. She moved as quietly as a cat with the noise of the generators drowning her footsteps out. She bolted from the wall and the railing and huddled behind a Jeep's back bumper. The computer stations were only twenty feet away. The ghostly wraith was no more than fifty feet away. She lined up the wraith in her gunsights.

"Say goodnight, you dirty dishrag." The pistol was loaded with blue-tipped bullets that were supposed to rip through anything. She squeezed the trigger and unloaded a burst that tore right through the wraith. The wraith, Fleece, didn't budge.

Big Apple pointed his finger at her and with gnashing teeth said, "Get her!"

Mandi cracked off two shots at the horned halfling.

The halfling dove behind the computer station.

Colonel Drew Dexter took cover behind the computer station and returned fire. He said, "You don't want to do this, Mandi! It's over. You're too pretty. I'd hate to see you die."

"Shut up!" She blasted over a succession of bullets at Drew. "You dirty liar." Bullets zinged over her head.

"I'm not playing games, Mandi!" Drew said. "Give up, or they will kill you."

She hunkered down behind the Jeep's wheel well, flattened out, caught a glimpse of Drew's feet, and fired.

"Ow!" Drew jumped behind the computer station. "She shot me in the foot!"

"The next bullet's going to take off more than your—hey!" The gun was ripped from her hand by an unseen force. The gun hurtled over to Big Apple, who snatched it out of the air. Mandi's entire body floated up into the air and flew into the cluster of her friends. Her head cracked against Sid's.

"Ow!"

"I told you to stay in the ambulance," Sid said.

"It looked to me like you needed some help. What was I supposed to do? I had the superpill," Mandi said.

"Supervitamin," Smoke corrected.

They were all jammed together in a human ball.

"It was for an emergency."

"This isn't an emergency?" she said with incredulity as the ball of bodies slowly spun around.

"Nope," Smoke said. "But I can see how by your standards you'd think so."

"Abraham, is that you?" she asked Ruger.

"No, young lady. It's me, Ruger." He winked at her. "I'm impressed with your bravery."

"Yes, so am I." Drew limped over to the group, pointing his gun at all of them.

Big Apple did the same. Eugene Drisk had managed to get back on his feet.

"I would have let you live if you hadn't shot me in the foot. I'm going to have to go on disability." Drew grimaced. "But I'm going to kill you last."

Eugene slammed his fists on the computer desk. "No! No! Impossible!"

Dr. Jack, who had been gloating, gaped at the screens. "This can't be right. This can't be right!"

"What is it?" Colonel Dexter asked. He limped over to the screens. "No, no, no, no! Where did my choppers go!"

"That bat thing destroyed them!" Eugene pounded the desk. "Now the Henchmen are routing our army! Oh my, they are in the tunnel. The Henchmen are coming! The Henchmen are coming!"

Dr. Jack glared at Big Apple and said, "Sic your wraith on them and stop them!"

"Don't talk to me like that. And don't worry," Big Apple said. "They aren't a match for the Underlord." He ran his finger underneath the black collar he wore. "As long as I have this, I control everything."

Ruger chuckled. "You spawn of a billy goat. You can't stop them. They are going to kill you. You're less than one hundred feet from death's door. And I'm going to enjoy watching you die. All of you."

"I've had enough of this chatter." Dr. Jack grabbed a nearby rifle and pointed it at the group. "I'm going to kill all of you." He took aim. "Then I'm going to kill all of the Henchmen."

The blaring alarms sounded again. The red emergency lights came on, and strobe lights flashed.

"What is going on now?" Eugene screamed. "Why is there a countdown on my screen? Detonation in five minutes?" He gave Jack a blank look. "Who did this?"

Smoke spoke up and said, "I did. Remember, I told you about those detonators. All of them are armed now. It's a safety mechanism that can't be turned off. In five minutes, this tunnel will go boom."

"He's bluffing!" Dr. Jack said.

"No, he's not." Sid pointed out the detonators. They were mounted on the Time Tunnel ring, the generators, and the power lines. "You can try to disarm them, but chances are you won't get half of them all done in time."

"Fleece!" Big Apple shouted. "Finish the Henchmen. We'll take care of them."

The bodies of Ruger, Smoke, Sid, and Mandi were separated and hovered over the ground. They lay still, paralyzed, slowly rotating in the air.

Big Apple tore the phone from Smoke's grip. A countdown was on it. "What's the passcode?"

"Eight. Six. Seven. Five. Three. Oh. Nine," Smoke said.

"That's it! I've had it with all of you." Big Apple tossed the phone to Eugene and started shooting.

A GREAT GUST of wind started up inside the tunnel. Abraham could see Fleece at the opposite end of the tunnel. The Underlord's arms made slow, arcane patterns in the air. Dead soldiers and their equipment went rolling down the tunnel, past Abraham's feet.

The Henchmen gathered in a knot behind Abraham. Like the tip of a spear, with the wind tearing at their faces, they trucked on.

"Forward, men! Forward!" Horace shouted with the wind tearing at his beard. For every step the group took forward, they slid half a step backward.

Abraham could see the light at the end of the tunnel. He could see his own body, Smoke, and Sid, spinning like rotisserie chickens on the other side. Then he saw another woman's hair dangling down. "Mandi!"

The Henchmen marched on against the tunnel tempest with the wind tearing at their cheeks. The farther they marched the stronger the winds became.

"Black Bane, can't you do something about this?" he shouted.

"Why would I do that? I'm quite fond of the breeze."

Big Apple started shooting into Abraham's friends.

"Nooo!" Abraham yelled. They were only twenty-five feet away from the haunting wraith. He set his eyes on the demon and said, "Iris! Now!"

The Henchmen hunkered down. Horace had his great arms locked around one of Iris's legs. Bearclaw had a hold of the other.

In her hand, Iris held Melris's Rod of Devastation, which glowed with the fire of a hundred burning purple stars. "Taste my purple power!"

A bolt of power rocketed out of the tip of the rod. The blast smote Fleece square in the chest and sent him flying backward out of the tunnel.

Mandi, Smoke, Sid, and Ruger fell to the ground. Ruger, in Abraham's body, popped up to his knees just as Fleece gathered himself.

On impulse, Abraham threw Black Bane at Ruger just as Big Apple pointed his gun barrel at Ruger's head. Ruger snatched the blade out of the air, and in a single lightning-quick stroke, he sliced off Big Apple's head.

Before the horned halfling's head hit the ground, Fleece glided back into the tunnel. At the same time, he pulled the collar from Big Apple's neck into his hand as if using a magnet. The wind had died, but he blocked Abraham and the Henchmen's passage. With the collar in one hand, he wagged his bony finger with the other. Fleece said in a deep, ghostly, but soothing voice, "No, no, no." The collar disintegrated in his hand. His dark robes shifted to light gray and white. Muscles and skin gathered over his bones in a miraculous transformation. "Ah. I am free now. The Sect thanks you, Abraham. Now I must go and restore order." He opened a portal of swirling mist and disappeared in a puff of misty smoke.

Abraham watched in fascination as Ruger Slade, using his own out-of-shape body, finished off the enemy. Ruger blocked a bullet fired by Drew Dexter and sliced him in half. Dr. Jack turned to run, but not before Ruger gored him in the back. He finally faced off with Eugene Drisk, who, on hands and knees, pleaded for his life. Ruger split the man in half.

———

"Come on, hurry up!" Sid said as she beckoned him to the other side of the Time Tunnel.

That was when Abraham heard the emergency alarms going off. With the bright flashing strobe lights in his eyes, he shielded his gaze and said, "What's the hurry? We won."

"I'm destroying the Time Tunnel," Smoke said. "You have less than two minutes left."

"But you guys were shot." He looked at Mandi.

She had a grimace on her face and held her hand over her ribs. "We have the sweetheart suits on. It hurts, but we'll live. Now are you coming home or not?"

Abraham looked back over his shoulder. There stood the Henchmen, battered, bruised, and bloodied from head to toe. They looked like cans that had been spat out of a meat grinder. Horace had a bullet hole through one cheek. Bearclaw showed two teeth busted out. Dominga was holding a flap of skin in place on her arm. Those strangers had given him everything they'd had.

"Uh"—he lifted a finger—"hold on." Abraham made his way around the group, shaking hands with everyone as he did so. He started with Horace.

"Horace, I couldn't ask for a more faithful friend. You can deliver beer with me anytime."

"Bearclaw, what can I say? If I didn't know you, you'd scare the hell out of me."

"Vern, you're a dick. But in an honest kind of way."

"Thank you, Captain," Vern said.

He hugged Iris. "You've been nothing but faithful and amazing.

"Dominga, wow." He kissed her on the cheek. "Just wow."

"Apollo and Prospero…" He shook their hands. "Every time I see a homeless person, I'll think of the two of you. And Nick Nolte."

He gave Tark and Cudgel brief hugs. "You both remind me of one of my closest teammates, Buddy Parker. I'll always keep you close to my heart."

"Skitts, you might not have the Brand, but you're a Henchmen."

The young brown-haired man nodded.

Abraham stood before Shades and gave the little fella an approving look. "What can I say? It was nice knowing you."

Shades sniffed. "Nice knowing you too, Captain."

He hugged Clarann and Clarice at the same time. "I pray that it all works out." He kissed Clarice on the cheek. "You deserve to know your father. Clarann, thanks for having faith in me in the beginning."

Clarann gave him a soft kiss. "Thanks for saving me. I would have been dead without you."

Sticks was the last one to thank. He laid his hands on her shoulders and studied her creaseless and expressionless face. "I want you to know that you meant the most to me out of everyone here."

"Don't get weepy on me. I know."

"I don't suppose you'd show me a smile, would you?"

"Nope."

He chuckled. "Thanks, Sticks. I'm truly going to miss you."

He gave her a kiss. She tightened her lips then suddenly kissed him back. They shared a long, passionate kiss. He broke it off and swallowed.

"That's the best good-bye I've ever had." He squeezed her hand and bumped into Iris.

Iris's smile was as big as a rainbow, and she said, "I bet I can top that." She puckered up, pulled Abraham down, and kissed him.

Abraham caught his breath, gave Iris a pat on the rear end, and headed over to Solomon. "What's it going to be? You coming home or staying here?"

Solomon stroked the hairs on his chin, looked at his friends, and said, "I've kinda gotten used to these guys. I think I'm going to stick around and see what happens."

Abraham reached up and squeezed Solomon's shoulder. "Thanks for believing me."

"Thanks for delivering."

Abraham moved toward the other side of the Time Tunnel, where he saw himself, Mandi, Smoke, and Sid waiting.

"Will you hurry up?" Mandi demanded.

"I'm coming." Before he crossed the threshold, he smiled and waved good-bye.

Then he met Ruger on the Time Tunnel's threshold. Ruger held out Black Bane. He grabbed the sword handle, and both men locked eyes. His soul slid from one body to the other. He found himself face-to-face with the one true Ruger Slade.

"I think I'm going to miss being you."

"I know. I missed me too," Ruger Slade said.

"Aren't you going to miss being me?"

Taking the sword with him, Ruger walked backward toward Titanuus, saluted with the blade, and said, "Well done, Abraham Jenkins. Well done."

The Henchmen gathered King Hector's body.

Smoke grabbed Luther and put the man over his shoulder. He stood in Titanuus for a moment and said, "Now I can say I've been here."

"Come on, John, we only have thirty seconds," Sid said.

The company ran to the ambulance and loaded in. Abraham got into the front seat with Mandi. As the ambulance made the turn in the tunnel, he waved one last time with the emergency lights flashing in his eyes. The Henchmen were gone.

The ambulance roared at full speed out of the tunnel. It hit the dirt road doing ninety. With purple lightning in the sky, the mountainside exploded. Everything went white after that.

89

C HAPTER 89 (Epilogue)

BEEP. Beep. Beep. Beep. Beep.

Abraham's nose twitched. That all-too-familiar hospital smell lingered in his nose. His eyes were closed. The sheets were stiff.

I don't want to look.

The last thing he remembered was riding out of the tunnel inside an ambulance. Mandi drove. Everyone else—Smoke, Sid, and a catatonic Luther—was in the back. A blinding flash of light was followed by an earth-shattering *kaboom*.

Time to face the music.

Taking a deep breath, he opened his eyes. He was right. There he lay in a hospital bed with an IV hooked to him. The curtain, with light sea patterns, was drawn. He blinked several times. His throat tightened.

Aside from the steady beeping of a vital-statistics monitor, he didn't hear anything else. He lifted his arms and saw no handcuffs, flexicuffs, or shackles of any shape or form. His limbs were free. With a grunt, he sat up and swung his legs over the side. His toes touched the cold floor. He rubbed his forehead with his fingers.

Let's see what is behind curtain number one, Monty.

With his pulse pounding behind his ears, he slowly pushed the curtain back. He was inside a single hospital room. A wooden door with a partial glass pane window was closed. A nurse walked by, stopped, and looked in. She was short and full-figured, with a blond ponytail and wearing black Hello Kitty scrubs.

Nurse Nancy. No!

Nurse Nancy opened the door and said, "Well, look who is finally awake." She checked the monitors, grabbed a clipboard, and jotted down some notes.

He studied her with wary eyes. She'd been close to Dr. Jack Lassiter, or so he thought.

Looking at the clipboard, she smirked.

"What?" he said.

She looked at him and replied. "What?"

"Uh... what time is it?"

"Morning time." She hooked the clipboard on the end of the bed. "And I'm finishing up a twelve-hour shift. So I hope you don't mind that I'm not very chatty. I'll let your friends or family know that you are awake. You seem to be in good shape, so the doctor will swing by and sign off your release."

"Doctor who?" he asked because he couldn't stop thinking about Jack Lassiter.

"No, not Doctor Who, the time-travel guy. Doctor Uy will come by. He's in a real good mood since he returned from his fishing trip. Don't worry, he won't release you if you ain't right." She looked him up and down. "You look fine to me. You've even slimmed down. Stay put, and I'll see to it that they bring you something to eat." She closed the door behind herself.

Abraham waited on pins and needles for another half hour. He lay in bed, uncertain what to think. His gaze was fixed on the door. He wasn't sure he wanted to know what was on the other side of it.

Did everything I remember happen, or was it all just a dream? He held his sheets with his fingers clutching in and out.

Mandi knocked on the door and quickly came inside. She had on a black polo shirt and blue jeans. Her bouncing brown hair hung down to her shoulders, and she carried a vase of flowers. "Hi!" she said cheerfully as she crept into the room and closed the door behind her.

"Mandi," he said with a shaky voice, "tell me what is going on. Did we just blow up a Time Tunnel or not?"

She set the vase of flowers on the table, unslung her purse, and set it on the chair. She sat down beside Abraham and took him by the hand. "No, we didn't blow up the Time Tunnel."

His shoulders sagged. "Oh."

"Smoke and Sid did."

He perked up. "What? It's all real." He grabbed her shoulders. "Don't mess with me, Mandi. Tell me it's over."

"Oh, it's over. I saved this for you." She pulled a newspaper out of her oversized purse. "Read."

He read the headline out loud: "Freak earthquake causes massive mountain slide." He skimmed the article. It didn't mention any names or report any injuries. It was vague and only stated that the National Guard was cleaning up. He looked at Mandi and asked, "So it's over?"

Mandi smiled brightly and nodded. "It's over."

He hugged her. She hugged back and kissed his face. Deep inside, he knew it was over. But he still wondered if all of it was even true. Giving her a black look, he said, "How do we even know that it happened?"

"Oh, we know." She opened his robe and gently ran her fingers over his chest. "And you'll have this."

He looked down to see a brand-new scar shaped like a crown on his chest. His jaw dropped. "How?"

Mandi shrugged. "I don't know, and I don't care. I'm just glad to have you back."

"Where are Smoke and Sid?"

"They are cleaning up things at Facility 117. Apparently, they have a lot of experience with this sort of thing. They told me to tell you hello and they hope to see you at the wedding."

"What wedding?"

"Our wedding," she said playfully. "You didn't think I'd go through all of that without marrying you?"

"Huh-huh," he was stunned, but he didn't mind her saying it. He felt peace. "Uh, what about Luther? Is he... gone?"

"No, he's alive and well back at the brewery—just, well, different." She patted him on a thigh. "Oh, wait, you don't want to forget this before we get out of here." Mandi moved to the clothing cabinet, opened the door, and reached up top. She tossed Jake's backpack onto the bed. "Just like you, it's been to Titanuus and back."

His eyes watered, not with tears of sadness but tears of joy. The guilt he'd felt for losing his family was gone. He realized it wasn't his fault, once and for all. He kissed the backpack. "I miss you guys."

Mandi wiped a tear away with a tissue. "You know they miss you too."

"Hmm... it feels heavier." He unzipped the backpack. The first thing he pulled out was the Rubik's cube. All the sides were solved. Immediately, he thought of the Crown of Stones and King Hector. He hoped King Hector made it. The second thing he pulled out was a leather pouch bigger than his fist. It had a lot of heft to it.

"What's that?"

"I don't know." He opened it to find the leather pouch was filled to the brim with gold and silver shards. He poured the coins into his hand. "Holy sheetrock."

TORCHED BY SIMON THE FENIX, the armies of Tiotan fled shortly after the Time Tunnel collapsed. On foot, Ruger Slade and the Henchmen started the journey back home. King Hector was alive and well, except he wasn't King Hector at all. He had the essence of someone else. And he was talking to Ruger and the queen.

"So I'm the King of Kingsland?" King Hector asked. He wore the Crown of Stones on his head, but the stones were missing. All of them had been buried in hundreds of tons of rubble behind him. "I've never been a king before."

Queen Clarann had her arm hooked in Hector's. "You'll make a fine king, Luther Vancross. I can see it in your eyes. Hector would approve."

With a cheerful tone, Hector said, "I can't wait to see my castle. Do I have a queen? A harem?"

"I'm your queen," Clarann said as she looked at Ruger. "But we need to talk about that. We have a delicate situation. You see…" She explained everything about her and Ruger's past.

Luther was very understanding. "We'll work it out." He stretched out a hand to Ruger. "So you're Ruger Slade. I've heard a lot about you."

Dominga and Tark returned from the front lines of the King's Army.

Dominga reported to Ruger, saying, "There's no sign of Leodor. One of the King's Guardians said that he jumped through a swirl in the sky."

Ruger nodded. "We'll find the snake on our next mission. Home first, before the House of Steel crumbles."

Shades strolled alongside Ruger, the thumb of his remaining hand hitched inside his belt, and said, "It's good to have you back once and for all, Captain."

"Hear, hear," Horace, Bearclaw, and Vern agreed.

"But we still have a problem," Shades added.

"What's that?" Ruger asked.

"Sticks is gone. And I didn't even see her leave," Shades said with a grim voice.

With one hand on his sword handle and the other hand on Shades's shoulder, Ruger said with a smile in his voice, "She isn't the only one that is gone. The presence within Black Bane is gone too. But I have a strong feeling that everything is going to be all right."

Abraham sat at the counter at Woody's Grill, eating a basketful of cheese fries loaded down with jalapeños. A tall chocolate milkshake he was sucking on was half empty. Mandi's stepfather, Herb, sat beside him, watching the TV. The old man was covered in age spots, his hair had thinned down to almost nothing, and he wore a Members Only jacket.

"Man, the Pirates really suck this year," Herb said. "I bet they wish that they had Jenkins the Jet back." He punched Abraham in the shoulder. "Man, could you throw a fastball."

Mandi's mother, Martha, came through the double doors leading into the kitchen. The older version of Mandi always had a warm smile on her face. She wore a maroon homemade apron that read in white letters, "Peace. Love. Joy." She wiped her hands off on a dish towel and asked, "Can I get you another milkshake, Abraham?"

"No ma'am. Mandi's probably gonna kill me for having this one," he said.

"You mean two," Herb said with a chuckle.

"Shhh..." Abraham said with a grin.

Herb spun around in his chair, eyed the front doors of the store, checked his watch, and said, "They're late. Aren't they late? I hate waiting. I haven't seen Luther in decades, and here I am waiting." He stuck his bottom lip out. "He probably won't come. Probably got abducted by aliens or something." He spun around on his stool and eyed the TV.

Abraham finished his fries and wiped off his fingers. Being back home was good, but a part of him felt as if he'd slip back into Titanuus at any moment. Now, however, he was content. He was more than happy to move on with Mandi.

"Oh, there they are." Martha took off her apron, revealing a black Woody's Grill T-shirt underneath. "My, I should have gotten fixed up. I look horrible."

"You never look horrible," Herb said.

"Oh, what do you know? You can't see a thing." Martha hurried to the door and opened it. Mandi was the first one through.

Luther Vancross came in next. His white hair was almost shaved down to the skin, and he sported a white moustache. In his flannel shirt and jeans, he looked strong and healthy. Even with the age spots, he didn't look a day over seventy. The woman accompanying Luther made Abraham jump off his stool.

"Sticks!"

Sticks still wore her brown hair tied back, showing her pretty, creaseless tomboy face. She'd donned a pair of jeans and a flannel shirt that was tied off over her belly button.

Abraham gave her a fragile hug. "Uh, I don't know what to say. Are you the only one?"

"Sort of," she said.

He looked at Mandi. "Why didn't you tell me?"

"I wasn't sure how I felt about your girlfriend from the other side. But we talked," Mandi said.

Sticks slapped him on the shoulder and said, "I like you, but..." she looked him up and down, "I like you better with Ruger's body. I guess I'm shallow."

Wringing her hands, Martha whispered to her daughter, "Who is Ruger, and where is the other side?"

"I'll explain later." Mandi hooked her mom by the arm and said, "Let's give them a moment."

"So why did you come?" Abraham asked Sticks. He noticed a knife strapped to the side of her leg, the Dagger of Death.

Sticks moseyed over to the stool beside him and sat down. She took in everything from the diner to the general store. "I thought it was time for a change."

"I see." He turned his attention to Luther. "And how are you doing?"

"The longer I stay, the better," Luther said.

Herb got right in Luther's face. His bulging eyes were squinting. "You look like Luther, but you don't sound like Luther. Who are you?"

"I assure you that I am Luther, Herb, but the years have changed me." Luther motioned to the diner booths. "Abraham, can we sit down?" He rubbed Herb's shoulder. "I'll be right back, and we'll catch up where we left off."

Abraham joined Luther and Sticks in the booth. He sat across from both of them with one knee bouncing up and down.

Luther scanned the diner as if he'd never been anywhere else before. He carried himself with a different air, much stronger than before. He asked, "Don't you know who I am, Abraham?"

"King Hector?"

"No." Luther's eyes fell on Martha. "It's good to see that this world is ripe with ample women."

Abraham's knee hit the table, making the salt and pepper shakers jump. "Black Bane!"

"Yes," Luther said with a glimmer in his eyes. "But that isn't my real name."

Abraham leaned forward. He noticed a Mona Lisa smile on Sticks's face. "So what is your name?"

Luther spread out his fingers. Tiny tendrils of blue lightning danced from fingertip to fingertip. "I am Boon."

Abraham had never heard the name before. He leaned back in the booth and asked, "So where are you from, Boon?"

"Bish."

ABOUT THE AUTHOR

Thanks for reading *The Henchmen Chronicles*! I have to tell you that this was one of the toughest projects that I've ever had to tackle. There were a lot of moving parts with this series, but I wanted to challenge myself and you with something new.

I attempted this portal fantasy because it thought it would be fun to include the modern vernacular that we are so connected to. I felt I had an original idea with the body-switching/soul-swapping angle too. (*Special note: The map of Titanuus is the same shape as my home state, West "by God" Virginia.)

I hoped to take you to a new world, where you could experience new backgrounds and races too. All in all, it's been a ton of fun, but this series was work! I'm glad it's done, but more importantly, I hope you enjoyed it. Let me know.

As I've mentioned, I have a lot of book series, and I'm slowly tying them all together. If Smoke and Sid piqued your interest and you like urban fantasy, give the *Supernatural Bounty Hunter Files* a try. It's a complete ten-book series. Collector's Set Link.

At the end, I reveal who the presence is inside the sword, Black Bane. This is the wizard Boon from my favorite series, *The Darkslayer* —pure hard-hitting action-packed sword and sorcery. You can check it out at The Darkslayer Omnibus Link.

I have written everything you could ask for in fantasy. Scroll on down and see more of what I have to offer.

Please leave a review. They are a huge help to me! Here is a link.

*I'd love it if you would subscribe to my mailing list: www. craighalloran.com.

*Follow me on BookBub at https://www.bookbub.com/authors/ craig-halloran.

*On Facebook, you can find me at The Darkslayer Report or Craig Halloran.

*Twitter, twitter, twitter. I am there, too: www.twitter.com/Craig-Halloran.

*And of course, you can always email me at craig@thedark-slayer.com.

ALSO BY CRAIG HALLORAN

Craig Halloran resides with his family outside his hometown of Charleston, West Virginia. When he isn't entertaining mankind, he is seeking adventure, working out, or watching sports. To learn more about him, go to www.thedarkslayer.com.

Check out all of my great stories …

Free Books

The Darkslayer: Brutal Beginnings

Nath Dragon—The Quest for the Thunderstone

The Henchmen Chronicles

The King's Henchmen

The King's Assassin

The King's Prisoner

The King's Conjurer

The King's Spies

The Odyssey of Nath Dragon Series (New Series) (Prequel to Chronicles of Dragon)

Exiled

Enslaved

Deadly

Hunted

Strife

The Chronicles of Dragon Series 1 (10 Books)

The Hero, the Sword, and the Dragons (Book 1)

Dragon Bones and Tombstones (Book 2)

Terror at the Temple (Book 3)

Clutch of the Cleric (Book 4)

Hunt for the Hero (Book 5)

Siege at the Settlements (Book 6)

Strife in the Sky (Book 7)

Fight and the Fury (Book 8)

War in the Winds (Book 9)

Finale (Book 10)

Box set 1–5

Box set 6–10

Collector's Edition 1–10

<u>Tail of the Dragon, The Chronicles of Dragon, Series 2 (10 books)</u>

<u>Tail of the Dragon #1</u>

Claws of the Dragon #2

Battle of the Dragon #3

Eyes of the Dragon #4

Flight of the Dragon #5

Trial of the Dragon #6

Judgement of the Dragon #7

Wrath of the Dragon #8

Power of the Dragon #9

Hour of the Dragon #10

Box set 1–5

Box set 6–10

Collector's Edition 1–10

<u>The Darkslayer, Series 1 (6 books)</u>

Wrath of the Royals (Book 1)

Blades in the Night (Book 2)

Underling Revenge (Book 3)

Danger and the Druid (Book 4)

Outrage in the Outlands (Book 5)

Chaos at the Castle (Book 6)

Box set 1–3

Box set 4–6

Omnibus 1–6

The Darkslayer: Bish and Bone, Series 2 (10 books)

Bish and Bone (Book 1)

Black Blood (Book 2)

Red Death (Book 3)

Lethal Liaisons (Book 4)

Torment and Terror (Book 5)

Brigands and Badlands (Book 6)

War in the Wasteland (Book 7)

Slaughter in the Streets (Book 8)

Hunt of the Beast (Book 9)

The Battle for Bone (Book 10)

Box set 1–5

Box set 6–10

Bish and Bone Omnibus (Books 1–10)

CLASH OF HEROES: Nath Dragon meets The Darkslayer miniseries

Book 1

Book 2

Book 3

The Gamma Earth Cycle

Escape from the Dominion

Flight from the Dominion

Prison of the Dominion

The Supernatural Bounty Hunter Files (10 books)

Smoke Rising: Book 1

I Smell Smoke: Book 2

Where There's Smoke: Book 3

Smoke on the Water: Book 4

Smoke and Mirrors: Book 5

Up in Smoke: Book 6

Smoke Signals: Book 7

Holy Smoke: Book 8

Smoke Happens: Book 9

Smoke Out: Book 10

Box set 1–5

Box set 6–10

Collector's Edition 1–10

Zombie Impact Series

Zombie Day Care: Book 1

Zombie Rehab: Book 2

Zombie Warfare: Book 3

Box set: Books 1–3

OTHER WORKS & NOVELLAS

The Scarab's Curse—Sword & Sorcery Novella

The Scarab's Power

<u>The Scarab's Command</u>

The Scarab's Trick

The Scarab's War